EXPECTING THE BILLIONAIRE'S BABY

BY
ANDREA LAURENCE

MILLS & BOON

First Published in Great Britain 2017
By Mills & Boon, an imprint of HarperCollins*Publishers*
1 London Bridge Street, London, SE1 9GF

© 2017 Harlequin Books S.A.

Special thanks and acknowledgement are given to Andrea Laurence for her contribution to the Texas Cattleman's Club: Blackmail series.

ISBN: 978-0-263-92815-0

51-0417

Our policy is to use papers that are natural, renewable and recyclable products and made from wood grown in sustainable forests. The logging and manufacturing processes conform to the legal environmental regulations of the country of origin.

Printed and bound in Spain
by CPI, Barcelona

Andrea Laurence is an award-winning author of contemporary romances filled with seduction and sass. She has been a lover of reading and writing stories since she was young. A dedicated West Coast girl transplanted into the Deep South, she is thrilled to share her special blend of sensuality and dry, sarcastic humor with readers.

To My Fellow TCC Authors—

I loved sharing a little blackmail between friends.
Looking forward to working with you all again!

And To Our Super Editor Charles—

If you can keep up with all twelve stories,
you're officially a superhero.
I'm going to buy you a cape.
Maybe some tights.

One

"You can do this, Cecelia."

Cecelia Morgan attempted to encourage herself as she looked over her portfolio for the hundredth time. Tomorrow, she was presenting her design plans to the board of directors of the new Bellamy Hotel. This was a big step for her and her company, To the Moon. The company she started after college specialized in children's furniture, bedding and toys. From the beginning she had targeted a high-end market, catering to wealthy parents who were looking for luxury products for their children.

The company had been a success from the very start. What had begun as a small online boutique had exploded into a series of stores across the United States after a celebrity posted on social media about how much they loved one of TTM's nursery designs. Cecelia had been forced to open her own production facility and warehouse outside her hometown of Royal, Texas, to keep up with the demand.

The portfolio on the desk in front of her, however, could take To the Moon to the next level. Designing furniture, toys and accessories for pampered little ones had been her first love, but now Cecelia was ready for her business to mature along with her tastes. The Bellamy Hotel was her chance to make this a reality.

The Bellamy was a brand-new five-star resort opening right outside Royal. Owner Shane Delgado had contacted Cecelia about decorating and furnishing the hotel about a month ago, after a previous designer had been fired well into the process. This would be a big step for Cecelia. If she could secure the contract with The Bellamy, it would give her the footing she needed to branch out into the luxury adult furniture market.

As her daddy always said, if you're not moving forward, you might as well be moving backward. She was successful, but that wasn't enough for the Morgans. Her subsidiary of To the Moon—Luna Fine Furnishings—could change everything for her.

She was shocked that Shane had reached out to her, given he was pretty clear he'd dismissed her as part of the mean girls clique, along with her best friends Simone and Naomi. Admittedly, she wasn't very nice to his girlfriend Brandee and recent gossip had been less than flattering about Cecelia and her friends.

Some even suspected them of being behind the recent blackmailings. Shane was taking a huge leap of faith inviting her to submit her ideas for this incredible opportunity; she wasn't about to screw this up.

Cecelia gathered up everything into her portfolio binder and slipped it into her leather briefcase. She'd probably gone over it a hundred times already. She needed to stop fiddling with it and just let it lie. It was perfect. Some of her best work yet. As usual, she was putting too much pressure on herself. Her parents certainly didn't help matters. They always held Cecelia, their only child, to very high standards and never accepted anything less than perfection

She supposed that was why she was so successful. Brent and Tilly Morgan were practically Texas royalty and had raised their daughter to follow in their footsteps. She went to the best private schools, rode horses and competed in dressage in high school, and went on to graduate summa cum laude with a business degree from a prestigious Ivy League university. Anything less for the younger Morgan would've been unacceptable.

While her parents had been supportive both emotionally and financially when it came to her company, Cecelia always worried that their support came at a price. If Luna Fine Furnishings wasn't the success that she hoped for, she might never hear the end of it. The last thing she needed was for her father to pat her on the back and tell her that maybe she needed to just stick with the baby things. You know…woman stuff. Or worse yet, to hand the business over to someone else and focus on settling down with Chip Ashford to make actual babies instead of baby furniture.

She wasn't opposed to settling down with Chip— he was her fiancé after all—but she certainly didn't want to throw away everything that she'd worked for in the process. Chip was a Texas senator, and he had been very supportive of her business so far. But Cecelia got the feeling that once they got married, Chip might feel the same way as her parents did.

It wasn't that she didn't want kids. Cecelia wanted her own children more than anything. But she was confident that she could be both a mother and the CEO of her own company. She didn't intend to set one ambition aside for the other.

A chime sounded on Cecelia's phone. She reached for it and tapped the screen to open up the Snapchat notification she'd just received for a private message. It took her a moment to realize what she was actually looking at. The picture was of a document with small text, but the header at the top brought a sinking feeling to her stomach. It read "Certificate of Birth" with the seal of the state of Texas on the bottom corner. The message across the screen was far more worrisome.

Somebody has got a secret.

Cecelia looked once more at the photo before it disappeared. It was then that she realized that this wasn't just any birth certificate, it was *her* original birth certificate. The one issued before she was adopted by the Morgans.

For a moment, Cecelia almost couldn't breathe. Her adoption had always been kept a secret. Everyone, including members of her extended family, believed that Cecelia was Brent and Tilly's biological daughter. Even Cecelia had believed it until her thirteenth birthday. That night, they'd told her that she was adopted but that they had kept it a secret for her own protection. The unfortunate truth was that her birth mother had been a junkie, and child services had taken Cecelia away from her when she was only a few weeks old. Her mother had overdosed not long after that, and she was put up for adoption. The Morgans thought that it was best if Cecelia's birth mother and that dark past were kept secret.

But someone had found out.

Cecelia didn't know how—she hadn't even seen her original birth certificate before. A new one had been issued when her adoption was finalized, so someone had done some serious sleuthing to find it.

Another image popped up on her screen. This one was a message written in letters cut from magazines like some sort of ransom note. She supposed that in some way, it *was* a ransom note. It demanded that twenty-five thousand dollars be wired to an account within twenty-four hours or her secret would be exposed to the entire town. It was signed, Maverick.

Considering everything that had been happening in Royal, Texas, lately, she should've known she would be targeted eventually. Maverick had been wreaking havoc on the lives of Royal residents for the past few months. This anonymous blackmailer had been the talk of the town, and everyone at the Texas Cattleman's Club had suspicions about who it could be. The most recent suspects had been Cecelia herself, along with Naomi and Simone.

Cecelia was a busy woman. She ran her own business, served as arm candy for her fiancé's various political events, was busy keeping up appearances for her parents and for Chip… She hardly had time in her schedule to get a manicure, much less to research and dig up dirt on her fellow residents. Her busy schedule and high standards made her come off as a bit snobbish, and Cecelia supposed she was, but she was no blackmailer. Unfortunately, the only way to prove it was to let everyone know that she was Maverick's latest victim.

That certainly wasn't an option. She couldn't have the whole town knowing that her entire life was a lie.

Unfortunately, this wasn't just her secret. Her parents had built their lives around their perfect "biological" daughter. They'd lied to countless family members and friends to keep up the charade, but they'd only done it to protect her. Paying Maverick was probably the only way to shield Brent and Tilly from the fallout.

But hers wasn't the only family she had to worry about. The Ashfords would have a fit. Chip came from a certain kind of family, and he believed that Cecelia was cut from the same cloth. Would Chip call off the engagement if he found out the truth? Their relationship was more about appearances and family alliances than love, but she hoped that Chip cared enough about her not to throw everything away if her secret got out. As far as she was concerned, she was a Morgan, through and through.

And as a Morgan, it was her responsibility to safeguard her and her family's reputation, or tomorrow's presentation would go down in flames. Her reputation where Shane was concerned was hanging on by a thread as it was. Surely, he wouldn't want a scandal to interfere with his hotel's grand opening.

But when did it stop? Would Maverick be content with the first payment, or would he drag this out until Cecelia was broke and her business was bankrupted?

Cecelia clutched her head in her hands and fought off a pending migraine. She'd suddenly found herself stuck between a rock and a hard place, and there was no easy way out of this. She either paid Maverick, or the truth of her adoption would be spread all over town. The clock was ticking.

She wasn't sure what her path forward would be, but Cecelia knew what she was doing next. In her life whenever a crisis arose, Cecelia always called her daddy. This conversation, however, was one that needed to be had in person. She didn't know how Maverick had found out about her adoption, but if her phone lines were tapped or her computer was being monitored, she couldn't risk anything but face-to-face communication.

It took Cecelia over an hour for her to reach her parents' mansion outside Houston. It was nearly ten o'clock by the time she arrived, but her parents would still be awake. As expected, she found her father sitting in his library. He was reading a book and smoking one of his favorite cigars.

Brent Morgan looked up in surprise when he noticed his daughter standing in the doorway of his library. "What are you doing here, sweetheart? Your mother didn't tell me were stopping by tonight."

Cecelia took a few steps into her father's favorite room and took a seat in the leather chair across from him. "She doesn't know I'm here. I'm in trouble, Daddy."

Furrowing his brow, he set aside his book and stubbed out his cigar. "What is it? Are you and Chip having problems?"

"No, this isn't about Chip." With a sigh, Cecelia told her father about the message she had received. His expression had morphed from concerned, to angry, to anxious as she spoke. "I've got twenty-four hours to wire them twenty-five thousand dollars, or everyone is going to know the truth."

"Our family can't afford a scandal like this. And imagine the pain this would bring to the Ashfords. Surely this isn't what you want. You're just going to have to pay him," he said, matter-of-factly.

Cecelia hated being put in a position where she had no options, and being under Maverick's thumb was the last place she wanted to be. The only real way to combat blackmail was by exposing the truth before the attacker could. If they beat Maverick to the punch they could put their own spin on her adoption and why they'd lied about it.

"Are you sure, Daddy? I mean, I know you and Mother were trying to protect me, but I'm a grown woman now. I'd rather the story not get out. However, would it be the end of the world if people discovered I was adopted? Does it change anything, really?"

"It absolutely does!" her father said with his face flushing red, making his salt-and-pepper hair appear more starkly white against his skin. "We've lied to everyone we know for thirty years. This would ruin our reputation. And what would the Ashfords think? They wouldn't understand. Neither would my customers or my friends. I could lose business. Hell, you could get thrown out of the Texas Cattleman's Club. It's social suicide, and your mother's heart couldn't take the scandal. No," he insisted. "This stays a secret. Period. I will loan you the money if you need it to pay the blackmailer, but you *will* pay him."

Cecelia noted the finality in her father's tone. It had been the same when she was an unruly child, the same when she was a teenager testing her boundaries. She was an adult now, but Brent Morgan was still in charge. She didn't have the nerve to go against him then, and she certainly didn't have the nerve to do it now. She'd come here for his advice, and she'd be a fool not to take it.

"No, I have the money. I'll make the transfer in the morning. I just hope it is enough to put an end to all of this."

"It has to be," her father said. "I refuse to have our family turned into laughingstocks."

Cecelia sighed in resignation and got up from her seat. "I'll take care of it, Daddy."

Deacon Chase turned his restored 1965 Corvette Stingray down the main street of Royal, Texas. It'd been thirteen years since he'd looked at this town in his rearview mirror and swore he'd never set foot in this narrow-minded, Texas dust trap again. The whole flight over from France, he questioned why he was coming back. Yes, it was good business, and working with his old friend from high school, Shane Delgado, had always been a pleasant experience. But when Shane mentioned that he wanted to build a resort in their hometown of Royal, he should have passed.

Then again, when else would he get the chance to show the town and the people who rejected him that he was better than them? Sure, back then he'd just been a poor kid with few prospects. He was the son of a grocery store clerk and the local car mechanic. He'd gotten to go to private school with all the rich kids only because his parents had been adamant that Deacon make something of himself, and they'd put every dime they had toward his schooling. Even then he had worked in the cafeteria to bridge the gap in tuition. Nobody else had expected much out of him, and those were the people who even acknowledged he existed. As far as most the residents of Royal were concerned, Deacon had never fit in, never would fit in and needed to accept his station in life.

No one had expected him to take his hobby of restoring cars and parlay the skills and money into restoring houses. They certainly hadn't expected him to take the profit from those houses and put it into renovating hotels. Now the kid who worked in the cafeteria was a billionaire and the owner of the most glamorous resort in Cannes, France, the Hotel de Rêve, among others.

The only person in Royal who had ever believed in him was Cecelia. Back in high school, she'd pushed him to be the best person he could be. Considering that she'd held herself to such high standards, he'd been flattered that she saw so much potential in him when most of the people in high school either ignored him or taunted him. Cecelia had said he was a diamond in the rough. *Her* diamond in the rough.

It'd certainly blown the minds of all the boys at school that Cecelia had chosen Deacon instead of one of them. What could he offer her after all? A free carton of milk with her lunch? It turned out that he'd had plenty to offer her. He could still remember how many hours they'd spent lying in the back of his pickup truck talking. Kissing. Dreaming aloud about their future together. Deacon and Cecelia had had big plans for their lives after graduation.

Step one had been to get the hell out of Royal, Texas. Step two had been to live happily-ever-after.

As Deacon came to a stop at the traffic light at the intersection of Main Street and First Avenue, he shook his head in disgust. He had been a fool to think any of that would ever happen. He might have fancy hotels and expensive suits, sports cars and a forty-foot yacht docked in the French Riviera, but Deacon knew, and everybody else knew, that Cecelia was too good for him.

It hadn't taken long for Cecelia to figure that out, too.

The light turned green, and Deacon continued down the road to where his father's old garage used to be. When he'd made his first million, Deacon had moved his parents out of Royal and into a nice subdivision in central Florida. There, they could enjoy their early retirement without the meddling of the snooty residents of Royal. His father had sold the shop, and now a new shopping center was sitting where it used to be. A lot had changed in the last thirteen years.

Deacon couldn't help but wonder how much Cecelia had changed. He tried not to cyberstalk her, but from time to time he couldn't help looking over the Houston society pages to see what she was up to. The grainy black-and-white pictures hardly did her beauty justice, he was certain. The last time he'd seen her, she'd been a young woman, barely eighteen. Even then, Deacon had been certain that she was the most beautiful woman he would ever see in person. He would bet that time had been kind to his Cecelia.

Not that it mattered. The most recent article he'd stumbled across in the paper had included the announcement of her engagement to Chip Ashford. He remembered Chip from high school. He was a rich, entitled, first-class douche bag. Deacon was fairly certain that that hadn't changed, but if Cecelia was willing to marry him, she certainly wasn't the girl that he remembered. Back then, she'd hardly given Chip the time of day.

Mr. and Mrs. Morgan must be so proud of her now. She'd finally made a respectable choice in a man.

Turning off the main drag, Deacon headed down the narrow country road out of Royal that led to his latest real estate acquisition. The rustic yet luxurious lodge that was to serve as his home base in the area stood on three acres of wooded land several miles outside town. He'd bought the property sight unseen when he decided to take on The Bellamy project with Shane. He couldn't be happier with the place. It was very much his style, although it was a far cry from the elegant European architecture and design that he'd become accustomed to.

He hadn't really needed to buy the home. Deacon had no real intention of staying in Royal any longer than he had to. But the businessman in him had a hard time passing up a good deal, and it seemed a shame to throw money away on renting a place while they built the hotel. He had no regrets. It was his happy retreat, away from the society jungles of Royal.

When he pulled up in front of the lodge, he was surprised to find Shane Delgado's truck parked out front. Deacon parked the Corvette in his garage, then stepped out front to meet his friend and business partner.

Deacon hadn't had many friends back in school. Basically none. But his side business of buying and restoring cars had drawn Shane's attention. Shane had actually bought Deacon's very first restoration, a

1975 cherry-red Ford pickup truck with white leather seats. Deacon had been damn proud of that truck, especially when Shane had handed over the cash for it without questioning his asking price. They'd bonded then over a mutual love of cars and had continued to keep in touch over the years. When they both ended up in the real estate development business, it was natural for them to consider working together on a few projects.

"What's wrong now?" Deacon asked as he joined Shane at the bottom of his front steps.

While the construction of The Bellamy had gone relatively smoothly, Deacon was the silent partner. Shane bothered him with details only when something had gone awry. He joked with Shane once that he was getting to the point that he dreaded the sight of his friend's face.

"For once," Shane said with a smile, "I'm just here to hang out and have a drink with my friend. Everything at the hotel is going splendidly. Tomorrow, Cecelia Morgan will be presenting her designs to the board, based on your recommendation. Assuming we like what Cecelia did, and I hope I'm not going too far out on a limb here, we'll be moving forward and getting that much closer to opening the hotel."

Deacon slapped his friend on the back of the shoulder. "I wouldn't have brought her on board if I didn't think she was the best designer for the job. Come on in," he said as they started up the massive stone stairs to the front door. "Have you eaten?" he asked as they made their way into his office for a drink.

Shane nodded. "I have. Brandee is constantly feeding me. By the end of the year, I'm going to weigh three hundred pounds."

"You're a lucky man," Deacon said as he poured them both a couple of fingers of whiskey over ice. Shane had recently gotten involved with Brandee Lawless, the owner of the nearby Hope Springs Ranch. She was a tiny blonde spitfire, and one hell of a cook. "I'd be happy to have Brandee feeding me every night."

"I bet you would," Shane said. "But you need to just stick with your cultured European women."

Deacon chuckled at his friend's remark. He had certainly taken advantage of the local delicacies while he was in Europe. Even though it'd been years since he and Cecelia had broken up, it had soothed his injured pride to have a line of beautiful and exotic women waiting for their chance to be with him. He would never admit to anyone, especially Shane, that not a one of them held a candle to Cecelia in his mind.

Deacon and Shane sat there together, sipping their drinks and enjoying each other's company. They didn't get a lot of opportunities to just hang out anymore. Deacon's office, however, just begged for gentlemen to spend time in comfortable chairs and shoot the shit. The walls were lined with shelves containing leather-bound books that, frankly, came with the house and Deacon would never read. They did create a nice atmosphere, though, along with the oil paintings of landscapes and cattle that hung there. It was all very masculine Texas style.

"Can I ask you something?" Shane asked.

"Sure. What?"

"You do know that Cecelia's business specializes in children's furniture, right?"

Deacon tensed in his chair. Perhaps his office made Shane too comfortable, since he felt like prying into Deacon's motivations for wanting Cecelia for the job. "Yeah, I know. I also know that she's managed to turn her small company into a furniture and accessories juggernaut since she started it. She's always had a good eye for design."

"She does, I won't argue that. But hiring her to decorate The Bellamy is a huge risk. She and Brandee aren't exactly fans of each other. And what if she and her friends are actually behind the cyberattacks? That's not the kind of publicity we'd want for our hotel. I don't have to remind you how much we stand to lose if our gamble doesn't pay off."

"That's why we just asked her to submit a proposal along with the two other design firms. We haven't hired anybody yet. If she's out of her depth in this, or acts suspicious in any way, we thank her for her time and send her on her way. It's not ideal, but not the end of the world, either."

Shane narrowed his gaze at him. He obviously suspected that Deacon had ulterior motives in wanting Cecelia involved in the project. Deacon understood. He wasn't entirely sure that he didn't.

"I'm not sold on either of the other firm's designs. She's last to present, so if she flops tomorrow, it's going to set the project back weeks while we find yet another designer and they start from scratch. We have hotel bookings starting day one. Every delay costs us money."

Deacon just nodded. He was well aware that he was taking a risk. But for some reason, he had to do it. Perhaps he was a glutton for punishment. Perhaps he was looking for any excuse to see her again. He wasn't sure. The only thing he was sure of was that everything would turn out fine. "Relax, Shane. The project will finish on time and on budget with the amazing decor you're hoping for."

"And how do you know that?" Shane asked, sounding unconvinced.

"Because," Deacon said confidently, "Cecelia hasn't failed at anything in her entire life. She's not going to start now."

Two

"Welcome, Miss Morgan. Please have a seat."

Cecelia took two steps into the boardroom and stopped short as she recognized the man's voice. She looked up and found herself staring into the green-and-gold eyes of her past. She couldn't take a single step farther. Her heart stuttered as her mind raced to make sense of what she was seeing. It wasn't possible that Deacon Chase, her first love, was sitting at the head of the boardroom table beside Shane Delgado.

Deacon had disappeared from Royal almost immediately after they graduated from high school. No one in town had seen or heard a word from him since then. She remembered being told that his parents had moved to Florida, and she had occasionally wondered what he had made of himself, but she hadn't had the heart to look him up and find out. She knew that it was best to keep Deacon a part of her past, and yet here he was, a critical element to the success of her future.

Cecelia realized she was standing awkwardly at the entrance to the conference room with the entire board of directors staring at her. She snapped out of it, pasting a wide smile on her face and walking to the front of the room where an empty seat was waiting for her. Beside him.

"Thank you, everyone, for having me here today. I'm very pleased to have the opportunity to present my designs for The Bellamy Hotel to the board. I'm really in love with what I have put together for you all today, and I hope it meets your expectations."

Deacon's cold gaze followed her around the room to where she had taken her seat, but she tried not to let it get to her. The man had every reason to hate her, so she shouldn't expect anything less.

She knew that Shane had a silent partner in The Bellamy project, but she'd never dreamed that it would be Deacon. She had a hard time believing it was even Deacon sitting there, considering how much he'd changed since she saw him last.

His lanky teenaged body had grown into itself, with broad shoulders and muscular arms that strained against the fabric of his expensively tailored navy suit. His jaw was more square and hardened now, as though he was trying to hold in the venomous words he had for her. The lines etched around his eyes and into his furrowed brow made it look like he didn't smile much anymore.

That made Cecelia sad. The Deacon she remembered had been full of life, despite the miserable hand that he had been dealt as a child. Back in high school, he'd had so much potential in him, Cecelia just couldn't wait to see what he was going to do with his future.

Now she knew. It appeared as though Deacon had done extremely well for himself. He had gone from the kid working in the cafeteria to the man who held her future in his hands.

Opening her portfolio, she sorted through her papers and prepared to give the presentation she had practiced repeatedly since Shane had called and offered her a chance to bid on the job. She pulled out several watercolor renderings of the designs, placing them on the easel behind her. Then, taking a deep breath and looking at everyone but Deacon, Cecelia began her presentation.

It was easy for her to get lost in the details of her plan for the hotel. Discussing fabric choices, wooden furnishing pieces, style and design was what she knew best. She had a very distinct point of view that she wanted to express for The Bellamy to separate it from all the other high-class resorts in the Houston area.

Judging by the smiles and nods of the people sitting around the conference room table, she had hit it out of the park. The only person who looked less than impressed, of course, was Deacon. His eyes still focused on her like lasers, but his expression was unreadable.

"Does anyone have any questions?" She looked around the room, ready to field any of the board's concerns. No one spoke up.

Shane finally stood up and walked around the table to shake Cecelia's hand. "Thank you so much, Cecelia," he said with an oddly relieved smile on his face. "I admit I was reluctant to believe you were the right designer for the job, but I must say I'm very impressed. You've done a great job. You're the last to present your designs, so we will have to discuss your proposal, and then we will get back to you about contracts. If we decide to go with Luna Fine Furnishings, how long do you think it will be before you can start work on the hotel?"

Her heart was pounding, but whether it was from Shane's question or Deacon being mere inches away, she couldn't say. "I have already started putting the major furniture pieces into production at my manufacturing facility," Cecelia said. Several of the designs were tweaks of her existing furniture, and it was easy to get them started. "I also put in an order for the fabric, and it should arrive tomorrow. I took the risk, hoping that you would accept my proposal. If you don't like what I've done, I'm going to have to find a new home for about two hundred and fifty dressers."

The people around the table chuckled. Shane just smiled. "A risk-taker. I like it. Well, hopefully we will find a good home for all those dressers. We hope to open the resort by the end of the month. Do you think you can make that happen?"

By the end of the month? Cecelia's stomach started to ache with dread. Even with construction complete, that was an extremely tight schedule. Two hundred and fifty suites in a month! Although she was expecting the fabric for the curtains and upholstered chairs, it would still take time to make the pieces. She wasn't about to say no, however. She could sleep when April was over. "Absolutely. We may have to have our craftsmen working around the clock to get all the pieces together and the wallpaper on the walls, but I think we can make it happen."

Cecelia tried to keep her focus on Shane, but Deacon's appraising gaze kept drawing her attention away. He still wasn't smiling like everyone else. But he wasn't glaring at her angrily anymore, either. Now he was just watching. Thinking, processing. She had no idea what was going on inside Deacon's brain because he hadn't spoken since he welcomed her into the room. Part of her wished she knew. Part of her didn't.

"That all sounds great. If you will give us just a few minutes, we're going to meet and will be right with you. Would you mind waiting in the lobby?"

"Not at all." Cecelia gathered her things up into her portfolio and, with a smile, stepped out of the room. The moment she shut the door behind her she felt like a weight had been lifted from her shoulders. Somehow, having that wall between her and Deacon seemed to make a difference. Thankfully, his laser-like vision couldn't reach her through the drywall and the expensive wallpaper of Shane's offices.

No question, he had rattled her. He'd probably intended to. After everything she'd done to Deacon, she deserved it. For the first time, she started to doubt that she would land this job. Yes, Shane had personally approached her about it, but perhaps Deacon had agreed to it just so he could have the opportunity to reject her the way she'd rejected him all those years ago.

She poured herself a glass of water at the nearby beverage station and took a seat, waiting anxiously for their decision. She was surprised they were moving so quickly, but if they needed the hotel done by the end of the month, there really wasn't a choice. She was the last designer to present her ideas, so the time to decide was here.

About ten minutes later, the door opened and a flow of board members exited the room. Cecelia waited patiently until her name was called and then stepped back into the conference room. The only person left in there was Deacon. She struggled to maintain her professional composure as she waited for him to finally speak to her. Now that they were alone, she was expecting him to lay into her about why she didn't deserve the job.

Instead, he smiled politely and stuffed his hands into his pants pockets. "I won't prolong the torture, Ms. Morgan. The bottom line is that everyone is very pleased with your designs and the direction that you'd like to take for The Bellamy. Shane has gone upstairs to have our contracts department write up something, and we will have it couriered over to your offices as soon as it's ready. Presuming, of course, that you will accept the job."

She'd be crazy not to. The budget that Shane had discussed with her was more than enough to cover materials and labor expenses and provide a tidy profit for her to add to her company's bottom line. She and her team would be working hard to earn it, but the very future of Luna Fine Furnishings was riding on the success of this project. *No* simply wasn't an option. She didn't want to seem too eager, however, especially where Deacon was concerned. "I'm happy to hear that you're pleased. I look forward to reviewing the contracts and touching base with you and Shane."

He nodded. "I understand the schedule is a bit hectic. The ground floor of the hotel has a business suite with several offices available for future hotel management. We're happy to offer you an on-site office location to help you better manage your team and their progress."

That would help. Especially if there was a cot in it where she could sleep. Perhaps she could finish a room so she could stay in it. "That would be lovely, thank you." She hesitated a moment before she spoke again. "May I ask you something?"

Deacon raised his brow in curiosity. "Of course."

She knew she should take the offer and run, but she wanted to know why they'd chosen her. Why *he'd* chosen her. "I am very grateful for this opportunity, but I'm curious as to why you chose to go with me instead of an established design firm. I'm sure you're aware that I've specialized in nursery and children's furnishings for the last few years. This is my first foray in adult luxury design."

Deacon nodded and thought over his response. "Shane and I requested your proposal because we knew the quality would be high. To the Moon is known for producing the best you can buy for a child's room. There's no reason for us to believe it would be any different with your adult designs. You're the best at whatever you choose to do, Cecelia. You always were."

There was a flicker of pain in his eyes as he spoke, but it was quickly masked by the return of his cold indifference to her. "If you'll excuse me," he said, before turning and marching quickly from the conference room.

Cecelia was left standing there, a little shell-shocked from their encounter. He said she was the best at what she did, but she could read between the lines—*except when it came to us*. She excelled in business but was a miserable failure when it came to love.

Deacon might be willing to hire her to do a job she was well capable of, but it was clear that he wasn't about to forgive her for what she'd done to him.

Deacon had made a mistake.

The minute Cecelia had strolled into that conference room, it had felt as though someone had punched him in the stomach. He'd tried to maintain the appearance of the confident, arrogant businessman, but on the inside he felt anything but. His chest was constricted, and he couldn't breathe. His heart was racing like he was in the middle of a marathon. He had thought he would be immune to her after all this time, but he was wrong.

Cecelia had been wearing a smart, tailored ivory-and-gold suit that accented every curve of her womanly figure. That certainly wasn't the body he remembered. She was still petite, but she had grown up quite a bit since he saw her last. He was still attempting to recover from the tantalizing glimpse of her cleavage at the V of her blouse when she smiled at him and flipped her long blond curls casually over her shoulder.

Instantly, he knew he was lost.

What the hell was he thinking coming back here? And an even better question, why had he insisted that Shane give Cecelia the opportunity to compete for the design job? He had all but guaranteed that he would come face-to-face with her like this. It was a terrible idea.

Cecelia had begun her presentation talking about fabrics and furniture details he really didn't give a damn about. He'd hardly heard a word she said. His mind was clouded with the scent of her perfume, reminding him of hot nights in the back of his pickup truck. It was the same scent she'd worn in high school. He'd had to save up for two months to be able to afford a bottle of it for her birthday.

Now all he could think about was her naked, willing body sprawled out beneath his own, his nose buried in her throat, drawing her scent deep into his lungs. They had dated for only six months during their senior year, but they had been some of the best months of his life. Deacon hadn't been sure what he was going to do with his life or if he was ever going to make something of himself, but he instantly knew that he wanted Cecelia to be a part of his future. He couldn't remember how many times they'd made love, but he knew it hadn't been enough.

Looking at her during the presentation, as she'd gestured toward a watercolor rendering of a guest suite, all he could see was the younger Cecelia sitting on his tailgate smiling at him.

Suddenly, every muscle in his body had tensed, every nerve firing sparks of need through him. Occasionally, Cecelia's gaze would flick over him and his throat threatened to close. He'd gripped the arm of his executive chair, trying to ground himself and calm down. It had been no way to act during a professional board meeting. If she had finished her briefing early, he wouldn't have been able to stand up to thank her without embarrassing himself.

Deacon thought that returning to Royal as a successful real estate developer would change things. But every ounce of cockiness and confidence seemed to fly out the window the moment he'd laid eyes on Cecelia. Suddenly, he was an awkward teenager again. His old insecurities washed over him. He hadn't been good enough for her then, and for some reason he didn't feel good enough for her even now.

Of course, it hadn't helped that their last conversation on graduation night had been her breaking up with him. He didn't know exactly what had made her change her mind. Up until that point, she'd been very enthusiastic about their plans and their future together. Then, suddenly, she'd turned a one-eighty on him and walked away.

Deacon had always known he wasn't the kind of boy the Morgans wanted for their daughter. He didn't come from a good family, he was poor and he worked with his hands. He was certain that Brent and Tilly were thrilled that Cecelia had chosen someone like Chip Ashford, former captain of the football team, Texas senator, son of one of the most respected and wealthy families in Houston. He had a bright future ahead of him, no doubt.

Damn him for putting himself in this position, knowing he would be drawn to Cecelia as he always had been, but once again unable to have what he wanted.

He had to remind himself that he hadn't returned to Royal to seduce Cecelia. That wasn't why he'd asked her to do this presentation, either. He had come back to prove to her, and everyone else in the small-minded little town, that he was better than them. To show them that he could take his humble beginnings and still manage to create an empire faster than any of them could manage to inherit. He'd come back to make Cecelia regret her decision. To make the Morgans regret their decision. Nothing more.

When he completed his mission and opened his new hotel, Deacon would return to Europe, indulge his vices and forget all about the cliquish and unimportant people of Royal, Texas.

Well, he doubted he'd forget about Cecelia.

He'd only *thought* it was hard being around Cecelia while she did her presentation. Being alone with her had been agonizing. What was he going to do now that she would be working at his hotel nonstop until it opened? He wouldn't be able to get away from her even if he wanted to. And he didn't.

He felt like an idiot as he strolled down the hallway to the office Shane had provided for him while he was in town. He felt like he'd run away from Cecelia. He should've been more confident, indifferent, as though she'd had no impact on him at all.

Just as he sat down at his desk, Shane appeared in his doorway. "A successful day, I'd say! We not only have a hotel, but the guests won't be sleeping on the floor. What do you say we go down to the Texas Cattleman's Club and celebrate with a drink?"

Deacon arched a brow at his friend. He'd never set foot in that building before. He hadn't even been good enough to clean their pool back in high school. "I'm not a member," he pointed out. "And I'm sure there are plenty of people in the club who would see to it that I never get to be one of them."

Shane dismissed him. "You are certainly welcome as my guest. And if you really wanted to be in the club I could sponsor you. I'm sure few people would have the nerve to speak up against me. Lately, the uproar has been more about the Maverick scandals, and I'm pretty sure that doesn't involve you. Aside from that, there are still a few folks sore that women can become members of the club. You should've heard some of the bitching when the billiards room was converted to a day care. I'm sure they'd be happy to admit you and counteract the appearance that it's turning into a henhouse instead of a clubhouse."

Deacon had never entertained the idea of joining the club. And all things considered, he really didn't want anything to do with an organization that had just decided in the past few years that women were worthy of participating. But he wouldn't be rude about it because he knew Shane was a member and enjoyed it. "No thanks. I think I'm going to finish up a few things here and call it a night. There is a T-bone steak in the fridge that's begging to be grilled tonight, and I can't disappoint it."

Shane smiled. "Okay, if you insist. But I'm going to drag you down there one day, though."

"Why? What's so great about a bunch of people sitting around in cowboy hats—which I don't own—talking about cattle and horses—which I'm not interested in?"

"Well, for one thing, the restaurant makes the finest steaks you'll ever eat. The bartenders pour a perfectly balanced dry martini. It's a nice place to hang out, have a drink and chat with friends."

Deacon supposed that to anyone else, it would sound very inviting. "Well, you're my only friend in town, so again, I'll pass. You go on and eat a finely prepared steak on my behalf."

Shane finally gave up, nodding and throwing up a hand in goodbye.

Deacon watched him go, relieved that he managed to get out of dinner. He had many reasons for avoiding the clubhouse, but the biggest one was Cecelia and Chip. He knew that both of them were members, and he had no interest in running into either of them tonight. Not after she'd spent the afternoon twisting his insides into knots.

No, he needed a little time before he saw Cecelia again. He needed to remind himself how badly she'd hurt him and how much he wanted her to regret what she'd done. To keep his head on straight, he had to stay away from her.

A steak, a stiff drink and a Netflix binge would do it.

He hoped.

Three

When Cecelia got back to her office later that afternoon, she found a giddy Simone waiting for her in the lobby. Cecelia loved Simone, she was one of her best friends in the whole world, but after the day she'd had—hell, after the week she'd had—she wasn't really in the mood. She had to jump on this Bellamy job right away if they were going to make the grand opening deadline.

Simone obviously didn't care, ignoring the stressed-out vibes Cecelia knew she was sending out. She followed Cecelia down the halls of To the Moon to her private office. "Have you heard the latest news?" Simone asked after she slipped into the room behind her.

Cecelia dropped her things down on her desk and

plopped, exhausted, into her chair. "Nope. There's news?"

Simone rubbed her hands together in excitement and rushed over to sit on the edge of her desk. "So," she began, "word is that Maverick is at it again. A message went out on social media to everybody in the Texas Cattleman's Club today."

Cecelia held her breath as she waited to hear the latest news. She'd been too busy with The Bellamy project to check her phone. Had Maverick taken her money and spread her secret anyway? "So, what did the message say?"

Simone pulled her cell out of her purse and flipped through it to find the message. Locating it, she handed the phone over to Cecelia. The message was short and blessedly vague. It read: Someone in the Texas Cattleman's Club is not who they say they are.

Cecelia shrugged it off and handed the mobile back to Simone, feigning disinterest. "That's hardly big news. I'd say half the people there aren't who they pretend to be."

Simone returned her phone to her bag. "And to think that folks still believe we're the ones behind the attacks!"

"I have to say I'm thankful this last message went out when I couldn't possibly have sent it. I've got a room full of witnesses."

Simone just shrugged. "That doesn't mean they don't still think Naomi and I are the culprits, that we're all in on it together. If I had the time, I just might be the kind to do it. You've got to give the guy credit. Royal has been pretty dull lately. Maverick has brought more excitement to town in the last few months than we've had since the tornados hit."

Excitement? Cecelia certainly wouldn't consider extortion or extreme weather exciting. They were both terrifying in their own right. "You know, you might not want to act so excited when that stuff comes out. It makes us look guilty."

"Hey, I thought you would enjoy this more. What's wrong with you today? You don't seem like your usual self."

Cecelia wanted to shout, *"Because the real Maverick is blackmailing me! That message was about me!"* But she wouldn't. Instead she said, "I'm just stressed out and tired. I had that big presentation today at The Bellamy."

Simone perked up again. "So, how did it go? Did you dazzle Shane with your designs? Is he going to dump Brandee and run away with you? Please tell me that at the very least he wasn't rude."

"He was fine. And Brandee didn't even come up. You could say that I dazzled him, since they offered me the contract. It seems I also dazzled his silent partner, Deacon Chase."

Simone's nose wrinkled in thought as she tried to place the name. "Deacon Chase. Why do I know that name?"

"Because," Cecelia explained, "that was my first boyfriend in high school."

Simone's eyes grew as wide as saucers. "Are you

kidding me? Is *that* Deacon Chase Shane's silent partner? Didn't you lose your virginity to him?"

Cecelia looked around nervously to make sure that none of her employees overheard their discussion. Getting up from her chair, she ran to her office door and shut it. "Say it a little louder, Simone. Yes, Deacon was my first." Those weren't exactly helpful memories considering he was in town at the moment, but they were true. Deacon had been the first boy she ever loved. The last boy she'd ever loved.

"Does Chip know he's in town?"

"Does that matter?" Cecelia asked. "Chip and I didn't date in high school. We didn't even date in college. He's got no reason to worry about Deacon."

Simone wasn't convinced. "Yeah, but he knows you two dated and were pretty serious. You don't think it's going to bother him that Deacon is back in Royal?"

If there was only one thing that Cecelia knew about Chip, it was that his ego was bigger than the state of Texas. In his opinion, Deacon was from a lower class of people. He wasn't competition in Chip's eyes, and never would be. "I don't think it would bother Chip. I mean, I agreed to marry Chip. I broke it off with Deacon after graduation, so I don't know why he would feel threatened by him."

Simone shook her head. "Chip may not have been threatened by the Deacon we knew back in high school, but if he is Shane's partner in the hotel, he's done well for himself. That may change things."

Cecelia wasn't sure about that, but she didn't really have time to worry. "Well, I'm sure that Deacon won't stay. He will be long gone once the hotel is finished. Speaking of Chip, I've got to get out of here. He and I are meeting for dinner tonight at the club. We're celebrating my new contract with the hotel."

"Excellent. I've really got to get out of here, too. I just stopped by on my way out of town to share the latest gossip. I'm meeting Naomi at the airport. We're flying out tonight to that fashion show in LA. We'll be there for a couple of days. You be sure to keep us posted if anything new happens with Maverick."

"I will, although I'm not sure you'd be so excited about his next attack if he were blackmailing *you*." Cecelia certainly didn't feel that way now that she was his latest victim.

"Oh, I'm sure he'll get to me eventually. He'll get to all of us eventually."

Simone practically skipped out of Cecelia's office as if Maverick's threats didn't bother her. Cecelia hadn't been bothered, either, until a few days ago. Now the worry was front and center.

He had to be alluding to her in his latest message. She had wired the money the way her dad had instructed her to, and yet he hadn't backed off. It was exactly what she was afraid of. Once you stepped into the cycle of blackmail, there was no good way to get out of it. She wouldn't be surprised to see another message tonight asking for more money. Despite what her father had told her, Cecelia knew she had to use a different tact with Maverick.

Her parents didn't want her to tell Chip the truth, but that might be her only option if Maverick didn't back down. Chip's family was not only wealthy, but they had connections. If she confided her secret in him perhaps he could help to protect her. The Ashfords could crush Maverick like a bug...*if* they wanted to. She hoped they would, because she didn't know who else to turn to. She would have to tell him tonight at dinner before things got worse.

She was counting on him to be her savior.

Cecelia was a ball of nerves as she pulled her BMW into the parking lot of the Texas Cattleman's Club.

The club wasn't where she would've chosen to have this important discussion with Chip, but he had made the arrangements without asking her. Inside, she found Chip seated in the far corner booth of the dining room. She let the host escort her back to the table. Chip got up as she approached and gave her a short embrace and a chaste kiss on the cheek. "There you are, kitten. You're late. I was starting to worry."

Cecelia looked at her watch as she sat down and it was exactly five thirty. She wasn't about to argue with him, though. To Chip, if you didn't arrive five minutes early, you were late. "I'm sorry. I got hung up with Simone. She wanted to talk to me before she left for California with Naomi."

Chip settled into the booth across from her and smiled. "And what did the lovely Simone have to tell you today?"

Cecelia considered her words. "Well, I wanted to wait to talk to you about this until after we ordered."

"I already ordered for us both," Chip interjected. "I got you the grilled mahimahi since you're watching your weight for the wedding."

Cecelia tried to swallow her irritation. She hated when Chip made decisions for her. Especially when those decisions were based on imaginary weight she had no intention of losing, *thankyouverymuch*. It was a portent of her future with him that she tried hard to ignore. She feared she would be going from spending all her time trying to please her parents, to trying to please her husband.

"Then I suppose I don't have to wait," she said, ignoring his comments. "Simone told me that Maverick is blackmailing somebody new."

Chip nodded thoughtfully and accepted the gin and tonic the waiter brought him before placing a glass of white wine in front of Cecelia. "I saw something come up this afternoon, but I was too busy to pay much attention to it. What does that have to do with Simone? Is she his latest victim? I wouldn't be surprised if she got into some trouble."

Cecelia steeled her nerves, thankful for the glass of wine even though she would've preferred a red. She took a healthy sip before she started the discussion. "No, he's actually blackmailing me."

"What?" Chip shushed her, leaning into her across the table. "Not so loud, people will hear you." He scanned the dining area for anyone who might hear. Fortunately, it was still early for the dinner crowd at the club. The closest table was involved in a lively discussion about steer and not paying any attention to them. "What is going on?" he asked when he seemed certain it was safe to continue their discussion.

Cecelia followed suit, leaning in and speaking in low, hushed tones. "I got a message from him. It seems he found something out about me from a long time ago, and he's trying to blackmail me with it. Well, I supposed he's been successful since I've already made one payment to him, but it doesn't seem like it was enough, given the post this afternoon."

Chip's expression was stiff and stoic, without any of the sympathy or concern for her that she was hoping for. "What is he blackmailing you about? You told me you had a squeaky-clean past. It's absolutely critical, if you're going to be the wife of a senator, that you don't have anything in your life that can be detrimental to my career."

Cecelia sighed. How did this become about him and his career? "I know. It's not really something I think about very often. It was completely out of my control. My parents chose to keep it secret to protect me, but in the end, I don't think it's that bad. It's hardly a skeleton in my closet, Chip."

Chip eyed her expectantly, but she hesitated. She hadn't said the words out loud in thirteen years. Only ever said them once, the night she confided in Deacon. Somehow she wasn't sure this would go as well. "I'm adopted," she whispered.

Chip flinched as though she had slapped him across the face. "Adopted? Why didn't you tell me?"

Cecelia gritted her teeth at his reaction. She could already tell this was a mistake. "No one was ever to find out. I was adopted by the Morgans when I was only a few weeks old. They decided to raise me as their own child and have never told anybody about my history…because of who my mother was."

"What's wrong with your mother?"

"She had a drug problem. I was taken away from her when I was only two weeks old. My parents told me that she was so distraught, she overdosed not long after that."

A furious expression came over Chip's face. "Are you telling me that your mother was a junkie?"

There was no way to make that part go down easier. "I guess so. She was never a part of my life, but yes, my mother had a serious and deadly drug problem."

Chip didn't appear to even hear her words. "I cannot believe you would lie to me about something like this." He flushed an ugly red with anger. She'd never seen her polished and professional fiancé like this. "I thought you were like me. I thought you were from a good family and would make a perfect wife. But you're nothing but an impostor playing a role. How could you agree to marry me when you were keeping something like that a secret?"

Cecelia's jaw dropped open in shock. She thought he might be surprised by the news, maybe even concerned about the potential backlash, but she certainly didn't think that he would accuse her of deceiving him. "I am not an impostor, Chip Ashford. You have known me my whole life. I was raised by the Morgans in the same Houston suburb you were. I went to all the best schools like you did. I am nothing like my birth mother, and I never will be. I couldn't control who my mother was any more than you could."

Chip just shook his head. "You can dress it up, but a liar is always a liar."

Cecelia's blood ran cold in her veins. "Chip, please, don't be like this. I didn't intentionally deceive you. My parents just thought it was best that no one know."

"Thank goodness for Maverick," Chip said. "Without him I never would've found out the truth about you. You and your parents would've let me marry you knowing that everything I believed about you was a lie."

Her eyes welled up with tears she couldn't fight. Was Chip about to break up with her over this? She couldn't believe it, but that's what it sounded like. "Chip…"

"Don't," he snapped. "Don't look at me like that with tears in your eyes and try to convince me that you are a victim in this. I'm sorry, Cecelia, but the engagement is off. I can't marry somebody I can't trust. You're a liability to every future campaign I run, and I'm not about to destroy my career for a woman who is living a lie."

Cecelia looked down at the gigantic diamond-and-platinum ring that she'd worn for the past six months of their engagement. She hadn't particularly liked the ring, but she couldn't say so. It was gaudy, but it was as expected for someone of his station. She didn't want to keep it, not when his words were like a knife to the heart. She grasped it between her fingers and tugged it off her hand, handing it across the table.

Chip took it and stuffed it into his pocket. "Thank you for being reasonable about that."

At least one of them could be reasonable, she thought as the pain of his rejection slowly morphed into anger. She never would've confided in Chip if she'd known he would react like this. Now, all she could hope for was damage control. "I hope that I can still count on you to keep this secret," Cecelia said. "Odds are it will get out eventually, but I would prefer it to be on my terms if you don't mind. For my parents' sake."

Chip got up from the table and shrugged it off. "What good would it do me to tell anybody? I've wasted enough time here. Have the waiter put dinner on my tab." He turned on his heel and marched out of the restaurant, leaving Cecelia to sit alone with their cocktails, a basket of bread sticks and an order for food they wouldn't even eat.

A hollow feeling echoed through her as she looked at his empty seat. Cecelia thought she would be more upset about her broken engagement, but she was just numb. The truth was that she didn't love Chip. Their relationship was more about strategic family connections than romance, but it still smarted to have him dump her like this when she was at her lowest point. They had planned a future together. They discussed how after The Bellamy deal they were going to sit down and make some solid wedding plans. Instead of finally getting one step closer to the family that she longed for, she was starting over.

Even if Chip kept his word and didn't spread her secret all over town, it would be embarrassing enough for everyone to find out about her broken engagement. Everyone would speculate about why they broke up if neither of them was talking. She wondered what Chip would tell them.

In the end, she was certain that her secret would come out anyway. One way or another everyone was going to find out that Cecelia was the adopted daughter of a junkie. Royal was a place where everybody was always in everyone else's business. They had all the drama and glamour that the Houston society provided, with all of the small-town nosiness that Cecelia could do without.

When the truth came to light, she wondered who would still be standing beside her. The members of the Texas Cattleman's Club were supposed to be like a family, but they were a fickle one.

Then there was the matter of her real family. How would her parents ever recover from the fallout? They'd built their lives on maintaining a perfect facade. Would their family, circle of friends and business contacts ever forgive the decades-long deception?

Reeling from the events of the evening, Cecelia picked up her purse and got up from the table, leaving a stack of bills to cover the tab. She could've let Chip pay for it all, but she didn't want to face the waiter and explain why she was suddenly alone with a tableful of food coming out of the kitchen.

As she got into her car, she leaned back against the soft leather seat and took a deep breath. At this moment, she needed her friends more than ever. But as Simone had said earlier, she and Naomi were already on a plane to California. They wouldn't be back for several days.

She couldn't talk to her parents about this. They would be more distraught about her breakup with Chip than how painful this was for her. She loved her parents, but they were far more concerned with appearances than anything else. She was certain that when word of her broken engagement got around to them, she would get an earful. She could just imagine her mother scrambling to get back in the Ashfords' good graces.

At the moment, Cecelia didn't really give a damn about the Ashfords. If they couldn't accept her the way she was, she didn't want to marry into their family anyway. So what if she wasn't of the good breeding that Chip thought she was? She was still the same person he had always known. The woman he had proposed to.

As she pulled her car out of the parking lot of the club, she found herself turning left instead of right toward the Pine Valley subdivision where she lived in a French château-inspired home. There wasn't much to the left, but Cecelia was in desperate need of a stretch of road to drive and clear her mind.

After a few miles, she realized that maybe all this was for the best. Perhaps Maverick was doing her a favor in the end. It was better that she and Chip break up now, while they were still engaged, than to have a messy divorce on her hands. And God forbid they'd started a family. Would Chip reject his own children if he found out that they were tainted by their mother's inferior bloodline?

Cecelia shuddered at the thought. The one thing she wanted, the one thing she'd always wanted, was a family of her own. She longed for blood relatives whom she was bound to by more than just a slip of paper. People who would love her without stipulations and requirements. Her parents did love her, of that she had no doubt. But the Morgans' high standards were hard to live up to. She had always strived to meet them, but lately she wondered how they would feel about her if she fell short. Would they still love and protect their perfect Cecelia if she wasn't so perfect?

As she made her way to the edge of town, she noticed lights on in the distance at the old Wilson House and slowed her car to investigate. She didn't realize anybody had bought that property. No one had lived in the large, luxurious cabin for several years, but someone was definitely there now.

She wasn't sure why she did it, but she turned her car down the winding gravel road that led to the old house. Maybe it was Maverick's secret hideout. There, out front, she spied a fully restored 1965 Corvette Stingray convertible roadster. She knew nothing of cars, but she remembered a poster of one almost exactly like this on Deacon's bedroom wall in high school. That one had been cherry red—his dream car.

This one was a dark burgundy, but she knew the

moment she saw it that the car belonged to Deacon. Instantly, she realized there was no place else she wanted to be in the whole world.

Deacon had known the truth about her. Years ago when they were in high school and completely infatuated with one another, they had confessed all their secrets. Cecelia had told him about her adoption and about her mother. She had even shown him the only picture she had of her mother. The old, worn photograph, given to her by her parents on her thirteenth birthday, had been found in her mother's hand when she died. It was a picture of her holding her brand-new baby girl, just a week before she was taken away.

Cecelia had spent a lot of time staring at that photo, looking for the similarities between her and her mother. Looking for the differences that made her better. She'd always been mystified by her mother's happy smile as she held her baby. How could she throw that all away? Every now and then she pulled the photo out to look at it when she was alone. Deacon hadn't judged her. Deacon had accepted her for who she was—the rich, spoiled daughter of the Morgan family and the poor, adopted daughter taken away from her drug-addled mother. Deacon had loved her just the same.

In this moment, she wanted nothing more than to feel that acceptance again. Without thinking, she drove up to the front of the house and got out of her car. She flew up the steps and knocked on the front door, not knowing what his reaction would be when he saw her. Judging by their interaction earlier that day, she didn't expect a warm welcome.

But she didn't care.

A moment later, the large door opened wide, revealing Deacon standing there in nothing but a pair of worn blue jeans. She had admired his new build during her briefing that day, but she could only guess what he was hiding beneath his designer suit. Now his hard, chiseled physique was on display, from his firm pecs to his defined six-pack. His chest and stomach were sprinkled with golden-brown chest hair she didn't remember from their times together in the past. Her palms itched to run her hands across him and see how different he felt.

Then her eyes met his, and the light of attraction and appreciation flickered there. Cecelia felt a surge of desire and bravery run through her, urging her on, so she didn't hesitate.

Before Deacon could even say hello, Cecelia launched herself into his arms.

Four

The last thing Deacon expected when he opened his front door was to find Cecelia standing there. If he had suspected that, perhaps he would've put a shirt on. Or perhaps not.

Instead, he'd been standing there half-naked when he opened the door and looked into the seductive gray eyes of his past. She'd seemed broken somehow, not as confident as she'd been during her earlier presentation. She'd appeared to almost tremble as her eyes glistened with unshed tears. Before he could ask what was wrong, or why she was here, she'd launched herself at him, and was kissing him.

At that point all Deacon could do was react. And in that moment, with the woman he had once loved in his arms again after all this time, he couldn't push her away. Their encounter that afternoon had only lit the fires of his need for her once again. The years of anger and resentment took a back seat to desire, at least for the moment. He had no idea what had brought her to his doorstep tonight, but he was thankful for it.

Now her mouth was hot and demanding as she continued to kiss him. These were nothing like the sweet, hesitant kisses of their teenage years. Cecelia was a grown woman who knew exactly what she wanted and how to get it. And from the looks of it, she wanted Deacon.

She buried her fingers in the hair at the nape of his neck, pulling him closer as she pressed her body against his bare chest. He could feel the globes of her full breasts molding against the hard wall of his chest through the thin silk of the blouse he had admired earlier that day. As her tongue slipped into his mouth, he felt a growl form in the back of his throat. She certainly knew how to coax the beast out of him. He tried not to think about how Chip Ashford could've been the one to teach her these new tricks.

That was the thought that yanked Deacon away from Cecelia's kiss. He took a step back, bracing her shoulders and holding her away from him. "What are you doing here, Cecelia?" he asked. "Shouldn't you be making out with your rich fiancé right now, instead of me?"

Cecelia silently held up her hand, wiggling the bare finger that had previously held the gigantic diamond he'd noticed that afternoon at the presentation. So, that meant the engagement was off, and just since he'd seen her last. That was an interesting development, although one he was certain had little to do with his arrival in town. Only in his fantasies would Cecelia cast aside Chip for him.

"May I come in?" she asked, looking up at him through thick, golden lashes.

His tongue snaked out over his lips as he nodded. "Sure." He took a step back, wondering what could've broken the engagement and driven Cecelia back into his arms, but before he could ask, she was on him again.

This time he had no reason to stop her. They stumbled back through the doorway, and he kicked it shut behind them. Without hesitation, he lifted Cecelia and started carrying her toward the bedroom. She clung to him, unwilling to separate her lips from his as he navigated through the house.

When they reached his bedroom, he sat her gently down at the edge of his king-size bed. Cecelia immediately started undoing his belt, sliding it from his jeans and tossing it to the floor. There was no question that this was what she wanted. And frankly, if he were being honest with himself, it was what he wanted, too.

He certainly didn't expect it to be dropped into his lap like this, but only a fool would ask questions instead of accepting the gift he'd been given. As she started to unbutton his pants, he reached for her hand and pulled it away.

"I've got this," he said.

Cecelia just smiled and began to undo her own blouse, button by button, exposing more of the creamy, porcelain skin he'd always admired. She was one of the few women he'd ever met who truly had a flawless complexion. There were no freckles, no moles—not even a scar. The Morgans would never allow their precious daughter to be injured. Her skin was like that of a china doll—smooth…even…perfect.

He remembered running his hands over it years ago and it feeling like silk against the rough, calloused palms he'd earned from working on cars. As she slipped her blouse off her shoulders and exposed the ivory satin of her bra, he ached to touch it and the flesh beneath it.

Her breasts nearly overflowed the cups as she breathed hard with wanting him. He took a step back as she stood to unzip her pencil skirt. The fabric slid over her ample hips and pooled at her feet. The sight of her nearly nude stole his breath away. She was just as beautiful and perfect as he remembered. Only now, she was a fully grown woman with all the curves that a man at his age could finally appreciate. As a teenager, Cecelia had been his first, and he'd hardly known what he was doing. He wouldn't have been able to handle a woman like Cecelia back then.

Cecelia's steely-gray eyes were fixed on him as she reached behind herself and unlatched her bra. Her breasts spilled free, revealing tight, strawberry-pink tips that were just as he remembered them. Thirteen years was too long to wait, and he couldn't resist reaching out to cup them in his hands. The hard peaks of her nipples pressed into his palms as he squeezed and massaged her sensitive flesh.

Cecelia sighed with contentment, leaned into his touch, tipped her head back and shook her blond waves over her shoulders. "Yes," she whispered. "I need your touch, Deacon. I need it now more than ever."

Deacon didn't respond. Instead, he dipped his head and took one of her tight buds into his mouth. He teased at it with his tongue until Cecelia was gasping and writhing against him. He wrapped his arm around her waist, holding her body tight against his, and then slipped one hand beneath her silky ivory panties.

He was surprised to find her skin completely bare and smooth there, providing no barrier for his fingers to slip between her sensitive folds and stroke her center. Cecelia gasped and her hips bucked against his hand, but he didn't stop. Instead he drew harder on her nipple, stroking her again and again until she came apart in his arms.

Cecelia cried out and clawed at his shoulders, more wild and passionate beneath him than she'd ever let herself be. She had gotten in touch with her sexuality, and he was pleased to be benefiting from it.

When her body stilled and her cries subsided, he lowered her gently onto the bed, laying her back against the brocade comforter. She watched beneath hooded eyes as he unbuttoned his jeans and slipped them off, along with the rest of his clothing. She watched him with appreciation as he sought out a condom from the nightstand and returned to where her body was sprawled across his mattress. He set the condom beside her on the bed, using both hands to grasp her panties and slide the fabric over her hips and down her legs.

With her completely exposed in front of him, Deacon could only shake his head in wonder. How had he gotten to this place tonight? He had anticipated grilling a steak on the back porch, drinking a few beers and watching the news. Instead, he would gladly go without his dinner and feast on Cecelia instead.

He opened the condom and rolled it down his length and then crawled onto the bed, positioning himself between her still-quivering thighs.

This was the moment he'd waited for, fantasized about, since the day he and Cecelia had parted ways. The last time they'd made love had been the night before their high school graduation. He'd had no idea that the next day Cecelia would be breaking up with him. He'd had no idea that he was holding her for the last time, kissing her for the last time, until it was too late. Then, all he could do was long for what he lost and search for it in the arms of other women.

"Please," Cecelia begged. "Don't make me wait any longer."

Deacon was more than happy to fulfill her wish. He slowly surged forward, pressing into her warmth until he was fully buried inside her. He gritted his teeth, fighting to keep control, as her tight muscles wrapped around him. She felt as good as he remembered. Maybe better.

Cecelia drew her knees up, wrapping her legs

around his hips and holding him close. She reached up for him, cupping his face in her hands and drawing his mouth down to her own. He began to move, slowly at first, and then picking up speed. Her soft cries and groans of pleasure were muffled by his mouth against hers.

It didn't take long for the tension to build up inside him. Cecelia was eager and hungry for him, and he was near his breaking point. He moved harder and faster as she clawed at his back. The sharp sting was a painful reminder that although he was enjoying this, he needed to remember who he was with. The Cecelia of his past, of his fantasies, was long gone. The woman beneath him was harder, shrewder and lacking the sweet innocence he'd always associated with her.

No matter what he tried to tell himself, Deacon knew that she was just using him. Whatever had happened between her and Chip tonight had driven her into his arms. She probably wanted to forget about everything that was going wrong in her life and was using Deacon as a reminder of when things were better. It had worked. Whatever tensions and worries she'd arrived with on his doorstep were gone.

Admittedly, his mood had improved, too. As Deacon focused on the soft warmth of her body, the stress of the day melted away and a new kind of tension took its place. Cecelia's cries grew louder beneath him, signaling that she was close to another release. He wasn't far behind her. Reaching between them, he stroked her center, pushing her over the edge once again.

"Deacon!" she cried out, writhing under him.

The tightening of her muscles around him drew him closer to his release. He thrust into her three more times, hard and fast, and it was done. His jaw dropped open with a silent scream as he poured himself into her willing body.

When it was over, Deacon pulled away from her and flopped back onto the bed. Staring up at his ceiling, he had a hard time believing everything that had just happened. He'd come back to Royal in the hopes that Cecelia might regret dumping him all those years ago.

This was way better.

Cecelia awoke with a start. She sat up in bed, her heart racing in her chest, as she looked around the unfamiliar room. For a moment, she couldn't figure out where she was, but the morning light streaming across the furniture and the shape of the man in bed beside her pieced it together.

Suddenly everything came back to her at once. She'd slept with Deacon. No, she'd thrown herself at Deacon and he'd had the courtesy not to turn her down and make her look like a fool. What was she thinking, running to him like that? Of all the people in Royal?

Then again, who else did she have to turn to? She couldn't blame last night on alcohol, but apparently the emotional trauma of her breakup with Chip was enough to dull her inhibitions. With the arrival of dawn, her good sense returned to her, and she realized that last night, however amazing, had been a terrible mistake.

She pulled back the blankets and slipped silently from the bed. She crept through the room, collecting her clothing, and carried it with her to the hallway, where she pulled the bedroom door closed behind her and got dressed.

She looked back at the door and pictured the man asleep beyond it only once before she disappeared down the hallway and out the front door. She practically held her breath until she had started her car and made it down the driveway without Deacon showing up at his front door to see her leave. It was better this way. Neither of them had to face the reality of last night and what it meant, which was a big nothing.

They were both under stress, and the sex had done its job and gotten it out of their systems. Hopefully, she would be able to finish her work at The Bellamy without this becoming a problem for her. She had enough to deal with, with the fallout of her broken engagement and the threat of Maverick looming overhead. She didn't need any weird sexual tension buzzing between them while she was trying to pull off the design coup of the century.

Two hundred and fifty guest suites in less than a month was no laughing matter. It would take all of Cecelia's focus and drive to make it happen. She didn't have time for any distractions in her life, but she most certainly didn't need Deacon, who would be at the hotel every day, reminding her of what they'd just done while she tried to work.

And yet, by the time she reached Pine Valley Estates, she was feeling guilty about running out. That was no way to treat Deacon, especially after how welcoming he'd been last night. He'd had every right to slam the door in her face when she showed up at his doorstep without warning. She was the one who had broken up with him because he wasn't good enough for her. How dare she just show up and throw herself into his arms and expect him to welcome her? And yet he had.

Now she felt worse than ever.

She pulled her car into the garage at her château just around the time her alarm normally would wake her. There was no time for her to dwell on her mistakes. She needed to shower, change, grab a double-shot latte and get to work on her first day of The Bellamy project.

Cecelia made a stop at her office to collect the things she would need while she was working at the resort. With her laptop bag slung over her shoulder and a small file box of necessary paperwork and designs in hand, she headed back out to the receptionist's desk.

Her secretary, Nancy, was sitting there when she arrived. "Good morning, Miss Morgan," she said.

"Good morning, Nancy. Mr. Delgado and Mr. Chase graciously offered me an office at the hotel so I can oversee our work there over the next few weeks. Tell anyone who needs to get a hold of me that I have my cell phone and my computer."

Nancy jotted the note on the paper pad beside her.

She waved as Cecelia turned and went out the front door with her things.

By the time Cecelia arrived at The Bellamy, work was in full swing for the day. She spied her painting team's truck, which meant that they were already laying a coat of steely-gray paint on the walls of every suite. By the time they were done, the wallpaper should have arrived and be ready to go on the accent walls and in the bathrooms.

She gathered up her things and started up the walkway into the back of the hotel, passing landscapers as they planted trees and bushes nearby. Inside she found an organized-looking woman in a headset and asked for directions. She pointed her down a hallway to the business suite of the hotel. There, she found one office designated for each of the owners, one for the hotel manager, one for the reservations manager, one for the catering manager and one empty office that had yet to be assigned. She assumed that would be hers for now.

She opened the door and turned on the light, finding a nicely appointed office space. She hadn't been contracted to decorate the interior management rooms, but it wouldn't be necessary. There was a desk, a rolling chair and a bookshelf. That was more than she would need while she was here. She busied herself unpacking her things and getting ready to dig into her work.

Once she was up and running, she started her day by making important calls. All of her suppliers needed to know that she had won the project bid and the pending orders needed to go forward as planned. Fabric, furniture and wallpaper were just the beginning. She had orders for paintings to go up in every single room, 250 matching small lamps to go on each nightstand, along with another 250 torch lamps for the corner behind the reading chair. Thousands of feet of carpeting needed to be ordered, in addition to ceramic tiles for the bathroom floors.

And all that needed to get here as soon as possible. As in yesterday.

Cecelia was lost in the minutiae of managing her inventory and orders when her cell phone rang. She looked down and noticed it was Naomi calling from California. She picked up the phone and answered it. "Hey, girl, how's California?"

"It's beautiful here," she said. "The weather is unreal. It makes me never want to come back to Texas, but of course I will, because you and Simone would kill me if I didn't."

"Is everything set up for the fashion show?"

Naomi just groaned. "I really don't want to talk about it. There's always last-minute chaos at these things. I didn't call to talk about all that anyway. I called because I got a text about you and Chip breaking up yesterday. Is that true?"

Cecelia had been hoping it would take longer for the news to get out, but apparently it was already making Royal's gossip rounds. "Yes, we've broken up, but really it's for the best. I think we just had different ideas of what our future was going to be."

"Hmm. So it didn't have anything to do with a *certain someone* coming back to town?"

Cecelia rolled her eyes. Simone must've told her about her run-in with Deacon. "No, it had nothing to do with him. I honestly doubt Chip even knows he's here yet. I didn't mention it."

"So what set all this off?"

She hesitated. She knew that she would eventually tell Naomi and Simone about her little blackmail problem, but now wasn't the time. "It was bound to happen eventually. Things just boiled over at dinner last night, so we called off the engagement. I'll tell you and Simone more about it when you get home. I wish you two were here."

"I'm so sorry that all this happened while we were gone, Cece. You've broken off your engagement and your two best friends aren't there to commiserate with you. That really sucks. I promise that when we get back, we will get together for some wine, a couple cartons of Ben & Jerry's and some good girl time. You'll put this whole thing behind you before you know it."

That sounded great. Cecelia really needed her friends to talk to. Had they been in town last night, perhaps she wouldn't have found herself in Deacon's bed.

"Good luck with the show," Cecelia said.

"Thank you. Hang in there. Oh, and don't forget that Wes and Isabelle's engagement party is coming up. You're not getting out of it, you know."

Oh, she knew. Cecelia said goodbye and got off the

phone. She needed to remember to pick up a gift for that. Frankly, she had been surprised to receive the invitation, but Isabelle was the kind of woman who wanted to be friends with everybody, even the girl who had spilled the beans about her secret daughter and upended her whole life.

She had RSVP'd two weeks ago, but now she was regretting it. She didn't really want to stroll into the Texas Cattleman's Club and have to face everybody after the breakup. More than a few people there would get a sick amount of pleasure from her misfortune. But she said she would go, so she would go.

Cecelia had just turned back to her computer when she heard a tap at the door. She looked up and immediately felt a surge of panic run through her. Deacon was standing in her doorway, a look of expectation and irritation on his face. She'd been hoping, in vain, apparently, that he would be too busy to come looking for her this morning. "Good morning, Mr. Chase. What can I do for you?"

Deacon arched a curious brow at her and just shook his head. "So this is how it's going to be, huh? It never happened?"

Cecelia smiled, putting on her most businesslike face as she tried to ignore the rough stubble on his jaw that she'd brushed her lips across only hours earlier. Her fingers tingled with the memory of running through his golden-blond hair and pulling him close to her. "I always like to keep things professional in the workplace."

"And later, when we're not in the workplace?" he asked.

"There's not much to say about last night, now or later, except that I apologize for the way I acted. It was inappropriate of me to burden you with my problems. After Chip broke off the engagement, I wasn't sure where to go or what to do. I made the wrong choice, and I'm sorry."

Deacon's green-gold gaze flickered over her face, studying her as though he could see the truth there. His jaw tightened, and finally he looked away. "The head of your painting crew is looking for you. He's waiting in the lobby."

Cecelia watched as Deacon turned and disappeared from her doorway without another word. The warm, attentive Deacon from last night was gone, leaving only the cold businessman behind. She hated that it had to be that way, and she wished he could understand. Now, more than ever, she needed his warmth and his compassion. All too soon, the rest of Royal would be turning their backs on her. But there was too much history between them, too many memories and emotions to cloud the present. She knew she had to put up a wall to protect her business and her reputation.

And her heart.

Five

He was a damn fool for thinking that their night together would go down any differently than it had.

Deacon knew better. He knew better than to just fall in the bed with Cecelia and think that things had changed. Just as before, he was good enough when they were alone, but not in public. He had thought that perhaps he had proved his worth, and that maybe things would go differently between them this time. Not so.

It had been a week since she'd shown up on his doorstep. They'd danced around each other at the hotel each day, both seemingly drawn to, and repelled by, each other. Cecelia avoided eye contact and stuck strictly to topics about work. But as hard as she tried to play it cool, it didn't change the underlying energy that ran through all of their interactions.

He wasn't about to give her the satisfaction of him chasing after her, however. The teenager whose heart she'd broken would've chased her anywhere if he thought he could have another chance. Real estate billionaire Deacon Chase didn't follow women around like a lost puppy dog.

But if there was one thing Deacon had learned in the past week, it was that she didn't regret that night. Not even one teensy, tiny, little bit. He'd seen the way her cheeks flushed when she'd looked up and seen him standing nearby. She had been hungry for the pleasure he happily gave her. That kind of hunger was nothing to be remorseful about. She'd come to him that night because she wanted to forget what a mess her life was for a little while, and he'd delivered in spades. More than likely, she regretted that she didn't regret their encounter.

Deacon hadn't lost too much sleep over it. They'd had sex. Amazing, mind-blowing sex, but just sex. It'd been thirteen years since they'd gotten together. They weren't in love with one another, and it was ridiculous to think that they ever would be. It would've been nice if she had said goodbye as she crept naked from his bedroom, but he supposed it had saved them from an awkward morning together.

No, what had bothered him the most during the past week was seeing who Cecelia had become over the years. Despite his feelings about her and their breakup, he had still loved the girl Cecelia had been. She'd been the sweetest, most caring person he had ever known outside of his own family. When the rest of the school, and the rest of the town, had turned their back on Deacon, Cecelia had been there.

The woman he watched stomping back and forth through the lobby of his hotel in high heels and a tight hair bun was not the Cecelia he remembered. She was driven, focused, almost to the point of being emotionless. What happened to her? When they had shared their dreams for the future as teenagers, being a hardnosed CEO had not been on Cecelia's list of ambitions.

If he looked closely, every now and then Deacon could see a flicker of the girl he used to know. It was usually near the end of the day, when the stress and the worries started to wear her down. That was when her facade would start to crumble and he could see the real Cecelia underneath.

He was watching her like that when Shane approached him. "She's quite a piece of work, isn't she?"

Deacon turned to him, startled out of his thoughts. "What do you mean?"

"I've always thought that Cecelia was a victim of a contradictory modern society. If she were a man, everyone would applaud her for her success and uncompromising attitude in the boardroom. Since she's a woman, she's seen as cold and bitchy. Heck, I see her that way after the way she treated Brandee. But there's no way she could've gotten this far in business if she wasn't hard."

"You make it sound like nobody likes her." That surprised Deacon, since she'd been the most popular, outgoing person in high school. Everyone had loved her.

"Well, she has earned quite the reputation in Royal over the years. Aside from her few close friends, I'm not sure that anybody really likes her, especially inside the Texas Cattleman's Club. Tell you what, though, it's not for their lack of trying. She's just not interested in being friends with most people. She and the rest of the mean girl trio tried to sabotage my relationship with Brandee. They thought it was a big joke. I don't know if folks are just not good enough to be her friends or what."

Deacon flinched. "That doesn't sound like her at all. What the hell happened after I left town?"

"I don't know, man." Shane shrugged. "Maybe you broke her heart."

Deacon swallowed a bitter chuckle. "Don't you mean the other way around? She's the one who broke up with me."

"Yeah, well, maybe she regrets it. I certainly would rather date you over Chip Ashford any day."

"Aw, that's sweet of you, Shane."

"You know what I mean," Shane snapped. "I'd be a bitter, miserable woman if I were dating him, too. I'm curious as to what will happen to her socially, now that she's broken it off with Chip, though. A lot of people in town tolerated her and her attitude just because she was his fiancée."

The discussion of her broken engagement caught Deacon's attention. "So do you know exactly what happened between her and Chip?"

Shane just shook his head. "I haven't heard anything about it, aside from the fact that it's over. It seems both of them are keeping fairly tight-lipped about the whole thing, which is unusual. I have heard that her parents are beside themselves about the breakup. They've been kissing the Ashfords' asses for years to get in their good graces, and I'm sure they think Cecelia has ruined it for them."

It grated on Deacon's nerves that Cecelia's parents were always more worried about appearances than they were about their own daughter. Couldn't they see that she was miserable with Chip? Probably so. They just didn't care. Deacon had never thought much of their family. They acted like they were better than everyone else. "Who cares about the Ashfords?" he asked.

"Everybody," Shane said before turning and wandering off, disappearing as suddenly as he had arrived.

Deacon watched him go, and then he turned back to where Cecelia had been standing a moment before. She was barking orders at a crew of men hauling in rolls of carpeting. When she was finished, she turned and headed in his direction with her tablet clutched in her arms. He braced himself for a potentially tense conversation, but she didn't even make eye contact. She breezed past him as though he were invisible and disappeared down the hallway.

A cold and indifferent bitch, indeed.

Looking down at his watch, Deacon realized he couldn't spend all of his time staring at Cecelia. The hotel opening was in a little more than three weeks, and they had a ton of work ahead of them. That was why he had returned to Royal after all—well, the official reason anyway. He turned on his heel and headed back toward his office to get some work done before the end of the day arrived.

When he looked up from his computer next it was after seven. It was amazing how time could get away from him while he was working. He couldn't imagine doing this job and having a family to go home to every night. He imagined he would have a very angry wife and very cold dinners. He stood up, stretched and reached over to turn off his laptop.

He switched off the light as he stepped out of his office, noticing the business suite was dark except for one other space. Cecelia's office. As quietly as he could, he crept down the hallway to peer in and see what she was doing here this late.

Cecelia was sitting in her chair with her back to him, but she wasn't working. She was looking at something in her hand. Deacon took a few steps closer so he could make out what it was. Finally, he could tell it was an old, worn photograph. One that he recognized.

She'd shown him the photo the night she confessed her biggest secret: that she was adopted. It was of a young woman, weary and worn but happy, holding a new baby. It was a picture of Cecelia's birth mother on the day she brought her daughter home from the hospital. Deacon hadn't given much thought to the photo back then. He had been more interested in Cecelia and the way she talked about it. She had always seemed conflicted about her birth mother. It was as though she wanted to know her, wanted to learn more about who she had been and why she had gotten so lost, and yet she was embarrassed by where she had come from. Deacon had no doubt that she had the Morgans to thank for that.

There was a lot going on with Cecelia. More than just regret over their one-night stand. More than just missing her mother. More than just being upset over her broken engagement. There was something else going on that she wasn't telling him. The whole town was convinced she was just a stuck-up mean girl, but he'd bet not one of them had looked hard enough to see that she was hurting. Of course, she had no reason to confide in him. While he'd proved himself trustworthy in the past, they weren't exactly close anymore. In that moment it bothered him more than in the thirteen years they'd been apart.

He wanted to go into her office and scoop her up into his arms. Not to kiss her. Not to carry her away and ravish her somewhere, but just to hold her. He got the feeling that it was a luxury Cecelia could barely afford. Chip didn't seem like a supportive, hold-his-woman kind of guy, and that was exactly what she needed right now.

But did he dare?

She had done nothing but avoid him since their night together. She'd made it crystal clear that she didn't want any sort of relationship with Deacon, sexual or otherwise. She just wanted to do her job, and so he would let her. The last thing he needed was to leave Royal for the second time with a broken heart and a bruised ego.

As quietly as he could, Deacon took a few steps back and disappeared down the hallway so he didn't disturb her. As he stepped out into the parking lot, there were only two cars remaining—his Corvette and her BMW. He stopped beside her car and stared down at it for a moment, thinking. Finally, he fished a blank piece of scrap paper out of his pocket and scribbled a note on it before placing it under her windshield wiper.

"I'm here if you need to talk—Deacon," it read.

Whether or not she would take him up on it, he had no idea. But he hoped so.

Things had been hard for Cecelia the past couple of weeks. She tried to lose herself in her work and forget about everything that was going wrong in her life, but in the evenings at the hotel, when it was calm and quiet, she had nothing to distract her from the mess of her own making.

Earlier that night, she'd gotten another message from Maverick. As she'd expected, the original payment was just that, and not nearly enough to keep him quiet. Another twenty-five thousand had to be wired by the end of the week, or her secret would be out and her family would be humiliated. Staring at the photo of her mother, she'd quietly decided that she wasn't giving him any more money. She felt a pang of guilt where her parents were concerned—surely they would face an uphill battle in restoring the trust of those they lied to—but it was time for her to take control of her life. Come what may.

Now, sitting in her car in the long-empty parking lot of the hotel, she clutched what might be her only lifeline. Finding the note on her windshield from Deacon had been a surprise. They hadn't really spoken since the morning she ran out on him, aside from the occasional discussion about the hotel. She thought she was doing a good job at keeping her worries inside, but Deacon had seen through it somehow. He'd always had that ability. In some ways, that made him someone she needed to avoid more than ever. In other ways, he was just the person she needed to talk to. The only person she could talk to.

But could she take him up on his offer?

At this point, she didn't have much to lose. Before she could second-guess herself, she put her car in Drive and found herself back on the highway that led to Deacon's place. Her heart was pounding in her chest with anxiety as she drove up the gravel path through the trees. His car was there, and the lights were on inside. Hopefully he was there alone.

She bit anxiously at her lip as she rang the doorbell and waited. This time, when Deacon answered the door, he was fully dressed in the suit he'd worn to the hotel that day, and she was able to control herself. Barely. "Hi," she said. It seemed a simple, silly way to start such a heavy conversation, but she didn't know what else to say.

Deacon seemed to sense how hard it was for her to accept his olive branch. Instead of gloating, he just took a step back and opened the door wider to let her inside.

"You said you were here if I needed to talk. Is this a good time?"

Deacon shut the door and turned to her with a serious expression lining his face. His green-gold eyes reflected nothing but sincerity as he looked at her and said, "Whenever you need to talk to me, I will make the time."

Cecelia was taken aback by the intensity of his words and their impact on her. She never felt like she was anybody's priority, especially Chip's. He always had an important meeting, a campaign to run, a fundraiser to plan, hands to shake and babies to kiss. Cecelia had been an accessory to him, like a nice suit or pair of cuff links. "Thank you," was all she could say.

Deacon led her through the foyer and into his sunken great room. The space was two stories high with a fireplace on the far end that went all the way to the ceiling with stacked gray-and-brown flagstone. He gestured for her to sit in the comfortable-looking brown leather sectional that was arranged around a coffee table made of reclaimed wood and glass. It was very much a cowboy's living room, reminding her of the clubhouse.

"Are you renting this place?" she asked.

"No, I actually went ahead and bought it. It was a good deal, and it came furnished. That made it easier for me to settle in and gave me a real home to come to each night. Despite the fact that I build hotels for a living, I don't exactly relish living in one. When the hotel is finished, I'll return to France, but I'll probably keep this place. Shane will be overseeing the business operations, but I'll also need to come back from time to time."

Deacon walked to a wet bar in the corner. "Can I get you something to drink?"

"Yes, please. I don't really care what it is, but make it a double."

She watched as Deacon poured them both a drink over ice and carried them over to the coffee table. Cecelia immediately picked up her glass and took a large sip. The amber liquid burned on the way down, distracting her from her nerves and eventually warming her blood. "I want to start by apologizing for that morning I ran out on you. I panicked and handled it poorly, and I haven't done any better since then."

Deacon didn't respond. He just sat patiently listening and taking the occasional sip of his own drink. She wasn't used to having someone's undivided attention, so she knew she needed to make the most of it.

"Everything in my life is falling apart," she said. "I don't know if you've been in town long enough to hear about Maverick, but he's been targeting members of the club since the beginning of the year. No one is sure who he is, or how he got the information, but he's been blackmailing people and spilling their secrets. I'm his latest victim."

That finally compelled Deacon to break his silence. "What could you have possibly done to be blackmailed for? Your parents always kept such a tight leash on you, I can't imagine you got into too much trouble over the years."

"He's not blackmailing me about something that I did. He's blackmailing me because of who I really am. Somehow Maverick has gotten a hold of my original birth certificate. He's threatening to tell everyone about my mother and her deadly drug habit. Up until now, no one has known the truth except for me, you and my parents."

Deacon frowned. "I don't see how anybody could hold something like that against you. Why don't you just tell people the truth and take his power away?"

Cecelia sighed. "I thought about doing that, but my parents were very strongly against it. They don't want to ruin the image of the picture-perfect family they've created over the years. I paid the blackmailer, but he still went ahead and started sending out messages to club members that alluded to me. I got another one from him today demanding another payment. There's no way out of this trap. I tried to confide in Chip, thinking that he could help me somehow, but he accused me of living a lie and broke off our engagement instead."

When Cecelia turned to look at Deacon, his jaw was tight and his skin was flushed with anger. "What a bastard! I can't believe you were going to marry a man who could be so careless with your heart. You deserve better than him, Cecelia, not the other way around. By the time he figures that out, I hope it's too late for him to win you back."

Once again, she was stunned by his words. She just couldn't understand how he could say things like that to her after everything that she had done to him.

"Why are you being so nice to me, Deacon? I don't deserve it."

Deacon reached out and took her hand in his. His warm touch sent a surge of awareness through her whole body, bringing back to mind memories of their recent night together. She pushed all of that aside and tried to focus on the here and now.

"What are you talking about? You've already apologized twice for the other night, unnecessarily I might add."

Cecelia met his gaze with her own. "I'm talking about high school. We were in love, we had made plans to run away and live this amazing life together, and I threw it all away. Don't you hate me for that?"

"I was angry for a while, but I have to admit that it fueled me to make more of myself. I couldn't hate you, Cecelia. I tried to, but I just couldn't. The girl I loved wasn't the one who broke up with me that day."

Cecelia felt a sense of relief wash over her. At least that was one thing she hadn't completely ruined. "I've never been strong enough, despite all my successes, to stand up to my parents. I made the mistake of telling them that after graduation, I was leaving with you. They had a fit and laid down the law. I wasn't going anywhere, they insisted. It broke my heart to break up with you, but I didn't know what else to do. And now, when they told me to keep my mouth shut and pay the blackmailer, I did it even though I didn't want to. I dated Chip for years because that's what they wanted. I probably would've married him to make them happy if he hadn't broken up with me. They've never really allowed me to be myself. I've always had to be this perfect daughter, striving to prove to them that I'm better than my mother was.

"I've only ever done two things in my life just because it made me happy. One was starting my business. Marriage and family didn't come as quickly as I'd hoped, so designing and decorating nurseries for a living was the next best thing."

Deacon stroked his thumb gently across the back of her hand as she spoke. "What was the other thing?"

She looked at him, a soft smile curling her lips. "Falling in love with you. You made me happy. You never asked me to be anybody other than who I was. You knew the truth about my mother, and it never seemed to bother you."

"That's because you were perfect just the way you were, Cecelia. Why would I ask you to change?"

No one had ever spoken to her the way Deacon did. His sincere words easily melted her defenses, cracking the cold businesswoman facade that she worked so hard to maintain. She'd always felt so alone, and she didn't want to be alone anymore.

Unwelcome tears started to well up in her eyes. Cecelia hated to cry, especially in front of other people. She wasn't raised to show that kind of vulnerability to anybody. In the Morgan household, she learned at a very young age that emotions made one appear weak, and that wasn't tolerated. Her birth mother had been weak, they'd told her, and look where she had ended up.

"I'm sorry," she said, pulling away from him to wipe her tears away.

"Stop apologizing," he said. He reached for her and pulled her into the protective cocoon of his strong embrace. Cecelia gave in to it, collapsing against him and letting her tears flow freely at last. He held her for what felt like an hour, although it was probably just a few minutes. When she was all out of tears, she sat up and looked at him.

Deacon's face was so familiar and yet so different after all these years. He still had the same kind eyes and charming smile she'd fallen in love with, there was just more maturity behind his gaze now. She found that wisdom made him more handsome than ever before.

In that moment, she didn't want him to just hold her. She wanted to surrender to him and offer him anything she had to give. Slowly, she leaned in and pressed her lips against his. This kiss was different from the one they'd shared before. There was no desperation or anger fueling it this time, just a swelling of emotion and her slow-burning desire for him.

Deacon didn't push her away, nor did he press the kiss any further. It was firm and sweet, soft and tender, reminding her of warm summer nights spent lying in the back of his pickup truck. It was a kiss of potential, of promise.

Cecelia wanted more, but as she leaned farther into Deacon, she felt his hands press softly but insistently against her shoulders. When their lips parted, they sat together inches apart for a moment without speaking.

Finally Deacon said, "That's probably where we should end tonight. I don't want you to have any more regrets where I'm concerned. Or expectations."

Cecelia didn't regret a thing about what had happened between them, but she understood what he meant. What future could they possibly have together? She was still picking up the pieces from her broken engagement, and he'd be back in France in mere weeks. She nodded and sat back, feeling the chill rush in as the warmth of his body left her.

Setting her drink on the coffee table, Cecelia stood up. "I'd probably better get going, then. Thank you for listening and being so supportive. You don't know how rare that is in my life."

Deacon walked her to the door, giving her a firm but chaste hug before she left. It felt good just to be in his arms. She felt safe there, as though Maverick—and Chip and her parents and the gossipmongers of Royal—couldn't hurt her while Deacon was around.

"I'll see you at work tomorrow," he said.

Cecelia waved at him over her shoulder, feeling an unusual surge of optimism run through her as she climbed into her car. For the first time in a long time, she couldn't wait to see what life had in store for her.

Six

"The chef has put together the tasting menu for the grand opening celebration. I didn't realize it was happening today, and I promised Brandee that I would go with her to shop for some things for the ranch. Can you handle it without me?"

Deacon looked up from his desk and frowned at his business partner. "I may have lived in Europe for the last few years, but I don't exactly have the most refined tastes. I am a meat-and-potatoes kind of guy. Are you sure you want to leave the menu up to me? That's a pretty important element of the party, considering we're trying to lure customers into the new tapas restaurant."

"I wouldn't worry about it. We hired the best Spanish chef in all of Texas to run the restaurant.

I'm pretty sure that anything Chef Eduardo makes is going to be amazing. If you're worried about it," Shane said with a wicked grin, "you could always ask Cecelia to join you. She's known for having excellent taste, in design and event planning."

Deacon sat back in his chair and considered Shane's suggestion. Since their kiss a few days ago, he had been considering his next move where she was concerned. He knew that he should back off before they both ended up in over their heads. The past had proven that his and Cecelia's relationship was doomed. They weren't the same people they were back in high school. Even so, he found his thoughts circling back to her again and again.

So what now? He wanted to spend some time with her. A date seemed too formal, especially since she might not want to be seen out with another man so soon after her engagement was called off. But this would be an interesting alternative if she had the time. "Okay, fine. You're off the hook. Get out of here and go buy some barbed wire or a horse or something."

Shane waved and disappeared down the hall. Deacon got up from his desk and went in search of Cecelia. He found her in the lobby directing the hanging of a large oil painting. It was a Western landscape, one of the few nods to Texas in her otherwise modern design.

"Perfect!" she declared after the level showed the frame was aligned just right.

"Well, thank you, I try," Deacon said from over her shoulder.

Cecelia spun on her heel and turned to look at him. "Very funny. Can I help you with something, Mr. Chase?"

Even now, always business first. Thankfully, he truly had a business proposition for her, even if his motivation was less than pure. "Actually, I was wondering if I could borrow you for an hour to help me with something."

"An hour? It's almost lunchtime."

"Which means...all your guys will be out in search of a taco truck and you will have nothing better to do than to join me for a private tasting at the new restaurant here in the hotel."

She arched an eyebrow at him, but she didn't say no. "Is the chef still working on the menu?"

"No, that's already set for both restaurants. What Chef Eduardo has put together for today is the menu for the grand opening gala. It features some of the items that will be on the restaurant's menu, but also some more finger-food-type selections that can be passed around by waiters. Shane was supposed to do this with me, but he's gotten roped into a shopping excursion with Brandee. That just leaves me, and I'm afraid I don't have the palate for this. I could use a second opinion."

Cecelia's gaze flicked over him for a moment, and then she nodded. She turned back to her crew. "Why don't you guys go ahead and take lunch? We'll finish up the rest of the paintings this afternoon."

She didn't have to tell them twice. The men immediately put down their tools and slipped out of the back of the hotel. Once they were gone, Cecelia turned back to Deacon with a smile. "Lead the way, Mr. Chase."

Technically, it wasn't a date, but Deacon felt inclined to offer her his arm and escort her down the hallway anyway. The Bellamy was designed with two dining options. The Silver Saddle was the more casual of the two, offering an upscale bar environment and featuring a selection of Spanish tapas in lieu of the typical appetizer selection. The other restaurant was the Glass House, a high-end farm-to-table restaurant, featuring all the freshest organic produce and responsibly sourced game available. The executive chef was even working on a rooftop garden where he intended to grow his own herbs and a selection of seasonable vegetables.

Normally, the Glass House would've been the appropriate venue for the grand opening, but Deacon had had other ideas. It wouldn't take much to lure the residents of Royal to the Glass House. That was right up their snooty, rich alley. Spanish tapas were another matter. Deacon had suggested that the food for the event be catered by the Silver Saddle instead, so they could introduce the town to what he and Shane hoped would be the newest hot spot in Royal.

When they arrived at the bar they found the executive chef waiting for them. Eduardo welcomed them with a wide smile. "Mr. Chase, I hope that you and your guest are very hungry."

"We are," Deacon replied. He'd seen a mock-up of the menu and knew they were in for a treat. He didn't actually expect to make many, if any, changes. Eduardo knew what he was doing. It was just good for him to know in advance what his guests had in store for them. "I can't wait to see what you put together."

Eduardo directed them to a corner booth. The decor of the bar was still a work in progress, but the majority of the key elements were in place. Along the edge of the room, the space was lined with burgundy leather booths and worn wooden tables. In the center was a rectangular bar that was accessible to guests on all sides. On the far side of the room from where they were seated, there was a stage for live music and a dance floor. Overhead, instead of a disco ball, Deacon had custom ordered a mirrored saddle, the bar's namesake.

They had gone for a cowboy atmosphere with a modern edge, much like Cecelia's room design, and Deacon was pretty sure they'd nailed it. In two months' time, he had no doubt that this place would be hopping on a Saturday night.

He helped Cecelia into the booth and then sat opposite of her. Before they could place their napkins in their laps, Eduardo called the first waiter to the table with a tray of four different beverages. He set them down and disappeared back into the kitchen.

"First, I wanted to start with the beverage selection for the evening. Of course we will have an open bar that will provide whatever beverages the guests would like. However, we will be showcasing the Silver Saddle's four featured drinks, as well." He pointed to the two wineglasses. "Here are our two signature sangrias. The first is a traditional red wine sangria, and this here is a strawberry rosé sangria.

"Next is our take on an Arnold Palmer, but instead of sweet tea, we use sweet-tea-flavored vodka and a sprig of rosemary in the lemonade. Last is the Viva Bellamy, designed exclusively for the hotel, with aged rye whiskey, sweet vermouth, blood-orange liqueur and orange bitters. Please enjoy, and we'll be out with the first round of tapas momentarily." Eduardo turned and disappeared into the kitchen.

"I have to say the best part of my job might be that I get to drink without ending up in the HR office," Deacon quipped with a grin as he picked up the old-fashioned glass containing the Viva Bellamy.

Cecelia opted for the rosé sangria. She took a sip and then smiled. "This is wonderful. It might be the best sangria I have ever had, actually. Try it."

She held the wineglass up to his lips and tipped it until the sweet concoction flowed into his mouth. It was a lovely beverage, but that wasn't what caught his attention. He was far more focused on Cecelia as she watched him. Perhaps Shane was smarter than Deacon gave him credit for. Feeding each other tapas could be quite the unexpectedly sensual experience for a weekday lunch at work.

Eduardo and the waiter returned a moment later with a selection of small plates. "Here we have stuffed piquillo peppers with goat cheese and seasonal mushrooms, seared scallops with English pea puree, chicken skewers with ajillo sauce, and black garlic and grilled lamb with rosemary sauce. Enjoy."

"Wow," Cecelia said. "This all looks amazing, and not at all what I was expecting from a place with a disco saddle hanging over the dance floor. I'd wager there's no place like this within a hundred miles of here. People are going to trip over themselves to get to your restaurant, Deacon."

He certainly hoped so. The array of food was both heavenly scented and visually impressive. He could just picture it being passed around on silver platters and arranged artfully along a buffet display. "Shall we?" he asked.

Cecelia nodded and looked around, considering where to start. "Do we share everything? I've never done tapas before, but this kind of reminds me of dim sum."

"Yes, it's similar. *Tapas* means small plates, so it's just tiny selections of many different, shareable dishes instead of large entrée. Just try whatever you like."

She started by reaching out and pulling a chicken skewer onto one of the empty plates they'd each been given to make the tasting easier. Deacon opted for the lamb.

Cecelia closed her eyes and made a moaning sound of pure pleasure that Deacon recognized from their night together. His body stirred at the memory of that sound echoing in his bedroom.

"Wow," she said as she swallowed her bite and opened her eyes. "I mean, I know I said that already, but it's true, this is so good. You have to try it." She slid a piece of the chicken off the wooden skewer, stabbed it with her fork and held it out to him.

Deacon took a bite and chewed thoughtfully. The flavors were excellent. Her feeding him wasn't bad, either, but he would much prefer to feed her. "That's good. Do you like lamb?"

She nodded. He took the opportunity to stab a small cube of lamb and feed it to her. She closed her eyes again as she chewed, thoroughly enjoying the food in a way he hadn't expected. She'd become quite the foodie since the last time they were together. He suddenly lost interest in trying the food himself, and wanted only to feed Cecelia.

He picked up one of the small stuffed peppers with his fingers and held it up to her. She leaned in, looking into his eyes as she took a bite. Her lips softly brushed his fingertips, sending a shiver through his whole body. When she finished, she took the second bite from his fingers. He tried to pull his hand away but she grabbed his wrist and held it steady.

"Don't you dare waste that sauce," she said. Without hesitation she drew his thumb into her mouth and sucked the spicy cream sauce from his skin.

Deacon almost came up out of his seat. The suction on this thumb combined with the swirl of her tongue against his skin made every muscle in his body tense up and his blood rush to his groin. She seemed unaffected. Cecelia pulled away with a sly smile, releasing his wrist. As though she hadn't just given him oral pleasure, albeit to his hand, she turned back to the selection on the table and chose one of the scallops.

She was just messing with him now. And he liked it.

* * *

The plates just kept coming out of the kitchen, and Cecelia found herself in food heaven. Her roommate in college had been the daughter of a famous Manhattan chef, and she'd exposed Cecelia to cuisines she hadn't tried back home in Texas. She'd developed a brave palate and high expectations by the time she'd graduated. The little diner in Royal had been fine before she left, but when she returned, she found herself trekking to Houston for cuisine with more flair and spice.

Now she'd have access to world-class dining right here in Royal. At that moment, Eduardo and his waiter brought out fried chorizo wrapped in thin slices of potato, a selection of imported jamón ibérico and Spanish cheeses, marinated and grilled vegetables in a Romanesco sauce, garlic shrimp and salmon tartare in salmon roe cones. By the time they got to the dessert selections, Cecelia wasn't sure she could eat much more. She loved her sweets, but she was far more interested in the tall, handsome dish across from her at the moment.

Cecelia would be lying if she said that she hadn't been thinking about Deacon since they shared that kiss Monday night. Part of her wondered if that had been his plan all along—to kiss her, send her home and leave her wanting more.

Cecelia did want more. There was no question of it. She just wasn't sure if indulging her desires was the best idea. There was certainly plenty of sexual attraction flowing between them, and their night of passion would be one she would never forget. But could she risk giving herself to Deacon when she knew she might fall for him again?

It happened so quickly the first time, Cecelia had hardly known what hit her. For a while after they'd broken up, she had thought that perhaps falling in love was easy to do. The years that followed would prove otherwise. No one, not even her ex-fiancé, had captured her heart the way Deacon had. She feared he still had that power over her.

The hotel opened in a little more than two weeks. Deacon had told her that once things were up and running, he would return to Cannes. She couldn't risk his taking her heart with him when he left. A few weeks didn't seem like much time to be together, but Deacon was a well-known commodity to Cecelia. She knew the kind soul she once loved was still there, so even that short time was enough for her to fall miserably in love with him again, just to have him disappear from her life like before.

Cecelia wouldn't let herself believe that this was a second chance to put things right between them. They could make peace, and already had, really, but a relationship between them seemed impossible. Even if he weren't returning to the French Riviera in a few weeks, they both knew she was in no position to start something promising with anyone. Not with Maverick's threat hanging overhead.

She wouldn't blame him for indulging while he was here and not getting attached. Hell, if *he* broke *her* heart this time, it would be some sort of karmic retribution somehow. She deserved it.

Maybe she was just a masochist, but she couldn't walk away from him. Not twice in a lifetime.

"I've got to sample dessert," Deacon said, oblivious to her train of thought. "I might explode or spend this afternoon napping in my office, but I told Shane that I would try everything." He eyed the selection of desserts on the table with dismay.

"I think you've still got room," she said. She reached out and picked up a berry tartlet, bringing it up to his lips. "Take a bite."

He didn't resist. Deacon bit down into the sweet treat, taking half of it into his mouth. Chewing, he watched as she brought the rest of it up to her mouth and finished it off with a satisfied sound.

"Yummy," she said and picked up another treat. This one was a small brownie with whipped cream and a dusting of what looked like chili powder. That would be interesting.

As they made their way through the rest of the desserts, Cecelia could feel them building toward something more. If it wasn't the middle of the afternoon, she was certain he would take her home and make love to her. As it was, she wouldn't be surprised if he escorted her into his office and locked the door. The entire meal had been the tastiest foreplay she'd ever had. It made her want to spend the weekend in bed with him, and she would if it wasn't for that pesky engagement party she had to go to tomorrow night.

It occurred to her that there might be one way to

get through the evening after all. "Deacon, can I ask you for a favor?"

He leaned in, causing the most delicious tingles as he smoothed his palm down her arm. "Anything."

"Would you go with me to Wes and Isabelle's engagement party at the club?" She had no doubt that the gossip would be flying about her breakup with Chip, and it would be so much easier if she had Deacon there with her to soften the blow.

Deacon narrowed his gaze at her. "The club? The Texas Cattleman's Club? Are you serious?"

Cecelia frowned. "Of course I'm serious. Why wouldn't I be serious? I'm a member. Everyone in town practically is a member now. What's the big deal?"

With a sigh, Deacon sat back against the leather of the booth. "The big deal is that I'm not a member. They would never *let* me be a member. I don't exactly relish hanging out someplace where I'm not wanted."

Sometimes Cecelia forgot how hard it was for Deacon to live in Royal back when they were kids. He had never fit in with the others driving the BMWs they got for their sweet sixteenth and going home to their mansions at night. She never really thought about it, because none of it ever mattered to her. He had simply been the most wonderful boy she'd ever known. The fact that he'd driven a beat-up pickup truck and lived in a small, unimpressive house on the edge of town hadn't been important.

But it had been important to him both then and now, gauging by his reaction. Even though he was successful, even though he could buy and sell half the people in this town, he still had a chip on his shoulder.

"You're not seventeen and broke anymore, Deacon. Stop worrying about all those other people and what they might or might not think. Actually, most of them are so self-centered that they won't be nearly as concerned with your being at the club as they will be about a million other things."

She leaned into him and took his hand. The touch of his skin against hers made her long for the night they'd spent together with his hands gliding over her naked body. Cecelia really did want him to go to the party with her, and not just as a buffer from the ire of the town. She wanted to go back to his place afterward and spend all night relishing the feel of him against her.

Cecelia looked in his eyes, hoping they reflected her intentions and thoughts. She stroked the back of his hand with her thumb in the slow, lazy circles guaranteed to drive him wild and get her exactly what she wanted. "Come with me. Please."

Jaw tight, his gaze dropped to his hand. With a soft shake of his head, he sighed. "Okay, you win. When is this engagement party?"

"Tomorrow night. Seven o'clock. Will that work for you?"

Deacon nodded. "I suppose. Will I get some sort of special reward for being your escort for the evening?" he asked with a grin lighting his eyes.

"You absolutely will," she promised. "Do you have anything in mind?"

"I do." Deacon took her hand and scooped it up in his own. He pressed his fingertips into the palm of her hand and stroked gently but firmly, turning her own trick on her. It was easy to imagine those hands on her body, those fingers stroking the fires that burned deep inside her. "What are you doing after work today?" he asked.

Her gaze met his, a small smile curling her lips even as he continued to tease her with his fingertips. "Nothing much," she said coyly. "What do you plan to do tonight?"

Deacon leaned into her, burying his fingers in the loose hair at the nape of her neck and bringing her lips a fraction of an inch from his own. She wanted to close the gap between them and lose herself in his kiss. It was all she wanted, all she could think of when they were this close. She could feel the warmth of his breath on her lips. Her tongue snaked across her bottom lip to wet it in anticipation of his kiss.

Instead he smiled and let his fingers trace along the line of her jaw. "Why, I plan to be doing *you*, Miss Morgan."

Seven

"So, are you friends with Wes or Isabelle?" Deacon asked as they slipped into the crowd mingling at the clubhouse.

Cecelia twisted her lips as she tried to come up with a good answer. "Neither, really. Wes and I are business rivals. We dated a while back, but that's it. I don't really know Isabelle that well, either."

"Why would he invite his ex to his engagement party?"

That was a good question, considering she was also the reason he'd gone years without knowing he had a daughter. She still felt bad about misjudging that whole situation. She'd helped to correct it in the end, but Wes would never get that time back, and that was her fault. "Well, in a roundabout way, I did help bring him and Isabelle back together after they broke up a few years ago."

"How's that?"

She shook her head and reached out for a flute of champagne being passed on a tray by a waiter in the standard black-and-white uniform of the club. Cecelia hesitated to tell Deacon what she'd done. He still saw her as the sweet girl he'd dated in school, and she didn't want him to see her any differently. "You don't want to know."

"Not good?" Deacon asked.

She shrugged. "Let's just say it wasn't my finest moment. But it all turned out well in the end, and since Isabelle invited me despite it all, I knew I needed to come and work on mending those bridges." Leaning into him, she spoke quieter so others nearby couldn't hear her. "I fear that before too long, I'll need all the friends I can get."

Deacon slipped a protective arm around her waist. "If anyone so much as says an ugly word to you tonight, I'll punch them in the jaw."

Cecelia smiled and leaned into his embrace. She wouldn't mind seeing Chip sprawled across the worn hardwood floor of the club, but that would cause more trouble than it was worth. And she probably deserved some of those ugly words. "That won't be necessary, but thank you."

As they turned back toward the crowd, the people parted and Isabelle rushed forward to give Cecelia a hug. She looked radiant tonight in a shimmering bronze cocktail dress that brought out the copper in her hazel eyes. "Cecelia, you made it! I'm so glad."

Cecelia accepted the hug and smiled as warmly as she could. Once she realized she'd been wrong about Isabelle's gold-digging ways, she found she really did like her. Now she just had to fight off the pangs of envy where Wes's fiancée was concerned. Soon, Isabelle would have the family that Cecelia had always wanted. She shouldn't hold that against her, though. It was a long time coming, raising Caroline as a single mother, in part because of Cecelia's meddling.

Turning to her date, Cecelia introduced them. "Isabelle, this is Deacon Chase. He's building The Bellamy with Shane Delgado."

Isabelle smiled and shook his hand. "I'm so excited for the hotel to open. It looks amazing from the outside."

Cecelia could tell Deacon was nervous, but he was handling it well. "Thank you," he said politely. "It looks amazing on the inside, too, thanks to Cecelia's great designs. Congratulations on your engagement."

"Thank you."

"It looks like a great turnout," Cecelia noted. "Even Teddy Bradford is here." That was a surprise to everyone, she was certain. She knew the CEO of Playco had been in merger negotiations with Wes before Maverick outed him as a deadbeat dad. Teddy espoused family values and had dropped Wes's Texas Toy Company like a rock when he found out about Isabelle and Caroline.

"I actually invited him," Isabelle confided. "I

haven't given up on the Playco merger, even if Wes thinks all is lost. I'm hoping that when he sees us together he'll reconsider the deal."

Cecelia could only nod blankly at Isabelle's machinations. The merger of Playco and Texas Toy Company wouldn't be good news for To the Moon and its bottom line, which is why Cecelia had kept her mouth shut where that was concerned. Wes was her biggest business rival. However, the success of Luna Fine Furnishings would make her untouchable if she could compete in both the adult and child luxury design markets. At the moment, things were going well enough that she didn't care if Teddy took Wes back.

"Good luck with that," she managed politely. "And congratulations on the engagement."

Isabelle crossed her fingers and said her goodbyes, slipping away to find Wes in the crowd. Once she was gone, Cecelia and Deacon continued to make their way through the room, saying hello and mingling appropriately. When they found the food, they each made a small plate and had a seat among some of the other guests. A long buffet had been set up for the party, with the centerpiece being a cake shaped like two hearts side by side with a third, smaller heart piped in pastel pink icing on top to represent their daughter. It was sweet.

They were perhaps an hour into the party, with no sign of Chip, and Cecelia was finally starting to relax. Maybe this event wouldn't be such a nightmare. Being there with Deacon had changed everything. She felt confident on his arm, which was a far cry from the times she'd gone to events with Chip. She was always on edge with him, wondering if she looked good enough, if she was saying the right thing... Now that it was over, she couldn't imagine a lifetime of being his wife. All she would have ever been was a prop he'd haul out at campaign rallies and fund-raisers. A Stepford wife in a tasteful linen suit with helmet hair and a single strand of pearls.

No way. Those days were behind her, and she'd never make that mistake again.

"I would like to propose a toast," Teddy Bradford said as he took position center stage with the microphone to draw everyone's attention. Cecelia noted that the boisterous old man was wearing his best bolo tie for the occasion. The crowd gathered around the stage to hear what he had to say. "Wesley, Isabelle, get on up here!"

The happy couple walked hand in hand to the stage and to stand beside Teddy.

"No one here is happier to see these two lovebirds tie the knot than I am. To me, and to the employees of Playco, family is everything. I had thought that perhaps Wesley felt differently, but I'm pleased—for once—to be proven wrong. Not only do I want to wish the couple all the happiness in the world, I want to wish it as Wesley's new business partner."

His words were followed by a roar of applause from the crowd. Wes turned to Isabelle with a look of shock on his face before he turned and shook Teddy's hand. Cecelia could only smile. Isabelle seemed sweet, but she was shrewd, as well. She had managed to accomplish tonight what Wes had been unable to over the past three months. Bravo. Perhaps she had more competition in the Texas Toy Company than she thought with Isabelle behind the scenes.

Wes turned back to Isabelle, they kissed and everyone in the club went wild. Deacon held Cecelia tighter to his side as though he sensed tension in her.

"Is this bad news for your company?" he whispered in her ear. Clearly, he knew it was or he wouldn't be asking.

"Perhaps, but I'm trying not to look at it that way. Those kinds of thoughts were what landed me such a miserable reputation in town. That's a worry for another day. Tonight I'd rather focus on the happy couple."

He nodded and pressed a kiss into her temple. "Then that's what we're going to do."

Cecelia sighed contentedly in his arms while Isabelle and Wes cut the cake and pieces started circulating around the room. "They cut the cake," she noted. "Cake is the universal sign at parties that it's finally okay to take your leave."

"Are you ready to go so soon?" Deacon asked. "I thought you were having a good time. And it looks like strawberry cake. We should probably at least stick around to have some. I love strawberry cake."

"When did you get such a sweet tooth?" Cecelia asked.

"It started back in high school when I couldn't get enough of your sugar."

Cecelia laughed aloud and leaned close. "You

don't need any cake, then. You're getting plenty of sugar once we get out of here. You've made it through the night with no complaints, and you should be rewarded."

Deacon smiled. "I'm glad you agree. It wasn't that bad, though." His glance moved around the room at the club and the people who frequented it. "I think I'd made more of this place in my mind because I couldn't be a part of it."

"No one would dare keep you out now."

Cecelia felt her phone vibrate in her purse, but she wasn't going to get it out just yet. As they waited on cake, she noticed quite a few people pulling theirs out.

"Oh, my God, honey." Simone ran up to her and clapped her hand over her mouth to hold back a sob.

Cecelia looked at her and again around the room in sudden panic. One person after another seemed to be looking down at his or her phone. The feeling of dread was hard for Cecelia to suppress. Especially when those same people immediately sought out Cecelia when they looked up.

Had Maverick's deadline already come and gone so soon? She had consciously decided not to pay the blackmail money again, but she never dreamed it would come out tonight, while she was at the club with everyone else.

"What is it?" she asked as innocently as she could, although she already knew the answer.

Simone held up her phone, showing the screen to her and Deacon. An old newspaper article about the drug overdose of Nicole Wood was there. It even featured the photo of Nicole and her infant daughter, the same one Cecelia carried in her purse. The section was circled in red and accompanied by a note:

Cecelia Morgan? More like Cecelia Wood—a liar and the daughter of a junkie and her dealer. No wonder the Morgans hid the truth. The homecoming queen isn't so perfect now, is she?

Deacon's arms tightened around Cecelia as she felt her knees start to buckle beneath her. It was only his support that kept her upright. She looked around the room, and it seemed like everyone was looking at her as though she smelled like horse manure.

Her head started to swim as she heard the voices in the room combine together into a low rumble. She could pick out only pieces of it.

"Who knew she was so low class?"

"I should've known she wasn't really a Morgan. But it looks like she's not Maverick, either."

"Her mother probably used drugs during her pregnancy, too. I wonder if that's why Cecelia is so incapable of empathy."

"Have they ever revoked someone's club membership for fraud?"

"You can see the resemblance between her and this Nicole woman. She never had Tilly's classically beautiful features."

Cecelia covered her ears with her hands to smother the voices. Her face flushed red, and tears started pouring from her eyes. Deacon said something to her, but she couldn't hear him. All she could feel was her world crumbling around her. She should've made the second blackmail payment. What was she thinking? That he would decide maybe that first payment was enough? That people wouldn't judge her the way she would've judged them not long ago?

It was a huge mistake, and yet, she knew this was a moment that couldn't be avoided no matter how much cash she shelled out. It wasn't about the money, she knew that much. He probably didn't care if he made a dime in the process. Maverick was set on ruining people's lives.

He would be a happy man tonight.

Deacon didn't know who Maverick was, but he sure as hell was going to find out. Why did this sick bastard get pleasure out of hurting people in the club? Deacon would be the first to admit this wasn't his favorite crowd of people, but who would stoop that low? If he could get his hands on Maverick right now, the coward would have bigger concerns than whose life he could make miserable next.

First things first, however. He could see Cecelia breaking down, and it made his chest ache. He had to get her away from this. With every eye in the room on them, he wrapped his arm around Cecelia and tried to guide her to the exit. She stumbled a few times, as though her legs were useless beneath her, so he stopped long enough to scoop her into his arms and carry her out. She didn't fight his heroics. Instead, she clung desperately to him, burying her face in the lapel of his suit.

The crowd parted as they made their way to the door. Half the people in the room looked disgusted. Some were in shock. A few more looked worried, probably concerned that their dark secret might be the next exposed by Maverick. There were only a few people in the room who looked at all concerned about Cecelia herself, and that made him almost as angry as he was with the blackmailing bastard that started this mess.

That was the problem with this town—the cliquish bullshit was ridiculous. It was just as bad in high school as it was now. It made him glad that he'd decided to leave Royal instead of staying in this toxic environment.

The problem was that most of the people in the town were in the clique, so they didn't see the issue. It was only the outsiders who suffered by their viper-pit mentality. Deacon had always been an outsider, and money and prestige hadn't changed that, not really. He'd gotten through the doors of the club tonight, but he still didn't fit in. And he didn't want to.

Yet if he had to bet money on Maverick's identity, he'd put it on another outsider. Whoever it was was just kicking the hornet's nest for fun, watching TCC members turn on each other so they would know what it felt like to be him.

Cecelia didn't need to be around for the fallout. This entire situation was out of her control, and she would be the one to suffer unnecessarily for it. Brent and Tilly should be here, taking on their share of the club's disgust for forcing her to live this lie to begin with. If they'd been honest about adopting Cecelia, there would've been nothing for Maverick to hold over her head.

He shoved the heavy oak door open with his foot and carried her out to the end of the portico. There, he settled her back on her feet. "Are you okay to stand?" he asked.

"Yes," she said, sniffing and wiping the streams of mascara from her flush cheeks.

"I'm going to go get my car. Will you be okay?"

She nodded. Deacon reached into his pocket to get his keys, but before he could step into the parking lot, a figure stumbled out of the dark bushes nearby. He didn't recognize the man, but he didn't like the looks of him, either. He was thin with stringy hair and bugged-out eyes. Even without the stink of alcohol and the stumble in his steps, Deacon could tell this was a guy on the edge. Maybe even the kind of guy who would blackmail the whole town.

"Cecelia *Wood*?" he asked, with a lopsided smile that revealed a mess of teeth inside. "Shoulda seen that one coming, right? Nobody is that perfect. Even a princess like you needs to be knocked off their high horse every now and then, right?"

Deacon stepped protectively between him and Cecelia. "Who the hell is this guy?" he asked.

"Adam Haskell," she whispered over his shoulder. "He has a small ranch on the edge of town. I'm surprised he hasn't lost it to the banks yet. All he does is drink anymore."

The name sounded familiar from Deacon's childhood, but the man in front of him had lived too many rough years to be recognizable. "Why don't you call a cab and sleep that booze off, Adam?"

The drunk didn't even seem to hear him. He was focused entirely on Cecelia. "You had it coming, you know. You can only go through life treating people like dirt for so long before karma comes back and slaps you across the face. Now you're getting a taste of your own medicine."

"Now, that's enough," Deacon said more forcefully. This time he got Adam's attention.

"Look at Deacon Chase all grow-w-wn up," he slurred. "You should hate her as much as I do. She treated you worse than anyone else. Used you and spit you out when she didn't need you anymore."

"Adam!" A man's sharp voice came from the doorway of the club. A lanky but solid man with short blond hair stepped outside with a redhead at his side.

"Mac and Violet McCallum!" Adam said as he turned his attention to them, nearly losing his drunken footing and falling over. "You're just in time. I was telling Deacon here how he's made a mistake trying to protect her. She's made her bed, it's time for her to lie in it, don't you think?"

Deacon's hands curled into fists of rage at his sides. He was getting tired of this guy's mouth. If he couldn't get his hands on Maverick, Mr. Haskell would do in a pinch.

"All right, Adam, you know you're not supposed to be here on the property if you're not a member of the club. They'll call the sheriff on you again. You can't afford the bail."

"Best sleep I ever get is in the drunk tank," he declared proudly, then belched.

"Even then." Mac came up to Adam and put an arm around his shoulder. "How about we give you a ride home, Adam? You don't need to be driving."

Adam pouted in disappointment, but he didn't fight Mac off. "Aw, I'm just having a little fun with her. Right, Cecelia? No harm done."

Mac just shook his head. "Well, tonight's not a good night for it. I'm pretty sure the party is over. If you stay around here any longer, it might be a fist and not the vodka that knocks you out tonight."

Mac was right. Deacon was glad the couple had intervened when they had or he might've had to get physical with the scrawny drunk.

"I can take anyone," Adam muttered.

"I'm sure you can," Mac agreed and rolled his eyes. "But let's not risk it tonight and ruin Isabelle's party any more than it already has been."

Mac led Adam toward his truck while Violet stayed behind with Deacon and Cecelia. "I'm so sorry, Cecelia," she said. "This whole thing with Maverick is getting out of hand. I can't imagine who would want to hurt everyone so badly. And the way people reacted...it's not right."

Cecelia came out from behind Deacon, still clinging to his arm. "Thank you, Violet."

The redhead just nodded sadly and followed Mac and Adam out into the parking lot. Cecelia watched her go with a heavy sigh. "There goes one of the five people in town who hasn't turned on me."

He hated hearing that kind of defeat from her. Cecelia was his fighter. He wasn't about to let Maverick beat her down. "You know what you need?" Deacon asked. "You need to get away from here."

She nodded. "Yeah, I'd like to go home if you don't mind."

Home wouldn't help. Word about her would just spread through town like wildfire, and soon everyone would know. Her parents would show up lamenting how embarrassing this was for them and making Cecelia feel even worse. Her friends would drop in to commiserate and reopen the wounds she was struggling to heal. No, she needed to get the hell out of Royal for a few days.

"I have another idea." Deacon took her hand and led her to his car. After the scene with Adam, he was too worried to leave her alone in case a partygoer came out of the club and had something nasty to say. When they got to his car, he opened the door and helped her in. "You're not going home."

She looked at him in surprise. "I'm not? Where are we going, then? To your place?"

Deacon shook his head and closed her door. He climbed into his side and revved the engine. He had bigger, better plans than just hiding her away at his wood-and-stone sanctuary. "I guess you could look at it that way."

He pulled out of the parking lot and picked up his phone. He dialed his private jet service and made all the necessary arrangements while Cecelia sat looking confused and beat down in the seat beside him.

Finally, he hung up and put the phone down. "It's all handled."

Cecelia turned in her seat to look at him. "You said we were going to your place, but that's back the other way. Then you have some vague conversation about going home for a few days. That doesn't make any sense. Where are we going, Deacon?"

He smiled, hoping this little mystery was enough to distract her from the miserable night. "Well, first we're stopping at your place so you can pack a bag and grab your passport."

He turned in time to see her silvery, gray eyes widen. "My passport? Why on earth…?"

Deacon grinned. This was a turn of events he hadn't expected, but it was the perfect escape. She needed to get away, he wanted to show her his crown jewel…it all worked out. By the time they returned to Royal, perhaps some new gossip from Maverick would crop up and make everyone forget about Cecelia's birth mother.

"Yes, and once you're packed, we're going to the airport where a private jet is waiting to take the two of us to one of my other properties, the Hotel de Rêve."

Cecelia sat in shock beside him. It took a few moments before she could respond. "Deacon, your other hotel is in *France*."

He pulled into her driveway and put the Corvette

into Park. "Yes. Hence the need for your passport. Pack for the French Riviera in the spring."

She shook her head, making her blond waves dance around her shoulders. Cecelia had really looked lovely tonight, in a beautiful and clingy gray lace dress that brought out the gray in her eyes, but he'd barely had time to appreciate it between the mingling and the drama.

"No, Deacon, this is crazy talk. I can't go to France tonight even if I wanted to. The Bellamy opens in two weeks. I have so much to do—"

"*Your staff* has things to do," he interrupted, "and they know what those things are. You're not carrying furniture and wiring lamps into the wall. You're the designer, and most of your work is handled. Shane will oversee everything else, I promise. You and I are getting out of this town for a few days to let this whole mess blow over. End of discussion."

The way Cecelia looked at him, he could tell it wasn't the end of the discussion yet. "Couldn't we just go to Houston or something to get away? Maybe New Orleans? No one would know where we were. We don't have to go all the way to France, do we?"

Deacon disagreed. He turned off the car and got out, opening her door. "Yes, we do."

"Why?" she persisted as she stood to look at him.

"Because I don't own a hotel in New Orleans. Now get inside and pack that bag. The plane leaves for Cannes in an hour."

Eight

Cecelia woke up in a nest of soft, luxury linens with bright light streaming through the panoramic hotel room windows. Wincing from the light, she pushed herself up in bed and looked around the suite for Deacon. She could see him on the balcony reading a newspaper and drinking his café au lait at a tiny bistro table there.

She wrapped the blanket around her naked body and padded barefoot to the sliding glass door. The view from the owner's suite of the Hotel de Rêve was spectacular. The hotel was almost directly on the beach, with only the famous Boulevard de la Croisette separating his property from the golden sands that lined the Mediterranean Sea. To the left of the hotel was a marina filled with some the largest and most luxurious yachts she'd ever seen. To the right, beautiful, tan tourists had already taken up residence on the beach.

The sea was a deep turquoise against the bright robin's-egg blue of the sky. There wasn't a cloud, a blemish, a single thing to ruin the perfection. It was almost as if the place wasn't real. When they'd first arrived the day before, Cecelia wasn't entirely certain that this wasn't a delusion brought on by jet lag. But after a quick nap, Cannes was just as pretty as it had been earlier. Of course, enjoying it with the handsome— and partially clothed—hotel owner hadn't hurt, either.

"*Bonjour, belle*," he greeted her. He was sitting in a pair of black silk pajama pants, and thankfully, he seemed to have misplaced the top. His golden tan and chiseled chest and arms were on display, and now she knew how he had gotten that dark. If she spent every morning enjoying the sun here, she might actually get a little color for her porcelain complexion, as well.

Cecelia didn't know why she was surprised to find that he was fluent in French, considering Deacon had lived here for several years and had to interact with guests, locals and staff, alike. She supposed it just didn't align with the Deacon she had once known— covered in motor oil or rinsing cafeteria trays—although it suited Deacon perfectly as he was now.

It made her wish she had kept up with her French studies after high school. She'd quickly lost most of her vocabulary and conjugation, really being able to function now only as a tourist asking for directions to the nearest restroom. "*Bonjour*," she replied in her most practiced accent. "That's about all the French I have for today."

Deacon laughed and folded his paper, which was also in French. "That's okay," he said, leaning forward to give her a good-morning kiss. "Perhaps later we can crawl back into bed and practice a little more French."

Cecelia couldn't suppress the girlish giggle at his innuendo. Deacon was smart to bring her to Cannes. There was just something about being here, thousands of miles away from Royal and all her worries, that made her feel like a completely different person. She liked this person a hell of a lot more than the woman who had very nearly married Chip Ashford. Apparently most of Royal hadn't liked her, either, judging by their reaction to her being knocked down a peg or two by Maverick's gossip.

Cecelia sat down at the table next to him, and he poured her a cup of coffee, passing her the pitcher of milk to add as much as she would like. He followed it with a plate of flaky, fresh croissants and preserves.

"Do you have anything in mind that you would like to do today?" he asked. "Yesterday we were too exhausted to do much more than change time zones, but I thought you might like to see a little bit of the town this afternoon. You haven't been to Cannes if you haven't strolled along la Croisette, sipped a beautiful rosé and watched the sunset. We could even take my yacht out for a spin."

She took a large sip of her coffee and nodded into her delicate china teacup. "That sounds lovely. I've never been to the French Riviera, so I would be happy to see anything that you would like to show me. I mean," she continued, "it's not like this is a trip that I've planned for a long time. I basically just let you sweep me off my feet and I woke up in France. I would be perfectly content to just sit on this balcony and look out at the sea if that was all we had time to do."

Deacon smiled. "Well, I figure there is no place on earth better suited to relax and forget about all your problems than the French Riviera. I've seen more than one tightly wound businessman completely transform in only a few days. After everything that has happened recently, I think it's just what the doctor ordered, Miss Morgan."

She couldn't argue with that. He was absolutely right. Here, the drama of Maverick and the fallout of her exposed secret felt like a distant memory, or a dream that she'd nearly forgotten about as she'd awakened. She had gotten a couple texts from Simone and her mother yesterday morning after they'd landed, but Deacon had insisted she turn off her phone. Overage charges for international roaming were a good excuse, he'd said, and once again he had been right. She didn't want talk to her mother or anyone else right now.

She just wanted to soak in the glorious rays of the sun, enjoy the beauty around her and relish her time alone with Deacon. They would return home soon enough to open the hotel, and she'd finally face everything she had been running from her whole life.

"I took the liberty of scheduling an appointment for you at our spa today. My talented ladies have been told to give you the works, so a massage, a mud bath, a facial... Whatever your little heart desires. That should take up a good chunk of your day, and then we can hit the shore later this afternoon, once you've been properly pampered."

Cecelia could only shake her head and thank her lucky stars that she had Deacon here with her through all of this. How would she have coped alone? Just having him by her side would've been enough, but he always had to go the extra mile, and she appreciated it. She just wasn't sure how she could ever repay him.

She idly slathered a bit of orange marmalade on a piece of croissant and popped it into her mouth. "You're too good to me, Deacon," she said as she chewed thoughtfully. "I don't deserve any of this VIP treatment. I'm beginning to think that maybe Adam Haskell was right, and all the negativity I've been breeding all these years was just coming back to haunt me. It had to eventually, right?"

"You're too hard on yourself," Deacon said. "The girl I fell in love with was sweet and caring and saw things in me that no one else saw. You might pretend now that you are a cold-as-ice businesswoman set to crush your competitors and anybody who gets in your way, but I don't believe it for a second. That girl I know is still in there somewhere."

Cecelia appreciated that he had so much faith in her, but she wasn't the innocent girl he knew from back in school. That girl had been smothered the day her parents forced her to break up with Deacon and put her life back on track to the future that they wanted for her. She had become an unfortunate mix of both her parents—a cutthroat business owner, a perfection-seeking elitist and, more often than she would have liked, a plain old bitch. He hadn't been around to see the changes in her, but she knew it was true. She was absolutely certain that most of the people in town were thrilled to see her taken down a notch. Maybe even a few of the people whom she'd once considered her friends.

"I'm glad you think so highly of me, Deacon, but I can't help but wonder if you're actually seeing me as I am, or as you want to see me."

"I see you as you are, beneath the designer clothes, fancy makeup and social facade you've crafted. That girl hasn't changed. She's still in there, you just haven't let her out in a long time."

Cecelia felt tears start to well in her eyes as her cheeks burned with emotion. She really hoped that he was right, and that the good person he remembered was still here. It seemed like over the past decade she had lost touch with herself, if she had ever really known who she truly was. She'd spent her whole life trying to live up to her parents' expectations, then Chip's expectations…

Who *was* Cecelia Morgan anyway?

She wiped her damp cheek with the back of her hand and reached for her coffee cup to give her something to focus on instead of the emotions raging just beneath the surface. "I don't know who I am anymore."

Deacon leaned forward, resting his elbows on the knees of his pajama pants. "That's the beauty of being in charge of your own life and not trying to live up to anybody else's standards. You can do whatever you want to do. If I had just sat back and accepted the life that everyone expected of me, we wouldn't be sitting on the balcony of my five-star hotel in France. I wanted to be more, so I made myself more. You can be who- ever you want to be, Cecelia, and if that means putting aside the mean-girl persona you've had all these years, and being the girl I used to know, you can do that, too."

"Can I?" she asked. "I'm not entirely sure that girl knew who she was, either. I was so easily manipulated at that age. I mean, all those plans we made, all those dreams we had for the future…that was important to me and I threw it all away. For what? Because my parents threatened to cut me off and throw me out of the house if I didn't."

Deacon's head turned sharply toward her. "What?"

Cecelia winced. "You didn't know that?"

His expression softened. "I suppose I knew they were ultimately behind your change of heart, but I thought you just wanted to please them as you al- ways did."

"I did want to please them, but not about this. I loved you, Deacon. I didn't want to break up with you. It broke my heart to do it, but I felt like I didn't have any choice. They were my parents. The only people in the world who had wanted me when no one else did. I couldn't bear for them to turn their backs on me."

"I wanted you."

Cecelia looked into Deacon's serious green eyes and realized she had made a monumental mistake that day all those years ago. Yes, she had a booming business and he had been successful on his own, but what could they have built together? They'd never know.

"I was a fool," she admitted. "I don't want to make the same mistake again. I want to make the right choice for my life this time."

Cecelia sipped her coffee and tried to think of who she wanted to be. Not who her parents wanted her to be. Not who Chip expected her to be. The answer came to her faster than she anticipated. She wanted to be the woman she was when she was with Deacon. When she was with him she felt strong and brave and beautiful. She never felt like she wasn't good enough. That was how she wanted to feel: loved.

But could she feel that way without him? Their time together had been exciting and romantic, but she had no doubt there was a time limit. Deacon had no interest in staying in Royal. He didn't like the town and he didn't like the people, and for a good reason. When The Bellamy was opened and running, he would return here to France, and she didn't blame him. This may very well be the most beautiful place she'd ever seen. She would be eager to return, as well.

She might feel like a superhero when she was with him, but once she was alone, could she be her own kryptonite?

"Dinner was wonderful," Cecelia said.

Deacon took her hand and they strolled along la Croisette together. The sun had already set, leaving the sky a golden color that was quickly being overtaken by the inky purple of early evening. The lights from the shops and restaurants along the walkway lighted their path and the crests of the ocean waves beyond them.

"I'm glad you enjoyed it. There's no such thing as bad food in France. They wouldn't allow it."

Cecelia laughed and Deacon found himself trying to memorize the sound. He hadn't heard her laughter nearly enough when they were in Royal. He missed it. In their carefree younger days, she'd laughed freely and often. He wanted her to laugh more even if he wasn't around to hear it. That was part of the reason he'd brought her here—to get her away from the drama of home in the hopes he might catch a fleeting glimpse of the girl he'd once loved.

Not that he didn't appreciate the woman she'd become. The older, wiser, sexier Cecelia certainly had its benefits. Looking at her now, he could hardly keep his hands to himself. She was wearing a cream lace fitted sheath dress. It plunged deep, highlighting her ample cleavage, and clung to every womanly curve she'd developed while they were apart. Falling for Cecelia was the last thing on his mind when he arrived in Royal, but it was virtually impossible for him to keep his distance from her when she looked like that.

"Can we walk in the water?" she asked, surprising him.

"If you want to."

They both slipped out of their shoes, and Deacon rolled up his suit pants. He hadn't thought she would want to walk along the shore and let the sand ruin her new pedicure. Yet with her crystal embellished stilettos in her free hand, she tugged him off the stone path toward the water.

The cold water that washed over them was a shocking contrast to the warm sand on his bare feet. He expected Cecelia to bolt the moment the chill hit her, but instead, her eyes got big with excitement and she laughed again.

"It's a little chilly," he said.

"It's April. It feels good, though. I can't remember the last time I put my toes in the sand and walked through the surf. Too long."

Deacon felt momentarily sheepish. He couldn't remember the last time he'd done it, either, and it was right outside his window the majority of the year.

"I understand why you'd rather be here than Royal," she said after they walked a good bit down the shoreline. "It's beautiful. And so different. I don't know that I want to go back, either." She chuckled and shook her head. "I will, but I don't want to."

Deacon felt the sudden urge to ask her why she couldn't stay. "Why go back?" he asked. "You don't have to do anything you don't want to do."

She looked at him through narrowed eyes. "Well, for one thing, I haven't finished your hotel yet. It opens in just a week and a half, if you'll recall. Plus, my company is in Royal. My employees. My friends and family."

"You could have all that here," he offered. "And me, too." Deacon surprised himself with the words, but he couldn't stop them from coming out. What would it be like to have her here with him all the time? Away from her parents' sphere of influence and the society nonsense she'd fallen prey to. He wanted to know.

Cecelia stopped walking, pulling him to a stop beside her. "You're not going to stay in Royal, are you?"

He shook his head. "You know I'm not."

Cecelia's gaze drifted into the distance. "I know. I guess a part of me was just hoping."

Deacon's heart sped in his chest. He hadn't given much thought to this fling with Cecelia lasting beyond the grand opening. He just couldn't disappoint himself that way. But it sounded like she was open to the possibility. "Hoping what?" he pressed.

"Hoping that you'd change your mind and stay awhile."

Deacon sighed. There were a lot of things he would do for her, but stay in Royal? He couldn't even imagine it. He didn't know why she'd ask him to, either. Didn't she realize how everyone treated him? How miserable it was for him? She didn't seem very happy there, either. "Royal, Texas, and I parted ways a long time ago."

Cecelia looked at him. "We parted ways, too, and yet here we are. Anything can happen."

He didn't want to argue about this and ruin their night. They were together now, and that was the most important thing. "You're right," he conceded. "Anything can happen. We'll see what the future brings."

Taking her hand into his, they started back down the beach. They were only a hundred yards or so from his hotel when he saw a child chasing after a dog on the beach. The little boy must've dropped the leash, and the large, wooly mutt seemed quite pleased with his newfound freedom.

In fact, the dog was heading right toward them. Before Deacon could react, the dog made a beeline for Cecelia. It jumped up, placing two dirty paw prints on her chest and knocking her off balance. Her hand slipped from his as she stumbled back and fell into the waves that were rushing up around their feet. She yelled as she tried—and failed—to find her footing in the icy water, soaking her dress and hair.

Deacon was in a panic and so was the little boy. They both lunged to pull the dog off her as it enthusiastically licked her face. It wasn't until the dog was yanked away that he realized Cecelia's shrieks were actually laughter. He stood, stunned for a moment by her reaction. Then he offered her his hand to lift her up out of the water, but she didn't take it. She was laughing too hard to care.

It was the damnedest thing he'd ever seen. The people back in Royal wouldn't believe it if Maverick circulated a picture of it. The perfect and poised Cecelia Morgan lying in the ocean fully clothed and covered in mud. The cream lace dress was absolutely ruined with dirty paw prints rubbed down the front. Her makeup was smeared across her skin, and her blond hair hung in damp tendrils around her face. She was a mess. But she didn't seem to care. And she couldn't have been more beautiful.

"*Je m'excuse, mademoiselle*," the little boy said as he fought with the dog that weighed a good ten pounds more than he did. "*Mauvais chien!*" he chastised the pup, who finally sat down looking smug about the whole thing.

"Cecelia, are you okay?" Deacon asked. He wasn't sure what to do.

She struggled to catch her breath, then nodded. Her face was flushed bright red beneath the smears of her foundation and mascara. "I'm fine." She reached up for Deacon, and when he took her hand, she tugged hard, catching him off guard and jerking him down into the water with her.

"What the—" he complained as he pushed up from the water, soaked, but the joyful expression on her face stopped him. He rolled up to a seated position beside her. "Was that really necessary?" he asked.

She didn't answer him. Instead, she wrapped her arms around his neck and pulled him into a kiss. Deacon instantly forgot about the water, the dog, the cost of his ruined suit... All that mattered was the taste of Cecelia on his lips and the press of her body against his. She was uninhibited and free in his arms, kissing him with the same abandon she had that first night after her breakup with Chip. There was no desperation this time, however. Just excitement and need.

He couldn't help but respond to it. This side of Cecelia was one he thought he might never see again. It was the side that had made out with him in the back of his truck, letting him get her hair and makeup all disheveled. It was the side that had sprayed him with the hose while he was detailing one of his restored cars and led to them getting covered in mud and grass as they wrestled on his front lawn.

Deacon had missed this Cecelia. Perfectly imperfect. Dirty. Joyful. Hot as hell. He realized that they weren't alone in the back of his truck, however. The little French boy and his dog were still standing there. He forced himself to pull away, looking over the mess she'd become.

The dress had been tight before, but wet, it was clingy and damn near see-through. He could see the hardened peaks of her nipples pressing through the fabric. He would have to give her his coat to cover her when they walked home.

"*Américains fous*," the little boy said with a dismayed shake of his head. He tugged on the dog's leash and headed back in the direction he'd come from.

"What did he say?" Cecelia asked.

"He called us crazy Americans." Deacon wiped the water from his face and slicked back his hair. "I have to say I agree."

Cecelia giggled into her hand and looked down at her dress. Her fingers traced over some of the sand and mud embedded in the delicate lace and silk. "My mother just bought me this dress for Christmas. It was the first time I'd worn it. Oh, well."

"I'll buy you ten new dresses," he said. Deacon pushed himself up out of the water and helped her up, too. He slipped out of his suit coat, wringing out the water before placing it over her shoulders.

"I don't want more dresses," she said, pressing her body to his seductively with the little boy long gone. A wicked glint lit her eyes as her lips curled into a deceptively sweet smile. "I just want you. Right now."

Deacon swallowed hard. "I think this walk along the beach is over, don't you?"

Nine

"Where are we going?" Cecelia asked.

Deacon smiled from the driver's seat of his silver Renault Laguna. In France he drove a French car. It seemed appropriate. They were only about ten minutes outside the city, and she was already keen to know everything. "It's a surprise."

Cecelia pouted. "Isn't it enough of a surprise to bring me to France on a whim in the first place?"

Perhaps. But last night, he'd gotten a sneak peek at the Cecelia he'd fallen in love with. There, lying in the surf, covered in muddy paw prints and soaked to the bone with seawater, he'd seen a glimpse of her. The radiant smile, the flushed cheeks, the weight of the world lifted from her shoulders in that moment... He wanted to capture that feeling in a bottle for her so she could keep it forever and pull it out whenever she needed to.

It also helped him realize he was on the right track with her. Getting her away from Royal was the best thing he could've done. It wasn't enough, though. Now Deacon wanted to get her even farther from the city, farther from people, to see what she could be like if she could truly let loose. There was nothing like the fields of Provence for that.

It was the perfect day for a picnic. The skies were clear and a brilliant shade of blue. It was a warm spring day, with a light breeze that would keep them from getting overheated in the sun. It was the kind of day that beckoned him outside, and the chance to make love to Cecelia in a field of wildflowers under this same sky was an opportunity he couldn't pass up.

The hotel's kitchen had put together a picnic basket for them, and he'd hustled her into the car without a word. Cecelia hadn't seen him put the basket and blanket in the trunk, so she was stewing in her seat, wondering what they were up to. He liked torturing her just a little bit. She was always in charge of everything at her company. Today, he wanted her to just let him take care of her and enjoy herself for once.

Of course, if he'd told her they were going to Grasse, she wouldn't know what that was. It was a tiny, historic French town surrounded by lavender fields that fueled their local perfumeries. It was too early for the lavender to bloom—that wouldn't happen until late summer—but there would still be fields of grasses and wildflowers for them to sit in and enjoy with a lovely bottle of Provençal rosé.

He found a tiny gravel road that turned off into a field about a mile before they reached Grasse. He followed it, finding the perfect picnic spot beneath an old, weathered tree. He turned off the car and smiled at Cecelia's puzzled expression.

"Where are we?"

Deacon got out of the car and walked around to let her out. "Provence. It's the perfect afternoon for a picnic in the French countryside with a lovely lady such as yourself."

Cecelia smiled and took the hand he offered to climb out of the Renault. She was looking so beautiful today. Her long blond hair was loose in waves around her shoulders. It was never like that in Texas. She always kept it up in a bun or twist of some kind that was all business, no pleasure. He liked it down, where he could run his fingers through the golden silk of it.

She was also wearing a breezy sundress with a sweater that tugged just over her shoulders. The dress had a floral pattern of yellows and greens that pulled out the mossy tones in her eyes. It clung to her figure in a seductive but not overtly sexual way that made him want to slip the sweater off her shoulders and kiss the skin as he revealed it, inch by inch.

"It's beautiful here," she said as she tilted her face to the sun and let the breeze flutter her hair.

Deacon shut the door and opened the trunk. He handed her a blanket and pulled out the picnic basket. "Let's go over by the tree," he suggested.

They spread the blanket out and settled down onto it together. "In the summertime," he explained, "these fields will be overflowing with purple lavender. The scent is heavenly."

She looked around them, presumably trying to picture what it would look like in only a few months. "I can see why you choose to live here, Deacon. I mean, who wouldn't want to live in France if they had the chance? It's beautiful."

"The scenery is nice," he admitted, "but it can't hold a candle to your beauty. Texas seems to have the market on that, unfortunately."

Cecelia blushed and wrinkled her nose. She shook her head, dismissing his compliment. "You're sweet, but I don't believe a word of it. Not compared to something like this." She looked away from him to admire the landscape and avoid his gaze.

There were days when Deacon wished he could throttle her parents. She was one of the most perfect creatures he'd ever had the pleasure of meeting, and she didn't believe him because the Morgans were always pushing her to be better. That was impossible in his eyes. "You don't believe me? Why not? Am I prone to hollow compliments?"

"No, of course not. It's just because," she began, looking down at her hands instead of staring him in the eye, "this is one of the most beautiful places in the world. People dream their whole lives of visiting a place like this one day. I'm just a pretty girl."

"You're more than just a pretty girl, Cecelia." Deacon leaned in and dipped a finger beneath her chin to tilt her face up to his. He wanted to tell her how smart and talented and amazing she was, but he could tell by the hard glint in her eye that she wouldn't believe him. Could she not tell by the way he responded to her touch? How he looked at her like she was the most delectable pastry in the window of Ladurée?

"What do we have to eat?" she asked, pulling away from his touch and focusing on the picnic basket.

"I'm not entirely sure," he admitted, letting the conversation drop for now. "The head chef put this together for me, so it's a surprise for us both."

Deacon opened the lid and reached inside, pulling out one container after the next. There was niçoise salad with hard-boiled eggs, olives, tuna, potatoes and green beans. Another contained carrot slaw with Dijon mustard and chives. Brown parchment paper was wrapped around a bundle of savory puff pastries stuffed with multicolored grape tomatoes, goat cheese and drizzled with a reduction of balsamic vinegar and honey. Another bundle of crostini was paired with a ramekin of chicken paté.

Finally, he pulled out a little box with a variety of French macarons for dessert. It was quite the feast, and very much the kind of picnic she'd likely never experienced back in Texas. There was more to food than barbecue, although you could never convince a Texan of that.

They spent the next hour enjoying their lunch. Together, they devoured almost every crumb. They laughed and talked as they ate, feeding each other bites and reminding him of that afternoon they shared at the Silver Saddle. Their second chance had truly started that afternoon with a tableful of tapas between them.

Now, a week later, here they were. This was not at all what Deacon had expected when he agreed to build The Bellamy with Shane and return to Royal. Sure, he knew he would see Cecelia. He figured they would converse politely and briefly over the course of their work together at the hotel, but never did he think he would touch her. Kiss her. Lose himself inside her.

He hadn't let himself fantasize about something like that because it hadn't seemed possible when he left Royal behind all those years ago. Then she'd shown up on his doorstep, devastated and suddenly single, and everything changed. Was it possible that he'd succeeded in being good enough for a woman like her? A part of him still couldn't believe it.

"What is it?" Cecelia asked. "You're staring at me. Do I have something on my face?"

Deacon shook his head. "Not at all. I was just thinking about how lucky I am to be here today with a woman as amazing as you are."

He expected the same reaction as before, but this time, when she looked into his eyes, the hard resistance there was gone. Did she finally believe him? He hoped so.

Cecelia thanked him by leaning close and pressing her lips to his. He drank her in, enjoying the taste of her, even as he slipped the sweater from her shoulders as he'd fantasized doing earlier. He tore his mouth from hers so he could kiss a path on the line of her jaw, down her throat and across the bare shoulder he'd exposed. She sighed and leaned into his touch.

"I was such a stupid little girl back then," she said with a wistful sigh. "All this time I could've had you, and I ruined everything. I don't know if I can ever forgive myself for that. Can you?"

Deacon's gaze met hers. "Yes," he said without wavering. It was true. As long as they ended up right here, right now, who cared about the past anymore?

Reaching out, Deacon swiped all the containers and food wrappers out of his way, leaving a bare expanse of blanket to lay Cecelia down on. Her blond hair fanned across the pale blue wool as she laid back and looked up at him with her mossy, gray-green eyes and soft smile.

"What are you doing?" she asked as he hooked a finger beneath the strap of her dress and pulled it down her arm.

Her right breast was on the verge of being exposed, and his mouth watered at the sight of her pink nipple just peeking out from the edge of her dress. He didn't answer her. Instead, he leaned down and tugged the fabric until he could draw that same nipple into his mouth. Cecelia gasped and arched her back, pressing her flesh closer to him.

"Someone could see us out here," Cecelia said halfheartedly. She certainly wasn't pushing him away.

"Do you want me to stop?" he asked, ceasing the pleasurable nibbling of her flesh.

"No," she whispered, excitement brightening her eyes.

"Good. Let them see us. I'm about to make love to you, Cecelia, and I don't care who knows about it."

It had been a long time since Cecelia had made love in a public place, and even then, it had been in the back of Deacon's old pickup truck while they parked in a secluded area by the lake on a Friday night. This wasn't quite as private, and it was broad daylight, but there was no way she would tell him no. Not when he looked at her the way he did and said things that made her resistance as weak as her knees.

If she were being honest with herself, she couldn't say no to Deacon, no matter what he asked of her. He was her knight in shining armor; the prince who swooped in and saved her when she felt like the walls of her life were tumbling down around her. She would give him anything he asked of her, even her heart.

She looked up at Deacon as he smiled mischievously at her and returned to feasting on her sensitive breasts. He still looked so much like the boy she remembered, even if he had grown into such a handsome and successful man. It made her think of the days and nights she'd spent in his arms and the future they'd planned together all those years ago. They'd both accomplished more than they'd ever dared to dream, but they'd both done it alone.

Cecelia didn't want to do it alone anymore. She wanted to live her life and chase her dreams with Deacon by her side. She felt her chest tighten as she realized that Deacon didn't need to ask for her heart. He already had it, even if he didn't know it. She was head over heels in love with him, even after such a short time together. It made her wonder if she had ever truly stopped loving him.

Her parents had been behind the breakup. She had done what she had to do, putting her feelings for Deacon on a shelf to protect her heart, but they'd never truly gone away. She hadn't loved anyone else. How could she? Cecelia had given her heart to him back in high school.

Deacon looked down at her, bringing her focus back to the here and now. She ran her fingers through the dark blond waves of his hair and then tugged him to her. He didn't resist, dipping his head to kiss her. Cecelia felt the last of her resolve dissipate. She wasn't strong enough to keep fighting her feelings and denying what they had. She was out of reasons not to love him. Out of reasons to push him away. She had to travel to the other side of the earth to feel like she was in control of her own life, but she wasn't going back to the way she was before they left Royal.

She was in love with Deacon, and she didn't care who knew it. It was really none of their damn business. Just as her birth mother's identity, and the challenges she'd had to face, was none of their business. Considering all the dirt Maverick was digging up on people in Royal, the residents of her small town really needed to tend to their own gardens and stop worrying about hers.

They broke the kiss, and a sly grin curled his lips. She could feel his hand gliding up her bare leg, pushing the hem of her long cotton dress higher and higher.

"Yes," she encouraged when his fingertips brushed along the edge of her lace panties. "I don't want to wait any longer."

Not to have him inside her. Not to have him in her life. Not to love him with all her heart and soul. She'd spent her whole life waiting for this.

Deacon removed her panties and flung them unceremoniously into the picnic basket. With his green-gold eyes solely focused on her, he traveled down her body, pressing kisses against her exposed breasts, her cotton-clad stomach and down where her panties had once been.

He parted her thighs and continued to look right at her as he leaned down to take a quick taste of her. Cecelia gasped as the bolt of pleasure shot straight through her. She was both thrilled and horrified by the idea of doing something like this outdoors in broad daylight. She wasn't a prude, but there was something so intimate about the contact that it seemed like the kind of thing that should be done in the semi-darkness of her bedroom.

Deacon didn't seem to care where they were. His tongue flicked across her flesh again before he began stroking her sensitive center with abandon. There was nothing Cecelia could do to stop the roller coaster she found herself on. She gripped the blanket tightly in her fists, hoping it was strong enough to hold her to the earth.

Deacon was relentless. His fingers and his tongue

stroked, probed, teased and tortured her until her breath was passing through her lips in strangled sobs. Her whole body was tense from the buildup inside her. She tried to hold back, to prolong the feeling as long as she could, but she couldn't. He stroked hard and slipped a finger inside her at the perfect moment, and she came undone. Deacon held her hips, tightly gripping them to continue his pleasurable assault even as she writhed and trembled beneath him.

"Please," she gasped at last when she couldn't take any more. "I can't."

Only then did he pull away, allowing her to finally relax into the blanket. She closed her eyes and reveled in the way her body felt fluid, almost boneless, as she lay there. Her climax had seemingly stripped her of the capacity to move. The sun was warm on her bare skin, heating the outside of her even as her insides were near the boiling point.

She was barely cognizant of Deacon hovering near her, and she pried open her eyes. He was propped on his elbow, looking down at her with mild concern.

"Are you okay?" he asked.

"I'll be better when you're inside me," she replied, her voice a hoarse whisper after her earlier shouts.

"I thought you might need a minute." Deacon grinned.

"All I need is you," Cecelia said, and she'd never meant words more in her life. He was all she wanted. In her bed, in her life, in her heart.

"If you say so."

Cecelia shifted her hips and pulled her dress out

of the way so he could position himself between her thighs. He fumbled with his pants for a moment, and then she got what she wanted. He filled her hard and fast, freezing in place once he was as deep as he could go.

She watched as he closed his eyes and gritted his teeth, savoring the feeling of being inside her.

"Do you know," Deacon began without moving an inch, "you feel exactly the same way you did when you were seventeen? It takes damn near everything I have not to spill into you right now, you're so tight."

Instead of responding, she drew her knees up to cradle his hips and tightened her muscles around him.

"Damn," he groaned and made an almost pained expression as he fought to keep control.

She didn't care. He'd certainly shown no mercy when she was resisting her release, and she wasn't about to, either. She lifted her hips, allowing him in a fraction of an inch farther.

He blew air hard through his nose and shook his head in defiance. "Not yet, Cecelia. Not yet. When I go, you're coming with me." Deacon bent down and pressed his lips against hers. She wrapped her arms around his neck and held him tight enough that her breasts flattened against the starched cotton of his green button-down shirt.

His tongue slipped over her bottom lip and into her mouth. Slowly, he stroked her tongue with his own. Cecelia expected him to mirror the rhythm with his hips, but he was frustratingly still from the waist down.

Unable to take any more of his slow torture, she pulled away from his kiss, leaving only the tiniest fraction of an inch between his lips and hers. "If you want me, Deacon, take me. I'm yours. I always have been."

That was as close to "I love you" as she was willing to go. At least for now. It was early to confess her feelings, and if he took the news poorly, she'd be stranded in a foreign country. No, that was a revelation best left to her hometown. He'd be more likely to believe her there as opposed to it being some kind of vacation-fling confession. Hell, she'd be more likely to believe herself there, too.

Her words had the intended reaction. Deacon buried his face in the small of her neck, planted a kiss just below her ear, then began to move inside her. It was slow and sweet at first, but before long, he was thrusting hard. The small break they'd taken allowed him to continue on, but she could tell by the tense muscles of his neck and the pinched expression on his face that it wouldn't be long.

She wouldn't be long, either. Despite just recovering from her orgasm only minutes earlier, she could feel another release building. She clutched Deacon's broad back and lifted her hips for the greatest impact. That was enough to make both of them groan with renewed pleasure.

"Yes, please, Deacon," she whispered into the summer breeze.

He didn't need the encouragement to act. Deacon reached between them and stroked her center as he continued to thrust into her. His fingers quickly brought her to the edge, making her scream.

Cecelia quickly buried her face in his shoulder to smother the cries before they drew someone's attention. Yet there was no way to smother the sensations running through her body. An intense wave of pleasure pulsated through every inch of her, curling her toes and making her fingertips tingle. Her heart tightened in her chest, reminding her just how different it was to make love instead of just having sex. It had been so long that she forgot there was a difference.

Her flutter of release sent Deacon over the edge. With a roar, he spilled himself into her and collapsed, pressing her into the blanket.

Cecelia held him against her bare bosom as their breathing returned to normal and their heart rates slowed together. As she held him, she looked up at the brilliant blue sky and wished this moment could last forever.

Unfortunately, the time together in France was coming to an end. It was time to fly back to Royal, debut The Bellamy and face the music.

Ten

Everything was perfect.

The hotel was flawless for its big debut. The black-tie-attired crowd filled the lobby of The Bellamy, flowing into the ballroom and out to the courtyard surrounding the pool. Even then it was almost elbow to elbow. It seemed as though the whole town had shown up to get their first peek at the resort. Unfazed by the crowd, the waiters moved expertly through guests with trays of delicious tapas and signature cocktails.

Shane and Brandee were beaming, and rightfully so. Deacon had heard nothing but compliments on the hotel so far. People loved the design, loved the food and couldn't wait to have guests stay at The Bellamy. Even people who at one time might've given Deacon dirty looks as they passed on the sidewalk stopped to congratulate him.

It was exactly what Royal needed, he was told. He certainly hoped so. He and Shane had a lot of money tied up in this place, and he hoped to get it back. If he could finally coexist with the upper-class circles of Royal, that would be even better. Maybe he'd be willing to stay a little longer than he'd planned after all. Deacon wasn't ready to make any big decisions, but the more time he spent in Royal, the easier it became. Cecelia might just talk him into becoming a Texan again before too long.

The only wrong tonight was the fact that he couldn't find Cecelia anywhere. Things had been crazy the minute they'd touched down in Texas. Their relaxing, romantic vacation came to a quick end with the final week of preparations that needed to be made for the opening of the resort.

He'd gotten used to having her in his bed and by his side, so it pained him to have her suddenly ripped away. He didn't even know what she was wearing tonight or if she was even here yet. He thought he saw her blonde head in the crowd, but he hadn't managed to get his hands on her with everyone wanting to congratulate him on the hotel.

"Mr. Chase?"

Deacon turned and found Brent and Tilly Morgan, of all people, waiting to speak to him. He made a poor attempt to mask his surprise, smiling and shaking Brent's hand although he had no idea why they wanted to talk to him. They never wanted anything to do with him before, and they certainly had never wanted him anywhere near their daughter.

"Mr. and Mrs. Morgan, so glad you could make it. How do you like the hotel?"

"It really is lovely," Tilly said. "Cecelia refused to give us any hints about her design, but I can see her refined aesthetic here in the lobby. I would love to see one of the guest rooms. Are any of them open to view?"

Deacon nodded, ignoring the fact that all of Tilly's compliments about the hotel were focused on their daughter's work and not on anything that had to do with him. "There's a gentleman near the elevators who is escorting guests to one of her suites on the second floor if you would like to take a tour. Cecelia really did an amazing job. Shane and I had no doubts in her ability to execute our vision here for The Bellamy. You should be very proud of her."

"Oh, we are," a man said from over Tilly's shoulder.

It'd been quite a few years since Deacon had laid eyes on Chip Ashford, but he instantly recognized him. Tall, blond—the perfect golden boy with an arrogant smirk and a spray-on tan. The people in Royal saw him as some sort of god, but he just looked like a game show host to Deacon—all smiles and no authenticity.

Deacon wasn't about to let Chip's treatment of Cecelia go unnoted after he stood there gloating about her as though they were still engaged. "I'm surprised to hear you say that, Chip. From what Cecelia tells me, you two didn't part very well. Something about her being an imposter."

"That was just a little misunderstanding," Chip said dismissively. "Wasn't it, Brent?"

Cecelia's father immediately nodded, as though he'd almost been coached with his response. "A little bit of nothing. Cecelia tends to get upset about the silliest things and make them into a bigger deal than they are. Nothing more than a little lover's spat."

Tilly nodded enthusiastically. Deacon was disgusted by how they sucked up to the Ashfords. The Morgans were a fine family on their own, and frankly, it was embarrassing.

"Brent, why don't you take Tilly upstairs to see one of Cecelia's rooms? I'd like to have a private chat with Deacon, if you don't mind."

"Not at all, not at all. Come on, Tilly." Brent put his arm around his wife and escorted her through the crowd to the wall of brass elevator doors that led upstairs.

Deacon watched them disappear, curious about what Chip had to say to him in private. The two of them had probably shared less than a dozen words between them. He imagined there was only one thing that Chip wanted to talk about: Cecelia. She was the only thing they had ever had in common.

The friendly expression on Chip's face vanished the moment the Morgans disappeared. When he turned back to look at Deacon, a scowl lined his forehead and drew down the corners of his mouth. "I've heard that you've been taking up with Cecelia."

Deacon did his best to maintain a neutral expression. He didn't want to give Chip any ammunition. "Have you? Good news travels fast."

"I wouldn't consider you making moves on my fiancée to be good news. Because of that whole dustup about the adoption, I am willing to be a gentleman and overlook the whole thing between you two. Especially since Cecelia has come to her senses."

Deacon tensed up and frowned at Chip's statement. "Come to her senses and realized marrying you was an epic mistake?"

Chip snorted in derision. "Hardly. You see, Chase, while you were busy getting ready to open this hotel, I was busy reconciling with my fiancée. I'll admit I reacted poorly to her news, but I apologized to her and she's accepted my apology. I presume, now that the hotel is open and the engagement is back on, that you'll crawl back into whatever European hole you climbed out of."

Deacon could hardly believe his ears. Chip couldn't be serious. There was no way that Cecelia would take him back after the way he had treated her. Deacon had been the one who'd comforted her when Chip broke their engagement. Deacon had been the one who'd whisked her away to France to avoid the cutting gossip after Maverick's revelation about her adoption. Deacon was the one who had held her in his arms, worshipped her body and accepted her for who she really was.

Would she really go back to the man who had shunned her after nothing more than a simple apology?

"You look surprised, Chase. I take it Cecelia hasn't gotten a chance to break the bad news to you yet. I would imagine the truth smarts a little, but you can't really be surprised. We all know who gets the girl in this scenario. I don't care how much money you've made over the years or who you've conned to get it. She wants a man from a good family with the connections and the power that only someone like I can give her. You might be a fun diversion in the sack, but you'll never be enough of a man in her eyes for anything more serious than that."

Deacon tried not to flinch at Chip's expertly aimed barb. Without fail, it hit him right in his most tender spot. He had worked hard to make more of himself, to be the man Cecelia always thought he could be. But he had always wondered if that was enough. It hadn't been enough back in high school when she broke up with him. She hadn't given him any reason to doubt her, but what really made him think that anything had changed?

Chip was right. He had money. But there were some things that money couldn't buy, things that Chip had been born with. If that really was the most important thing to her, Deacon would never be good enough.

"Besides, I've been doing a lot of thinking and talking to my campaign manager, and we've decided that her past isn't the career bombshell I thought it might be. In fact, it might even be an advantage. I'm not polling well with the working-class demographic. Having a fiancée with a tragic backstory like hers—

adopted with a drug-addicted mother and humble origins—might give me an edge come election time. It makes me more relatable to the masses."

Deacon looked at Chip's smug expression and felt his hands curl into fists at his side. Cecelia was nothing more than a campaign prop to him. Chip might be more connected than him, but he wasn't stronger. He had no doubt that he could lay Chip out on the floor without much effort. It would be amazingly gratifying to feel his knuckles pound into the man's jaw. He could just imagine the stunned looks on the faces of everyone around them as Chip lay bleeding on the newly laid marble floor.

But he wouldn't do that. He liked to think that he'd gained some class along with his money over the years. Starting a brawl at the opening gala of his five-star resort wouldn't earn him any new friends in this town. He wouldn't ruin this night for Shane and Brandee, or any of the hotel's employees. They had all worked too hard to make tonight a success, and he didn't want to undo their efforts with his brash behavior. Chip wasn't worth it.

Besides, if Chip *was* telling the truth and Cecelia had chosen to return to him after everything he'd done to her…she wasn't the woman he loved. The Cecelia he wanted was the one he'd fallen for again in Cannes. There, she had been happy and free of all the pressures this damned town put on her. That woman wouldn't have returned to Chip after his cold betrayal. But perhaps that woman had stayed behind in France.

Deacon eyed Chip coolly before swallowing his

pride and holding out his hand like a gentleman would. "Well, congratulations on your engagement. You two certainly deserve each other."

Chip narrowed his gaze at Deacon's backhanded compliment, but chose to grin and accept it anyway.

"If you'll excuse me," Deacon said, walking away before Chip could respond. He had to get away from him before he reconsidered punching him in the face. Instead, he sought out Shane and Brandee. He knew this was his party, too, but he couldn't stand to be here another moment. He certainly didn't want to be a witness to Cecelia and Chip's reconciliation. Seeing her on that bastard's arm was more than he could take. It was better that he leave now than risk causing a scene and ruining the whole night.

When he found Shane, he leaned in and whispered a few things to him. Shane turned to him with a surprised look on his face but knew better than to start a discussion about it right now. He simply nodded and clapped Deacon on the shoulder.

Deacon turned and disappeared into the bowels of the hotel where only staff were allowed to go. He wasn't entirely sure where he was headed, he just knew that he had to put some distance between himself and the woman he had been foolish enough to fall in love with the second time.

Shame on him.

Cecelia circled the ballroom for the third time, still unsuccessful in locating Deacon. She had been anxious about tonight—her first public appearance since Maverick spilled her secrets—but as she maneuvered through the crowd, everyone had carried on as if nothing had happened.

She was glad because she refused to have tonight ruined by old drama that was out of her control. She had more important things to tend to. She was bubbling over with nerves and excitement, eager to find Deacon, but so far she was having no luck. She was certain he was here—she had seen him earlier, and his car was still in the lot—but now he had vanished into thin air.

Arriving late to the party had not been a part of her plan for the evening, but it had been unavoidable. She'd had to make an unplanned stop to confirm something she had suspected since they got back from Cannes. Now that she knew for certain, she couldn't wait to find Deacon, but he was lost in a sea of tuxedos and cocktail dresses.

She was on the way to the office suites to see if he was hiding out and working instead of enjoying the party. That was when she found herself face-to-face with her ex-fiancé in a secluded hallway.

Chip was wearing his favorite Armani tuxedo, showing off his good looks the way he'd always liked to do. There had been a time when Cecelia could have been swayed by his handsome appearance, but that was in the past. There was no comparison between him and Deacon, and she couldn't understand how she let herself waste so much time on a man with few redeeming qualities outside of his social standing.

"There you are, kitten. I have been looking all over for you, tonight."

Cecelia folded her arms over her chest and narrowed her gaze at him. "I can't imagine why. And please don't use pet names, Chip. I'm not your kitten. I'm not your anything, if you recall us breaking up a few weeks ago."

Chip smiled, oozing all the practiced charm that he used on women and constituents alike. "Listen, I'm sorry about how all that went down. It was wrong of me, and I reacted poorly."

Cecelia was stunned by his apology, although it meant very little to her now. She didn't understand why he was bothering her, much less cornering her at the opening, when she had more important things to be doing. What was he after? "Thank you. Now if you'll excuse me I—"

Chip reached out and caught her arm, stopping her from pushing past him and returning to the party. "What's the rush, kitten? We really need to talk about some things. I've been doing a lot of thinking about us."

"Us? We don't have anything to talk about, Chip, but especially not about *us*." Cecelia was desperate to escape, jerking away from his grasp. She glanced over his shoulder, hoping to catch the eye of anybody who could come and rescue her, but there was no one in sight. The party was carrying on at the other end of the hallway. "I would rather have a root canal than talk to you right now."

Chip just smiled. "My favorite part of my kitten is

her claws. Now just relax and give me five minutes. We were together a long time, certainly you can spare a moment or two. That's all I ask."

Cecelia sighed. "Okay, fine. Five minutes, that's it. And stop calling me kitten. Do it one more time and I walk."

He held up his hands defensively. "Okay, okay. No more pet names. Cecelia, I came here looking for you tonight because the last few weeks apart have helped me realize that I was a fool. My feelings for you are stronger than I thought, even stronger than my concerns about your background. I've realized they're unfounded. I need you by my side going into this next reelection."

Cecelia could hardly believe her ears. When she was a liability, he couldn't dump her fast enough. Now that he decided she could be an asset to his campaign, he was crawling back. He was delusional to think she would go along with nonsense like this. "Chip, you've lost your mind."

"No, hear me out. You and I are good together. We always have been. We make the perfect American couple. Voters are just going to eat up the classic, traditional values we represent. This is a win-win for us both, Cecelia."

She could only shake her head. "You never wanted *me*, Chip. You just wanted some trophy wife you can parade around at fund-raisers and rallies. That's not what I want out of my marriage."

Chip didn't look dissuaded. He was well versed in debate, and she could tell that he wasn't going to give up until he won. "It wasn't so long ago that I was everything you wanted, Cecelia. You were so anxious to plan our wedding and start our life together. What about the children we were going to have? The future we planned? Are you willing to just throw all that away?"

"You threw it away, Chip, not me. And yes, I am willing to walk away from what you've offered me. I have found something infinitely better."

Chip chuckled bitterly. "You mean Deacon? Seriously? I'm offering you the chance to be the first lady of the United States, Cecelia. I'm going all the way to the White House one day, and I want to take you with me." He reached into his pocket and pulled out the engagement ring she'd returned the afternoon they broke up. He held it up like a gaudy offering to the diamond gods. "You're going to turn this down and walk away from the amazing life that we have ahead of us because you've got feelings for that loser?"

"As a matter of fact I am, Chip. Your five minutes are up." Cecelia brushed past him and the engagement ring she'd once worn and pushed into the crowd, hoping he didn't follow her. How she ever could've agreed to marry a man like that was beyond her. What was she thinking? She knew. It was what her parents wanted for her. She was tired of that. Now she wanted what she wanted for herself, whether they liked it or not.

She was about to start a new phase in her life, and she wanted to start it with Deacon. *If* she could find him. Finally, she spotted Shane and went up to him, hoping he could help her track Deacon down.

Shane spotted her and smiled in a polite, yet oddly cold fashion. "Good evening, Cecelia."

"Evening, Shane. Have you seen Deacon anywhere? I've been looking for him all night, and I haven't managed to find him."

Shane nodded. "Deacon had to leave, but he told me to tell you congratulations on your engagement."

Cecelia's blood went ice-cold in her veins. "What engagement?" she asked.

"You and Chip. Both he and your parents have been telling everybody at the party that you two have reconciled and the wedding is back on. It's all anyone can talk about tonight. Quite a shrewd tactic to suppress the other scandal, I have to say."

Her jaw dropped. She couldn't even believe what she was hearing. Chip was such an arrogant bastard that he'd gone around announcing their engagement before he'd even talked to her about it. How dare he tell people that they got back together without even consulting her! "I can't believe this," she said. And then she realized the depth of what this meant.

Deacon thought that she had taken Chip back. How could he believe such a thing? He hadn't even asked her if it were true. No wonder he had left the party early. She dropped her head into her hands and groaned.

"What's the matter?" Shane asked.

She couldn't even answer him. She didn't want to waste another minute talking to him when she could be tracking down Deacon and clearing up this whole mess. She turned and ran as fast as she could, weaving through the crowd to find the nearest exit and get to her car.

Cecelia was almost out of the ballroom when she heard her father's sharp, demanding voice say her name. She stopped and turned, seeing her parents standing a few feet away with a typically disappointed expression on their faces. "I can't talk right now, Dad."

"You can and you will, young lady. Chip tells us that you turned your nose up at his apology and proposal. What are you thinking? Do you know how hard we had to work to stay in the Ashfords' good graces after all this blew up? After Maverick released your information, you were nowhere to be found. Your mother and I had to deal with the backlash."

"Please reconsider, dear," her mother said in a less authoritative tone. "I really do think Chip is a good choice for you. He has so much potential, and he's from such a good family. We should be thankful that they're willing to reconsider the engagement after the truth about your lineage came to light. What are they going to think when Chip tells them that you've rejected him for the son of a mechanic?"

Cecelia's hands curled into fists at her side. If she'd gotten nothing else from her time in Cannes, it was that she wasn't going to let her life be dictated by her parents anymore. "Honestly, I really don't care what they think of me. I don't want anything to do with them, much less become one of them. I am not marrying Chip Ashford. If he hasn't ruined it for me tonight, I intend to marry Deacon Chase."

Both her parents looked at her with an expression of shock and dismay, but she didn't care. She cut her father off before he could start telling her why she was wrong. "I am tired of working so hard to meet your approval. If you truly love me, you will love and accept me for who I am, not for who you want me to be, and certainly not for whom I do or do not marry. If you can't agree to that, then I don't want you in my life any longer."

She didn't wait for their response. Right now, all that mattered was finding Deacon. Outside the ballroom, Cecelia slipped out of her high heels and ran through the back door of the hotel with them clutched in her hand.

She scanned the parking lot, but she didn't see his Corvette anywhere now. She rushed over to her own car and headed straight for his place. When she pulled up the gravel driveway, she was disappointed to find his car wasn't there, either, and all the lights were out. He'd told Shane he was leaving. Cecelia thought he had meant he was leaving the party, but now she had a sick ache in her stomach that made her think that perhaps he meant he was leaving Royal altogether.

She whipped her car back out onto the highway and rushed to the small executive airport where he had chartered the private jet to take them to France. If he was really, truly leaving, his car would be there.

At the airport, she found only more disappointment. The airport was mostly empty, with only one other car in the parking lot, and it wasn't Deacon's. She put her car in Park and sat there, unsure of what to do next. She didn't know where else to look for him.

Frustrated, she leaned back into her seat and let her tears flow freely down her cheeks. This was not the way she envisioned tonight going. Tonight was supposed to be happy. She was supposed to be sharing the most amazing and exciting news with the man she loved, and instead she was sitting in an empty parking lot alone, feeling as though everything she had ever wanted in life was slipping through her fingers.

Her whole life, all she ever wanted was her own family. Blood, love and a bond that nothing could split apart. Today, when she'd gotten home from the drugstore, she had looked at the two lines on the pregnancy test and thought that her dream was finally coming true. She had rushed to The Bellamy, anxious to share the good news with Deacon, only to have her dream intercepted by her delusional, lying ex.

And now, if she didn't find a way to clear things up with Deacon, she was going to find herself in a position she never expected: a single mother.

Eleven

Deacon was nowhere to be found.

It'd been three days since the grand opening of The Bellamy, and no one, not even Shane, had seen him. Or at least that's what he'd said. He wasn't likely to roll on his friend if his friend didn't want to be found. Deacon hadn't shown up at the hotel offices to work. His laptop was missing from his docking station. He hadn't been seen at his house. It was like he had simply vanished off the face of the earth.

Cecelia had tried contacting him on his cell phone, but he wasn't responding to her calls or texts. She didn't even think his phone was turned on because it immediately rolled to voice mail. That or he'd blocked her. She supposed that if she dropped the news on him in a text, he would respond. However, it just seemed wrong to tell a man he's going to be a father that way.

She caught herself constantly checking her phone for a missed message, each time frowning in disappointment and putting the phone back down. When her phone did ring, it was people she didn't want to talk to. Her father was too stubborn to reach out, but her mother had called three times and left messages. Still, Cecelia wasn't quite ready to speak to them. They had sold her out to get back in the Ashfords' good graces, and it would be a long time before Cecelia would be calm enough to sit down with them and have an adult conversation about how she planned to live her life from now on. If they ever wanted to see their grandchild, they'd adjust to the new Cecelia pretty quickly.

She was even ignoring calls from Naomi and Simone. She knew if she spoke to them she would spill the news about the baby, and Deacon needed to be the first to know, no question.

She was starting to get desperate. With the job at The Bellamy complete, Cecelia had moved back into her business offices. Now was the time that she was supposed to leverage her high-profile job at The Bellamy and launch her adult furniture line, but she found her heart just wasn't in it. It required a level of dedication and focus that she simply didn't have at the moment. Perhaps it was pregnancy brain. She'd heard that it could cause difficulty concentrating.

Or maybe it was simply the fact that Chip had potentially ruined the future she'd always wanted with

Deacon. That made everything, including the success of Luna Fine Furnishings, seem insignificant in comparison.

Sitting back in her office chair, Cecelia gently stroked her flat belly. Her doctor, Janine Fetter, had calculated her to be four weeks along, but she would be showing before she knew it. How was it that her life had changed so drastically in such a short period of time? It seemed like only yesterday that she was getting ready to pitch her designs for The Bellamy to Shane, planning her wedding with Chip and paying off Maverick with blackmail money.

Now the job at the hotel was over, her engagement was broken, her secrets were public knowledge and she was pregnant with the child of a man who seemingly didn't want her any longer. She supposed she could blame the entire situation on Maverick. If he hadn't started meddling in her life, she wouldn't have had to confess to Chip and break their engagement. She wouldn't have thrown herself at Deacon because he was the only one who knew the truth and wouldn't judge her. She wouldn't have hopped on a flight to France with him to avoid the backlash of her secret being exposed to the entire town. She wouldn't have fallen in love with him again in a lavender field.

She also wouldn't be pregnant. It was a little ironic that the one thing she'd always wanted, the baby she'd dreamed of since she was a teenager, had come to be through the complicated machinations of the town blackmailer. If she ever found out who was behind it all, she supposed she should send him an invitation to the baby shower.

Cecelia's stomach started to sour. She reached for the roll of antacids in her desk drawer only to find she'd chewed the last one an hour ago. She didn't know whether it was thinking about Maverick or the latest in her constant bouts of morning sickness, but the Rolaids and saltine crackers she'd been eating lately weren't cutting it. At this rate, she'd be the first pregnant woman in history to lose weight.

With a sigh, she slammed the drawer shut and eyed the clock on her computer monitor. It was almost lunchtime. Time to run a few errands. She needed to go in search of something nausea friendly like chicken noodle soup and maybe a big glass of ginger ale to go with it. Her next stop would be the drugstore to restock her medicinal supplies before heading back to the office.

Pushing away from her desk, Cecelia picked up her purse and swung it over her shoulder. The offices of To the Moon were fairly close to downtown Royal, so she was able to walk the two blocks to the Royal Diner.

The Royal Diner was one of the few places in the town proper to eat, or at least it had been before The Bellamy opened with their high-class offerings. The diner was far more informal, complete with a retro '50s style. As Cecelia stepped in, the sheriff's wife and owner, Amanda Battle, waved at her from behind the counter. She opted for one of the unoccupied red leather booths. Sitting at the counter would invite too much conversation, and her heart just wasn't in it today.

There was chicken and wild rice soup on the menu. She ordered a bowl of that with crackers and a ginger ale. Amanda wrote down the order and eyed her critically, but didn't ask whatever questions were on the tip of her tongue.

Amanda returned with a tray a few minutes later and started unloading everything. "I brought extra crackers," she said, her tone pointed. "You look like you need them."

Cecelia looked up at her, wondering if she looked that awful. "Thank you."

"When I was pregnant," Amanda began, "I had the worst morning sickness you can imagine. Do you know what helped?"

Cecelia tried not to stiffen in her seat. Why was Amanda telling her this? It was one thing for her to look green around the gills, another for the woman to know she was pregnant.

"Those bracelets they give you when you go on a cruise. It puts pressure on some part of your wrist that makes the nausea go away. You can get them at the drugstore. If it wasn't for those and ginger ale, I might've never made it to the second trimester. That one is a lot more fun."

"Thank you," Cecelia repeated. "I'll look into that."

Amanda smiled, seemingly content to help and not at all concerned about the juiciness of the information she had inadvertently unearthed. "I'm glad you've got some new joy coming into your life. I felt so bad over those posts about your birth mother. That stupid Maverick can't ruin everything, no matter how hard he might try."

At that, Amanda turned and walked away, leaving Cecelia with her soup and her thoughts. She was right. Everything was a mess at the moment, but she knew things would work out.

Perking up in her seat, Cecelia had a thought. Maverick had managed to spread gossip to damn near everyone in town with hardly any effort at all. Maybe she could use his tricks to get Deacon back, as well. The power of social media had worked well for him, so why wouldn't it work for her?

Cecelia quickly finished her lunch, left money for the tab on the table and headed down the street to the drugstore. The morning sickness that had dominated her thoughts faded to the back of her mind as she formulated her plan with each step. She quickly restocked her supply of antacids, grabbed a bottle of prenatal vitamins and, on Amanda's recommendation, picked up a special nausea wristband designed for pregnant women.

After checking out, she rushed back to the office and immediately started drafting a message. She kept it short and sweet, using Maverick's hashtag. Plenty of people in town were following it, so the news should spread like wildfire. And, if Maverick himself was a little perturbed that he hadn't managed to ruin her life by exposing her latest tidbit of gossip, all the better.

She started with Snapchat and a photo of her bare ring finger. She followed it up with Instagram and

Twitter. Finally, she posted to Facebook. Everyone in town, including her parents, the Ashfords and Deacon himself, should be using one or more of those platforms.

"Despite persistent rumors to the contrary, I am not, and never will be, engaged to Chip Ashford ever again. I would much rather be Mrs. Deacon Chase, and I hope that after everything that has happened between us, he will believe that and know how much I love him."

That done, she sat back in her chair and hoped for the best. There was a new flutter of butterflies in her stomach, but this time it had nothing to do with morning sickness and everything to do with putting her heart on the line. Every word of the post was true. Even if Deacon never looked in her direction after what happened, she wasn't about to go back to the life she'd escaped with the Ashfords. Being with Deacon had helped her to realize that there was more to a relationship than arm candy and photo ops.

She wanted a real, loving relationship with a man who respected and appreciated her no matter what. And she knew now, more than ever, that she wanted that relationship with Deacon. Their baby would be the icing on the cake, completing the family she'd always wanted.

Surely Deacon didn't really believe that she would take Chip back after everything he had done to her? He'd torn off, taking Chip at his word. She couldn't imagine what Chip had said to him to send him into hiding without even asking her first. If she knew,

Chip would probably be earning a well-deserved black eye. Let Maverick tweet about that.

Cecelia had done her part to put things right between them. The message was traveling through the interwebs, hopefully on its way to Deacon's inbox. She could already hear her cell phone buzzing in her purse, so the message was spreading at the speed of Royal gossip. Her father was probably having a heart attack on the imported living room rug at that exact moment, and her mother was calling to chastise and disown her. That was fine by her. She was more interested in being a Chase than a Morgan anyway.

If everyone else was seeing it, Deacon should, too. Surely when he read the message he could come out of hiding and seek her out. She couldn't very well locate him, if the last few days were any indication. No, she'd left a digital breadcrumb trail for Deacon to follow, and all she could do was to sit back, wait for the love of her life to sweep her off her feet and brace herself for her world to change forever.

Deacon was used to being invisible in Royal. As a kid, most people had paid him no mind, and not much had changed over the years, despite his Cinderella moment at The Bellamy grand opening. He'd considered bailing on the town entirely after the fiasco with Chip, but something had kept him here. Whether it was his obligation to Shane or his misguided feelings for Cecelia, he wasn't sure. Either way, he knew he wasn't staying long, but in the meantime, the most

effective course was for him to hide in plain sight—
at The Bellamy itself.

He pulled the laptop out of his bag and set it up at
the modern glass-and-chrome desk that was a feature
of the penthouse suite. He could go downstairs to his
office, but he ran the risk of running into someone
and having to answer questions. Shane knew he was
up here, but he had respected his space so far and
promised he wouldn't reveal his whereabouts.

He'd never actually left the hotel that night. He'd
marched through the bowels of the building trying
to burn off his anger, then he'd had the front desk
code him a key for the unoccupied penthouse suite,
and he'd been there ever since. He'd left only to move
his car from the employee lot to the virtually empty
parking garage for guests.

He'd returned to the lobby just long enough to see
Chip holding Cecelia's hand as they spoke to one
another in a dark, quiet corridor near their offices.
Hearing Chip boast had been bad enough, but it was
like a knife to his gut to see them together like that.

He doubted anyone missed him, or was even looking for him, but if they were, they wouldn't expect
him here. Why would he stay in a hotel with a perfectly lovely and secluded home only a few miles
away?

To avoid Cecelia.

It was childish, he knew that. And perhaps she
didn't give a damn where he was or what he was
doing. She might be off making lavish wedding plans
with Ashford for the social event of the year. If she

was looking for him, it might just be to apologize for leading him on or to thank him for the lovely trip to France. Thanks, bye.

Either way, he didn't want to know what she had to say to him. He'd heard plenty that night from Chip. She'd made her decision, wrong as it might be, and he would live with it. He just didn't have to stick around so they could rub it in his face. He was going to make sure the hotel was running smoothly, hand over the reins to Shane, put his rustic lodge up for sale and return to his role as The Bellamy's silent, and invisible, partner.

Hell, if Shane could buy him out, he'd let him. Then he'd have no reason or need to ever set foot in the state of Texas again.

Maybe once he returned to Cannes, he could wipe Chip's smug face from his memory. Deacon hadn't even known they were competing for the same woman until Chip announced that he had won. Of course he'd won. Chip didn't believe for a moment that Deacon was his competition. And despite the strides he'd made over the years, Deacon wasn't sure he was Ashford's competition, either.

They offered Cecelia different things. They both had money and good looks, so with that canceling out, Chip had things Deacon simply couldn't give her. Could never give her. Like a good family name, political connections and peace at home with her parents. That couldn't be bought, no matter how much money he made.

Then again, Chip didn't deserve a woman like Cecelia in his life. Not even with all that he could offer her, because he just wasn't a good person. He wasn't nice to Cecelia, much less to the little people whose votes he was constantly chasing. The only question was whether Cecelia knew that and appreciated what that meant for her future. If she even cared.

In France, away from her parents and the pressures of Royal, she had been free to be the person she wanted to be. That was the person he loved. But apparently those two Cecelias couldn't coexist back home. Within days of returning to Texas, she'd not only changed her mind about Deacon…changed her mind about who she wanted to be and how she wanted to live…but she'd decided to take Chip back. Never mind how cruel he'd been, or how he'd kicked her when she was down. Once he was willing to "overlook" her shortcomings and take her back, she'd fallen into his arms.

Apparently she preferred being the good robot her parents wanted her to be than the happy, free spirit he saw inside her. And if that was the case, Deacon was fine moving on without her in his life. He didn't want *that* Cecelia anyway.

The suite doorbell rang, pulling Deacon from his thoughts. He didn't know who it could be. He hadn't ordered room service, and housekeeping had already visited for the day. With a frown, he got up and went to the door. Through the peephole, he spotted Shane. Reluctantly, he opened the door. If something was wrong at the hotel, he needed to man up and deal with it, not barricade himself in the penthouse, even if it meant he might see Cecelia downstairs. "Hey," he said casually, trying to act as though they didn't both know he was hiding up here after getting his heart trampled.

"Hey." Shane had a strange expression on his face. It was a weird mix of excitement and apprehension, which made Deacon even more curious about this unexpected visit. "Have you been online?" Shane asked.

Deacon took a step back to let his business partner into the suite. "No," he admitted. "I've done some work, read some emails, but I haven't really felt like seeing what the rest of the world was up to the last few days." He certainly didn't want to see a new engagement announcement for Cecelia and Chip, or run across any type of society buzz about their upcoming wedding being back on despite her tragic, secret past. He intended to be far, far away from Royal, Texas, by the time that event took place.

Shane charged in, nearly buzzing with nervous excitement. "So you really haven't seen it?"

Deacon closed the door, slightly irritated at the intrusion. "Seen what, Shane? I told you, I've been living in a cave for the last few days."

"Wow. I'm so glad I came up here, then. You need to see this." Shane turned his back on him without elaborating further, ratcheting Deacon's irritation up a notch, and walked over to the computer. He sat down at the desk, silently typing information into the web browser.

"Can't you just tell me?" Deacon asked as he came up behind him.

"No," Shane said. "You have to see this for yourself."

Deacon tried not to roll his eyes. He crossed his arms over his chest and waited impatiently for Shane to pull up whatever important news had to be seen firsthand. At the moment, all he could see was that he'd pulled up Facebook. Deacon didn't even have a Facebook account. He didn't need a social site to remind him that he didn't really have any friends to keep up with online.

"Here," Shane said at last. He pointed to the screen as he got up from the chair. "Sit down and read this."

Deacon didn't argue. He sat down and looked at the post Shane had pointed out. It was a post from Cecelia's Facebook account. Her screen icon was a selfie that the two of them had taken when they were walking on the beach in Cannes. That was an odd choice for a woman who was engaged to another man, he thought. Then he read the words, and his heart stopped in his chest.

"Despite persistent rumors to the contrary, I am not, and never will be, engaged to Chip Ashford ever again. I would much rather be Mrs. Deacon Chase, and I hope that after everything that has happened between us, he will believe that and know how much I love him."

Deacon sat back against the plush leather of his computer chair and tried to absorb everything he'd read. She wasn't engaged to Chip? Had the smug bastard lied to Deacon's face about the whole thing? Was he so arrogant that he'd assumed she'd take him back if he only asked? That was a bold bluff, he had to give Chip that. From the sound of that post, it was a bluff that hadn't succeeded. If they really weren't together, that meant she still wanted to be with him.

Judging by her words, she wanted to be more than just with him. She wanted to spend the rest of her life with him.

She loved him.

It was a damn good thing Shane had made him sit down.

"Can you believe it?" Shane asked. "When I saw her that night at the party after you left, she seemed really confused by my congratulations on her engagement. I thought maybe she was just annoyed that the news got out before they could make an official announcement, but now it looks like it was because she didn't know what the hell I was talking about."

Deacon almost didn't believe what he was reading. He had been jerked around so many times where Cecelia was concerned that he was afraid to think it could really be true. He wanted it to be true, though. He'd made the mistake of letting himself fall in love with her again these past few weeks. He'd never intended on it, but after that afternoon in Provence, he couldn't help himself. He was madly in love with Cecelia Morgan. Could she really, truly be in love with him, as well?

"What are you going to do?" Shane pressed.

"I have no earthly idea," he answered. And that was the truth. He didn't want to screw this up. If he and Cecelia got back together, that was it. It was for life. He was going to marry her, make it official and never let that sweet creature out of his sight again. Even if that meant living in Royal for the rest of his life. It was the sacrifice he was willing to make to have her as his wife.

"Well, are you just going to sit here? Why aren't you rushing out the door to sweep her off her feet? She wants to marry you, Deacon. Stop hiding in this damn penthouse suite and do something about it."

Deacon closed his laptop screen and turned to face Shane. "I want to do this right. I can't half ass it on a whim. She deserves better than that. I don't think the little jewelry store in town is going to have what I need. Care to join me for a trip to Florida to get the perfect engagement ring?"

Shane grinned. "Florida? Just for a ring? There're some great places in Houston."

Deacon shook his head. "There's only one ring in the world for Cecelia, and it's in Florida."

"Okay," Shane agreed. "Do we need to have my assistant book some first-class tickets?"

"First class?" Deacon smirked, then shook his head as he reached for his phone. "Nope. We're taking a private jet."

Twelve

Cecelia slipped the key card into the elevator panel, allowing her to go to the restricted top floor of The Bellamy. When her message went out into the universe and everyone but Deacon seemed to receive it, she decided it was time to take some drastic measures. Someone had known where he was. Her money had been on Shane, but she'd opted to approach his fiancé instead. It was a risk, considering how Brandee probably felt about her, but she was her only hope. Brandee would likely have had the information without that pesky sense of loyalty to a friend.

It turned out she was right. Brandee not only gave her Deacon's location, but the access card to get her there. She had seen the posts online and, despite everything, was all too happy to help Cecelia reunite with Deacon.

The elevator chimed and the doors opened. Cecelia stepped out onto a small, elegant landing. There were doors at each end of the hallway. One was labeled the Lone Star Suite and the other the Rio Grande Suite. Brandee said that Deacon was in the former, so she took a deep breath to steel her courage and turned left toward his room and, hopefully, her future.

Facing the massive oak door, she raised her hand to knock but was surprised when the door whipped open before she could make contact.

Deacon was standing there, looking just as startled to find Cecelia on his doorstep. He was wearing an immaculately tailored dark gray suit with a sapphire-blue shirt that reminded her of the color of the ocean in Cannes. It clung to every angle and line of his body, making him look impossibly tall and more handsome than she could even remember.

Their sudden face-to-face stole the words from Cecelia's lips.

"Cecelia? What are you doing here?" he asked.

She bit anxiously at her lip. "Brandee told me where you were. I'm sorry, but I had to talk to you about something. It looks like you're headed out the door, though, so I guess I'll come back."

"No!" Deacon shouted, catching her upper arm before she could turn away to leave. "No, I was going to find you."

Cecelia felt a bit of the pressure crushing her rib cage lift. "You were?"

"Yes, please come in." Deacon stepped back and held out his arm for her to follow him into the suite.

She made her way into the room and over to the seating area with the modern couches she'd designed and had manufactured. It felt a little weird to be sitting on them as a guest. "You're a hard man to find," she admitted.

Deacon sat down on the sofa beside her, angling his shoulders and hips to face her. "I didn't want to be found. Especially by you."

The words were like a kick to her gut, but she had to understand where he was coming from. He didn't know the truth. "You know that Chip is a boastful liar, right? I hadn't seen or spoken to him since we broke up, and I certainly hadn't agreed to marry him before you two had your run-in at the party."

Deacon nodded. "I know. Shane showed me your post yesterday."

"Yesterday?" He'd seen it and done nothing. Why had he waited? She'd put her heart on the line, and he'd sat back and thought about it overnight. She'd been in misery, on pins and needles, waiting to hear from him. That was the only reason she'd come after him. If he wasn't swayed by her declaration of love and desire to marry, he at least needed to know he was going to be a father.

"I had a lot to think about after I saw that."

"Well, I came here today because I have more to say to you than can fit in one hundred and forty characters. I also need to say things that don't need to be posted for the whole world to read. Not because I'm ashamed of them or you, but because some things are meant to be private, and between two people."

She closed her eyes for a moment to gather her thoughts. She had a lot to say, and she wanted to say it just right. "First, I wanted to thank you."

"Thank me?" Deacon looked surprised.

"Yes. You've taught me how to feel again. To love again. After we broke up, it hurt so badly to lose you that I shut down inside. I couldn't bear the pain, and I didn't want to fall in love with someone else and lose them, too. I decided I was done with love and I was going to focus on my career instead. I built baby furniture because a part of me thought it would be as close as I would ever get to having children. At least with a loving partner. I convinced myself that a loveless marriage that made good business sense was the right choice.

"I was wrong about everything. I didn't know I was starving until you gave me a taste of what I'd been missing. Then I knew I was wrong to close off my heart, wrong to think Chip was the kind of person I needed in my life… But most of all, I was wrong to think that I could ever stop loving you, no matter how hard I tried to suppress it."

She hesitated for a moment and turned to look at him so he would be able to sense and feel how much she meant the words she was about to say. "You are the only person I've ever known who loved me just the way I was. No restrictions, no requirements. So I wanted to thank you for that."

Deacon stared at her silently for a moment, and

then he reached out to take Cecelia's hand in his own. "I've never stopped loving you, Cecelia. Even when I was angry or hurt, I still loved you. You're the reason I haven't left Royal yet. There was no reason to stay, but a part of me just couldn't leave you behind, even if you'd chosen that greasy politician over me."

"I would never do that. He doesn't hold a candle to you. I don't understand why my parents can't see what kind of man he really is, but in the end it doesn't matter. In France, I decided I was going to live my own life on my own terms, and that hasn't changed. If my parents come around, they can be in my life, but if they don't, I'm okay with that. I'm never choosing them over you again."

Deacon squeezed her hand as she spoke. "You have no idea how happy I am to hear you say that. I've got a few things I need to tell you, as well."

"I wasn't finished," Cecelia said, but he raised his hand to shush her. She hadn't gotten to the critical news yet.

"I've been doing a lot of thinking while I've been holed up in his hotel suite. Your message and your arrival here today made things easier, but I was determined to change things between us before that happened. I walked away that night when I was faced with Chip's challenge, and I shouldn't have. Suddenly, I was eighteen again and not good enough for you. I walked away that night all those years ago, and I walked away again, instead of fighting for your love the way I should have. I'm not making that mistake again because you are worth fighting for.

"When I ran into you at the door just now, I was coming to tell you how much I loved you. Even if Chip had convinced you to take him back, I was going to steal you away, and I knew I could because he could never give you what you really needed. I'm the only one who can love you the way you need to be loved. I want to give you that life you've dreamed of, the family you've always wanted. I am determined to give you everything your heart desires. Starting with this."

Deacon reached into his coat pocket and pulled out a black velvet box. "I was on my way to find you and give you this. You said you wanted to be Mrs. Deacon Chase, and I didn't want to make you wait a moment longer. I didn't immediately come running to you because I wanted to have the right ring, the right words, the right suit…I wanted this moment to be perfect."

Cecelia shook her head with tears glistening in her eyes. "It is perfect, Deacon. You could be in jeans with a grape ring pop and I would say yes because you're the best thing that's ever happened to me."

Deacon smiled. "This is a little better than a grape ring pop."

He opened the box, revealing the prettiest vintage ring she'd ever seen. It had a round diamond set in a thin rose-gold band. A circle of small diamonds set in rose gold surrounded the center stone, and intricate scrolls were cut into the setting and along the sides. Cecelia had never seen anything like it.

"I didn't want to compete with Chip to get you the

biggest, gaudiest diamond I could. Instead, I wanted to get you the most meaningful ring I could. This one belonged to my grandmother. Shane and I flew to Florida yesterday to get it from my parents."

Deacon plucked the ring from its velvet bed and held it up to her. "Cecelia, this question has been a long time coming, but will you be my wife?"

Cecelia had been asked that question one time before, but this was completely different. There were butterflies in her stomach, her heart was racing and she couldn't take her eyes off the beautiful ring. When Chip proposed, she didn't know what it should feel like. Accepting his proposal had been like signing the paperwork to buy a new car—nice and satisfying, but not exactly a moment to cherish for a lifetime. This blew everything out of the water.

"Yes!" she said, bubbling over with love and enthusiasm. "I've been waiting to be Mrs. Deacon Chase since I was seventeen years old."

Deacon slipped the ring on her finger. It fit perfectly. The minute he read the message from Cecelia online, he knew this was the ring for her. His grandmother had told him as a child that her ring was to be kept so he could give it to the love of his life one day. Her marriage had been full of love and laughter, and she wanted the same for him. Even in their hardest financial times, his parents refused to sell the ring. He would need it one day, they insisted.

And based on the light in her eyes and the smile on her face, she liked it. The anxious muscles in his neck and shoulders started to relax now that she'd said yes. He snaked his arms around Cecelia's waist and tugged her to him. Their lips met, and suddenly it felt as though all was right with the world. Cecelia was going to be his wife. Nothing else mattered.

When their lips finally parted, Deacon studied Cecelia's face for a moment. "You've been waiting a while to be married to me. How much longer do you want to wait to make it official? We can be on a jet to Las Vegas in an hour."

Her nose wrinkled as she considered his offer. The idea of her being his wife before the sun went down was intriguing. Their relationship had come apart so many times, he was keen to make it legal once and for all before she could slip through his fingers again.

"No," she said at last. "I want to be your wife more than anything, but I don't want to elope. I want this whole town to put on their best cowboy boots, go down to the church and witness you and me making vows to love one another until the end of time. I want my parents to see it. The Ashfords to see it. I even hope Maverick will be sitting in those pews, so he'll know that he didn't win this time, not with me."

Deacon couldn't have been more proud of his fiancée than he was in that moment. Even if he had come to terms with this town and what people thought of him, it made him happy to see that she was proud to be his wife. "They'd better get used to having me around anyway."

Cecelia perked up beside him. "Does that mean you're willing to move here?"

He hadn't given it a lot of thought, but yes, if that was what she wanted. "I'd live on the moon if that's where you were. I'll have to travel quite a bit to my various hotels, but if you want Royal to be home, that's fine with me."

"Can we spend the summers in France?"

Deacon grinned. "You bet. I can't say no to you. If you want to live here, we'll live here. If you want a big church wedding with four hundred guests, let's do it. I happen to know the guy who owns the big new hotel in town, if you want to have a reception there. Anything you want, you'll have it. The white dress, the church, the flowers, the whole thing. Go buck wild, baby."

"I won't go too crazy," she said, although he could already see the wheels turning in her head with wedding plans. "I still want to marry you as soon as possible. Maybe not tonight, but soon."

That was fine by him. All he wanted was to be married. Cake, flowers and all the other trappings of the ceremony were unnecessary distractions to him, but he understood their importance to her. "Okay. We'll get the engagement announcement in the Sunday paper. Or shall we go post the good news online before Maverick can beat us to the punch?" Deacon asked in a joking tone.

Cecelia shook her head. "Not yet. I want to keep this just between us for a day or two. And besides that, Maverick doesn't know everything. I've got another little secret of my own."

Deacon's brow raised in curiosity. What other big news could she possibly have to share? "What's that?"

She untangled her fingers from his and placed his hand across her stomach. "I'm having Deacon Chase's baby."

Deacon didn't think that he could be stunned speechless, but she'd just done it. His baby? She was pregnant with his baby? He looked down at his hand and the still-flat belly beneath it. "You're pregnant?"

"Yes. You're happy, aren't you? Please say you're happy."

He pinned her with his gaze so there were no doubts in her mind about how he felt. "I'm thrilled beyond belief. I'm just not sure how it happened. We were careful, weren't we? How far along are you?"

"Four weeks. I think it happened that first night we were together, when I threw myself at you."

Deacon arched an eyebrow. "The day you sneaked out on me?"

"Yes," she admitted with a sheepish grin. "I guess I would've been back no matter what."

Deacon couldn't even imagine how he would've taken the news if she had shown up after her disappearing act and announced she was having his baby. He was nearly blown off his feet as it was. "How long have you known?" he asked.

"I started feeling poorly on the flight back from Cannes. I thought I was just airsick, but when it persisted a few days, I realized there might be more to it. I bought a pregnancy test the night of The Bellamy's grand opening. That's why I was late to the party. When I did arrive, I was looking all over for you to tell you the news, but you'd already left after arguing with Chip. When I realized what had happened, I was heartbroken, but I couldn't find you to tell you the truth."

Deacon squeezed his eyes shut to keep from getting angry. Not at her, but with himself. He'd ruined that moment they would've shared together because he thought so little of himself that he let Chip scare him off. There she'd been, searching the crowd to tell him they were having a baby, and he was licking his wounds in the penthouse.

"I am so sorry," he said. "I let Chip ruin that night for us. We should've spent this week together picking out baby names and planning our future together."

"I don't care about that," Cecelia insisted. "It's just a few days in the scheme of things, and it gave us both some time to figure out what we really wanted, baby or no baby. What matters is that you and I love each other, we're getting married and we're having a baby. I've always wanted a family of my own, and now I'm going to have it. With you."

Deacon pulled Cecelia close again, this time tugging her all the way into his lap. He cradled her in his arms, capturing her lips in the kind of kiss he'd fantasized about since they got back to Texas. She melted into him, reminding him just how much he'd missed her touch these last few days.

"If you're having my baby, maybe we should reconsider the Vegas option and get married tonight."

Cecelia shook her head. "This isn't a shotgun wedding, Deacon, and I don't want anyone to think so. Besides, I think a baby is the perfect wedding gift, don't you?"

It sounded good to him. "If that's what you want, I'm glad to be the one to give it to you."

Cecelia laid her head on his shoulder and sighed contentedly. Deacon could feel her warm breath against his skin, and it sent a shiver through his body. He was tired of talking about plans and exes and blackmailers. He wanted to lay claim to the mother of his child. He stood without warning, making Cecelia squeal and cling to his neck.

"What are you doing?" she asked.

"I'm making good use of the king-size bed in the penthouse suite to make love to my fiancée."

She didn't complain. She just held on until he placed her gently on the bed. "After everything that's happened, do you think everyone will be surprised to find out that you've won me back?"

Deacon hovered over her and planted a soft kiss on her lips. His fingers sought out the buttons of her blouse and started working them open. He slipped one hand inside to cup her breast through the lacy fabric she liked. She gasped, arching up off the bed.

"I didn't win you back, Cecelia. You've always been mine."

* * * * *

Quinn's blue eyes locked on her with an intensity that stirred an unexpected heat in her belly.

Even when she knew with 100 percent certainty it was all an act.

She licked her lips, her mouth gone suddenly dry. She should say something. Prevent this farce that no one would ever believe. But then again…hadn't she promised herself she would make this a performance worth watching?

A show of passion?

"Now." His gaze never left hers even as he continued to address the media. "I am going to ask you to check Ms. Koslov's schedule for a new interview time tomorrow. Because tonight we have something private and wonderful to celebrate."

The camerawoman gave a quiet squeal of excitement. A few people clapped halfheartedly. Sofia wondered how she'd ever dared to ask Quinn McNeill for a temporary fiancé. She couldn't believe he'd granted her wish

And not with his brother. But with Quinn himself as her fake groom.

The cameras captured every moment of this absurd dance as she clutched a bouquet in one hand while Quinn tucked the mysterious black velvet box into the other. Then, leaving no doubt as to his meaning, he slanted his lips over hers and kissed her.

* * *

The Magnate's Mail-Order Bride
is part of the McNeill Magnates trilogy:
Those McNeill men just have a way with women!

THE MAGNATE'S
MAIL-ORDER BRIDE

BY
JOANNE ROCK

First Published in Great Britain 2017
By Mills & Boon, an imprint of HarperCollins*Publishers*
1 London Bridge Street, London, SE1 9GF

© 2017 Joanne Rock

ISBN: 978-0-263-92815-0

51-0417

Four-time RITA® Award nominee **Joanne Rock** has penned over seventy stories for Mills & Boon. An optimist by nature and a perpetual seeker of silver linings, Joanne finds romance fits her life outlook perfectly—love is worth fighting for. A former Golden Heart® Award recipient, she has won numerous awards for her stories. Learn more about Joanne's imaginative Muse by visiting her website, www.joannerock.com, or following @joannerock6 on Twitter.

To Maureen Wallace, the empathetic
and efficient property manager on-site at the
vacation rental where I finished this book.
When construction work outside my rental
made writing impossible, Maureen listened to
my tale of woe and found another spot for me,
making sure I could get work done the next
day and have a gorgeous water view to boot!
Thank you for going above and beyond to help.

One

"It's no wonder her performances lack passion. Have you ever seen Sofia date anyone in all the time we've known her?"

Normally, Sofia Koslov didn't eavesdrop. Yet hearing the whispered gossip stopped her in her tracks as she headed from the Gulfstream's kitchen back to her seat for landing.

A principal dancer in the New York City Ballet, Sofia had performed a brief engagement with a small dance ensemble in Kiev last week. Her colleagues had been all too glad to join her when her wealthy father had offered his private plane for their return to the United States. But apparently the favor hadn't won her any new allies. As one of the most rapidly promoted female dancers currently in the company, Sofia's successes had ruffled feathers along the way.

She clutched her worn copy of *A Midsummer Night's*

Dream to her chest and peered toward her father's seat at the front of the jet, grateful he was still engrossed in a business teleconference call. Vitaly Koslov had accompanied the troupe on the trip to the Ukraine, his birthplace. He'd used their rare time together as an opportunity to pressure Sofia about settling down and providing him with grandchildren who might be more interested in taking over his global empire than she'd been.

"That's not fair, Antonia," one of the other dancers in the circle of four recliners snapped, not bothering to lower her voice. "None of us has time to meet people during the season. I haven't had a lover all year. Does that make me passionless when I go on stage?"

Sofia told herself she should walk back to her seat before the pilot told them to buckle up. But her feet stayed glued to the floor. She peered down at her notes on Shakespeare's play, pretending to reread them for an upcoming role as Titania if anyone happened to notice her.

"But Sofia's been with the company since ballet school and have we ever heard her name connected romantically with anyone?" Antonia Blakely had entered ballet school at the same time as Sofia, and had advanced to each level with the company faster than her. "Actually, her dad must agree that she's turning into a dried-up old prune, because—*get this*." She paused theatrically, having relied on showmanship over technical skill her entire career. Now, she lowered her voice even more. "I overheard her father talking to the *matchmaker* he hired for her."

Sofia's stomach dropped even though the plane hadn't started its descent. She gripped the wooden door frame that separated the kitchen from the seating area. For over a year she'd resisted her father's efforts to hire a matchmaking service on her behalf. But it was true—he'd stepped up the pressure during their visit to Ukraine, insisting she think about her family and her roots.

Marriage wasn't even on her radar while her career was on the upswing. Would Dad have signed her up with his matchmaker friend without her approval? Her gaze flicked back to the proud billionaire who made a fortune by trusting his gut and never doubting himself for a second.

Of course he would proceed without her agreement. Betrayal slammed through her harder than an off-kilter landing.

"Seriously?" one of the other dancers asked. "Like a private matchmaker?"

"Of course. Rich people don't use the same dating web sites as the rest of us. They try to find their own kind." Antonia spoke with that irritating assurance shared by know-it-alls everywhere. "If Papa Koslov gets his way, there'll be a rich boy ready and waiting for his precious daughter at the airport when we land."

Sofia lifted a hand to her lips to hold back a gasp and a handful of curses. She wasn't wealthy, for one thing. Her father might be one of the richest people in the world, but that didn't mean she was, too. She had never even spent a night under his roof until after her mother's death when Sofia was just thirteen. She'd followed her mother's example in dealing with him, drawing that financial line and refusing his support a long time ago. Her father equated money with power, and she wouldn't let him dictate her life. Ballet was her defiance—her choice of art over the almighty dollar.

Her father knew he couldn't control her choices. Not even Vitaly Koslov in all his arrogance would arrange for her to meet a prospective date in front of twenty colleagues. Not after an exhausting overseas dance schedule and nine hours in the air across seven time zones. Would he?

A ringing noise distracted her from the question and she peered around, only to realize the chime came from her pocket. Her cell phone. She must not have shut it off for the plane ride. Withdrawing the device, she muted the volume, but not before half the dancers on the plane turned to stare. Including the group nearby who'd been gossiping about her.

None of them looked particularly shamefaced.

Sofia hurried toward an open seat and buckled into the wide leather chair for descent. She checked the incoming text on her phone while the pilot made the usual announcements about the landing.

Her closest friend, Jasmine Jackson, worked in public relations and had agreed to help Sofia with a PR initiative this year to take her dance career to the next level. Jasmine's text was about the interview Sofia had agreed to for *Dance* magazine.

Reporter and one camera operator for Dance will meet you in terminal to film arrival. We want you to look like you're coming off a successful world tour! Touch up your makeup and no yoga pants, please.

Panic crawled up her throat at the idea of meeting with the media now when she was exhausted and agitated about the other dancers' comments. Still, she pulled out her travel duffel and fished around the bottom for her makeup bag to comply with Jasmine's wise advice. Chances were good that Antonia had misinterpreted her father's conversation anyhow. He might be high-handed and overbearing, but he'd known about the *Dance* magazine interview. She'd told him there was a chance the reporter would want to meet her at the airport. He wouldn't purposely embarrass her.

Unless he fully intended to put her on the spot? Prevent her from arguing with him by springing a new man on her while the cameras rolled?

Impossible. She shook off the idea as too over the top, even for him. She already had the lip gloss wand out when her phone chimed with another message from Jasmine.

WARNING—the camera person freelances for the tabloids. I'm not worried about you, of course, but maybe warn the other dancers? Good luck!

The plane wheels hit the tarmac with a jarring thud, nearly knocking the phone from her hand. Capping the lip gloss, she knew no amount of makeup was going to cover up the impending disaster. If Antonia was correct about her father's plans and some tabloid reporter captured the resulting argument between Sofia and her dad—the timing would be terrible. It would undermine everything she'd worked for in hiring a publicist in the first place.

Celebrated choreographer Idris Fortier was in town this week and he planned to create a ballet to premiere in New York. Sofia would audition for a feature role—as would every other woman on the plane. Competition could turn vicious at the slightest opportunity.

Maybe it already had.

Steeling herself for whatever happened in the terminal, Sofia took deep breaths to slow her racing heart. Forewarned was forearmed, right? She should consider herself fortunate that her gossipy colleague had given her a heads-up on her father's plan. With cameras rolling for her interview, she couldn't afford the slightest misstep. She could argue with him later, privately. But she wouldn't sacrifice a good PR opportunity when she had the chance of a lifetime to be the featured dancer in a new Idris Fortier ballet.

She would think of this as a performance and she would nail it, no matter what surprises the public stage had to offer. That's what she did, damn it.

And this time, no one would say her performance lacked passion.

"Don't do something stupid because you're angry." Quinn McNeill tried to reason with his youngest brother as he strode beside him toward the terminal of the largest private airport servicing Manhattan. They'd shared a limo to Teterboro from the McNeill Resorts' offices in midtown this afternoon even though Quinn's flight to Eastern Europe to meet with potential investors didn't leave for several hours. He'd canceled his afternoon meetings just to talk sense into Cameron.

"I'm not angry." Cameron spread his arms wide, his herringbone pea coat swinging open as if to say he had nothing to hide. "Look at me. Do I look upset?"

With his forced grin, actually, yes. The men shared a family resemblance, their Scots roots showing in blue eyes and dark hair. But when Quinn said nothing, Cameron continued, "I'm going to allow Gramps to dictate my life and move me around like a chess piece so that I can one day inherit a share of the family business. Which I don't really want in the first place except that he's drilled loyalty into our heads and he doesn't want anyone but a McNeill running McNeill Resorts."

Last week, Quinn, Cameron and their other brother, Ian, had all been called into their grandfather's lawyer's office for a meeting that spelled out terms of a revised will that would split the shares of the older man's global corporation into equal thirds among them. The news itself was no surprise since the McNeill patriarch had promised as much for years, grooming them for roles in his company even though each of them had gone on to develop their own business interests. Malcolm McNeill's apathetic only son had taken a brief turn at the company helm and proven himself unequal to the task, so the older man had targeted the next generation to inherit.

None of them *needed* the promised inheritance. But Cam was the closest to their grandfather and felt the most pressure to buy into Malcolm McNeill's vision for the future. And the catch was, each of them could only obtain his share of McNeill Resorts upon marriage, with the share reverting to the estate if the marriage ended sooner than twelve months.

Out of overinflated loyalty, Cameron seemed ready to tie the knot with a woman, sight-unseen, after choosing her from a matchmaker's lineup of foreign women eager to wed. Either that, or he was hoping a ludicrous trip to the altar would make their grandfather realize what a bad idea this was and prompt him to call the whole thing off.

It had always been tough to tell with Cam. For Quinn's part, he was content to take a wait-and-see approach and hope their grandfather changed his mind. The old man was still in good health. And he'd conveniently booked a trip to China after the meeting in his lawyer's office, making it next to impossible to argue with him for at least a few more weeks.

"Cam, look at it this way. If it's so important to Gramps that the company remain in family hands, he wouldn't have attached this new stipulation." Quinn ignored the phone vibrating in his pocket as he tried to convince his brother of the point.

"Gramps won't live forever." Cameron raised his voice as a jet took off overhead. "That will might be ludicrous, but it's still a legal document. I don't want the company to end up on the auction block for some investor to swoop in and divvy up the assets."

"Neither do I." Quinn's coattails flapped in the gust of air from the nearby takeoff. "But I'd rather try to convince the stubborn old man that forcing marriage down our throats might backfire and create more instability in the company than anything."

"Who says my marriage won't be stable? I might be on to something, letting a matchmaker choose my bride. It's not like I've had any luck finding Ms. Right on my own."

Cameron had a reputation as a playboy, a cheerful charmer who wined and dined some of the world's most beautiful women.

Quinn shook his head. "Since when have you tried looking for meaningful relationships?"

"I don't want someone who is playing an angle." Cameron scowled. "I meet too many women more interested in seeing what I can do for them."

"This girl could be doing the same thing. Maybe you're her ticket to permanent residence in the United States." Shouldering his way through a small group of businessmen who emerged from the terminal building stumbling and laughing, Quinn opened the door and held it for his brother. "How much do you know about your bride? You've never even spoken to this woman. Does she even speak English?"

Where the hell was their master negotiator brother, Ian, for conversations like this? Quinn needed backup and the reasonable voice of the middle son who had always mediated the vastly different perspectives Cameron and Quinn held. But Ian was in meetings all day, leaving Quinn to talk his brother out of his modern-day, mail-order bride scheme.

All around him, the airport seethed with activity as flights landed and drivers rushed in to handle baggage for people who never paused in their cell phone conversations.

Cameron led them toward the customs area where international flights checked in at one of two counters.

"I know her name is Sofia and that she's Ukrainian. Her file said she was marriage-minded, just like me." Cam pulled out his phone and flashed the screen under Quinn's nose. "That's her."

A picture of a beautiful woman filled the screen, her features reflecting the Eastern European ideal with high cheekbones and arched eyebrows that gave her a vaguely haughty look. With her bare shoulders and a wealth of beaded necklaces, however, the photo of the gray-eyed blonde bombshell had a distinctly professional quality.

Quinn felt as if he'd seen her somewhere before. A professional model, maybe?

"This is probably just a photo taken from a foreign magazine and passed off as her. Photography like that isn't cheap. And did you pay for a private flight for this woman to come over here?" Not that it was his business how his brother spent his money. But damn.

Even for Cameron, that seemed excessive.

"Hell, no. She arranged her own flight. Or maybe the matchmaker did." He shrugged as though it didn't matter, but he'd obviously given this whole idea zero thought. Or thought about it only when he was angry with their grandfather. "Plus she's *Ukrainian*." He stressed the word for emphasis. "I figured she might be a help once you secure the Eastern European properties. Always nice to have someone close who speaks the language, and maybe Gramps will put me in charge of revamping the hotels once I've passed the marriage test." He said this with a perfectly straight face.

He had to be joking. Any second now Cameron would say "to hell with this" and walk out. Or laugh and walk out. But he wasn't going to greet some foreigner fresh off an international flight and propose.

Not even Cameron would go that far. Quinn put a hand on his brother's chest, halting him for a second.

"Do not try to pass off this harebrained idea as practical in any way." They shared a level gaze for a moment until Cameron pushed past, his focus on something outside on the tarmac.

Quinn's gaze went toward a handful of travelers disembarking near the customs counter. One of the women seemed to have caught her scarf around the handrail of the air stairs.

"That might be her now." Cameron's eyes were on the woman, as well. "I wish I'd brought some flowers." Pivoting, he jogged over to a counter decorated with a vase full of exotic blooms near the pilots' club.

Vaguely, Quinn noticed Cameron charming the attendant into selling him a few of the purple orchids. But Quinn's attention lingered on the woman who had just freed her pink printed scarf from the handrail. Although huge sunglasses covered half her face, with her blond hair and full, pouty lips, she resembled the woman in the photo. About twenty other people got off that same plane, a disproportionately high number of them young women.

Concern for his brother made him wary. The woman's closest travel companion appeared to be a slick-looking guy old enough to be her father. The man held out a hand to help her descend the steps. She was waif-thin and something about the way she carried herself seemed very deliberate. Like she was a woman used to being the center of attention. Quinn was missing something here.

"She's tiny." Cameron had returned to Quinn's side. "I didn't think to ask how tall she was."

Quinn's brain worked fast as he tried to refit the pieces that didn't add up. And to do it before the future Mrs. McNeill made it past the customs agent.

The other women in front of her sped through the declarations process.

"So who is supposed to introduce the two of you?" Quinn's bad feeling increased by the second. "Your matchmaker set up a formal introduction, I hope?" He should be going over his notes for his own meeting overseas tonight, not worrying about who would introduce his foolish brother to a con artist waiting to play him.

But how many times had Cameron stirred up trouble with one impulsive decision or another then simply walked away when things got out of hand, leaving someone else to take care of damage control?

"No one." Cameron shrugged. "She just texted me what time to meet the plane." He wiped nonexistent lint off his collar and rearranged the flowers, a glint of grim determination in his eyes.

"Cam, don't do this." Quinn didn't understand rash people. How could he logically argue against this proposal when no logic had gone into his brother's decision in the first place? "At least figure out who she really is before you drag her to the nearest justice of the peace." They both watched as the woman tugged off her sunglasses to speak with the customs agent, her older travel companion still hovering protectively behind her.

"Sofia's photo was real enough, though. She's a knock-out." Cameron's assessment sounded as dispassionate and detached as if he'd been admiring a painting for one of the new hotels.

Quinn, on the other hand, found it difficult to remain impassive about the woman. There was something striking about her. She had a quiet, delicate beauty and a self-assured air in her perfect posture and graceful walk. And to compound his frustrations with his brother, Quinn realized what he was feeling for Cameron's future bride was blatant and undeniable physical attraction.

Cameron clapped a hand on his shoulder and moved toward the gate. "Admit it, Sofia is exactly as advertised."

Before Quinn could argue, a pair of women approached the doors leading outside. They were clearly waiting for someone. Both wore badges that dangled from ribbons around their necks, and one hoisted a professional-looking camera.

Reporters?

Cameron held the door for them and followed them out.

And like a train wreck that Quinn couldn't look away from, he watched as Cameron greeted the slender Ukrainian woman with a bouquet of flowers and—curse his eyes—a velvet box. He'd brought a *ring*? With his customary charm, Cameron bowed and passed Sofia the bouquet. Just in time for the woman with the camera to fix her lens on the tableaux.

Quinn rushed toward the scene—wanting to stop it and knowing it was too late. Had Cameron called a friend from the media? Had he wanted this thing filmed to be sure their grandfather heard about it? Whatever mess Cam was creating for himself, Quinn had the sinking feeling he'd be the one to dig him out of it.

Cold, dry, winter wind swept in through the door and blasted him in the face at the same time Cameron's words hit his ears.

"Sofia, I've been waiting all day to meet my bride."

Two

Sofia had mentally prepared to be approached by a suitor. She had not expected a marriage proposal.

In all the years she'd danced Balanchine on toes that bled right through the calluses, all the times she'd churned out bravura fouetté turns fearing she'd fall in front of a live audience, she'd never been so disoriented as she was staring up at the tall, dark-haired man bearing flowers and…a ring?

The way she chose to handle this encounter would surely be recorded for posterity and nitpicked by those who would love nothing more than to see her make a misstep offstage. Or lose a chance at the lead in Fortier's first new ballet in two years.

In the strained silence, the wind blew Sofia's scarf off her shoulders to smother half her face. She could hear Antonia whispering behind her back. And giggling.

"For pity's sake, man, let's take this inside." Sofia's father was the first to speak.

Vitaly Koslov maintained his outward composure, but Sofia knew him well enough to hear the surprise in his tone. Was it possible he hadn't foreseen such a rash action from a suitor when he arranged for a matchmaker for her without her consent? The more she thought about it, the more she fumed. How dare this man corner her with his marriage offer in a public place?

She stepped out of the wind into the bright lobby, wishing she could just keep on walking out the front exit. But the camerawoman still trailed her. Sofia needed to wake up and get on top of this before a silly airport proposal took the focus of the *Dance* magazine story away from her dancing.

"Ladies." Sofia turned a performer's smile on the reporters, willing away her exhaustion with the steely determination that got her through seven-hour rehearsals. "I'm so sorry. I forgot I have a brief personal appointment. If you would be so kind as to give me a few moments?"

"Oh, but we've got such a good story going." The slim, delicately built reporter was surely a former dancer herself. She smiled with the same cobra-like grace of so many of Sofia's colleagues—a frightening show of sweetness that could precede a venomous strike. "Sofia, you never mentioned someone special in your life in our preliminary interview."

The camera turned toward the man who'd just proposed to her and the even more staggeringly handsome man beside him—another dark-haired, blue-eyed stranger, who wasn't as absurdly tall as her suitor. They had to be related. The second man's blue eyes were darker, frank and assessing. And he had a different kind of appeal from the well-muscled male dancers she worked with daily who honed their bodies for their art. Thicker in the shoulders and arms, he appeared strong enough to lift multiple ballerinas at once. With ease.

Tearing her eyes from him, she pushed aside the wayward thoughts. Then she promised the reporter the best incentive she could think of to obtain the respite she needed.

"If I can have a few moments to speak privately with my friend, you can film my audition for Idris Fortier." Sofia recalled the magazine had been angling for a connection to the famous choreographer. As much as she didn't want that moment on public record—especially if she failed to capture the lead role—she needed to get those cameras switched off now.

Her father wasn't going to run this show.

After a quick exchange of glances, the reporter with the camera lowered the lens and the pair retreated to a leather sofa in the almost empty waiting area. In the meantime, the rest of the troupe who had traveled with Sofia lingered.

"May we have a moment, ladies?" her father asked the bunch. And though some pouting followed, they went and joined the reporters, leaving Sofia and her father with the tall man, still holding a ring box, and his even more handsome relation.

Belatedly she realized she had mindlessly taken the orchids the stranger had offered her. She could only imagine how she looked in the pictures and video already captured by the magazine's photographer.

The same woman her publicist warned her moonlighted for the paparazzi. How fast would her story make the rounds?

"Sofia." The tall man leaned forward into her line of vision. "I'm Cameron McNeill. I hope our matchmaker let you know I'd be here to take you home?"

Even now, he didn't lower his voice, but he had a puzzled expression.

She resisted the urge to glare at her father, afraid the reporter could use a long range-lens to film this conversation. Instead, Sofia gestured to some couches far removed from the others, but her suitor didn't budge as he studied her.

His companion, still watching her with those assessing blue eyes, said something quietly in the tall man's ear. A warning? A note of caution? He surreptitiously checked his phone.

"How do I know that name? McNeill?" Her father's chin jutted forward in challenge.

"Dad, please." After a life on stage studying the nuances of expressions to better emote in dance, Sofia knew how easily body language could tell a story. Especially to her fellow dancers. "May I?" Without waiting for an answer she turned back to Cameron. "Could we sit down for a moment?"

Her father snapped his fingers before anyone moved. "McNeill Resorts?"

As soon as he uttered the words, the quiet man at Cameron's shoulder stepped forward with an air of command. He seemed a more approachable six foot two, something she could guess easily given the emphasis on paring the right dance partners in the ballet. Sofia's tired mind couldn't help a moment's romantic thought that this man would be a better fit for her. Purely from a dance perspective, of course.

He wore the overcoat and suit of a well-heeled Wall Street man, she thought. Yet there was a glint in his midnight-blue eyes, a fierceness she recognized as a subtler brand of passion.

Like hers.

"Vitaly Koslov?" Just by stepping forward into the small, awkward group, he somehow took charge. "I'm Quinn McNeill. We spoke briefly at the Met Gala two years ago."

A brother, she thought.

A very enticing brother. One who hadn't approached her with a marriage proposal in front of a journalist's camera. She approved of him more already, even as she wondered what these McNeill men were about.

She needed to think quickly and carefully.

"Sofia's got family in New York," Cameron informed Quinn, as if picking up a conversation they'd been in the middle of. "I knew she wasn't some kind of mail-order bride." He smiled down at Sofia with a grin too practiced for her taste. "The reporters must be doing some kind of story on you? I saw their media badges were from *Dance* magazine."

"Mail-order bride?" Her father's raised voice made even a few seen-it-all New Yorkers turn to stare, if only for a second. "I'll sue your family from here to Sunday, McNeill, if you're insinuating—"

"I knew she wasn't looking for a green card," Cameron argued, pulling out his phone while Sofia wished she could start this day all over again. "It was Quinn who thought that our meeting was a scam. But I got her picture from my matchmaker—"

"There's been a mix-up." Quinn stood between the two men, making her grateful she hadn't pulled the referee duty herself. "I told my brother as much before we realized who Sofia was."

Sofia couldn't decide if she was more incensed that she'd been mistaken for a bride for hire or that one of them wanted to marry her based on a photo. But frustration was building and the walls damn well had ears. She peered around nervously.

"Who is she?" Cameron asked Quinn, setting the conspicuous velvet box on a nearby table. Sofia felt all the eyes of her fellow dancers drawn to it like a magnet even from halfway across the waiting area.

"Sofia Koslov, principal dancer with the New York City Ballet." He passed Cameron his phone. He'd pulled up her photo and bio—she recognized it from the company web site. "Her father is the founder of Self-Sale, the online auction house, and one of the most powerful voices in Ukraine, where I'm trying to purchase that historic hotel."

The two brothers exchanged a meaningful look, clearly wary of her father's international influence.

While Cameron whistled softly and swiped a finger along the device's screen, Sofia's father looked ready to launch across the sofa and strangle him. Maybe her dad was regretting his choice of matchmaker already. Sofia certainly regretted his arrogant assumption that he could arrange her private life to suit him.

"You call that a *mix-up*?" Her father's accent thickened, a sure sign he was angry. "Why the hell would you think she needed a green card when she is an American citizen?" Her father articulated his words with an edge as he got in Quinn McNeill's face. "Do you have any idea how quickly I can bury your hotel purchase if I choose to, McNeill? If you think I'm going to let this kind of insult slide—"

"Of course not." Quinn didn't flinch. "We'll figure out something—"

Sofia missed the rest of the exchange as Cameron leaned closer to speak to her.

"You're really a ballerina?" He asked the question

kindly enough, but there was a wariness in his eyes that Sofia had seen many times from people who equated "ballerina" with "prima donna." Or "diva."

"Yes." She lifted her chin, feeling defensive and wondering if Quinn could overhear them as he continued to speak in low tones with her father. The older brother drew her eye in a way men seldom did. And was it her tired imagination or did his gaze return to her often, as well? "I competed for years to move into a top position with one of the most rigorous and respected companies in the world."

Men never apologized for focusing on their careers. Why should she?

Cameron nodded but made no comment. She sensed him rethinking his marriage proposal in earnest. Not that it mattered—obviously a wedding wasn't happening. But how to dig herself out of this mess for the sake of the cameras and her peers? If she wasn't so drained from the long flight and the demanding practice schedule of this tour, maybe her brain would come up with a plausible, graceful way to extricate herself.

She noticed the members of her dance troupe moving steadily closer, no doubt trying to overhear what was going on in this strange powwow. Every last one of them had their phones in hand. She could almost imagine the tweets.

Will Sofia Koslov be too busy with her new fiancé to give her full attention to Fortier?

The dance world would go nuts. A flurry of speculation would ensue. Would Fortier decide he didn't want to work with a woman who didn't devote all of her free time to dance?

Her stomach cramped as she went cold inside. That would be so incredibly unfair. But it didn't take much to lose a lead role. It was all about what Fortier wanted.

"And you were not actively seeking a husband?" Cameron asked the question with a straight face.

Did he not realize she'd forgotten him completely? Her eyes ventured over to Quinn, hoping the man truly had an idea about how to fix this, the way he'd assured her father.

"No," she told him honestly. "I didn't even know my father had hired a matchmaker until shortly before we landed. He signed me up without permission."

"Then I apologize, Ms. Koslov, if I've caused you any embarrassment in my haste to find a bride." Cameron lifted her hand and put it to his lips, planting a kiss on the back of her knuckles. The gesture had the flair of a debonair flirt rather than any real sentiment. "My brother warned me not to rush into this. And, once again, it seems the ever-practical Quinn had a good point."

He straightened as if to leave, making her realize she would be on her own to explain this to the reporters. And the dance community. But she didn't blame Cameron. She blamed her father.

"You were really willing to marry someone without even talking to them?" She couldn't imagine what would drive him to propose to a stranger out of the blue.

"I was leaving it in the hands of professionals." He shrugged. "But next time, I will at least call the bride ahead of time. Good luck with your dancing, Sofia." He stuffed his hands into his coat pockets. "Quinn's flight doesn't take off for a few hours. If you need help with the reporters, my brother has a gift for keeping a cool head. He'll know what to do."

"You're…leaving?"

"I only came to the airport to see you. It's Quinn who has a flight out." He nodded toward his brother, who had captured the full attention of her father. "But he'll come up with a plan to help you with the reporters first. He's the expert at making the McNeills look good. I'm the brother who seems to stir up all the trouble."

It didn't occur to her to stop Cameron McNeill as he pivoted and stalked away from her, the necks of her traveling companions all craning to follow his progress through the airport terminal. She noticed other women doing the same thing.

But then, these McNeill men were uncommonly handsome.

The whole thing felt too surreal. And now the two reporters turned from the large windows on the other side of the terminal and headed her way again. The sick feeling returned in the pit of her stomach. She should have been using this time to come up with a plan. Maybe she could tell the reporters that the proposal had all been a joke?

Except she'd trip over any story she tried to concoct. Unlike her PR consultant, Sofia was not a master of putting the right spin on things. Besides, her colleagues' words about her not dating still circled around in her head.

About her lack of passion.

What would they say now that her suitor had ditched her publicly?

Her father and Quinn McNeill converged on her.

"You should listen, Sofia. McNeill has a fair plan." Vitaly nodded his satisfaction at whatever they'd decided.

Fear spiked in her chest as the reporters drew closer. These men didn't understand her world or the backlash this little drama would cause. How could she win the part in the Fortier ballet while her whole dance company gossiped gleefully about her five-minute marriage offer?

"No. I will handle this." She looked to Quinn Mc-Neill. "I need to save face. To come up with something that doesn't make it look like I've been jilted—" Hell, she didn't know what she needed. She couldn't even explain herself to Quinn. How would she ever make sense in front of the reporters?

Quinn's blue eyes gave away exactly nothing. Whereas his younger brother was all charm and flirtation, this man's level stare was impossible to read. He seemed at ease, however. He leaned closer to her to speak softly while her father discreetly checked his watch, positioning himself between her and the oncoming dancers.

"Your father is livid at my brother's antics." Quinn's voice was like a warm stroke against her ear. It gave her a pleasant shiver in spite of her nervousness. "I'd like to appease him, but it's more important to me that you're not embarrassed by this. How can I help?"

She blurted the first thing that came to mind. "Ideally, I'd like a fiancé for the next three weeks until I have a ballet part on lockdown." As soon as the words tumbled out, of course, she realized that was impossible. Cameron McNeill was already gone.

But Quinn did not look deterred. He nodded.

"Whatever I say, please know that it's just for show." His hand landed on her spine, a heated touch that seeped right through her mohair cape. "We'll give a decoy statement to the media and then you and I can iron out some kind of formal press release afterward. But I can have you happily engaged and out of here in less than five minutes. Just follow my lead."

She didn't even have time to meet his eyes and see for herself his level of sincerity, because the cameras were rolling again, the bright light in her eyes. Excited whispering from the other dancers provided an uncomfortable background music for whatever performance Quinn McNeill was about to give.

Strange that, when her reputation hung in the balance, the main thing she noticed was how his hand palmed the small of her back with a surety and command even a dancing master would appreciate.

Her father hung back as the flashing red light on the Nikon handheld swung her way. Blinking while her eyes adjusted, she thought she saw her father reclaim the velvet ring box Cameron had left behind and hand it to Quinn. Which made sense, she supposed. The brother of empty gestures left a diamond behind while the practical brother reclaimed it. Hadn't Cameron assured her Quinn would take care of everything?

"Ladies." Quinn's voice took on a very different quality as he turned to the camera and the small audience of her colleagues who clutched their cell phones, surely eager to send out updates on this little drama. "Forgive me for spiriting away Sofia earlier. In my eagerness to see her again, I failed to remember her interview with the magazine. I didn't mean for a private moment to be caught on film."

Sofia could almost hear the collective intake of breath. Or was that her own? Her stomach twisted, fearing what he might say next while at the same time she couldn't make herself interrupt. Like any strong partner, he led with authority.

Besides, he said it was only for show.

"Where is your brother?" one of the reporters asked. "He said he couldn't wait to meet his bride."

No doubt they'd all been surfing the internet to figure out who Cameron and Quinn were.

"My brother was teasing. Cameron hadn't met Sofia yet and, in the way brothers sometimes do…" He deployed a charming grin of his own, one even more disarming than his brother's had been, only now she realized how practiced the gesture could be. "Cam only said that to rattle me on the day he knew I was going to ask her something very important myself."

Quinn turned to her now, his blue eyes locking on her with an intensity that speared right down to her belly to stir an unexpected heat. Even when she knew with one hundred percent certainty it was all an act.

"He just so happened to have a ring in his pocket?" the reporter asked, gaze narrowed to search out the truth.

"I had no idea he brought an old ring of our mother's from home," Quinn continued easily. "Then he grabbed some flowers from the customer service desk." He pointed out a half-empty vase nearby. "Trust me when I tell you, my brother doesn't lack for a sense of humor—a somewhat twisted one."

Even Sofia found herself wondering about his story. Quinn looked convincing enough, especially when he gazed down at her as if she was the only woman in the world.

She licked her lips, her mouth gone suddenly dry. She should say something. Prevent this farce that no one would ever believe. But then again...hadn't she promised herself she would make this a performance worth watching?

A show of passion?

"Now—" his gaze never left hers even as he continued to address the media "—I am going to ask you to check Ms. Koslov's schedule for a new interview time tomorrow. Because tonight, we have something private and wonderful to celebrate."

Somewhere behind that bright light the camerawoman gave a quiet squeal of excitement while someone else—

a colleague from the ballet company, no doubt—made a huff of disappointment. That the story hadn't panned out how she'd wanted? Or that she'd have to wait until tomorrow for answers? A few people clapped halfheartedly. The dancers who had hoped for a scandal were clearly disappointed while Sofia wondered how she'd ever dared to ask Quinn McNeill for a temporary fiancé. She couldn't believe he'd granted her wish.

And not with his brother but with Quinn himself as her fake groom.

The cameras captured every moment of this absurd dance as she clutched the bouquet in one hand while Quinn tucked the mysterious black-velvet box into the other. Then, leaving no doubt as to his meaning, he slanted his lips overs hers and kissed her.

Three

Normally, Quinn McNeill knew how to stick to the talking points. He'd delivered enough unwelcome news to investors during his father's failed tenure as the McNeill Resorts' CEO that Quinn had a knack for staying on script.

But all bets were off, it seemed, when an exotic beauty fit into his arms as if she'd been made for him. One moment he'd been delivering the cover story to explain Cam's behavior and still give Sofia Koslov a fiancé. The next, he was drowning in her wide gray eyes, her full lips luring him into a minty-flavored kiss that made the mayhem of the airport fade away.

This was so not the plan he'd come up with to smooth over business relations with Sofia's ticked-off and powerful Ukrainian father. He'd told Vitaly Koslov he would publicly apologize and explain away the proposal as a joke between friends. But when Quinn had seen the panic on Sofia's face, he'd known his only option was to help her in whatever way she needed.

Although, it occurred to him as he kissed her…

What if she'd meant she wanted that fake engagement with his brother?

Forcing himself to edge back slowly, Quinn peered down at her kissed-plump lips and flushed cheeks. She couldn't have possibly meant she wanted anything to do with Cameron. Not after that kiss.

Still, he'd just complicated things a whole lot by claiming her as his own.

"So you're engaged to Ms. Koslov?" one of the reporters asked him while the other one flipped off the power button on her camera.

"A full statement will be issued tomorrow morning," Vitaly Koslov snapped before Quinn could respond, the older man's patience clearly worn thin as he shot a dark glare at Quinn.

The hotel deals he was working on in Kiev and Prague were now seriously compromised. The man had threatened to block the sales by any means necessary if Quinn didn't smooth things over with the media, and Quinn was guessing that taking Cameron's place as Sofia's suitor wasn't what Vitaly Koslov had in mind.

Right now, however, Quinn had promised the man to get his daughter out of the terminal and home as quickly and privately as possible.

"Come with me," Quinn whispered in Sofia's ear, a few strands of silky hair brushing his cheek as he bent to shoulder her bag for her. "Your father will divert them. We are too happy and in love to pay attention to anyone else."

He started walking toward the exit, hoping she would continue to play her part in this charade. She did just that, moving with quick, efficient steps and glancing up at him in a way that was more than just affectionate.

Hell. Those gazes sizzled.

"How fortunate we are," she muttered dryly. Her tone was at odds with the way she was looking at him, making him realize what a skilled actress she was.

Had the kiss been for show, too? He liked to think he could tell the difference.

"I regret that we have to do this. I hope my brother at least had the decency to apologize before he made his escape." Quinn had already texted his pilot to reschedule his own flight, a delay that would add to the considerable expense of closing this deal that might never happen anyhow.

He held the door for Sofia and flagged the first limo he spotted, handing off her luggage to the driver to stow. The wind plastered her cape to Quinn's legs, bringing with it the faint scent of a subtle perfume.

"He did apologize." She tucked the mohair wrap tighter around herself, waiting on the curb while the driver opened the door and she relayed the address of her apartment. "He told me he was sorry right before he assured me you'd take care of everything." She slid to the far side of the vehicle, distancing herself from him. "Tell me, Quinn, how often do you step in to claim his discarded fiancées?"

He understood that she was frustrated, so he told himself not to be defensive.

"This would be a first," he replied lightly, taking the seat on the opposite side of the limo. "I tried to talk him out of hunting for a wife in this drastic manner, but he was determined."

The driver was already behind the wheel and steering

the vehicle toward the exit. Darkness had fallen while they were inside the terminal.

"It would not have been so awkward if there hadn't been any media present." She seemed to relax a bit as she leaned deeper into the leather seat, pulling the pink scarf off her neck to wrap it around one hand. "Then again, maybe it would have been since I had the rest of the dance ensemble with me and there are those who would love nothing more than a chance to undermine my position in the company."

"Your father told me that you were recently promoted to principal." He only had a vague knowledge of the ballet, having attended a handful of events for social purposes. "Does that always put a target on a dancer's back?"

"Only if your name is mentioned for a highly sought-after part in a new ballet to premiere next year. Or if you rise through the ranks too quickly. Or if your father sponsors a gala fund-raiser and angles for you to be featured prominently in the program." She wound the scarf around her other hand, weaving it through her fingers. "Then, no matter how talented you are, the rumor persists that you only achieved your position because of money."

In the glow from the streetlights, he watched her delicate wrists as she anxiously fumbled with the scarf. She hadn't been this skittish back in the airport. Did he make her nervous? Or was she only allowing herself the show of nerves now that she was out of the spotlight?

He found himself curious about her even though he should be focusing on the details of their brief, pretend engagement and not ruminating on her life. Her kiss.

"You move in a competitive world." It was something he understood from the business he managed outside of

McNeill Resorts since his bigger income stream came from his work as a hedge fund manager. His every financial move was watched and dissected by his rivals and second-guessed by nervous investors.

"The competition led me to hire a PR firm at my own expense, which is costly, considering a dancer's salary. But they secured the feature for me in *Dance* magazine."

He had no idea what a professional ballerina earned, but the idea that she'd hired a publicity firm suggested a strong investment in her career. Quinn found it intriguing that she would pay for that herself considering her father's wealth.

That wasn't all he found intriguing. The spike of attraction he felt for her—a heat that had intensified with that kiss—surprised him. He'd been adamantly opposed to his grandfather's marriage ultimatum and yet he'd found himself jumping into the fray today to claim Sofia for his own.

Not just for McNeill Resorts. Also so Cameron couldn't have her.

As soon as he'd seen her today, he'd felt an undeniable sexual interest. No, hunger.

"I realize that my brother created an awkward situation and you have every right to be frustrated."

"And yet you helped me out of a tricky situation when I was tongue-tied and nervous, so thank you for that." She settled her hands in her lap and stared out the window at the businesses lining either side of Interstate 17 heading south toward Manhattan. "I have a difficult audition ahead of me and I know I wouldn't have been able to focus on it if the debacle in the airport was the topic on everyone's lips." She gave him a half smile. "If I didn't have a fiancé, everyone would badger me about what happened. But since I actually *do*? I don't think anyone will quiz me about it. Sadly, my competitors are more interested in my failures than my successes."

He understood. He just hoped her father would support her wishes regarding their charade.

"Yet tonight's events leave you a loophole, Sofia, if you want to give a statement that you refused me." He hadn't thought about it until now, but just because he'd implied he was asking for her hand didn't mean she would necessarily accept. "If you change your mind about this, I can have someone work on a statement for the press that expresses my admiration for you, my disappointment in your refusal—"

"Expedient for you, but not for me." She tipped her head to the window, her expression weary. He noticed the pale purple shadows beneath her eyes. "Just because I issue a statement that says it's over doesn't mean there won't be questions about my love life given the back-stabbing in my company this season. An abrupt breakup when everyone wants a story could make the press start digging into how we met. And until I know the truth about where Cameron got my contact information, I'm not comfortable letting the media look too closely at how we connected. I never wanted anything to do with a matchmaker, and I'm concerned that whoever my father hired posted my information in a misleading way. I don't understand why your brother thought I was Ukrainian. Or why he didn't know I was a dancer."

"We could work on a cover story—"

"I am exhausted and my body thinks it's midnight after the time I spent in Kiev. I have rehearsal tomorrow at ten and what I need is sleep, not a late-night study session to keep a cover story straight." She folded her arms and squared her shoulders, as if readying herself for an argument.

Did she realize how many complications would arise if they continued this fictional engagement? He'd really thought she would jump at the chance to say she'd turned down his proposal. But then again, he couldn't deny a surge of desire at the prospect of seeing her again.

"I'm willing to continue with the appearance of an engagement if that's simpler for you." He wanted to right the mess Cameron had made. And this time, it wasn't for Cameron's sake.

It was for Sofia's.

"It would be easier for me." She twisted some of her windblown blond hair behind her ear and he noticed a string of five tiny pearls outlining the curve. "Just for three more weeks. A month, at most, until the rumor mill in my company settles down. I need to get through that important audition."

She glanced his way for the first time in miles and caught him staring.

"Of course," he agreed, mentally recalibrating his schedule to accommodate a woman in his life. He would damn well hand off the trip to Kiev to Cameron or Ian since Quinn would need to remain in New York. "In that case, maybe we should draw up a contract outlining the terms of the arrangement."

With Vitaly Koslov threatening to block his business in Eastern Europe, Quinn needed to handle this as carefully as he would any complicated foreign acquisition.

"Is that wise?" Frowning, she withdrew a tin of mints from her leather satchel and fished a couple out, offering him one. "A paper trail makes it easier for someone to discover our secret."

He took a mint, his eye drawn to her mouth as her lips parted. He found himself thinking about that kiss again. The way she'd tasted like mint then, too. And how an engagement would lead to more opportunities to touch her. The idea of a fake fiancée didn't feel like an imposition when he looked at it that way. Far from it.

"Quinn?" Her head tipped sideways as she studied him, making him realize he'd never responded. "If you really think we need the protection of a legally binding contract—"

"Not necessarily." He should keep this light. Friendly. Functional. "But we'll want to be sure both of our interests are protected and that we know what we're getting into."

"A prenup for a false engagement." She shook her head. "Only in New York."

"Your father will want to ensure your reputation emerges unscathed," he reminded her.

The limo driver hit the brakes suddenly, making them both lurch forward. On instinct, Quinn's arm went out, restraining her. It was purely protective, until that moment when he became aware of his forearm pinned against her breasts, his hand anchored to her shoulder under the fall of silky hair.

A soft flush stole over her cheeks as he released her and they each settled back against their respective seat cushions. The awkward moment and the unwelcome heat seemed to mock his need to put the terms of this relationship in writing.

"That's fine," she agreed quickly, as if she couldn't end the conversation fast enough. "If you want to draw up something, I will sign it and you can be sure I will not cause a fuss when we end the engagement."

She wrapped her mohair cape more tightly around her slight figure, the action only reminding him of her graceful curves and the way she'd felt against him.

Damn. His body acted as though it'd been months since he'd been with a woman when…

Now that he thought about it, maybe it had been that long since he'd ended a relationship with Portia, the real-estate developer who'd tried to sell him a Park Avenue penthouse. In the end, Quinn hadn't been ready to leave the comfort of the Pierre, a hotel he'd called home for almost a decade. He hadn't been ready for Portia, either, who'd been more interested in being a New York power couple than she had been in him.

Somehow he'd avoided dating since then and that had been…last year. Hell. No wonder the slightest brush of bodies was making him twitchy. Gritting his teeth against the surge of hunger, he told himself to stay on track. Focused. To clean up his brother's mess and move on.

The sooner they got through the next month, the better.

Sofia breathed through the attraction the same way she'd exhale after a difficult turn. She ignored the swirl of distracting sensations, calling on a lifetime's worth of discipline.

She controlled her body, not the other way around. And she most definitely would not allow handsome Quinn McNeill to rattle her with his touch. Or with his well-timed kisses that were just for show, even if the one she'd experienced had felt real enough.

With an effort, she steered him back toward their conversation, needing his captivating eyes to be on something besides her.

"I'm curious about the plan you developed with my father. I'm certain it didn't involve us being engaged." She would rather know before her father contacted her. Her powerful parent would never stop interfering with her life, insisting he knew best on everything from which public relations firm should promote her career to hiring a matchmaker she didn't want.

They'd butted heads on everything since her mother had died of breast cancer during Sofia's teens, ending her independence and putting her under the roof of a cold, controlling man. Until then, she and her mother had lived a bohemian lifestyle all over the US and Europe, her mom painting while she danced. When her mother died, she'd been too young to strike out alone and her father had been determined to win her over with his wealth and the opportunities it could afford.

She'd wanted no part of it. Until he'd found that magic carrot—ballet school in St. Petersburg, Russia, an opportunity she truly couldn't ignore. But she'd been paying for the privilege in so many ways since then, her debt never truly repaid.

"He wanted me to write off Cam's behavior as a private joke between old friends." Quinn shifted conversational gears easily. "But I'm sure he'll be glad that your preferences were considered."

"Vitaly has never concerned himself with my preferences." She already dreaded the phone call from him she knew was coming. He would be angry with her, for certain. But she needed to remind him that *he* wasn't the injured party here. "But he is not the only one affected by his decision to hire a matchmaker without my permission. I need to call him and demand he have that contract terminated immediately. I don't want my photo and profile posted anywhere else."

"Would you like me to tell him?" Quinn asked. She must have appeared surprised because he quickly added, "I don't mean to overstep. But he and I have unfinished business and I plan to find out exactly where Cameron found your profile. I'm not sure who is at fault for the miscommunication between your matchmaker and his, but I plan to look into it as a matter of legal protection for McNeill Resorts since your father threatened to sue at one point."

Sofia sighed. "I'm ninety percent sure that was just blustering, but I honestly don't blame you. And since I'd rather not speak to my father when I'm so upset with him, I'd actually be grateful if you would handle it."

It was a sad commentary on her relationship with her father that, while she hardly knew Quinn, she was already certain he would deal with her dad more effectively.

"Consider it done. And for what it's worth, he seemed to care a great deal about you when I spoke with him." Quinn said the words carefully. Diplomatically. No wonder Cameron relied on him to take care of sticky situations. "But I'm most concerned about your expectations going forward." He narrowed his gaze as he turned back toward her. "For instance, how often we need to be seen together in public. If we're going to do this, we'll need to coordinate dates and times."

"Really?" She was too tired and overwhelmed by the events of the evening to maintain the pragmatic approach now that it was just the two of them. "Although it's been a while since I dated, I'm sure that we managed to schedule outings without a lot of preplanning. Why don't I just text you tomorrow?"

His short bark of laughter surprised her as the limo descended into the Lincoln Tunnel toward Manhattan. Shadows crossed his face in quick succession in spite of the tinted windows.

"Fair enough. But maybe we could find a time to speak tomorrow. I'd like to be sure we agree on a story about how we met since you'll be talking to the media."

A stress headache threatened just from thinking about how carefully she would have to walk through that minefield, but damn it, she'd worked too hard to land that feature in *Dance* magazine to allow her pretend love life to steal all the spotlight.

"I have a rehearsal tomorrow at ten and I'll be jet-lagged and foggy-headed before that." She could barely think straight now to hammer out the details. "What if I just avoid reporters until we speak later in the day?"

Tomorrow's challenges would be difficult enough. She couldn't believe she'd also offered for *Dance* magazine to film her private audition with Idris Fortier the following week. She would be stressed enough that day without having her mistakes captured on video.

"This news might travel fast." He frowned, clearly disliking the idea of waiting. "But I understand about jet lag making conversation counterproductive in the morning. Can I pick you up after rehearsal then?"

His voice slid past her defenses for a moment; the question was the kind of thing a lover might ask her. Was it certifiable to spend so much time with him this month? He was the antithesis of the kind of men she normally dated—artists and bohemians who moved in vastly different worlds from the Koslov family dynasty. Quinn, on the other hand, was the kind of polished, powerful captain of industry who liked to rule the world according to his whim. The tendency was apparent from the moment he'd strode into her personal drama today and quietly taken over.

His assistance had been valuable, without question. But would she regret letting herself get close to a man like that? Especially one with such unexpected appeal?

"After rehearsal will work." She steadied herself as the limo driver jammed on the gas, trying to make some

headway down Fifth Avenue despite the rush-hour traffic.
"I'll be done by four. Do you know where the theater is?"

"Of course." He shifted his long legs in front of him,
his open overcoat brushing her thigh when he moved.
"Is there a side door? Somewhere to make a more discreet exit?"

She crossed her legs, shifting away from him.

"Good idea. There's a coffee shop on Columbus Avenue." She checked the address on her phone and shared
it with him as the car finally turned down Ninth Street
in the East Village where she lived. Her phone continued to vibrate every few minutes, reminding her that the
whole world would have questions for her in the morning.

"Do you live alone?" he asked as the car rolled to a
stop outside her building.

The question shouldn't surprise her since the neighborhood wasn't the kind of place where hedge fund managers
made their home. Her father hated this place, routinely
trying to entice her into rooms at the Plaza or a swank
Park Avenue place.

"Yes." Her spine straightened as if she was standing
in front of the ballet barre. "I love it here."

He got out of the car to walk her to the door while the
driver retrieved her bag. In the time it took her to find
her keys in her purse, two older men stumbled out of a
local bar, boisterous and loud. She noticed that Quinn
kept an eye on them until they passed the entrance to
her building.

"Thanks for the ride." She opened the front door and
stood in the entryway, very ready to dive into bed.

Alone, obviously. Although the thought of diving
into bed with Quinn sent a warm wave of sexual interest through her.

"I'm walking you to your apartment door," he insisted,

eyes still scanning the street out front that was filled with more bars than residences.

Too weary to argue, she gave a clipped nod and led the way through the darkened corridor toward the elevator. She was vaguely aware that he had taken her bags from the limo driver and was carrying them for her. A few moments later, arriving at apartment 5C, Quinn stepped inside long enough to settle her luggage in the narrow foyer. Strange how much smaller her apartment seemed with him in it. She watched as his blue gaze ran over the row of pendant lamps illuminating the dark hardwood floor and white grass-cloth walls covered with dozens of snapshots of ballet performances and backstage photos.

Maybe it was a sudden moment of self-consciousness that made her grab her cell phone when it vibrated again for what seemed like the tenth time in as many minutes. Checking the screen, she realized the incoming texts weren't from curious colleagues or her father.

Half were from the publicity firm she'd hired. The other half were from the ballet mistress. A quick scan of the content told her they were all concerned about the same thing—social media speculation had suggested she wasn't serious about the Fortier ballet and was focusing on her personal life. She felt her muscles tighten and tense as if she were reading a review of a subpar performance, the stress twisting along her shoulders and squeezing her temples.

"Is everything all right?" Quinn's voice seemed distant compared to the imagined shout of the all-caps text messages.

"You were right. News of our engagement traveled quickly." Swallowing hard, she set the phone on an antique cabinet near the door. "My publicist urged me to wear an engagement band tomorrow to forestall questions until she writes the press release." Anger blazed through her in a fresh wave, shaking her out of her exhaustion. "It is a sad statement on my achievements that a lifetime of hard work is overshadowed by a rich man's proposal."

She wrenched off her scarf and fumbled with the buttons on her cape, anger making her movements stiff.

"It's because of your achievements that anyone is interested in your private life," Quinn reminded her quietly, reaching for the oversize buttons and freeing them.

She might have protested his sudden nearness, but in an instant he was already behind her, lifting the mohair garment from her shoulders to hang it on the wrought-iron coatrack.

"It still isn't fair," she fumed, although she could feel some of her anger leaking away as Quinn's words sank into her agitated mind. He had a point. A surprisingly thoughtful one. "No man would ever be badgered to wear a wedding ring to quiet his colleagues about his romantic status."

"No." He dug into his coat pocket and took out the small, dark box that had caused such havoc at Teterboro. "But since you've been put in a tremendously awkward position, maybe we should see what Cameron had in mind for his proposal."

He held out the box. The absurdity of the night struck her again as she stared at it. Who would have suspected when she boarded her plane in Kiev so many hours ago that she would be negotiating terms of an engagement with a total stranger in her apartment before bedtime?

"Why not? It's not like I'm going to be able to sleep now with all this to worry me." Shrugging, she backed deeper into her apartment, flipping on a metal floor lamp arching over the black leather sofa. "Come in, if you like. I haven't been home in three weeks so it feels nice to see my own things. I'm glad to be home even if it has been a crazy day."

She gestured toward the couch, taking a seat on the vintage steamer trunk that served as a coffee table.

"Only for a minute." He didn't remove his coat, but he did drop down onto the black leather seat. "I know you must be ready for bed." Their eyes connected for the briefest of moments before he glanced back at the ring box. "But let's take a look."

He levered open the black-velvet top to reveal a ring that took her breath away.

Quinn whistled softly. "You're sure you never met my brother before today?"

"Positive." Her hand reached for the ring without her permission, the emerald-cut diamond glowing like a crystal ball lit from within. A halo of small diamonds surrounded the central one, and the double band glittered with still more of them. "It can't possibly be real with so many diamonds. Although it looks like platinum."

"It is platinum." He sounded certain. "My brother goes all-in when he makes a statement." Gently he pried the ring from the box. "And given how much trouble his statement caused you today, I think it's only fair you wear it tomorrow."

Dropping the box onto the couch cushion, he held the ring in one hand and took her palm in the other. The shock of his warm fingers on her skin caught her off guard.

"I can't wear that." She sat across from him, their knees bumping while his thumb rested in the center of her palm.

Awareness sparked deep inside her, a light, leaping feeling like a perfectly executed cabriolé jump. Her heart beat faster.

A slow smile stretched across Quinn's face, transforming his features from ruggedly handsome to swoonworthy.

"We agreed on an engagement. Don't you think it makes more sense to use the ring we have than to go shopping for a new one?"

The insinuation that she was being impractical helped her to see past that dazzling smile.

"I never would have guessed your brother would spend a small fortune on a ring for a woman he never met." She edged out of his grip. "I thought he was a romantic, not completely certifiable."

Quinn's smile faded. "I assure you, Cameron is neither." He set the ring on the steamer trunk beside her. "I'll let you decide whether or not to wear it in the morning. And in the meantime, I'd better let you get some rest."

He rose to his feet, leaving a priceless piece of jewelry balanced on last month's *Vogue*.

"Quinn." She stood to follow him to the door then reached back to grab the ring so she could return it. "Please. I don't feel right keeping this here."

He turned to face her as he reached the door, but made no move to take the glittering ring.

"If you were my bride-to-be, I would spare no expense to show the world you were mine." His blue eyes glowed with a warmth that had her remembering his kiss. Her breath caught in her chest and she wondered what it might be like for him to call her that for real.

Mine.

"I'm—" *At a total loss for words.* "That is—" She folded the diamond into her hand, squeezing it tightly so the stones pressed into her soft skin, distracting her from her hypnotic awareness of this man. "If you insist."

"It's a matter of believability, Sofia."

"It's only for one month." She wasn't sure if she said it to remind him or herself.

"We'll work out the details tomorrow." He reached to smooth a strand of hair from her forehead, barely touching her and still sending shimmers of pleasure along her temple and all the way down the back of her neck. "Sleep well."

She didn't even manage to get her voice working before he was out the door again, leaving her alone in a suddenly too empty apartment.

Squeezing the ring tighter in her fist, she waited for the pinch of pain from the sharp edges of the stones. She needed to remember that this wasn't real. Quinn McNeill had only agreed to this mad scheme to clean up his brother's mess. Any hint of attraction she felt needed to be squashed immediately, especially since Quinn was cut from the same mold as her father—focused on business and the accumulation of wealth. Her world was about art, emotions and human connections.

Her mother had taught her that people did not fall into both camps. In Sofia's experience it was true. And since she wanted her own relationships to be meaningful bonds rooted in shared creativity and ideals, she was willing to wait until she had more time in her life to find the right partner. Romance could not be rushed.

"It's only for a month," she said aloud again, forcing herself to set the engagement ring on the hallway table.

Surely she could keep up her end of a fake engagement for the sake of appearances? She'd made countless sacrifices for her career, from dancing on broken toes to living away from her family on the other side of the globe to train with Russian ballet masters.

Ignoring the sensual draw of Quinn McNeill couldn't possibly be more difficult than those challenges.

Yet, even as she marched herself off to bed, she feared she was lying to herself that she could keep her hands off the man anywhere near as easily as she'd set down the ring.

Four

Quinn pulled an all-nighter, working straight through until noon the next day. He rearranged his schedule to accommodate more time in the city over the upcoming month. He'd avoided the office and shut off his phone for all but critical notifications, not ready to address the questions about his relationship with Sofia until they'd worked out a game plan.

Sofia.

Shoving away from the overly bright screen on his laptop, Quinn leaned back into the deep leather cushioning of his office chair. His grandfather's old chair, even after decades of use, seemed to retain class and grace, a steady touchstone in a career that constantly demanded invention and innovation to stay competitive. Eyes wandering to the corner of his walnut desk, he absently skimmed over the open newspaper. Even with news apps on his phone, Quinn still read the paper every morning, feeling a sense of connection to the ink and paper. And he couldn't ignore what was printed in today's society section—a photograph of the lithe ballerina.

She hadn't been far from his thoughts all morning and now was no different as he shut down his computer and headed out of the office building to his chauffeur-driven Escalade. And damn if Sofia didn't continue to dance through his mind as he rode toward the site of McNeill Resorts' latest renovation project in Brooklyn. Quinn powered down his laptop and stored it in the compartment beside the oversize captain's chair. He tried to prep himself for the inevitable confrontation with Cameron, who was slated to be on site in their grandfather's absence.

Even though his brother had walked away from his would-be ballerina bride yesterday, Quinn guessed that Cameron would still have something to say about the turn of events after he'd left. And though Quinn hoped he'd quelled some of Sofia's father's anger, he knew the engagement would make waves with his brother. If anything, Quinn hoped that this would make Cameron come to his senses about tying the knot with a woman he'd never met.

Running his hand through thick hair, Quinn let out a low sigh. He needed Cameron to be rational today.

He pressed the switch for the intercom as the Escalade rolled to a stop.

"I shouldn't be long, Jeff," Quinn told his driver before he stepped out of the vehicle in front of the converted bank on Montague Street in Brooklyn Heights. Coffee in hand, he headed onto the site, his well-worn leather shoes crunching against the gravel and construction dust.

Glancing at the scaffolding on the building, he nodded at the progress as the smell of fresh-cut wood and the sounds of hammering filled the air.

"Morning, Giacomo." Quinn nodded to the site foreman before picking up a hard hat to enter the building.

Giacomo—a sought-after project manager who specialized in historic conversions—gave a silent wave, his ear pressed to his cell phone while he juggled a coffee and a tablet full of project notes. The guy pointed to the roof of the building, answering Quinn's unasked question about his brother's whereabouts. Out of respect, the only time the McNeills showed up at each other's job sites was to talk family business.

Or, in this case, family brides.

Mood darkening as he anticipated an argument, Quinn climbed the temporary stairs installed during the renovation stage to connect the floors that had been stripped down to the studs. A swirl of cement dust kicked up from some kind of demo work on the second floor, and he quickened his steps. He passed some workers perched on scaffolding outside the fourth floor, debating the merits of salvaging some of the crumbling granite façade. Quinn had practically grown up on job sites like this, frequently travelling around the country with his grandfather to learn the business.

At least, that had been the family's party line. The larger reason was that, during the six months of the year his father had custody of his sons, Liam McNeill was usually too busy thrill-seeking around the globe to bother with parental duties.

Cliff-jumping in Santorini, Greece, or white-water rafting down a perilous South Korean river always seemed like more fun to Quinn's father than child-rearing. So Malcolm McNeill had stepped in more times than not, teaching his grandsons about property development and the resort industry from the ground up.

Reaching the rooftop, Quinn spied his brother looking out at the skyline from the structure's best feature— a sunny oasis on the roof that would one day be a space for outdoor dining, drinks and special events. Even at noon the view was breathtaking. But at dusk, when the sun slipped behind the Manhattan skyline, there was no finer perspective on the city than right here.

Cameron sat in a beat-up plastic patio chair that looked like a Dumpster salvage, the legs speckled with various-colored paints. He had dragged the seat close to the edge of the roof, his laptop balanced on his knees and his hard hat sitting on a section of exposed trusses at his feet. His dark jeans sported sawdust, his leg bouncing to some unheard rhythm.

Quinn must have made a noise or cast a shadow because Cameron looked toward him.

"I'm not sure I want to see you right now." Cameron didn't smile, his attention returning to his computer screen. "The headlines I've seen so far don't exactly fill me with confidence about what went on last night after I left."

"The key point there being—you left." Quinn had never connected as well with Cam as he did with Ian, and that made it tougher to see Cameron's side now when his younger brother seemed so clearly in the wrong.

"So you felt compelled to stick around and play white knight?" Cameron flipped the screen of his laptop to face Quinn, showing a headline that read Two McNeill Magnates Propose to Former Sugarplum Fairy.

The accompanying photo showed Sofia pirouetting across a stage in a tutu. Damn. So he hadn't really imagined how hot she was. The levelheaded, practical side of

Quinn reeled at the absurd headline and the media circus that would continue to send in the clowns until the official "engagement" story aired.

But his rational side didn't seem to be in full control. Sofia's petite body, her lean and limber pose, made him recall their kiss and the heat of that impromptu moment.

Cameron set his jaw, daggers dancing from his eyes. Accusatory and angry, sure. It was all Quinn needed to be drawn back to the problem at hand.

Quinn crossed his arms, undaunted. Cam had to realize what was at stake.

"You piss off her father, one of the wealthiest men in the world, who also happens to have enough Eastern European connections to run our deal for the new resorts into the ground, and call it none of my business?" Quinn shook his head and dragged a crate over to where Cameron was sitting. He planted a foot on it.

Cameron's mouth thinned, his voice a near growl. "You crossed a line into my personal affairs and you know it. You don't just propose to your brother's girl five minutes after they're through." Cameron tipped back in the plastic chair like it was a rocker. It teetered on two legs.

The move put Quinn's teeth on edge but not nearly as much as his words. Cam would think no more of walking across exposed truss beams at two stories than he would at twelve.

"Sofia was never yours," Quinn reminded him, more irritated than he ought to be at the idea, as a protective fire suddenly blazed in the pit of his chest. "And you lost any chance you had of salvaging something with her when you walked out of the airport yesterday."

For once, however, Quinn couldn't be disappointed

with in Cam's impulsive ways The thought of her sharing that kiss with anyone but Quinn was intolerable.

"Think what you want of my motives, but I saw how you were looking at her." Cameron drummed his fingers along the back of the laptop case.

That stopped him. He couldn't deny that he'd felt something as soon as he'd seen her in person.

Cam shook his head. "And I still wouldn't have walked out, except I saw her looking at you that same exact way. It's one thing for me to turn my back on a bar fight or a heated investors meeting, but, contrary to popular belief, I wouldn't leave the woman to fend off nosy journalists if I hadn't seen the looks darting back and forth between you two."

"In that case…thank you." Stunned by a depth of insight he'd never given his brother credit for, Quinn wasn't sure how to handle the new information. Had Sofia been as drawn to him as he was to her? "After speaking to her father, I'm beginning to think her privacy was compromised by the matchmaker he hired. Bad enough Vitaly Koslov contracted the consultant without her knowledge. But I don't think he would have ever sanctioned his daughter's photo and contact information on the kind of pick-a-bride profile site you described to me."

"I thought the same thing after I left the airport yesterday." Cameron turned his laptop screen so Quinn could see the web banner for a Manhattan matchmaker, Mallory West. "I called my own matchmaker and she reminded me that I knowingly chose a match off a third-party web site Mallory West's clients can access, so I was informed ahead of time that Ms. West didn't know those women personally. She simply facilitated the meet. She gave me a full refund and assured me she would speak to the person who vetted the women on the web site I viewed."

Quinn sank down onto the crate and looked out across the bay on the sprawl of Lower Manhattan anchored by the Freedom Tower. Now that he'd seen firsthand how much havoc Cameron's bride hunt had caused for Sofia, he was thoroughly invested in the whole debacle.

"How can a matchmaker match people she doesn't actually know?" That sounded unethical. "I didn't think that's how they worked."

Cameron nodded as he signed into a private web page.

"They don't. But I was in a hurry and didn't want to jump through a lot of hoops since I wasn't really looking for true love everlasting." Cameron shrugged. "And Mallory's right—she was just a facilitator. I was paying special attention to the women listed on that third-party web site."

"Defeating the whole purpose of a matchmaker." Quinn ground his teeth together. "You might as well have gone shopping for a bride online. Why the hell would you pay the rates for a private matchmaker only to meet a woman whose name you pulled out of a damn hat?"

Cam seemed to take the question seriously. "I wanted to speed up the process and I hoped that the matchmaker's résumé lent credibility to the women I met."

Quinn wished he'd paid better attention when Cameron had first told him about his visit to the matchmaker's office, but at the time, he'd been focused on talking Cam out of jumping into a marriage.

"So she's taking no responsibility and she gave you your money back, which makes me wonder if she's worried about that web site, too. Can you still access that page?"

"No. Now that I've given up my membership with

Mallory West, I can't, but Ms. West said Sofia's profile is no longer included on the page."

"And once you told her you were interested in meeting Sofia, she texted you the flight details?"

"Correct." Cameron closed the laptop.

"I'll pass that information along to Sofia's father. I'm hoping to defuse some of his anger. After all, he was the one who released her photo in the first place. It's not your fault he hired an incompetent matchmaker." Quinn raised his voice as a jackhammer went to work somewhere in the building. The roof vibrated with the noise.

"I find it ironic that I ran out to marry a woman because of Gramps' will, and Sofia was my match based on her father's equally manipulative tactics to see her wed." Cameron picked up his hard hat and juggled it from one hand to another, his eyes never leaving some distant point to the northwest.

"Right. But I don't understand why Vitaly was surprised to see you in the airport if he shared the flight information with Sofia's matchmaker, who shared it with yours." Quinn's teeth rattled as the vibrations under his feet picked up strength. "I don't think his surprise was an act. Which means something doesn't add up."

He'd already hired a guy in his company's IT department to research any information about Sofia Koslov that had been posted online in the last month. Even if the third-party web site had deleted her profile, this guy could usually find reliable traces. For Quinn, it would help to show Vitaly where Cameron had found Sofia's profile. How could Sofia's father block the sale of the hotels the McNeills wanted if they were blameless in this matchmaking snafu?

But hiring an investigator served a second purpose, too—protecting Sofia's privacy.

Rising to his feet in one fluid motion, Cameron picked up his hard hat and shoved it onto his head.

"It makes sense to figure out what happened with Sofia's personal information before you move forward with your engagement." Cam checked his phone and put it in his pocket. "Or your wedding."

"Whoa." Quinn clapped a hand on his brother's back. Hard. "We're not getting married, as you damn well know."

The thought of spending a night with her revved him up fast, though. He didn't need that image in his head when he was on his way to meet her and talk through a plan for their fake engagement.

Then again, it wasn't as if he'd promised to keep his hands off her or anything. And she wanted the engagement to be believable. Already he was giving himself permission to get closer to her.

Much, much closer.

"You keep on telling yourself there's nothing going on." Cam shook off his hand and stalked toward the stairwell. "But no matter how much you play it off like Gramps' will doesn't matter to you, I know it's got to be in the back of your mind that you need to get married." Cameron rested a hand on the brick half wall that housed the stairs and faced Quinn. "Soon."

A dark expression clouded Cameron's features as he turned away, his steps echoing in the sudden silence as the jackhammer stopped. Quinn watched his brother walk away before he could argue. He was not getting married for the sake of McNeill Resorts, damn it. He was just running some damage control for the family business after his brother had made such a damn mess of things.

But maybe Cameron had a point. Quinn was attracted

to her. He had to pretend to be her fiancé. There was no reason in the world he couldn't use this time to get closer to Sofia.

To enjoy Sofia.

To find out if that kiss had been a fluke or if the heat between them was every bit as scorching as he imagined.

Five

Sofia braided her wet hair in the large, shared dressing room after her shower, unwilling to attend her meeting with Quinn while drenched in sweat from her second class of the day. The writer Anton Chekov had once famously said that he knew nothing about the ballet but that the ballerinas "stink like horses" during the intervals, and the man had a point.

Digging in her bag for a hair tie, she scuttled past some of the junior dancers before she dropped into a chair near one of the makeup mirrors. The afternoon classes tended to have more of the sixteen-to eighteen-year-olds who could give her a run for her money physically, which had been just what she'd needed. After a day in the air yesterday, her body had felt off during her first class of the morning. So after her show rehearsals, she'd joined an afternoon session as well to will her body back into show shape. A day missed, and a dancer noticed. Besides, cramming every second of her day with hard work meant there were less opportunities for her older colleagues to quiz her about yesterday.

Or the huge rock on her finger.

She hadn't left the breathtaking ring on for long, but she'd worn it from the cab to the dressing room before removing it for dancing, causing a room full of whispers and raised eyebrows before the dancing master put everyone to work. She retrieved Quinn's gift now that she was in street clothes and slid the beautiful piece onto her finger. The few junior ballerinas remaining at the end of the day were in a heated discussion about the romantic availability of one of the male dancers.

"Holy crap, honey, look at that thing." Jasmine Jackson's voice surprised her, even though she should have been expecting her friend and publicist to meet her backstage for a quick meeting.

Jasmine rushed toward her, the heavy exit door banging shut behind her as she wove around stored stage lights and rolling racks of costumes covered in plastic. Petite with glossy hair so black it looked blue in certain light, Jasmine had attended ballet school with her in North Carolina for a year before Sofia's mother had caught the travel bug to tour Europe. Jasmine had quit dancing at thirteen with the arrival of hormones and serious curves. Many women would envy her figure, but Sofia had taken the phone calls from her distraught friend when her breasts had moved well into C-cup range—one of many physical changes that made dancing more difficult and casting directors overlook her. She'd been devastated.

Jasmine had ended up attending Syracuse University for communications and went on to work in advertising and promotions for the fitness industry. Her job paid well and brought her to New York, much to Sofia's delight. They'd shared an apartment for two years before Jasmine's budget had seriously outstripped hers and her friend had upgraded to a bigger place.

Sofia squeezed her hand in a fist to keep the ring in place. "I know. I'm terrified of losing it. And it seems really weird that it fits me, doesn't it?" Had her father shared such personal details with the matchmaker he'd hired? She had considered speaking to him today to assess how much her privacy had been breached. But she was still so angry with him over his presumptuous matchmaking tactics.

Jasmine bent to lift and examine Sofia's hand. A strand of silky black hair trailed over Sofia's wrist as her friend peered at the ring in the lights of the makeup mirror. As always, Jasmine looked so put together—her knee-length, gray-and-taupe sweater dress was formfitting underneath a tailored swing coat she left open. Bracelets clinked as she moved, everything about her girly and feminine. By contrast Sofia sported leggings and a man's dress shirt left untucked, with a black blazer—kind of her go-to work outfit in the colder months. With her wet hair braided, she felt more than a little dull next to glamorous Jasmine.

"Wow. Those diamonds are the real deal." Her Southern accent had softened over the years, but the lilt was still there. "Come on. Let's walk and talk so I can bring you up to speed before we meet with your very sexy fiancé."

Leave it to Jasmine to maintain the façade of this fake engagement in public. She was great at her job and a great friend, too. Jasmine had tried refusing payment for the work she did to promote Sofia's career, but she wouldn't hear of it. As it was, she knew the rate Jasmine gave her was far less than what her friend billed her corporate accounts.

"You're going into the coffee shop with me?" Sofia led the way out of the building, taking the less conspicuous path over West Sixty-Fifth Street instead of cutting through Lincoln Center. "I've been second-guessing myself and nervous about seeing him all day." She squeezed Jasmine's arm like a lifeline, grateful for a true friend after the past weeks of being on her guard at all times.

"Well, I hadn't planned on it." Jasmine frowned, oblivious to the male heads she turned as they navigated streets getting busier as rush hour neared. "The two of you have a lot to figure out."

"I know. But you're a major part of that." If Jasmine was there, it was like a business meeting—a way to coordinate schedules.

"Since when do you need a babysitter for a date? I'll say hello, but then I've got to go. I have an appointment downtown for happy hour drinks." Her work in PR happened over dinner and cocktails as often as it happened in a boardroom. "So fill me in on what happened today."

"Not much, thankfully." She'd been pleased with her plan to avoid talking about the engagement by outworking everyone in the room. "The only one who really cornered me about it was the ballet mistress, and she just warned me to remember that Idris Fortier would surely prefer any woman he worked with to devote one thousand percent to his ballet."

"Did you tell her that one thousand percent was a bit much?"

"Would I still have a job right now if I did?" The lighthearted moment ended quickly as Joe Coffee came into view and Sofia thought about seeing Quinn again.

Had she overestimated his appeal last night in her trancelike jet lag? She hoped so.

"How are your knees?" Jasmine asked. It was the only question that could rattle her more than Quinn.

Prone to knee problems, Sofia had injuries the same way all dancers had injuries. That is, always. Ballet was hard on the body and a dancer never knew when her time might be up. She feared for the length of her career, especially when she remembered the devil's bargain she'd made with her father as a teen. Two months after her mother died, he'd refused to let Sofia pursue a dance opportunity in St. Petersburg, insisting she finish her education in the US. But after weeks of begging and crying—it was what her mother had wanted for her—he'd offered her a trade. She could go to Russia for dance school, but only if she promised that when her dance career was finished, she would come to work for him.

Which was not happening. He couldn't hold her to a deal she'd made as a teen. But she worried for her future with no backup plan after dance. Saying no to him when she had no prospects would be difficult. Staying in this expensive city would be virtually impossible. She willed away the ache in her knee and vowed to ice it longer tonight. It'd have to do.

"I had some twinges in my right knee in Kiev, but nothing that kept me off the stage." She tucked her shoulder bag closer as a family with two strollers pulled up beside them on the crosswalk. Horns and squeaky brakes mingled with the occasional sound of a doorman whistling for a cab in a cacophony her ears welcomed after six hours of Tchaikovsky and Stravinsky.

"Don't overdo it," Jasmine warned. "Staying healthy is more important than Idris and his ballet, no matter what you think."

"On the contrary, Idris and his ballet are my ticket to a post-dance career." She knew that a starring role and working closely with the superstar choreographer would completely change her profile in the dance world. It would open doors for a creative project she had in mind, but she needed someone like him to be on board. So she just had to nurse her knee through this opportunity.

Jasmine laughed. "You're the same as ever, Sofia. I think I could replay the conversations we had at nine and they'd be exactly the same ones we have today. You've always had a plan, I'll give you that."

Sofia slowed her step outside the door of Joe Coffee, grabbing Jasmine's arm.

"Not with Quinn McNeill, I don't." She wasn't intimidated by him or his money. Yet there was something about the way he made her feel that kept her anxious. Was it just physical attraction? Or did that anxiety mean something more worrisome?

Was it her gut telling her he was untrustworthy?

A messenger on a bicycle slammed his bike into the rack near them before entering the coffeehouse. The scent of fragrant Arabica beans and baked goods drifted through the door in his wake. Hunger reverberated in Sofia's stomach. Her diet was controlled and disciplined. Most days, she didn't mind. The sacrifice of cheesy fries and pizza had yet to outweigh the worth of her dream. But the smell of food tempted her so.

"He's just a man. The same as any other." Jasmine pursed her lips. "Your everyday average billionaire." She linked her arm through Sofia's and tugged her ahead. "Come on. I've got a few details to go over before I head out."

Squaring her shoulders, Sofia headed inside, determined not to let Quinn see that he made her uneasy. Distracted.

And far too interested in the attraction she'd felt for him the first moment their gazes had connected.

*   *   *

Head high, Sofia Koslov strolled into the coffee shop like a dancer and Quinn took notice from his seat at a table in the back corner. She carried herself differently than other women, a fact he'd picked up on yesterday before Cameron had proposed to her.

At that time he hadn't known what it was about her perfect posture and her graceful movements. Now he recognized it as her dance training that made her move like that. He couldn't picture her ever playing the Sugar Plum Fairy, however, despite the news clippings.

The Black Swan in *Swan Lake* maybe. She had a regal elegance, a sophistication. Her hair was pulled back into a damp braid that highlighted the long neck traditional in ballerinas. Her clothing was simple and understated so that the only thing that shone was the woman herself. And the ring on her left hand, he amended with satisfaction. Even staring at her across a crowded coffee shop, Quinn wanted her.

Damn.

He rose to greet the two women as they made their way through milling patrons juggling cups and cell phones. Her friend continued to shadow her step for step, a fact that disappointed him since he'd been eager to speak to Sofia privately. Or as privately as he could in a Manhattan java shop. He would have lobbied to meet at his apartment or in a quiet restaurant, but Sofia had been tired and rattled last night when they'd made these plans and he had the impression she'd purposely chosen someplace more public.

"Sofia." He greeted her the way he would greet a woman he loved, sliding an arm around her waist and kissing her cheek, mindful of the public atmosphere but still appropriately warm. He thought it better to be cautious since he didn't know her friend and wanted to be sure he played the part of Sofia's husband-to-be at all times.

Besides, it felt good to touch her.

The cool skin of her cheek warmed as his lips lingered for a moment. When he backed away, he spied the hint of color in her face before he extended a hand to her friend.

"Quinn McNeill," he introduced himself.

"Jasmine Jackson. I'm the best friend as well as the publicist. And total keeper of all her secrets." Her grip was firm and professional, and her eyes made it clear she knew full well about their ruse. "Shall we have a seat so I can go over my suggestions for the two of you?"

"Of course. Right this way." He gestured toward the table he'd secured in the back. Jasmine went first, and he palmed the small of Sofia's back to guide her along. Having his hands on her again made him realize how much he'd looked forward to acting out the part of fiancé.

He claimed the seat beside Sofia while Jasmine took the spot across from them and set down the leather binder on the maple surface between them.

"I've made copies of my ideal social calendar for both of you." She slid matching papers their way. "I've already sent Sofia the digital file so she can forward it to you, Quinn."

Taking in the extensive notes on dates and events, he was impressed. She had details about the status of their invitations, directions, suggested attire, a who's who list of people they should try to speak to at each event and potential spots for photo ops. Clearly, the woman had done her homework and she'd done it in a hurry.

"I see you know the New York social calendar," he remarked, wondering if his company's PR firm would do half as good of a job. "This is ambitious."

As Sofia's finger followed the lines of type, the diamond engagement ring caught the last of the pale winter sunlight. As impressive as the piece was, and he was glad she'd worn it, he felt a ridiculous urge to replace it with something of his own choosing.

He hoped that normal brotherly competitiveness accounted for that instinct and not some latent sentimental notions. No way would he let his grandfather's dictate to marry get to him. He had decided to use this time with Sofia as a way to enjoy their obvious attraction. Not romanticize it.

"As I said." Jasmine closed her binder and folded her manicured fingers on top of the leather. "This is simply a wish list that would serve several purposes at once for Sofia."

"You got in touch with *Dance* magazine to reschedule our interview?" Sofia asked, her finger now stalled on a line item toward the bottom of the page.

"Yes. I told them today was full for you but that you could meet with them Friday night during the welcome reception for Idris Fortier." Jasmine reached across the table to point out the event listed at the top of the paper. "In the meantime, I promised to release your statement about yesterday's events to them first." Jasmine pulled another set of papers from the binder and passed them across the table. "Here's a tentative release. If you could make your changes and send the digital file back to me before seven tonight, I can get it to the reporters for a blog post spot they're holding for you."

Quinn scanned the release, approving of the minimal personal details it included.

"'When we met'?" Sofia read a highlighted yellow section aloud. "'When we fell in love'? Is that really necessary?" Her gray eyes darted his way then back to her friend.

"Those are two questions everyone will ask. Better to save yourself answering it twenty times over and put out the information up front that you want people to see." Jasmine gave Sofia's forearm an affectionate squeeze. "But I will let you two discuss that since I need to run to another appointment."

Secretly pleased to have Sofia all to himself, Quinn rose as Jasmine took her leave. Sofia neatly folded the papers and tucked them into the black leather satchel she carried.

"Maybe we could talk through the rest of this while we walk? The park is close by. I know I suggested this place, but I wasn't thinking about how noisy it would be."

"Good idea." He left the waitress a tip even though they hadn't ordered, then escorted Sofia out onto the street. With a hand on her hip, he could feel the tension vibrating through her. Stress? Nervousness? He had a tough time reading her. "I live on the other side of the park. We could at least head in that direction."

The traffic would be gridlocked soon anyhow and he knew the paths well enough on the southern end of Central Park.

"Sounds good." She seemed slightly more relaxed outdoors. "And I'm sorry if this situation is cutting into your time. I probably wasn't in the best frame of mind to make decisions yesterday."

"Attending these events will only benefit my business." He turned down West Sixty-Ninth Street toward the park, plucking her bag off her shoulder to carry it for her. Fake fiancé or not, she would be his top priority for the upcoming weeks. She didn't seem like the type of woman who allowed other people to take care of her.

But from where Quinn stood, she was in need of some spoiling—something this media ruse might let him do for her. "I haven't done much networking in the last year and it always lifts the company profile."

He wanted her at ease. Enjoying herself. Hell, he wanted to get to know her better and this would be the perfect time. So the less she worried about inconveniencing him, the better.

"That's a generous way to look at the situation. Thank you."

"I wouldn't call it generous." He tipped his head up to the skies as a few snowflakes began to fall. "Are you going to be warm enough for this?"

Her blazer was heavy but now that the sun was almost down, the temperature was hovering just below freezing.

"My cape is in my bag," she said, pointing to the satchel on his shoulder. He lifted his arm so she could rifle through it and pull out the same mohair garment she'd worn the day before.

"Let me." Drawing her to the quieter side of the street near the buildings, he took the cape and draped it over her shoulders, then turned her so he could fasten the two big buttons close to her neck. His eyes met hers and, for half a heartbeat, that same awareness from their kiss danced in the air between them.

"I can get them," she protested, trying to sidle away politely.

He held fast, hands lingering on the placket as the snowfall picked up speed, coating her shoulders.

"But the more comfortable we get with each other now, the easier it's going to be to fool everyone on Friday." He looked forward to it.

Very much.

Part of it had something to do with the way her heartbeat quickened at his touch. He could feel the quick thrum beneath his knuckles right through her layers of clothing. He wanted to kiss her again, to taste her rosy lips where a snowflake quickly melted. But instead, he reached for the wide hood of her cape and drew it over her head to keep the snow off.

"Then I will try to think of this day as a dress rehearsal." She sounded so damn serious.

That, combined with some of the things she'd shared with him the night before, reinforced his notion of her as highly driven. He admired her work ethic and her dedication to her career. He'd always been the type to pour himself into a work project, too. Duty and perseverance were the cornerstones of his approach to the world.

"In that case, we can't go wrong." Readjusting her bag on his shoulder, he pressed a light hand to the small of her back to guide her through a left on Central Park West and the quick right to get on the path that would take them toward his apartment. "From what I gleaned about you last night as I read up on your career, it sounds like you've succeeded at everything you've set out to accomplish."

Even with the hood pulled up, he could see the way she smiled.

"Either that or I have an excellent publicist."

That surprised a laugh out of him as they strode deeper into the park, which seemed a bit busier than usual, the fresh snow bringing out kids and kids-at-heart. They passed people walking dogs and packs of middle-school-aged children in uniforms, still wearing backpacks.

"Jasmine does seem determined to package your career—and you—in the best possible way."

"She's a good friend and an equally awesome public relations manager."

"And this reception she wants us to attend. That's

for the choreographer you mentioned who's putting together the new ballet." He'd read about the guy a good bit last night. "The media can't use enough superlatives about him gracing New York with his presence." It had been a bit much in Quinn's mind, but then, he was far from an expert.

"You have been doing your research." She rewarded him with an approving smile that renewed the urge to kiss her.

But he also liked finding out more about her that would help him get closer to her. He would wait.

"This is a dress rehearsal for me, too, Sofia." He watched a few kids try to shake a radio-controlled helicopter down from some tree limbs; they were attracting an audience. "I'm trying to get my part down."

"You're doing well. If you were one of my students, you'd be promoted to the next level."

"You teach?" He paused on the outskirts of the crowd.

"A lot of the dancers do." Sofia's gaze went up to the helicopter and the kids shaking any branches of the old oak they could reach. "It's a way to pick up some extra income and give back to the company. The School of American Ballet is like our farm system…it feeds the City Ballet."

"Give me one second." He hated to interrupt her, but he also couldn't let the kids kill a tree that—for all he knew—could predate the damn park itself. He set down Sofia's bag and grabbed a football at one of the boys' feet as he strode into the group. "Guys, back up a minute."

The group did as he asked, a few calling out taunts that he'd never be able to reach the branch where the helicopter teetered. Which he welcomed, of course, since the ribbing only ensured that he'd throw twice as hard.

He'd grown up with brothers, after all. He spoke the language.

"I get three shots," he insisted. "Only because I haven't warmed up my arm."

"I'll give you six, old man," shouted a wiry redhead who seemed to be the ringleader. "That thing is straight-up stuck."

Old?

Quinn told himself that he was only interested in saving the tree, but with a beautiful woman he wanted to impress watching from the sidelines, there was a chance he was fueled by another motivation altogether. Far from old…he was acting like a damn kid.

Backing up a step to adjust his aim, he cocked his arm and let the football fly.

Like in an ESPN highlight reel, the thing connected with the toy helicopter on the first try, earning cheers of admiration. And, because it had been so high up, the kids had time to run underneath the tree where the mouthy redhead caught it, scoring some of the victory for himself.

"Sorry about that." Quinn jogged back to Sofia, who stood on the path under a halo of light from a cast-iron street lamp. He grabbed her bag and hitched it higher on his shoulder.

With her hooded cape and the snow falling all around her, she looked like some exotic character from one of her ballets. A Russian princess, maybe.

"You appeared to have performed that trick a few times before," she observed.

"With two brothers? Of course. We got plenty of things caught in trees as kids. Kites were the worst to get down. By comparison, the helicopter was a piece of cake." His warm breath lingered in the cool air, making it seem as though his words hung in the space between them. A gust of wind sent a slight chill through him. Glancing at Sofia, he noticed her hair was still wet.

"I can't imagine what it would be like to have siblings." The loneliness in her words was evident.

"Your bio doesn't say much about your family." He knew because he'd scoured it for details about her.

"In the past, I tried to keep my personal life and work life separate. Not that I have a lot of personal life to speak about." She stared up at Tavern on the Green as they passed. The restaurant looked sort of otherworldly in the snowfall with the trees and white lights all around. "But my mother died when I was thirteen and I am not close with my father."

"I'm sorry about your mother." He took her hand for the dash across West Drive before they reached quieter roads through the middle of the park. "That must have been a really difficult age to lose a parent."

He didn't let go of her hand since her fingers were chilled. And because he wanted to touch her. Besides, they would be in the public eye again soon enough, where they would have to sell themselves as a loving couple.

As if she understood his motivations, she leaned into him and the spicy smell of her currant perfume wafted up to him. Hooking her arm through his, she drew closer.

"I was devastated. All the more so because my mother hated my father, which meant I hated him, too. Then, suddenly, after her death I was left with him." Sofia pushed off her hood as they reached denser growth that limited how much snow fell on them. Maybe she'd just been looking for a reason to untwine their fingers. "To this day, I don't know what drew the two of them together since he represented everything she despised. She called the privileged wealthy a 'soulless culture.'"

"What about you?" Quinn wondered where that left him in her world view. "Do you agree with your mother?"

"Wait." She turned around to look at the path they'd just traveled, tugging on his arm so they stood off the walkway to one side. "Let's stop for a second and take it in."

She didn't have to explain what she meant. This part of the park was beautiful on any given day. But in a fresh snowfall, with the Tavern on the Green glowing from within and the tree trunks and branches draped in white lights, the view was like no other in the city. The snow dulled the sounds from the streets nearby, quieting rush hour to white noise.

Standing with Sofia at his side made it all the more appealing. The glow of the white lights reflected on her face.

"Beautiful." His assessment, while simple, was heartfelt.

"But you know what my mother taught me about beauty?" Sofia asked, a mischievous light in her liquid silver eyes. "It is not a matter of just looking beautiful. It should surround us." She held her hand out, palm up to catch snowflakes. "Feel special." Inhaling deeply, she smiled with her eyes closed. "Have a unique scent when you breathe it in. And if you can catch it on your tongue, the taste will be beautiful, too."

He watched, transfixed, as this aloof and disciplined dancer stuck her tongue out and tipped her head to the sky.

Another time, he might have laughed at her antics. But she seemed lost in a happy childhood memory, and he didn't want to spoil it. Reaching for her hand full of snowflakes, he warmed her palm with his and peered upward through the white branches at the hint of stars beyond.

"You're right." He felt the beauty around him, that much was certain. But it had more to do with the slide of her damp fingers between his. With the tattoo of the pulse at her wrist that he felt on his palm.

"Did you catch one?" She lowered her chin to meet his gaze, her eyes still alight with a glow of happiness.

But she must have seen another expression reflected in his face because her smile faded.

"No." He reached for her jaw to thumb a snowflake from her creamy cheek, her skin impossibly soft to the touch. Capturing her chin in his hand, he angled her lips for a taste. "But I'm about to."

Six

Transported by the snow, the city and the man, Sofia hadn't been expecting the kiss, and maybe it was her total lack of defenses that let her feel the pleasure of it. She delighted in the warm pressure of his mouth in contrast to such a cold day. The soft abrasion of his chin where the new of growth of whiskers rubbed over her tender skin oversensitive from the wind. The gentle way he touched her face to steer her where he wanted, to better delve between her lips.

Answering his demand by stepping closer, craving the warmth of the man, Sofia lost herself.

Quinn's kiss was the second act of *Swan Lake*. Or maybe *Giselle*. Or maybe it was every romantic moment she'd ever danced and never felt deeply until this moment. She squeezed his hand where he'd entwined their fingers, enjoying the way her body fit against him. They weren't like two dancers with bodies that complemented one another. But like a man possessing a woman, lending her his strength so she didn't have to draw from her own.

It was a moment of heaven.

When he slowly pulled away from her and she felt the snowflakes fall on her skin again now that he did not completely shelter her, the cool ping of the tiny drops urged her out of her romantic swoon. And no doubt about it, she stood in Central Park swooning on her feet for a man she'd met the day before.

"Quinn, we have a lot of work we should be doing." She blurted the words with no segue and zero grace. "If we want to get that press release out on time, that is."

Untangling her fingers from his, she brushed by him to continue walking…east? Her brain scrambled to regain thought. Yes, east. What on earth had gotten into her? Had that kiss been part of the role he seemed determined to play for her? Or had he truly felt inspired to kiss her?

"You're right." Quinn didn't need to walk fast to keep up with her as she practically jogged through the park. His longer strides ate up the ground easily. As he glanced at her, the light reflected devilishly in his eyes. "But I want you to know I liked kissing you, Sofia. Very much. There's no reason we shouldn't enjoy ourselves over the next few weeks."

Sharp, cold air entered her lungs. "Just because we are within easy reach doesn't mean we should automatically start touching." She didn't want to be a convenient outlet for him. "But what's our story for how we met or when we met?"

"I was introduced to your father at the Met Gala. Were you there with him?"

"Of course not. Do you have any idea what a ticket costs to that event?" At moments like this she could understand how her mother might have come to believe the wealthy were living in a different universe from regular people. The Met Gala was so far beyond her price range it was laughable.

"Actually, no." He stuffed his hands into the pockets of his overcoat, his profile in shadow as they walked. "I was on the guest list because I made a donation to the museum."

Right. Which meant he'd paid more than the ticket price that was almost half her annual salary. Like her father, Quinn belonged to a world of wealth and unreality. A world she had purposely avoided.

"Suffice it to say, we didn't meet there." She wished she'd worn warmer clothes for their walk. Her knees were feeling the effects of the cold.

"What if we say we met here? In the park? We bonded over rescuing a kid's toy stuck in a tree last spring." As a bicyclist churned through the growing snow cover, Quinn slid a protective arm around her, his hand an enticing warmth through her cape before his touch fell away again. "At least we don't have to make up something fictional. We base it on today, but say it happened when I was walking home one evening and you were taking a break in the park."

"That could work." She nodded, locking down the time frame in her mind and trying to envision today's scene in a different season. "Although I would never give a stranger I met in the park my contact information."

"Maybe I started taking that route home every day, hoping to see you. Two weeks later, bingo. There you were again. We fell in love over the next few months, and that should be all we need to fill out Jasmine's press release." He slowed as they passed Central Park Zoo and headed toward Fifth Avenue. "Are you all right?"

"Of course," she answered automatically. "Why?"

"You're limping."

"No I'm not." She couldn't be. Refused to be. She excelled at hiding injuries on stage. Perhaps she just didn't give much thought to her gait in her private time. "Just hurrying to get home."

She couldn't read his expression in the dark.

"I should have insisted on a car. We're almost there."

"I'm fine. And if you can point me to the closest subway station? I thought there was one on Fifth?"

"Come inside and warm up first. I'll drive you home."

"That's not necessary. As you pointed out, we have enough for the press release. I'll send it over to Jasmine when I get home."

"We haven't firmed up plans for the Fortier reception." As they emerged from the park, he crossed Fifth Avenue at East Sixty-First. "Besides, my building is right here. I can send out that release for you, and I'll call you a car afterward." He stopped outside the Pierre.

He lived in the hotel?

Of course he did. It was a gracious, old New York address with five-star service. The small part of her that was still her father's daughter could already envision the kind of food room service provided here.

"Sofia." Quinn lowered his voice as they stood under the awning in front of the building. "We're committed to this course now. Let's be sure we deliver a believable performance."

"Believable because we show up for all of those public appearances as a couple?" She lowered her voice even more in deference to the doorman who was pulling open a cab door for a newcomer. "Or believable because we're kissing in our spare time?"

Quinn seemed to weigh the idea carefully. "If you truly think that the kiss was a bad idea, we'll make sure all future displays of affection are strictly for show and limit them to the public sphere."

She wasn't sure if she was disappointed or relieved. Maybe a little of both.

"That might help." At least then she'd be prepared before he kissed her again. She'd have her guard up. Her body would receive a warning before he stoked it to life with a mere flick of his tongue. "Thank you."

"Will you come inside, then? We can have dinner sent up while we fill in the blanks for Jasmine and send out the statement." Quinn had been both patient and reasonable.

Of course, he was only doing any of this for the sake of his business concerns, protecting the McNeill interests from the threats her father had made at the airport last night. She needed to remember that, even if his kisses told a different story. Quinn was simply more experienced. Worldly. Maybe even jaded. Some people could kiss solely for passion's sake, not love, but she'd never been that kind of woman.

Or so she thought. Maybe she'd just never met a man she could truly feel passionate about? Unlike her friends, she'd never been a boy-crazy teenager. Her attention and love had always belonged to the stage.

"Okay," she agreed, the chill in her bones making the decision for her, damn it. Or maybe it was the promise of something more delicious than the banana and crackers that awaited her at home.

It wasn't Quinn's fault she was far more attracted to him than she'd ever been to any man. Deep in thought as they entered the hotel, they rode a private, key-operated elevator to his floor. Even the elevator was opulent, inlaid with gold, and the deep rich scarlet carpet showed no signs of wear. The doors swished opened into a large foyer and a view through the living room to Central Park.

The apartment took up an entire floor.

She should have guessed from the engagement ring she still wore that he would live this way. His family owned a resort chain, while he himself managed a hedge fund. Exactly the kind of man she would have never envisioned herself with. But in spite of the multimillion-dollar views, his apartment was decorated with tasteful restraint. Coffee-toned walls were a warm backdrop for sleek, gray furnishings punctuated with some rust-colored accents—a vase, matched roman shades that covered the top third of the huge windows. Comfortable and attractive, the room pulled her forward as Quinn switched on the fireplace and put in a call to the hotel's kitchen.

An hour later, picking over the remains of her chicken fricassee while seated on a giant leather couch that wrapped around a corner of Quinn's apartment, Sofia had to admit she felt glad to be there. The snow had stopped outside the living room windows, but peering down into the park with all the street lamps lit was sort of like looking into a dollhouse with hundreds of different tiny rooms. He was putting the finishing touches on the press release on his laptop. A fire crackled in the fireplace, warming her feet and knees, and she'd even accepted a throw blanket made of the softest cashmere ever.

With silent apologies to her mother, Sofia decided that no one truly soulless would help a scrappy thirteen-year-old retrieve a toy. Or help Sofia carry off a mad scheme to pretend to have a fiancé. Quinn was an exception to her mother's rule about rich people.

"Just confirming…when did we know we were in love?" Quinn had taken the easy chair diagonally across from her, maintaining a professional amount of space between them.

"How about when you ordered the chicken fricassee for me?" she offered, trying to stick to the truth the way he'd showed her earlier.

"No one could blame you for being wooed by the food here." He quit typing and peered over at her in the firelight.

They hadn't put any other lights on in this room, although there was a glow from the kitchen. Sofia had been enjoying looking outside and the view was easier to appreciate with less light behind her.

"Dancers are perpetually starving," she admitted. "So I'm more susceptible than most to good food."

"Why are you always starving?" Quinn set aside the laptop long enough to clear their plates and set the dishes on a serving cart that had been delivered half an hour ago.

"It's a figure of speech. I expend a great deal of energy, for one thing. And, for another, the body preferred by most directors is very slender."

The topic had come under more debate over the last few years with a move to recognize healthy bodies of all sizes in dance. But ballet was rooted in traditions on every level, and she didn't know any company that truly embraced this philosophy yet.

"I'm surprised. I would think the moves require a great deal of strength."

"They do. But we need to build that strength in different ways. Repetition of lighter weights, for example."

"But why?" He took the seat closer to her now, sharing the couch even though he was a couple feet away. He'd brought his laptop with him but hadn't opened it yet.

"Choreographers like a company of dancers that are all roughly the same size and build. There's more symmetry to it when we all move."

"And you'd still get that if you all agree to be ten

pounds heavier. And wouldn't more muscle minimize injury?"

"Yes and no. Some say a lighter frame puts less strain on the joints."

"You can't eat enough. You work constantly. You're subject to intra-squad jostling for position—so much so you're willing to fake an engagement to keep your detractors quiet." He counted off the negatives on his fingers. "So if you're willing to go through all that, I have to think there's one hell of an upside for you."

"There is." She shifted positions, straightening as she warmed to her subject. "I watched *Sleeping Beauty* with my mother as a child. It was a performance in the middle of nowhere—a tiny troupe traveling through Prague. And I was captivated by Aurora like any other little girl who attends the ballet." Sliding off the couch, she moved to an open spot on the floor to show him. "I thought the dancer was the most beautiful and elegant woman in the world." She took a position for the Rose Adagio dance in her stocking feet, imagining a princely suitor before her as she mimicked Aurora's questioning pose with one leg raised and curved behind her. "When she took the roses from each of her four suitors..." She mimed the action, having danced the role many times herself. "I knew I wanted to *be* her. Not just Aurora, but the dancer who brought her to life."

Quinn's blue gaze tracked the movement of her arched foot as she lifted it in the exaggerated extension that her Russian teachers had stressed. The warmth in his eyes—his attention to her body—did not inspire the same feelings as when she captured an audience's imagination on stage. This felt personal in a way that heated her skin and made her all too aware of her appearance.

Not just her body, which was perpetually displayed in

dance. But the stroke of her braid against one arm. The rush of air past her lips as her breath caught.

"So you dance for the love of it. Because it was your dream." He kept the conversation focused, which she appreciated since she'd forgotten what they were talking about for a moment, distracted by the sparks that crackled between them.

"I have never wanted to do anything else." Which was why she feared the end of her career, a moment that could sneak up on her on any given night, with her body constantly battling injuries.

She needed to reach the top of her field now—as quickly as possible—to achieve the fame necessary to parlay the experience into success afterward. And she needed to dance the starring role for Fortier to make that happen.

"Ballet is your passion." Quinn let the word simmer between them for a long moment before returning his attention to the laptop. "And I think I know when we fell in love."

He began typing.

"You do?" Her heartbeat stuttered in her chest. She forced herself to sit back down and resume normal conversation in spite of the nerve endings flickering to life all over her body.

Too late she realized she had sat closer to him than she'd been before. She told herself that was only so she could peer over his shoulder at whatever it was he was typing. She caught a hint of his male scent, something clean like soap or aftershave that made her want to breathe deeply.

"It was the first time I saw you dance." His fingers paused on the keyboard, the sudden quiet seeming to underscore the moment and stirring to life a whole host of complicated feelings.

His words should not affect her this way. Especially since they were spinning tall tales for the media and not discussing anything remotely real.

"Name the performance. I'll tell the whole world how your movements on the stage captured me. When I watched you dance, I saw how passion guides you and knew we were a match."

"You toy with me," she accused, scuttling back to her previous position on the couch. "Your words are like your kisses—all for show. But I find them confusing."

"I'm not toying with you." He passed her the laptop. "You should read this over."

How could she concentrate on the words when her blood ran too hot and she kept imagining the way his eyes had followed her body while she danced?

"I'm sure it's fine." She set the laptop on the couch between them. "Jasmine will review it before she sends it out."

"Sofia?" He moved the laptop to the coffee table, edging closer. "I don't know how else to approach this to make you more comfortable. But *you* wanted to put on this show. I'm trying to help you."

His voice, deep and masculine, sent a shiver through her.

"Thank you. But I would prefer if this remained a performance for the benefit of others. I don't want to play at the game when we are alone." She felt his nearness in the same way that she knew without looking where her dance partner would be at all times. Except that was practiced, a trick she'd learned through study and repetition. With Quinn, her cells seemed to seek out his presence, attuning themselves to him without her even thinking about it.

"The only reason I kissed you in the park is because I'm attracted to you. I won't pretend otherwise." With a shuddering breath, his eyes, which a moment ago blazed with heat, seemed to ember as his voice lilted with resignation. "But I can put a rein on that, and I have."

"How? How do you put a rein on it, as you say?" She wondered if he had tricks of his own. Something she might learn for herself.

"It's not easy. And it gets tougher the longer I'm with you." He lifted his hand toward her face the way he'd done in the snowfall right before he'd kissed her. But then he lowered his fingers again, hand falling to his side. "We have an agreement, however, and I'll do what it takes to see it through. If that means we play this your way, I'm going to do everything in my power to keep my hands to myself unless we're in public."

"The way we will be on Friday." At the reception for Idris Fortier. Her first real public appearance with Quinn as a couple, and it would be a major moment in her career.

Butterflies fluttered through her belly at the thought of being on this man's arm all evening. Feeling his hand at her waist or grazing her hip through a thin evening gown.

Pretending to be in love.

Her lips tingled as she wondered if he would kiss her.

"Yes." His gaze dipped to her mouth as if he could read her mind. "I'm already looking forward to it."

Seven

Tossing generous handfuls of Epsom salt into the tub, Sofia ran the hot water, anticipating the effects of the bath. Her muscles ached and it was only Wednesday.

As she let the water fill the tub, she pumped toning soap onto her hands and then her face, before splashing water from the faucet to wash away a day of sweat and stress. A candle flickered on the sink's countertop, sending a soothing scent of lavender into the air. When she was a small girl, her mother would always burn lavender candles after a long day. Although only a small connection to life before her mom passed away, the fragrance still relaxed her.

And she needed that now more than ever.

Deep breath in. Deep breath out.

Washing the rest of the soap from her face, Sofia tried to focus on preparing for the private audition for Idris Fortier in less than a week. That should be her sole thought.

But instead thoughts of Quinn pushed into her head. It had been two nights since they'd walked through the park and a day since her interview with *Dance* magazine where she'd relayed the love story she and Quinn had manufactured. The details seemed all too real. And she kept replaying their brief time together. His lips, his touch. How she was attracted to him, though she knew better.

Even after her bath, she was frustrated as hell. She stepped out of the tub, water dripping from her body onto a bath mat, and tested her knee carefully. And, thank heaven, it held. It felt better if not perfect. She shrugged on a short, fluffy bathrobe and yanked the tie into a knot.

Patting her face dry with a semi-plush hand towel, she examined her reflection in the mirror. She could do this. She could nail the audition and be the star that Idris Fortier wanted for his next ballet. That connection would do so much for her. Give her career legs after her physical ones quit giving her the lift and height she needed on her jumps.

Stashed on the corner of the countertop was a collection of reviews from the most reputable critics about Fortier's last ballet. Jasmine had sent this particular stack over to her apartment. When Sofia had an audition on her radar, she always poured over press releases and reviews, trying to glean a better sense of her audience.

Sifting through the documents once more, a headline caught her eye.

Affair.

She eased herself down onto the edge of the tub and put her feet back in the water as she devoured the article. Apparently the choreographer had had an affair with the star of his last production. The weight of that information unsettled her.

Her phone chirped, startling her. Pulling it out of the pocket of her robe, she glanced at the screen.

Quinn.

"Hello." Heart fluttering, she felt a mixture of excitement and nerves crash in her chest.

"Hello, Sofia." His voice incited a flush of warmth over her skin beneath the robe.

"Quinn." His name felt like an endearment on her tongue. "Hello," she said again. To cover her surprise.

She closed her eyes and saw him there—with her—in the tub. Her mouth went dry.

"I thought you might like an update about the matchmaker situation," he continued.

Something that felt an awful lot like disappointment pounded in tandem with her heartbeat. Had she really just wanted him to call for no reason? If this faux engagement was going to work, she'd have to keep her emotions in check.

"Of course. Tell me." The news clipping about Idris's affair was still in her hand; she stared at it while Quinn's baritone voice filled the speaker, willing her pulse back to normal.

She hadn't called her father since announcing her engagement at the airport, despite how angry she'd been with him at the time. That night, she'd been too exhausted to do battle with him, and Quinn had told her he would take care of making sure her dating profile was removed from wherever it had been posted.

"I'm not sure if I mentioned that Cameron's matchmaker is Mallory West. He contacted her for an explanation the day after he proposed to you."

The name meant nothing to Sofia, but as her dancing peers had noted, she wasn't part of the Manhattan singles scene.

"Did she say where she got my flight information?" She had thought about that more than once. How could Cameron's matchmaker have known her arrival time in New York, while her father claimed to be ignorant of Cam's appointment to meet her?

She dipped her hand into the bubbles in the tub, skimming her fingers across the soapy tops.

"She told Cameron she would look into it." Quinn's voice was as potent as his touch. If she closed her eyes, she could imagine him beside her. "But since then, her phone has been disconnected and her email generates an autoreply that she's out of the country on an extended trip."

Sofia forced her eyes open, thinking about that bit of peculiar news. Her cheeks puffed with a hefty exhale. "What do you think it means?"

"For now, it simply means that she is a dead end in our hunt for information. I'm sorry, Sofia. But I will continue having my IT technician hunt for any sign of her online. And, for what it's worth, he's seen no traces of a dating profile for you online, so I think the matchmaker your father hired made good on her promise to pull it down."

"At least that part is good news." She really needed to call her father and ask him more about the situation herself, if only to find out whom he'd hired to help her with her dating prospects. She would feel better once she told that person in no uncertain terms that she wasn't interested.

"It is. And we'll figure out the rest of it, Sofia," Quinn assured her before his tone shifted and his voice got lower. "But that isn't the only thing we have to figure out."

"No?" Sensations tripped down her spine at that sexy rasp in his voice. "What else should we be discussing?"

A half laugh sounded from the other end of the call and nothing else, no background noise, just him. He must be somewhere private. Alone. "Something more fun. So, Sofia, what kind of dress should I buy you to wow and woo the crowds at Idris Fortier's reception on Friday? Do you have a favorite boutique?"

Buy her a dress? The gesture was sweet. But it was too much. Far too much.

"That is kind of you, but definitely not necessary." Still, she imagined what he would choose for her. What it would be like to slide on a garment handpicked by Quinn?

"I'll take you shopping anywhere you'd like."

She tried not to think about the beautiful things a man like Quinn McNeill could afford.

"You are thoughtful, Quinn, but I can't accept more gifts." She felt guilty enough about wearing that massive diamond on her left hand, but he'd convinced her the ring was a necessity. "And I already have something in mind." She didn't mean for her voice to sound so clipped.

"Are you nervous?" he pressed, the deep tones of his whiskey-rich voice warming her moist body.

Her instincts kicked in; she could tell he was interested. He actually wanted to know.

"A bit. I...I just..." Her voice trailed off. Social gatherings and big parties were not her thing. She disliked superficial small talk, preferring meatier conversations.

Music.

Dancing.

"Yes?" he prompted.

"I'm terrible at galas. And around large masses of humanity in general."

"Seriously?" Surprise colored his voice. "But you dance in front of large audiences."

"Yes, seriously. I have stage fright in social scenarios

where I'm forced to talk. But when I'm on stage, ballet feels like poetry, like breath. It's different. Completely different." Chewing her lip, she felt a ball of anxiety begin to form.

Deep breath.

"Luckily for you, I'm quite the pro at these galas. I'll be there to guide and help you, if you want to follow my lead, that is."

"If you can speak in coherent sentences, you'll be one step ahead of me. I'm notoriously awkward in interviews. Jasmine has tried to coach me, but I get very tense."

"I hope that having me there helps. But either way, we'll get through it. And if you want to leave early, I'll give everyone the impression that it's my fault because I can't wait to have you all to myself."

The images that came to mind heated her skin all over again. So much so, she needed to pull her feet out of the hot water.

"How generous of you," she observed, feeling tongue-tied already but for a very different reason.

"I do what I can." The smile in his voice came right through the call. "So can I ask what you plan on wearing?"

A playful tone from him? Now, wasn't that a surprise. Smiling, she glanced out of the bathroom and into her bedroom, eyeing her closet where she had exactly nothing appropriate.

While her father would have loved to write her monthly checks or set up a trust fund for his sole heir, she'd resisted all of his efforts to share his wealth with her in any way. Her mother had always blamed him for his refusal to focus on the things that really mattered in life. Like love. Family. Art. All the things that mattered most to Sofia.

She would do without a dress.

"Something stunning," she told Quinn finally, wondering if she could get something on loan from the costume department.

"Something sexy?" He pressed and she heard his smile through the phone.

"Extremely," she said, forgetting that she was supposed to keep herself in check around him.

Chuckling, his voice was low like a whispered promise. "I look forward to seeing every sexy inch of you on Friday."

And before she could close her gaping jaw, he'd hung up.

Quinn stepped from the limo outside Sofia's apartment building shortly before seven on the night of the reception for her big-deal choreographer.

He hit the call button near the door and waited to be buzzed in before heading inside and taking the elevator to her floor. They'd spoken by phone the last two nights and their conversations had allowed him to get closer to Sofia without the in-person surge of attraction getting in the way. She seemed more at ease on the phone, as if she needed that cerebral connection before she'd allow herself to admit the physical chemistry that had been apparent to him since the first moment he'd seen her.

He'd even talked her into letting him send her a gown for tonight, a feat it had taken him a lot of effort to pull off. He'd only gotten his way by arguing that it would make their engagement more believable. He would absolutely want his fiancée to appear at such an important event for her career in an unforgettable, one-of-a-kind dress. Especially since this would be their first formal public outing as an engaged couple.

Now, as he rang the bell outside 5C, he mentally reviewed the game plan. *Let the attraction build. Don't rush her.* But once they were in the spotlight and she needed to sell their relationship as a stable, happy union that wouldn't detract from her dancing, he planned to deliver. She would be in his arms as often as possible to prove it.

And he looked forward to that more than he'd anticipated any date in a long time. So much for the idea that all this was for show or to smooth over relations with her father. Quinn wasn't going through with it just to ease those European deals and to save his brother from embarrassment.

When the door opened, the sight of her hit him in his chest like a physical blow. Not because she was beautifully dressed, although she damn well looked incredible in her navy-silk gown with subtle, breezy feathers covering much of the skirt to the floor-length hem, her blond hair artfully arranged so it was half up and half down, the tendrils snaking along her neck. He would have been affected if she'd been in a T-shirt and shorts.

He'd missed her. And that realization rocked him.

"You look incredible, Sofia." She looked like the woman he wanted more than any other. Her wide, smoke-colored eyes picked up hints of silver when she wore navy. Diamond roses glittered in her ears.

"You clean up rather nicely yourself." She reached to touch him, surprising the hell out of him in the best possible way, but in the end she merely rubbed the fabric of his tuxedo sleeve appreciatively. "That's a gorgeous tux."

"Thanks," he answered absently, his mind on stun at a simple brush of her fingers. He wanted her touching all the rest of him that way. But he breathed deep and stuck to the game plan.

"Are you ready to go?" He stepped inside her apartment, following her while she retrieved a beaded purse.

"Almost. I couldn't get the hook at the top." She presented him with her back. A soft scent like vanilla mingled with musk drifted up from her hair as he swept aside some of the blond tendrils to find the clasp.

What was it about the nape of a woman's neck that drove a man insane? The vulnerability of it? The trust in exposing it? Quinn wanted to lean closer and lick her there, kiss his way to the back of her ear and then down the column of her throat again.

He settled for taking his time with the clasp, his knuckles lightly brushing beneath the fabric of her dress. He felt the answering quiver in her body. They were that close. Sealing his eyes shut for a moment—needing to control his runaway thoughts—he finished the job and reached around her to take the evening wrap, settling it on her shoulders.

"Time to leave," he urged, wanting nothing so much as to get her in public so he could touch her. How backward was that? Most men couldn't wait to get a woman home to be alone. But he'd promised her their physical contact would be just for show. "Do you have a coat?"

Quinn needed a public audience as an excuse to put his hands on her.

But maybe tonight would change that. Make Sofia realize the effort of staying away from each other wasn't worth it when they could explore the heat between them to their thoroughly mutual satisfaction.

"A cape." She reached for a long black cape with fur around the oversize hood. Lovely. Elegant. Like her.

Before she could move further, he took it from her and draped it reverently over her shoulders. She looked like a timeless screen star in that movie *Doctor Zhivago*.

Damn, he was getting downright sentimental. He needed air. Bracing, cold air.

Leaving her apartment behind—thank God the elevator was crowded to keep him in check—he offered his arm and was glad she took it as they walked toward the vestibule. As a dancer used to working on her toes, she must be comfortable in the sky-high silver heels he glimpsed beneath the dress hem as she walked. But with damp spots on the hall floor from the snow tracked indoors, it helped that she could hold on to him for support.

Once they were inside the limo and headed uptown to the gala venue, Sofia placed a hand on her chest.

"Can I just tell you I'm a nervous wreck?"

"Just remember, you're a professional at the top of her career about to impress a choreographer who is probably already very eager to work with you." Quinn had read up on Idris Fortier over the course of the week, as well as the dance world's frenzied reaction to his New York arrival.

"You don't know that. Some of my reviews are solid." She spoke quickly, settling her purse beside her as they stopped at a red light. "But I have received plenty of harsh criticism, too, and I know my own shortcomings, so Fortier might decide—"

"I read your reviews, Sofia. They're more than solid." He wanted to halt her before she strayed too far down that road of what-ifs and worry. "Some say you favor technique over artistry, the sport of it over the dancing, and you don't trust your partners enough." He'd scoured the praise and the criticism in an effort to understand her more, to be closer to her. "But I compared your reviews to the rest of the stars in the company, and I don't see anyone who comes away more favorably. In fact, critics agree you are the most exciting talent to work here in years. If I can glean that as a novice, an insider like Fortier will be well aware of you."

"I'm not so sure about that." She wound one of the long, loose feathers of her skirt around her finger where the cape had fallen away. He noticed how her nails were polished a clear pink, and her engagement ring was practically glowing in the limo's dome lighting.

But her movements suggested she was more than a little nervous.

"May I make a suggestion?" He covered her hand where she'd gently destroyed the single feather, breaking his own rule about not touching her in private.

"I don't suppose it could hurt." The tension in her body was so obvious she practically vibrated with it. "What is it?"

"Considering that you're visibly anxious about tonight…" he began. But before he could propose the idea, she made a small sound of distress. Uncrossing and re-crossing her legs in the opposite direction, her foot nudged his calf and then began to jitter.

"Oh, God." She swallowed hard. "I *will* get it together. Even though there is so much riding on making a good impression—"

"Listen. We make a good team. Remember how easily we ran off the journalists from *Dance* magazine at the airport? I know your goals tonight and I'm good at things like this. Follow my lead and you'll be fine." He twined his fingers through hers, hoping to impart some calm, not just because he wanted to touch her.

"You think I can after reading how I don't trust a partner?" she asked dryly. "I've gotten dropped on several occasions. It doesn't inspire confidence."

Sofia's forced smile and raised brow struck him. He

needed to assure her that he wasn't one of those types of partners. He'd be there.

Pulling her gaze away from his, she stared out the window, eyes actively scanning the buildings and pedestrians on the sidewalk.

"I can imagine." He smoothed his thumb over the back of her hand, liking the feel of her skin and the way his touch relaxed her. He could sense some of the tension leaking away as her musky vanilla perfume seemed to invite him closer. "But I would never let you fall."

"Well. Thank you." Her gaze fell to their locked fingers, as if she were surprised to see the way they were connected. "I will admit that I could use a steadying presence tonight."

A car horn blared outside and a faint crescendo of sirens filled the air. Oh, New York.

"Good. Now, about my suggestion." He traced the outline of her engagement ring with his finger, extraordinarily aware of her calf still grazing his knee. "It might help if you allowed me to distract you."

"Distract me?" She arched an eyebrow at him, skeptical but no longer nervous. Her jittering foot came to a rest.

If anything, the sudden stillness of her body suggested she just might be intrigued.

"It's completely up to you." He wanted nothing so much as to gather her up and settle her on top of him. But he had a plan and he would take his time. Let her get used to the idea of enjoying every moment of their time together. "But we could rechannel all that nervous energy. Give it a different physical outlet."

Her jaw dropped.

"I am not the kind of woman who has sex in a limousine," she informed him, not looking quite as scandalized as she might have.

He, on the other hand, was plenty surprised her mind had gone there.

"Well, damn. That's an incredible thought, but I wasn't suggesting we take things that far. You look too beautiful to mess up before your big night, Sofia."

"Then be more clear," she snapped, her cheeks pink and her eyes alight with new fire. "Because I have no idea what you mean."

In a blink, he shifted positions, releasing her hand so he could bracket her shoulders between his arms, pinning her without touching her. He held her gaze, lowering himself closer until his chest came within inches of her breasts. Even with her dress and cape between them, he could see their gentle swell.

He spoke softly in her ear.

"Distraction." He articulated it clearly so there would be no mistake. "I could kiss you somewhere that wouldn't mess you up. A spot along the curve of your lovely neck, maybe." His eyes wandered over her, assessing the possibilities. "Or beneath your hair."

A shiver ran through her while his breath warmed the space between her skin and his mouth. Careful not to touch her, he let the idea take hold. If nothing else, he felt damn certain just this conversation would rewire her thoughts for a while, taking them off the choreographer she was so anxious to impress.

The notion satisfied him. A lot.

"That is a crazy idea," she whispered back. "Letting you kiss me might give me more heart palpitations than I was having before."

He wanted a taste of her. So. Badly.

"But the heart palpitations I could give you would be the pleasurable kind." Dragging his attention off the rapid pulse at her throat, he heard her quick intake of breath, saw her eyelids flutter once. Twice.

"You are way too sure of yourself, Quinn McNeill." Her hands lifted, hovering near his shoulders as if she debated touching him there.

He willed her palms closer.

"No. I'm sure of what's between us even though you don't want to acknowledge it."

"We're only pretending," she insisted, her eyebrows furrowing as the limo slowed to another stop, jostling her closer to him. She braced her palms on his chest. Torture. Pure torture.

He hoped their destination was another hour away because he was locking that limo door if anyone tried to open it now.

"I only agreed to pretend because I was attracted to you to start with." The words were out of his mouth. He couldn't take them back, and what surprised him was he didn't want to.

"What are you saying?" She shook her head, squinting as she tried to process. "Next month, this will be all over—"

"I know." Gently he edged her wrap back and smoothed aside a few locks of silky hair that curled around her neck and rested against the fur-lined hood. "But until then, I want this."

Pressing his lips to the curve of her shoulder, he soaked in the warmth and fragrance unique to this woman. Sweet and musky at the same time, her scent made him instantly hard. Not moving, he wanted to take his cue from her, only advancing this game as far as she'd let him.

When her hands finally landed on his shoulders, for a moment he thought she might push him away. Instead her fingers tunneled under his open coat, then farther inside his jacket, splaying out over his tuxedo shirt until he could feel the soft scrape of her short nails through the cotton.

The sensation raked over his senses, arousing a fierceness in him that had no place in a limo five minutes before a party. He opened his mouth to taste her, lick her, nip her. His chest grazed her breasts, her delicate curves arching hard against him as she pressed deeper into him.

Her response was everything he wanted, everything he could have hoped for, and the damn reception of hers was just a minute farther up the road. But his heart slammed in his chest in a victory dance, his body too caught up in the feel of hers to get the message that this was not the time to take all he wanted.

Damn. Damn.

"Sofia." He kissed her neck below her ear, bit the tender earlobe just above her earring and forced himself to lean back. "We're here."

Eight

Games and lies, Sofia reminded herself later that night while Quinn fielded another question about their relationship from the reporter who wanted to do a follow-up interview with her and her fiancé. They were seated in a private room off the skylight lounge where City Ballet was holding the party for Idris Fortier, the music from a chamber orchestra filtering in through the open door along with the sounds of laughter, clinking glasses and the rumble of conversation.

The space was crowded and warm, especially for those who danced.

Or those who were overwrought with the sensual steam of longing.

Quinn and Sofia had been dealing in games and lies all week, so she could hardly be upset with her handsome, charming date for spinning a moving tale about how he fell in love watching her dance. She'd signed off on the story, after all. She'd agreed that it was easier to root the lies in some element of truth so they had shared memories to trot out at moments like this.

How could she fault Quinn now for being a much better liar than her, especially since she was the one who'd pressed for the pretend engagement?

"But I won't take the focus away from Sofia's dancing," Quinn was saying as they sat side by side on a black leather sofa in the sparse, modern room full of bistro tables and areas for private conversations. "If you'll excuse me, I'll let her finish up the interview." He turned toward her, his tuxedo not showing a single crease as he stood and kissed her hand. "Save me the first dance when you finish?"

His blue eyes had a teasing light. It bothered her that he was good at this, rousing suspicions of his motives no matter that he claimed to be attracted to her.

"Of course. Thank you." She smiled up at him, playing her part but knowing she wasn't as skilled as he was. And her body still hadn't completely recovered from the kisses in the limousine.

If he hadn't pulled away when he had back in the vehicle, she would have sacrificed the most beautiful gown she'd ever worn to press herself against all that raw masculine strength and follow where the attraction led.

"Your future husband was one of the city's most eligible bachelors, Sofia," the reporter—Delaney—observed. The woman's eyes followed Quinn as he strode out the open door into the party in the lounge. "The McNeill heirs are rich, charming and exceedingly good-looking." She tore her eyes from Quinn as she picked up her digital tablet where she'd been taking notes. "His brother must have made quite an impression on you when he proposed at the airport. But I'm surprised you dated Quinn for so long without meeting Cameron? Cameron tends to be the most visible of the three."

Sofia fought back nerves, not wanting to drop the ball after Quinn had set her up so skillfully to talk about something else.

"That may be, but I don't have much time outside of ballet for socializing. What time I do have, I spend with Quinn. But I'd prefer to talk about work, if you have any questions for me."

Delaney pursed her lips in a frown.

"Very well." She changed screens on the tablet. "Perhaps you'd like to address your critics. Your work has been called mechanical and without artistry. What makes you think you will capture the leading role in the Fortier project when the choreographer is such a decided fan of mood and emotion in his work?"

The biting tone of the query told Sofia just how much she'd accidentally offended the reporter by asking to change the subject. Maybe she should have asked Jasmine to be here for this follow-up interview to help smooth over awkward moments and ensure Sofia didn't embarrass herself. But it cost enough just to have Jasmine set up these kinds of appointments, and she had attended a video interview earlier in the week.

The upside of all the press coverage was that she ought to have a great feature piece by the time they were finished, right?

"I strive every day to balance the physical demands of the dance with all the artistry I can bring to each piece. I hope that I'm always improving on both fronts. An artist should always aspire to improve." She should explain how. Give the reporter more to work with. Except that her nerves had returned in full force.

"And what is your impression of Mr. Fortier so far?" the woman asked, tapping her stylus on the tablet.

Was she waiting for the quotable bit that would torch Sofia's career for daring to stick to the topic?

"I have the same impression everyone else has. He's a brilliant talent and our company is extremely fortunate to work with him." She couldn't believe she'd invited this woman to her private audition with Fortier.

The last thing she needed was to be nervous on that day, too. She was usually so solid when she danced. She didn't need Delaney getting in her head.

"Are you aware that his last two featured leads have moved in with him during the creative process?" The woman watched Sofia's reaction closely. "That he was romantically linked to both of them?"

She hadn't known about that. Although she had read about the affair with the previous one, she'd assumed that was just a one-time thing. People working together fell in love all the time.

But the same scenario twice?

"No." With an effort she coaxed her lips into a smile. "I'm sure it's not a requirement for the job."

Outside the private room, the chamber group paused in their play and someone took the microphone. Sofia peered over her shoulder, wondering if Idris was about to be introduced.

"I'm sure it's not." Delaney gestured toward the open door. "But don't let me keep you. I plan to speak with several more of your colleagues tonight."

"Have you got all the material you need?" Sofia had hoped for a feature in the magazine, not a snippet about her engagement to a hedge fund manager.

"Plenty." Delaney flipped off her tablet and stood. "And I'll be there to film your audition for Mr. Fortier, which will be something our readers will want to hear all about."

Sofia knew she'd made a misstep with the woman, but had no idea how to correct it now. She settled for being polite as she rose to her feet.

"Thank you, I look forward to it," she lied, although not nearly as well as Quinn could have in this situation. Funny how he'd become her biggest ally this week, their unlikely partnership providing her with an outlet at a stressful time in her career.

Maybe she shouldn't be so quick to write off his ability to put on a façade in public. She would do better to learn the trick from him.

"Enjoy that handsome fiancé of yours," the reporter called after her. "You're so lucky to have found someone special. I was thinking of resorting to a matchmaker myself."

Sofia nearly tripped over her feet, the shock of the words like an icy splash to her nerves. Turning, she saw Delaney tapping her chin thoughtfully with her stylus.

"You don't happen to know any good ones, do you?" the woman asked.

A gauntlet had been dropped.

Sofia understood the implication. The woman knew something about what had happened at the airport. Had she learned that Sofia's father had hired a matchmaker? That in itself was certainly not a big deal. But what if she knew more than that? That her engagement was a lie. That Sofia had only done it to quiet the gossip among her peers so she could focus on her dancing.

Maybe she should have straightened it out that night. Stuck with the truth. But since she was in no position to untangle any of it right now, Sofia simply smiled.

"I don't, but I've heard that's a very popular option

these days." She rushed to melt into the crowd and find Quinn.

In the pressure cooker of her work world, her fake fiancé had become her best source of commiseration.

And he wanted to be even more than that. He wanted to give her pleasure, a heady offer that had teased the edges of her consciousness all evening long. With her heart ready to pound out of her chest, she realized he was the only person she wanted to see right now.

If only she could truly trust him. But even as she raced to find him, she reminded herself to be careful. He might genuinely be attracted to her. But he wouldn't be helping her right now if it didn't serve McNeill interests.

"I need to speak to you."

Sofia's whisper in Quinn's ear was the sexiest thing he'd heard since that small gasp she'd made in the limo when he'd kissed her neck. He'd been ready to get her alone ever since then.

Maybe this was his moment.

He stood on the fringes of the crowd listening to the guest of honor speak at a podium about his eagerness to work in New York and to let the city inspire him. The guy said all the right things, but something about him irritated Quinn from the moment he'd opened his mouth. Perhaps it was just because he held power over Sofia's career and Quinn didn't like thinking that the subjective opinions of one man could mean so much to her.

More likely, it was because Idris Fortier laughed at his own jokes and occasionally referred to himself in the third person. The well-heeled crowd in attendance hung on his every word, however.

"Should we listen to this first?" Quinn asked Sofia quietly, surprised her interview had finished so soon.

"The reporter asked me if I could recommend a good matchmaker." The soft warmth of her breath teased over his ear, but the seductive sensation couldn't cancel out the anxiety in her words.

And no wonder she was nervous.

"He's almost done speaking." Quinn wrapped an arm around her waist, to bring her as close as possible, wanting to give every appearance of being deeply in love and lost in one another. "It will be easier to talk once the dancing begins." His lips moved against the silk of her hair. "And I don't want your reporter friend to see us darting off in a corner to whisper."

Nodding, she relaxed against him ever so slightly. That small show of trust was something he'd been working hard for all week long. He'd put her needs first, letting Cameron fly to Kiev to handle the hotel acquisitions. He'd asked his brother Ian for help running down more information about Mallory West, giving himself more time to gain Sofia Koslov's trust.

To help her, of course. They'd agreed to as much. But things had gotten more complicated as he admitted the depth of his attraction. He wanted her. And after the heat they'd sparked in the car on the way over here, he thought he knew where things were headed between them.

Would she act on that attraction if she knew this engagement was helping him as much as it helped her? That he'd purposely delayed drawing up that contract he'd discussed with her that first night they'd met because he now wondered if the relationship could help him around his grandfather's marriage dictate.

Quinn still hoped he could help Malcolm McNeill see that he didn't need to call the shots in his grandsons' love lives. That he could trust them to find spouses on their own terms and in their own time. Quinn would at least try to talk him into scrapping the marriage stipulation from the will. But failing that? He was confident he could work out some kind of agreement with Sofia that would help him to fulfill the terms.

As the crowd around him erupted into applause for the choreographer, a violinist struck a dramatic, quavering note. It cracked through the air, stirring the room. The unmistakable trill of a Spanish bandoneon followed in the opening note of a tango, a rare dance Quinn knew well. It transported him back to the small Buenos Aires pub where he'd learned the steps afterhours with his work crew while overseeing renovations on one of the family's resorts. He recalled the packed dance floor crowded with passionate couples and knew, with fierce certainty, that he wanted to share this with Sofia.

"Dance with me," he murmured in her ear, his nostrils flaring at the vanilla scent of her skin. It rose around him and heated his blood.

Her large gray eyes were hesitant, questioning as they swerved to his. He trailed his fingertips up her spine, feeling the sweet curve of her back through silk. "I am classically trained," she murmured in a breathy rush. "The tango is a ballroom dance."

"Then it will be a welcome chance for me to partner you on the floor." He drew her toward the square parquet tiles near the musicians.

"Since when do hedge fund managers learn sexy Argentinian dances?" She was light on her feet as she backed into position, joining the handful of couples taking the floor.

"I must have known I'd need to impress a woman one day." He tightened his grip on her, urging her closer as they entered the counterclockwise flow. Her lithe body moved gracefully against his, but this wasn't a pretty dance. It was primal and raw.

She watched the other dancers long enough to gather her bearings, then turned her gaze back to him.

"You are full of surprises, Quinn McNeill." For an aching moment her body cradled the growing hardness concealed by his tuxedo. Then she twisted her hips sideways and kicked her foot through the long slit up one side of her dress, shooting him a coquettish look from beneath the sweep of her long lashes.

At last he'd distracted her completely. She was no longer worried about the reporter, the choreographer or her career. All her focus was on him.

The throbbing notes of the violin wove with the cry of the bandoneon and echoed the seething heat she stirred inside him.

Before she could slip too far away, he hauled her close again then bent her backward. Her spine arched and her head dipped to the floor, exposing the creamy, satin skin of her elegant neck, the slender column of her body. Their hips brushed as they swayed and then he snapped her upright so that their mouths touched. They breathed each other in and their gazes tangled.

Tension whipped between them. His body grew taut; need and craving pounded through him. He felt the pressure of it all licking through his blood. When he stepped with his left foot, she followed, her limbs seeming to loosen and grow molten, her movements more languid. The arm curled around his neck singed his flesh and her fingers burrowed into his hair, her nails raking his skin.

He steered her expertly, felt her respond to the lightest of touches, the smallest pressure. She seemed to surrender to the dance, to him, as her eyes closed and she let him lead her the way he wanted to.

Yet just when she looked defenseless, a staccato rhythm seemed to break her trance and she whirled around him, improvising mouthwatering steps as he stood rigid, watching. Wanting. He couldn't tear his eyes off her. She held his hand then shimmied lower, her body sinuous. She rose slowly. Out of nowhere, her lips curved into a tempting smile, her expression full of promise.

His mouth dried and his tongue swelled. They cross-stepped for several more beats and the world fell away. His senses narrowed, homing in on the beautiful woman who didn't back down when he pushed forward, who stood her ground and stalked him as well until at last, they stood, foreheads pressed together, breaths coming in fits and starts as the tango ended.

"Come home with me," he commanded. Her eyes burned into his and dimly he heard another song, slower, strike up.

Her grip tightened on his. "Yes."

Victory surged through him. He wanted to pick her up and carry her out of the crowd and downstairs to the waiting limo this minute. But he didn't want to end her time at a work function without accomplishing one more key goal that her friend Jasmine had clearly laid out as an objective for the evening.

"Excellent." He released her slowly, peering through the crowd to find the man who held Sofia's professional future in his hands. "We'll pay our regards to the man of the hour and then we're free to spend the rest of the night however we choose."

He felt her go still beside him. But she didn't tremble or fidget the way she had earlier in the evening.

"Good idea." She nodded. "I'll say hello and then I'll text Jasmine from the car to let her know about Delaney's comment to me. I want to give Jasmine some advance notice if the reporter plans a story about the matchmaking mix-up."

"I'll ask my own public relations department to circulate some stories about our engagement, as well."

That would lend their union all the more credibility. And for the first time Quinn found himself wondering what Sofia would say if he asked her to extend a fake engagement into a year-long marriage like his grandfather's will stipulated...

But of course he wouldn't do that. His grandfather's terms were out of line and unfair. He needed to talk him into rewriting the will. Right now, he would keep his focus on Sofia.

They stood waiting while an older woman dressed in an exotically colored caftan finished her conversation with the famed choreographer. When Sofia turned worried eyes toward him, Quinn took great pleasure in skimming a touch along her hip. And discreetly lower. Her eyes went wide so that she was thoroughly distracted by the time the older woman bid Fortier good-night.

"Sofia Koslov." The boyishly built Frenchman opened his arms wide. "My dear, I've been dying to meet you."

Quinn released her so she could be swept into a hug he personally found too damn enthusiastic, but then, he might have thought as much about anyone who put their hands on a woman he wanted this badly.

"Welcome to New York, Mr. Fortier," she greeted him. Her wooden delivery was an endearing sign of her nerves, Quinn realized.

He liked knowing things about this very private woman that other people didn't.

"Call me Idris. I insist." The man didn't spare a glance for Quinn as his eyes raked over Sofia with what Quinn hoped was professional interest.

Her body was the medium for her dance, he reminded himself even as he ground his teeth together.

"Idris," she corrected herself with quiet seriousness. "We are thrilled to host you at City Ballet. We are all excited to hear your plans for your new work."

Quinn found himself hanging on her words, wanting her to succeed since it clearly meant so much to her.

"And I sincerely hope you will be the first to hear those plans, Sofia. I look forward to your audition."

Before Sofia could reply, the celebrated choreographer turned to greet a young man who'd come to stand behind Sofia, effectively dismissing her.

Sofia tucked against Quinn's side with gratifying ease, whispering, "Did I offend him?"

If she wasn't so intent on securing the man's good opinion, Quinn might have told her that—on the contrary—Fortier's behavior had been rude. But he didn't want her to worry.

"You were perfect," he assured her honestly as he guided her through the crowd toward the coat check. "Jasmine would have been thrilled."

"Speaking of Jasmine." Sofia opened her purse and withdrew her phone. "I need to let her know what happened with that reporter." She lowered her voice for his ears only. "We should be prepared if the woman releases a story about me using a matchmaker."

Quinn nodded his agreement as he excused himself to retrieve their coats. But he already knew his plan B if the matchmaker story leaked. If anyone questioned the legitimacy of their engagement, it would pave the way to convince Sofia to marry him for a year and secure that damned inheritance anyhow.

Just in case.

Nine

Twenty minutes later Sofia watched the numbers light up above the elevator in Quinn's building as they waited for the private conveyance.

Ten, nine, eight…

Quinn's hand brushed the small of her back and circled, his touch burning her as it had on the dance floor. The white-gloved bellhop near the concierge desk spoke with a deliveryman wheeling in a silver cart full of insulated dishes—presumably a five star meal from an area restaurant. Behind them, an elegantly attired elder gentleman strode through the building's thick glass doors, the smell of diesel and roasting nuts carrying on the rush of crisp, evening air that trailed after him.

Was she out of her mind for being there?

Probably.

Their arrangement was for public events only, yet here she stood, ready—no, *wanting* this intimate privacy with Quinn.

Seven, six, five…

Every nerve ending had come alive since the moment he'd guided her through the most passionate dance she'd ever performed. Only, it hadn't been a performance. Every unchoreographed move had been born out of the sensuous desire he'd incited. Never before had she completely let go that way and she felt so empowered. Impassioned.

Nearby, other elevators with more white-gloved attendants took patrons to their floors, but she and Quinn were waiting for the private one direct to his floor.

Four, three, two…

Yet she hadn't come home with Quinn just because she was crazy with lust. She wanted to take this risk with him and open up as she had on the dance floor. He'd helped her navigate a stressful time in her life just as he'd led her through the tango—with certainty, command, giving as well as taking.

While she'd appreciated his strength and cool head this week, his passionate moves had given her another glimpse at the enigmatic man, made her want to know him more. Following his lead, as she had earlier, gave her confidence to let go and trust that he wouldn't let her down.

In fact, she suspected he would bring her to greater heights than she'd ever known. Her past relationships had all been as careful as her professional life, each step rehearsed until she felt safe about moving forward. And where had that gotten her?

It had been bloodless companionship that amounted to little more than friendships, causing her peers to think she led some kind of sad, passionless existence.

There was nothing passionless about what she felt for Quinn. Nothing scripted. Just heat and wild fire.

The elevator bell chimed, the doors opened and he

ushered her inside the wonderfully empty space. She held her breath as the door swooshed closed and, in an instant, he backed her up against the paneled wall. Hand burrowing in her hair, he loosened the few pins that held its shape so that the fragrant locks tumbled around her face, releasing the scent of her shampoo. Her cape slid from her shoulders to pool on the floor and she shoved his wool overcoat off in a quick, deft sweep.

She melted at his appreciative, predatory growl. When his lips brushed hers, she rose on tiptoe and fit her body against the hard length of him. A feminine thrill shot through her when he deepened the kiss. His tongue slid over the seam of her mouth, demanding entrance, and she moaned in the back of her throat. She felt winded, light-headed and incredibly turned on as he crushed her to him, his mouth slanting over hers, their tongues tangling in their own passionate dance.

His heart drummed against her chest, hard enough that she could feel it through his tuxedo jacket. Her head tipped back at the crescendo of sensations as he dropped his mouth to the crook of her neck, his tongue sweeping in intense, hot circles, his breath sounding harsh in the small space.

She gasped when he traced the outline of her rib cage through her dress. Her breasts swelled and ached as his fingers skimmed over her neckline before dipping inside to tease each tight peak. A sizzling tremble ran rampant through her body. His blue eyes burned into hers when the elevator lurched to a halt and he stepped away.

She pressed her hand to her chest as though she could slow the runaway beat of her heart. This was all going so fast, but she needed that speed now that she'd made up her mind not to wait anymore. She'd wanted Quinn, probably had from the moment he'd captivated her full attention at the airport even through her jet-lagged exhaustion. No more holding back. Their tango had been a prelude of what was to come and she wouldn't waste another minute out of his arms now that she'd made the decision to take this risk.

To trust her partner.

When the elevator arrived at his floor, he backed her inside the apartment, guiding her through the vaulted great room and open kitchen that she remembered from the first time she'd been there. Tearing at each other's clothes, they moved as one down a hallway she hadn't seen before, and into a dimly lit bedroom where a lamp shone on a large painting of the Manhattan skyline. In the sitting area, she spied a large desk against one wall and a bank of shade-covered windows on another. When he made as if to tumble them both to the bed, she sidestepped at the last minute.

Just long enough to catch her breath.

Her lips burned from his kisses, her skin tingling everywhere underneath the sensuous silk gown he'd had delivered to her apartment today, complete with a tailor to ensure the hem fell just right. Then the gown had felt like a lover's caress against her skin, the hand-sewn, designer original a decadent luxury. But now, she only wanted the real thing—Quinn's hands all over her. No extravagant dress would do.

"Are we moving too fast?" he asked, brushing his knuckles down her bare arm. "We can slow things down. Take our time. Would you like a drink?"

"No." She didn't need anything to cloud her head. "I just want a moment to take it all in. Savor the sensations."

She rested her hands on his broad chest, admiring the contrast of her pink nails against the crisp white tuxedo shirt, her glittering ring a reminder of all they pretended to be to each other. But she needed this much to be real.

He lifted her hand to kiss the back of her knuckles. The back of her hand. The inside of her wrist. Even that brush of his lips in such an innocuous spot made her simmer inside.

Somewhere in the suite of rooms, a clock chimed twelve. A fairy-tale time...only she wasn't turning into a pumpkin or the girl she'd been before tonight.

Now that she'd stepped onto this path, she was desperate to see where it led. What she would discover. Most of all, she wanted to dance with him. The kind of dance they'd begun at the party and would continue here to its fiery conclusion.

She turned her back and peered over her shoulder. "I might need a hand." She pulled her hair to one side, revealing the zipper. "I want to be careful with the gown."

"Damn the gown." His teeth flashed in the darkened room. "I want what's inside." He eased the zipper down past her hips and she felt the room's temperate air caress her bare skin.

"Are you sure?" She slid the fabric from one shoulder and smiled at him, loving that he let her go at her own pace, giving her time to enjoy this kind of teasing pleasure.

"Lady, I've never been more sure of anything in my life," he growled, unadulterated male appreciation roughening the edges of his voice. Still, he held himself back and she loved the command he exerted over every aspect of his life—even hers. It steadied the out-of-control tilt of her world and made her feel as though she might stop spinning for tonight at least.

The silk whispered as the gown fell around her silver heels. She stepped out of it then turned slowly. He gaped at her, his amusement gone, replaced by an intent, hungry expression that made her stomach clench and warmth pool at the apex of her thighs. As a dancer, she'd always been aware of her body. She'd felt every muscle, sinew and bone, commanded them to move and pose at her will. Yet now she felt less in control and more aware of her body than ever. Standing there half-nude in her black lace bra and panties, she felt her skin heat everywhere his gaze fell. With Quinn, she wasn't just a dancer but a woman brimming with desire and needs that transcended her ambitions, her career, her future. She wanted to gulp down every second of this encounter with him.

When she slid each bra strap down over her arms, his eyes grew hooded. Exhilaration fired through her at his reaction. She commanded attention in a way that had nothing to do with her training, her skills, and everything to do with who she was…or maybe who she was discovering herself to be.

She turned again, unhooked her bra then dangled the scrap of lace from an extended hand, letting the lingerie drift to the polished wood floor. At his guttural groan she smiled, pressed an arm across her aching breasts and turned, crossing one leg over the other as his eyes drifted down then rose slowly, lingering.

"Enjoying yourself?" She stepped between his legs and her knees brushed the edge of the bed.

"Not as much as I'm about to," he vowed then tumbled her down on top of him.

Sofia absorbed the feel of him, from the hard planes of his chest through the starched cotton shirt to the silken glide of his pants along her bare thighs. The metallic pinch of his belt buckle pressed against her abdomen, just above the jutting length of his erection.

He cupped her bottom, fitting her to him in a way that aligned the neediest part of her with that straining length.

"I've thought about doing this," she admitted, skimming a finger along the edge of his jaw. "All week, I thought about it when I was on the phone at night with you."

"When we were talking about the missing matchmaker? Our career hopes and the demands of ballet?" He captured her finger in one hand and brought it to his lips for a gentle bite. "All that time, you were thinking about being naked on top of me?"

"Maybe not every second. But the idea definitely crossed my mind a few times. Especially right after I disconnected the calls." Those had been oddly lonesome moments. She'd felt a growing attachment to him but she hadn't been sure if it was friendship, a sense of being allies at a time when they needed one another, or if it was simply attraction. But each night when confronted with the silence of her apartment, she'd thought about how much she wanted to see him again.

Touch him. Undress him.

His expression grew serious. "I thought about you then, too. It was like the quiet echoed louder once we stopped talking."

His words so nearly matched the way she felt she fought a desire to squeeze him tighter and kiss him senseless. She was already taking a risk tonight in being with him. She wasn't ready for a more emotional leap that might bare too much of her soul.

So, instead, she kissed him.

And for the first time she took the lead in the kiss, exploring the fullness of his lips and taking teasing swipes at his tongue. She tasted and tested, liking the feel of his body under her as she moved around him. Her nipples tightened at the friction of the pleats on his shirt. Her hair slid down to pool on top of him, curtaining them in silky privacy. She could have kissed him for hours, but then he ended the game by rolling on top of her.

A new game began, becoming hotter and more fervent until she became lost in him and the way he made her feel. He palmed her breasts, cradling each in turn as though they were precious weights, his thumb gliding over each tip until the peaks ached with sensitivity. Only then did he lower his tongue to first one, then the other, making her back arch to increase the delicious friction.

She lifted her hands to his shirt, flicking open the buttons and tugging the fabric from his pants. He must have loosened his tie and the top button earlier, because the knot slipped free easily, his shirt suddenly open to her questing hands.

He felt even better than she'd imagined, his bare skin simmering with heat. From the sprinkling of hair on his chest, she followed the lightly furred line down the center of his abs to his pants, but he reared up on his knees and stopped her, unfastening the buckle himself and lowering the zipper to her avid gaze.

Built like an athlete, he had the thighs and butt of a soccer player, his whole composition heavier than a dancer's. Sturdier. Immovable. And yet he'd been light on his feet when he'd taken her around the floor in that surprising tango tonight. Proving he knew how to use all that muscle to enticing effect.

"I want you inside me." She didn't know she'd said the words aloud until her throat rasped on a harsh breath. Reaching to touch his hip, she followed the path of his boxers as they slid from his thighs.

"And I can't wait to be there." He stretched over her, his thigh parting hers as he gave her more of his weight.

Sofia sighed into him, wrapping her arms around his neck, molding her breasts to his chest and fitting her hips to his. He rolled them, as one, to the side of the bed where he tugged a box of condoms from a nightstand drawer. He left them there, a tangible assurance she would get what she wanted.

She cried out when he shifted against her, his thigh pressed at the juncture of hers where she ached for him. Where she wanted more of him. But in an instant, he replaced his thigh with his palm, his fingers playing lightly along the damp silk of her panties, now the only scrap of clothing between them.

Their gazes collided in the half light and the intensity of his expression quieted her hunger for a moment since she could see the same need in his eyes. He wanted her, too. Badly. But he must be holding back for the right moment, spinning out the beauty of the dance until act three instead of jumping straight to the climax.

Who would have thought she'd be the one desperate for more, faster, while Quinn took his time with every delicious sensation, burning this night into her memory—she knew—forever. So, closing her eyes, she gave herself over to him and his sure hands, allowing her mind to savor each shock of pleasure he ignited with his fingers. He pressed gently, testing what made her sigh and gasp, only sliding beneath the silk when she twisted her hips in a silent plea.

And, *oh.*

The slick glide of one blunt finger down the center of her set off one heady contraction after another, her body racked with spasms in a release that shook her to her toes. The waves of pleasure broke over her again and again.

Quinn whispered sweet words in her ear, beautiful encouragement she only became dimly aware of as she floated back from her brief trip to carnal oblivion.

"I can't wait to taste you," he breathed against her ear, the sensual promise alone almost sending her body into another orgasmic frenzy.

"I'm too new to this," she reminded him. "That is, I'm not *totally* new to this, but it's never been like this for me before." She kissed his shoulder, her tongue tasting a hint of salt on his skin. "I might lose consciousness if I have much more pleasure in one night."

He grinned, his male pride evident as he tightened his hold on her waist. "I don't think that's possible, but it could be an interesting experiment."

"I think I'd rather be fully in control of my senses for all of this." She roused herself to draw the arch of her foot up the back of his leg, gratified to see his smile slip, his pupils dilate. "You could take it easy on me this first time."

"As long as there are more times." Hooking a finger in her panties, he dragged them down and off, the action stirring a feather that must have fallen in the sheets from her discarded dress.

Quinn plucked it from the air, drawing it over her hip and up her rib cage, circling her breast. Sweet chills skipped along her nerve endings.

"There will be more times," she promised, knowing this night had to mean something more than simple pleasure. Didn't it?

Refusing to overthink it, telling herself that simple pleasure might be a very good thing, she helped herself to the box of condoms and withdrew a single packet.

Handing it to him, he set aside the feather and went to work ripping open the foil. She took the opportunity to kiss along his biceps, feeling the muscles flex against her lips as he moved. The raw power in his body fueled the fire in her.

When he positioned himself between her thighs, she bit her lip at the sensation of him right there, where she needed him most. Their eyes met. Held. He gripped her hips with one hand and tilted her chin toward him with the other.

Brushing her lips with his, he took his time entering her, letting her get used to the feel of him. Even if it hadn't been a long time for her, it still would have felt brand new for being so different. Quinn wasn't like any man she'd ever met and he treated her body in ways no one ever had before.

So by the time they were joined fully, the sweat on his brow told her how much his gentleness cost him. She kissed his cheek and his jaw, grateful for the tender care. But now, with her body easing around him and the delicious pleasure building again, she could give herself over to the sensations. Let him guide her.

Rolling them over again, he settled her on top of him, giving her a sense of control. His hands remained on her hips, though, setting the pace for each toe-curling thrust. For long moments she lost herself in it—the heat of the friction, the musky scent of his skin, the silken sheets that brushed against her calves. But then, remembering the way Quinn's eyes had heated on the dance floor earlier, she swiveled her hips with the grace and strength that a ballerina had at her disposal, taking him with her on a sensual slow ride.

His eyes closed as he hissed a low, ragged breath, giving her a tantalizing peek at the man behind the sleek, controlled exterior. When his eyes opened, she saw blue fire even in the dimly lit room.

Spinning her to her back, he kept one arm anchored beneath her, his forearm aligned with her spine, one hand at her neck. Nose to nose, he thrust deeply—again and again—until the pleasure was too much to bear. She came in a blinding rush, a cry rising from her throat while the spasms trembled through every part of her.

Quinn held her tight, his release following hers a moment later so that his breathing was as sharp and ragged as hers in the quiet afterward. They lay together in the middle of the king-size bed, limbs still twined and sheets wound around their feet in a soft love knot.

Sofia wanted to remain there, boneless and sated, for as long as possible. She felt so good, for one thing. And for another, she had no idea how to follow up something like that with casual conversation. All her life, she'd been better using her body to express herself than her words and she'd done that tonight, as well.

But as Quinn tucked her against his chest and stroked her hair, she knew there was one significant difference.

She'd built some kind of friendship with him, too. That long walk in the park and their talks on the phone at night had all helped her to feel closer to him and to give her the sensation that maybe he cared about more than just protecting his resorts business from the wrath of her father.

She might have been able to drift into sleep on that hopeful note, but one disturbing truth had emerged from the party tonight. As their breathing returned to normal, Sofia couldn't help but share her worry.

"I hope that journalist was just taking shots in the dark tonight when she brought up the matchmaker." She didn't want that story to come out now. Or ever. Antonia Blakely could whisper her gossip all day long, but if there was no proof her father hired a matchmaker, she wouldn't share the story with the media.

Antonia might be venomous, but she wouldn't risk casting a shadow on her own career.

"It seems an awfully specific detail to pick out of a

hat," Quinn observed in a dry voice. He pulled the blankets over her, tucking her in next to him.

Even so, her skin cooled thinking that Delaney from *Dance* magazine might really have her big scoop.

"Jasmine texted me that she'd look into it." Nervous tension crept into Sofia's shoulders, spoiling the languid pleasure she'd been feeling.

"And you know she will. If she has any advance notice, she'll let us know." His hand roved rhythmically along her arm, then rested on her hip. "But if the reporter actually writes that your father hired a matchmaker, we simply toast to the fact that you got lucky on your first try. And then stay engaged for as long as you need to prove you were committed to finding true love." The five-o'clock shadow on his jaw caught against her hair, a tender intimacy that would have soothed her if not for the direction of a conversation that made her worried.

"I can't tie you up forever." She scooted up to a sitting position, her shoulders tensing. "Maybe we should just come clean. It was all a mix-up anyhow."

Quinn shook his head.

"We're in too deep now. And the backlash could hurt my family's business as much as you."

Those tentative, hopeful feelings of trust she'd put in him earlier now seemed misplaced. Quinn really was staying with her to protect his business interests. To ensure her father's goodwill by doing what she'd asked of him.

"So what would you suggest?" she asked, clutching the sheet to her chest.

"If it comes down to it, we can always get married for real." His teeth flashed white in the darkened room, but his expression was more grimace than grin. "No one would dare to question our love then."

"Only our sanity." Frustrated, she debated calling Jasmine anyhow—if only to reassure herself she was worrying needlessly. She wanted real answers, not a glib treatment of the problem. "I'm serious, Quinn."

"Unfortunately, so am I." He leveled a look at her from across the pillow before dropping a kiss on her temple. "Instead of a fake engagement, we make it a fake marriage. We give it a year and call it quits. Our critics are quieted. Scandal averted."

"You would be willing to go that far?" To *actually* marry. "To share a name, a house and a life when it's all for show?"

And she thought she was the performer in the relationship. Perhaps Quinn was a better actor than she knew. Even with her.

"There's too much at stake now. It's not only your career or your father's threats to McNeill Resorts' European acquisitions." His arms went around her, but the temperature in the room had cooled considerably. For her, at least. He didn't seem to realize the effect his words had as he continued. "My name is on a hedge fund. My clients could pull billions of dollars out if they don't trust my word."

She let the realizations roll over her, remembering all the times her mother had warned her to follow her passions and not chase material successes. As much as she'd tried to do that, she still found herself naked in the arms of a man who would always put his fortune first. It was a timely reminder not to wade any deeper into her feelings for Quinn.

But that didn't stop the truth from cutting deep.

Ten

Two days later, Quinn paced around his personal library at the McNeill Fund headquarters in the Financial District, one floor above the McNeill Resorts' offices.

His brother Ian had returned from Singapore earlier in the week. After giving him a day to recover from the trip, Quinn had asked for his help tracking down Mallory West to ask her some follow-up questions after Cameron's too brief interview with her. Ian had texted both Cameron—returned that morning from Kiev—and Quinn to meet this afternoon to share new information that concerned them both.

Now, with Ian leaning a hip on the front of Quinn's massive desk and Cameron commanding the leather executive chair behind it, Quinn stood at the window looking out over the view of the city, the Woolworth Building in the foreground with other towers stretching as far he could see in the wintry, gray haze.

"So is it true that Mallory West closed up shop?" Cameron asked, pushing back from the desk to test the range of positions available on Quinn's leather chair. "When I spoke to her the last time—"

"That wasn't her you talked to." Ian slanted a glance at their younger brother over his shoulder. Closer in height to Quinn than Cameron, Ian had more of their Brazilian mother's coloring—dark eyes and deeper skin tone—but the shape of his face and features echoed the rest of the McNeills.

His clothes were the most casual today—dark jeans with a gray blazer and a button-down. But that was normal since Ian spent most of his time on job sites around the globe.

"Dude. I think I know who I talked to." Cameron smoothed a hand over his bright blue-and-yellow tie that was as unconventional as the wearer. He might sport a Brooks Brothers suit, but his socks were usually straight out of a Crayola box or else covered with weird graphics from video games. "It was the same woman who spoke to me the first time. Who was helping me find a wife."

"Right," Ian told him dryly. "First of all, you don't order a wife the same way you get a snack from the room service menu. Second, the woman you spoke to on both occasions was Mallory's assistant, Kinley."

"She lied to me?" Cameron stopped messing with the settings on the chair and sat straighter.

Quinn pivoted back toward the room, giving Ian his full attention.

"Kinley has been lying to all of Mallory's clients for nearly a year—almost since the inception of Mallory's debut as a matchmaker—impersonating her employer to protect the woman's real identity." Ian hitched his leg higher on the desk so he could face his brothers better.

"I'm trying to trace her real identity now. But I wonder if part of the reason the matchmaking service closed down was because something went wrong with Cameron's date."

"But the more relevant question is where did Sofia's contact information originate, and who would have added her to the web site that Cameron viewed?" Quinn asked. "The obvious answer is that it was the matchmaker her father hired, but Vitaly swears the woman he hired speaks little English and was tasked to find a Ukrainian husband for Sofia through personal connections, not online." Quinn wanted to bring reassurance to Sofia after the way things had ended on a strained note two nights ago.

He'd run through the events dozens of times in his mind, trying to pinpoint exactly when her attitude toward him had shifted from red hot interest back to overly cautious regard. Was it simple morning-after awkwardness? Or had he upset her and not realized it? Whatever it was, he had the sense they'd taken one step forward and two steps back after the Fortier reception.

She certainly hadn't liked the idea of marriage. And he wasn't any more eager to go down that path than her, even if it would fulfill his end of his grandfather's will. But if he had to marry to help Sofia with damage control in the press? Then he'd be an idiot *not* to at least stick with the marriage for a calendar year to take that family pressure off him.

"Are you kidding? If the woman doesn't speak English, it's all the more likely she was confused about what she posted online." Cameron folded his arms on the desk and pulled himself forward on the wheeled chair. "Talk to Koslov's matchmaker and your problem is solved."

"Possibly." Quinn regretted exploring this end of the matchmaking equation more when he'd already guessed it was a dead end. But how much did he dare look into the Ukrainian woman who was Vitaly Koslov's personal friend?

After assuring Sofia he would ask her father to make sure her dating profile was removed from circulation, Quinn had phoned Koslov, but the guy hadn't exactly been forthcoming with much information. All Vitaly had told him was that he'd hired a close personal friend named Olena to search for a husband for Sofia. But when Quinn suggested the woman must have given out Sofia's travel plans to a US matchmaker to relay to Cameron, Vitaly had gotten angry all over again about Cam's public proposal.

"I'm still going to look for Mallory West, just for the principle of the thing." Heading over to the bookshelves, Ian tipped a silver weight that was part of a perpetual motion machine, sending the oddly shaped pendulum piece swinging and glinting in the fluorescent lights.

"Thank you for all you've done." Quinn appreciated the way his brothers came together as a family even if they didn't always see eye to eye. "If Sofia's father doesn't want to come clean about the role he played in all this, I'm not sure I want to ruffle his feathers anyhow. I had one of my IT techs search for any traces of Sofia's dating profile, and he found nothing. So I feel sure her digital privacy is intact."

"It's unlike you to use company resources for something personal," Ian noted while Cameron just grinned. And grinned.

And grinned.

Damn it.

"Obviously the guy needs overtime and I'm paying him out of pocket." Hadn't that been clear? "And what happened in Kiev, Cam? What's the holdup now on those hotels?"

His brother had taken Quinn's place at the most recent round of meetings on the Eastern European acquisitions, but no paperwork had come through for the purchase.

"Officially, we're waiting on some government bureau to sign off. But if you ask me, it's an excuse they trotted out to hide the fact that Koslov is blocking the sale. His name came up more than once during the meeting."

Thwarted on every front, the day was going to hell in a hurry. "Why would he interfere with the deal after I made it clear I acted in his daughter's best interests?"

"Maybe he's waiting to see how it all plays out," Ian offered. "She's not off the hook yet, especially if that reporter is hinting that she knows something about a matchmaker."

"Which would be his fault, not ours." Quinn hated having to dance to the guy's tune, but as far as the hotel deal went, clearly Sofia's father had plenty of foreign influence.

Quinn debated speaking to that reporter himself to get a better feel for what was going on. He could run interference for Sofia while she was auditioning since the same reporter would be covering it for her magazine.

Besides, he wanted to see Sofia again. Soon.

His cell phone vibrated on the desk, but before his brothers could use the call as an excuse to leave the meeting, the Caller ID flashed their father's name.

"It's Dad," Quinn announced. "Maybe you'd better stick around."

Both of his brothers went stone silent. Their father communicated with them less than ever since he left the family business. He hadn't been in New York for over a year.

"Hi, Dad," Quinn answered, finger hovering over the

button to broadcast the call to the room. "I'm with Ian and Cam. Mind if I put you on speakerphone?"

"No," Liam answered, his voice sounding unusually hoarse. "That will save me having to call them, too."

Concerned, Quinn turned on the feature. "Is everything okay? Where are you?"

A perpetual thrill-seeker, Liam McNeill had gotten himself into some tight spots over the years.

"I'm in China. I figured I'd check out that Mount Hua Shan ascent since your gramps is over here anyhow."

Quinn hadn't heard of it, but he knew the kinds of climbs that attracted his father's attention. "You're with Gramps?"

"Not yet, but I'm heading to Shanghai now. He called me to see if I could come get him out of a local hospital."

All three brothers froze. Quinn could feel the tension in the room as a chill shot over his skin.

"Why?" Ian barked into the phone. "What's wrong?"

"He was on a tour of the city, I guess, and the guide brought him in. There are language barrier issues, of course, but apparently they think he had a minor heart attack and they want to keep an eye on him."

Cameron swore quietly, speaking for every last one of them. No matter his age, Malcolm McNeill had always seemed invincible.

"How far are you from the hospital?" Cameron asked, already loading a map on his phone.

It occurred to Quinn, while his brothers took down the necessary information, that they had taken over his usual role as the leader. He'd froze the first moment he'd heard the word *hospital*.

"Call us when you see him," Quinn barked, finally adding to the conversation. Their father agreed to do so and ended the call.

The three of them didn't say much as they parted. Their father was already in China, so it wasn't as if they needed to jump on the first plane. He'd let them know if they should come to Shanghai.

After his brothers left, Quinn could think of only one person he wanted to see. Needed to see.

And it wasn't about marriage, damn it, even though honoring his grandfather's will now seemed like something he needed to take more seriously.

Right now, he didn't care about that. He just wanted Sofia's arms around him and he was too numb to think about what that might mean.

The night before the most important audition of Sofia's life, the downstairs intercom buzzed.

"Hello?" she asked, not expecting anyone and figuring it was probably a fast-food delivery guy having a hard time getting in the building. How many times had her neighbor ordered a pizza and then decided to walk her dog or get in the shower?

"Sofia, it's Quinn. I need to see you." His tone set off an answering response in her body before her brain had the chance to think it through.

But something in his voice alerted her that it was serious. This was not the sound of her tango-dancing lover or even her friend who could talk her through her nervousness. Something was wrong.

"Of course." She buzzed him inside and shut down the video of one of Fortier's first ballets she'd been watching. She was dancing a piece from it for her audition, hoping to capture the mood of it better than his star had at the time.

But now her focus shifted to Quinn, as it had so often since they'd met, and even more often since they'd shared a night together. Yes, she needed to guard her emotions more around him. Yet she couldn't simply turn her back on their pact when it had been her idea to stay together for appearance's sake.

Or maybe she just really wanted to see him tonight. The idea seemed like a worrisome possibility as she checked her reflection in a mirror over the couch. Her eyes were bright and her color high. She tugged her black cashmere cardigan closer around her, covering the pink tank top she was wearing with silky, gray lounge pants.

"Get a grip," she reminded herself as she moved toward her front door. She was almost there when a sharp rap sounded.

As she swung the door wide, Quinn's gaze snapped up to meet hers. Everything about him looked tense. His flexing jaw. The flat line of his mouth. The set of his shoulders beneath a black wool coat tailored to his broad form.

And yet some of the tension seemed to ease as he looked at her.

"Sofia." He didn't step inside even though she'd made a pathway clear. "May I come in?"

She waved him in and shut the door behind him. He brought a hint of the cold air with him and a slight hint of the aftershave that she remembered on her skin following the night they'd spent together. Like an aphrodisiac, it pulled her closer and she breathed deep for a moment while she stood behind him.

"Can I take your coat?" Idly, she wondered what he thought of her tiny apartment as she hung the beautifully made wool garment on a simple iron coatrack she'd bought at a salvage shop in Long Island.

She might have connections to Quinn McNeill's extravagant world through her father, but she'd never let herself be a part of it. Last week's ill-fated private flight aside, she paid her own way in life in spite of her father's wealth.

"I apologize for stopping by unannounced. My grandfather had a heart attack twelve hours ago." Quinn's stark statement changed the track of Sofia's thoughts instantly.

"I'm so sorry." She'd never forget the pain of her mother's battle with cancer. The hurts were etched on her forever, pain that went so much deeper than anything her profession could ever wreak on her knees or her feet. "Is he okay?"

She reached for him, needing to offer some kind of comfort in spite of all her warnings to maintain her guard around him. She could never deny someone comfort in the face of that kind of hurt.

"I'm waiting for my father to call from Shanghai with an update, but with the time difference…" He shrugged, still wearing the jacket of his black, custom-tailored suit that looked like something off Savile Row. His burgundy tie and crisp, white shirt were an elegantly simple combination. "I don't know how long it might be." He glanced around the apartment beyond the small foyer. "Am I interrupting anything? I told the driver to wait in case you were busy."

Of course he did. Because hedge fund managers didn't just drive themselves around the city. But even that reminder of their very different lives didn't stop her from wanting him to stay.

"I was just going over some notes for my audition tomorrow—"

"I forgot." Shaking his head, he halted his steps before the living area. "Hell, Sofia. I know how important that is—"

"It's fine. I was only getting more nervous anyhow."

She drew him forward, gesturing toward her well-worn couch. "I don't want you to wait for that phone call alone."

No matter that she'd hoped to put up more barriers with him.

He'd been kind to her when she'd been nervous at the reception for Idris. Helped her maintain a façade of an engagement when she'd asked him to. She wouldn't betray their unlikely friendship even if he was better at guarding his heart than she was.

"If you're sure." He still didn't take a seat, however. "I'll stay a little longer." He stopped at a framed photo above an antique wooden rocker. "Is this your mother?"

"Yes." She remembered that moment so well, standing on a rocking boat deck, her mother's arm slung around her shoulders and a new sunburn already making her skin itch. "That's the summer before she died. We went to Greece and sailed with a group of art students around the islands."

"What a year that must have been." He reached to trace Sofia's face in the photo, a gesture she swore she felt on her own skin. "From so much happiness to mourning her."

"She gave very explicit instructions about that." Her throat tightened as she remembered. "We were supposed to celebrate her life. Not mourn. She wanted her ashes taken out to the Aegean so she could sparkle in the sunlight one more time." Sofia smiled at the memory of her saying the words. "She said if I did it, maybe she'd come back as a mermaid. Which, in all my thirteen-year-old wisdom, I called bullshit. But she said I would understand the truth about beauty and magic when I was older."

"And you have." Quinn turned away from the photo, his eyes full of warmth.

"Not really." She rubbed her arms briskly to ward off

a sudden chill despite the cashmere cardigan. "I work hard to create beauty on stage, but I still haven't found anything magical about the sweat, blood and stress fractures that go into ballet."

She hated to sound like a cynic. But perhaps she resented—just a little—that she hadn't inherited more of her mother's free-spirited joy.

"But you saw it that first time you watched *Sleeping Beauty* when you were a girl," he reminded her. "It showed when you told me about that performance. And you admitted yourself that the skill wasn't necessarily impressive. Maybe you only see the magic from the audience."

"Maybe." She conceded the point mostly because she didn't want to bring him down on a night that was already stressful for him. "What about you?" She tugged him to sit beside her on the couch. "Do you see your mom often? I think I read that she's a Brazilian native."

A surprise smile appeared on his handsome face. "Studying up on your fiancé?"

"I had to be prepared to field questions about you since we've been dating for months." She had a lot of her own questions about him. She felt like the man she knew wasn't necessarily the one she read about online.

Lowering himself to the couch cushion beside her, Quinn gave a tight nod. "My mother moved back to Brazil after the divorce. She has a place just outside Rio de Janeiro. I make an effort to call her often, but…"

"But it's complicated?" she offered, touching his hand softly, then linking their fingers.

His mouth cocked into a jaded smile and he rubbed his thumb along the inside of her wrist. "Families are usually more complicated than they seem, aren't they? My parents were married for seven years. My father, for lack of a better description, marches to his own drummer. He's a thrill-seeker, an adrenaline junkie who swept my mother off her feet. He showed up at a bar where she was singing one night after he'd had a close call with a hang glider on a mountain near Rio."

Giving his hand an encouraging squeeze, she nodded at him. "Your mother sings?"

"Not often anymore, but yes. She has a beautiful voice. The night they met, she thought my dad finally saw the error of his ways and was going to stop taking stupid risks." Quinn barked out a low laugh. "But that didn't last long. By the time the rib fractures healed, he was right back to his old tricks. After seven years together, she said she wouldn't follow him anymore and be complicit in watching him kill himself."

From her quick internet searches, Sofia had read that Liam McNeill was a reckless adventurer. And from what she could tell about Quinn, he was almost the exact opposite. Quinn's practical, steady and calculating nature was probably part of what made him such a successful hedge fund manager. His fund set records two years straight for its profit margins. In some ways he reminded her of her own father.

"Your dad didn't try to change?"

"No. He got a lawyer to divide things up evenly— much to my grandfather's frustration—and my mother returned to Brazil permanently. My brothers and I split our time between Rio and New York. Six months with Dad, six months with Mom."

Sofia's brow rose in surprise. "Do you speak Portuguese?"

"Not as well as I did as a child, but yes. Some Spanish, too. The languages definitely help both my businesses, but I'm not sure I'd recommend raising children on two continents to make it happen." The genuine regret in his voice gave her a small peek into his upbringing and the things he must have overcome. How hard would it have been to be away from his mother for half the year at such a young age?

She wanted to know more about him. But with him sitting so close and her feelings about him all over the map, she didn't know how wise it would be to keep up this intimate conversation when their thighs were almost touching.

Plus, he might ask more about her and her own complicated relationship with her wealthy father.

"A man of many talents," she said, pushing off the couch. "Tea?"

She needed to put some distance between them, even just for a moment, to resurrect some fragile emotional boundaries.

"Please. Thank you, Sofia."

Her apartment was small and she moved quickly from the couch to the kitchen area. Sofia kept her teakettle on her stove for easy access. Filling the yellow kettle with water, she placed it on the burner, twisting the knob to high.

"So that tango at the gala…your globe-trotting background explains why you moved so beautifully. It's part of your identity." Leaning up against the stove, she stared at him, remembering the way his body had kept rhythm with hers.

Apparently going to the kitchen wasn't going to prevent her from wanting him. He looked far too good in her home.

"Yes. But I always gravitated more toward life with my grandfather, who ended up caring for my brothers and me more than my dad. Gramps was the one that pushed me—and my brothers—toward responsibility and productivity. In some ways, I'm much closer to him than I am to either of my parents." His expression darkened. No doubt he was worried about the older man.

"I'm sure we'll hear some news about him soon." She remembered the fear of wondering if a loved one was going to be okay. There were nearly two months of her life she'd spent waiting and terrified when her mother was sick. For the first time she really thought about the fact that her father hadn't been much comfort. But then, he was one to lose himself in work—the same way he pushed her to do now and then. Work more. Dance more. Move forward with life and quit worrying about what might be, until sometimes she felt like she was pirouetting so quickly her world was a blur—

The kettle whistled, startling her from her thoughts, and she poured the boiling water into two teacups. They, like the kettle, were flea market finds. Mismatched. But sturdy, full of character. Artistry of a different kind. She plopped the tea diffuser into the cups, the jasmine green tea mixture instantly turning the water a pale, spring green.

As she placed the cups on the fancy serving tray—another mismatched item—she felt his eyes on her. Glancing around her apartment, her cheeks flushed.

What did he think of her and her piecemeal apartment when his life operated at a whole different frequency? She shouldn't care. And it didn't matter. But she felt a rush of stiff-necked pride anyhow.

She carried the tea to the sofa, nearly spilling the whole thing when his cell phone rang. The chime seemed to blare through the small space, unnaturally loud. Rushing to settle the tray, she sat beside him as he answered the call.

"Dad." Quinn sat forward on the couch, his elbows on his knees, all his attention focused on the call.

Sofia wondered if she should give him privacy. But what if he needed her? She moved closer to him in spite of everything. Damn it, she would have wanted someone sitting by her any of those times she'd gotten bad reports about her mom from doctors who didn't know who else to tell. Her father hadn't been there, unaware of her sickness since Sofia's mother hadn't wanted to tell anyone.

"So that's encouraging news, right?" Quinn glanced over his shoulder and their gazes collided.

She hoped, for his sake, that his grandfather would make a strong recovery. Quinn listened to his father while Sofia stared at Quinn's broad back. Even now, she wanted the right to touch him, to be the woman who sat by his side and could loop her arm through his whenever she chose. What madness was this that gave her such strong feelings for him so fast?

Her heart thumped hard as she took a careful sip of the scalding tea and tried not to cavesdrop. But she was so very worried for him.

"You sure you don't want me to call them?" Quinn was asking. "Thanks, Dad."

He disconnected the call and set aside the phone, pivoting to look at her.

"It was minor and they are keeping him for two days for observation. Gramps' doctor in New York is being consulted, because even though it was minor, they want to put a pacemaker in."

"Can it wait until he comes home?" Arranging for medical care in foreign countries was a challenge. She and her fellow dancers had experienced that more than once in their travels.

"We'll let his doctor make the call after he reviews

the tests from the hospital in Shanghai. But Dad says Gramps looks good." Quinn looked better, too. Some of the tension seemed to have rolled off his shoulders since he'd walked through her door.

"I'm so glad to hear it." She set her cup aside and reached for him. She planned to rub his shoulder, maybe. Or squeeze his forearm.

But as she moved toward him, he opened his arms wide and hugged her. Hard.

"Thank you, Sofia." He stroked her back with his big hands, tucking her against his chest. "I was so damn worried."

She would have replied, but her cheek rested against his chest, preventing her from speaking. His arms still squeezed her tight. She settled for planting a kiss on his shirt to one side of his tie. His body was warm beneath the fabric. She could feel his heartbeat beneath her ear. Hear how it picked up rhythm. For a moment time stood still as she thought about what that rapid heartbeat meant. And how the rest of this night might unfold.

He would leave if she asked him to.

She knew without question that how things proceeded from here was her call. But as she edged back to look up at him, she knew she didn't stand a chance of sending him away. Not when her own heart beat faster and her whole focus had narrowed to him.

He was the only man she'd ever met who could make the rest of her world disappear. And the night before the most important audition of her life, maybe she needed the chance to lose herself in the raw passion only Quinn could give her.

Eleven

He wanted to lose himself in her.

Quinn had tried giving her an out, offering to leave so she could focus on her audition. But she had insisted he stay. And after the hellish worry of the last few hours, he was only too glad to shift gears. All that pent-up, tense energy found an enticing outlet in the irresistible woman beside him.

"Sofia." He threaded his fingers through her hair and pulled her to him.

Everything about her was soft and welcoming, from the cashmere sweater to the creamy-smooth skin beneath. He brushed the backs of his knuckles under the cardigan to trace the edge of her tank top. The slow hiss of her breath between her teeth stirred him, calling him to touch her just the way she wanted. Just the way she needed.

"I've missed you." He'd thought about her so often since their last night together. Had it only been two nights ago?

It seemed like two months. He'd wanted her in his bed every moment since.

"I thought I dreamed how good this felt." She kissed the words into his cheek as she undid the buttons beneath his tie.

Quinn tugged at the knot, wanting all the barriers between them gone. He'd taken off his jacket earlier. Now he cursed French cuffs to the skies and back as he undid one and Sofia unfastened the other.

"It was no dream." He tore the shirt off, tossing it on a slipper chair nearby. "I was there, remember? It was better than anything I could have imagined."

"For me, too." She studied his exposed chest. Her gaze hot and admiring, but he wanted her hands all over.

Closing the distance between them, he lifted her against him, startling a squeak of surprise from her while she wrapped her arms around his neck and—much to his pleasure—her legs around his waist.

"Bedroom." He gripped her splayed thighs, cradling them at hip level as he started walking toward a hallway in the back. Her vanilla and floral scent teased his nostrils, bringing back heady memories of things they'd done that night after the welcome reception.

He hadn't wanted to shower the next day, but wanted to savor her fragrance on his skin.

"On the right," she murmured between kisses, her teeth raking gently down his neck. "Hurry."

Her hands smoothed over his back and shoulders, feeling everywhere she could reach. As she moved, her hair stroked his chest, a tantalizing brush of silk each time. She reached to flick a light switch dimmer as they entered the hallway, casting a warm glow where he'd bared one shoulder.

Black cashmere falling away, he nudged aside the tank top strap with his teeth.

"You taste so good." Selfishly, he wanted to keep her up all night, tasting her and tempting her, driving her to that precipice again and again.

But he knew she needed her rest for the audition. This time together had to be enough for tonight.

"You can tell from just one bite?" she teased in a whisper, the hint of her passionate nature setting him on fire.

"I'm hoping like hell I can confirm the facts." He turned them sideways to edge through a partially open door and into her bedroom.

A very white bedroom. A single bedside reading lamp illuminated a high, four-poster painted white with hints of gray details around the carved woodwork and an eggshell-colored duvet atop floor length pale linens. An antique chandelier hung over the bed. Even in the dim light from the bedside, the glass prisms cast small rainbows around the room. Behind the bed, there was a triangular bookcase instead of a headboard, hundreds of leatherbound volumes adding the room's only color.

Quinn set her in the center of the bed, hating to let go of her, but giving himself a moment to unfasten his belt and step out of his shoes. Sofia watched him, rolling one shoulder and then the other out of her sweater until she was down to her pink tank top and pajama pants. When her eyes lowered to where he unzipped his pants, his blood rushed south, turning him to steel.

It made the unzipping an effort, but seemed to inspire Sofia to sidle out of the cotton spandex, revealing that she was wearing absolutely nothing underneath her shirt. At the sight of her pink-tipped breasts, he forgot about his pants and dived onto the bed with her, drawing her down into the thick duvet with him.

Her moment of laughter turned to a gasp of pleasure as he fastened his mouth around one taut peak, drawing her in for a thorough exploration. She twisted beneath him, her hips seeking his. No woman had ever lit him up as fast as she did, heat blistering across his back, and they weren't even naked yet.

Hands raking off the rest of her clothes—the lounge pants and bikini panties—he traced the muscles of her bare calves and thighs, hugging her legs to his chest as he worked his way back up her body. He kissed a path along her hips, relishing the growing warmth in her skin and liking that he'd put it there.

Heart hammering, he ignored his own needs to focus on hers. Parting her thighs to make room for himself there, he kissed her deeply. Thoroughly. Listened to every sigh and hitch in her breath to learn what she liked best as he stroked her over and over with his tongue.

He brought her close to release twice, feeling her body go taut and still. Both times he backed off, not ready to finish. If this was his only time to be with her tonight, he wanted her fully sated. Boneless with the pleasure he gave her. But the third time she tensed, her fingers gripping his shoulders, he took her the rest of the way, helping her savor every last sweet thrill until she collapsed beneath him.

Elbowing his way higher on the bed, he undressed the rest of the way while she caught her breath. He retrieved a condom from his wallet before he tossed aside his pants, placing it on the bed nearby. When he was done, he moved to cradle her against him so he could stroke her hair while she recovered. He wasn't expecting her to rise up from the bed like some kind of pagan goddess and straddle him, but she did just that, arching her eyebrows at him as though she was daring him to object.

As if he ever would.

"You're beautiful," he told her simply, watching her as she positioned herself above him.

She bent low to kiss him and retrieved the condom. She unwrapped it and rolled it into place, her touch tempting him far too much. He took deep breaths. Steadied himself.

Damn, but he wanted her. Now.

When she lowered herself on him, he ground his teeth together to hang on to the moment. And when she started to move, her beautiful body a tantalizing gift, he knew that moment would be seared on the backs of his eyelids forever. She gave him this and so much more tonight.

His body roaring with a new fire, he had no choice but to roll her to her back and hold her there for a long moment. Pulling himself together, he steeled his body for the incredible sensual onslaught of this woman.

After a long pause he kissed her, thrusting deep inside her. She surrounded him with her softness and her scent, her arms winding around his neck, her feminine muscles clamping him tight. Sweet sighs turned to needy cries as he increased the pace, but she met every thrust, driving him higher.

By the time the heat in his blood reached a fever pitch, he'd brought Sofia to that heady precipice again, her body tensing under his. Sweat beading on his brow, he drove inside her once more, propelling them both over the edge.

Breath, limbs and shouts tangling, they held on tight to one another while the pleasure swelled and spent itself. They lay there, heartbeats syncing as they slowed.

Quinn pulled a corner of the duvet over her, covering her pale limbs with the white, downy spread. Her blond hair danced along her jaw as the air shifted around her from the movement of the blanket.

She lay her cheek on his chest and he had a sudden pang at the realization that it all felt too damn right. After the way she'd welcomed him, her care for him extending to his family when she'd urged him to stay until his father called, Quinn couldn't pretend this arrangement of theirs was strictly for show. Something had shifted between them and it was a whole lot more than sex.

He didn't know what it was. But he'd dated women for months without feeling the kind of connection he had to Sofia after a week together. And with his grandfather's health on the line now—because, damn it, the heart attack had scared the hell out of him—Quinn couldn't ignore the idea that had been rolling around his head to cement their relationship.

Too bad she'd already told him that marrying for show was a bad idea. He still didn't understand how that was so much worse than a fake engagement, but he knew where she stood in regard to a fake marriage.

But what if it was for his grandfather's sake?

"I can almost hear you thinking," she said, peering up at him from her spot on his chest, her hair a tousled, sexy mess. "Everything okay?"

Quinn could fulfill the terms of the will and keep her by his side in one move. And maybe help her focus on her career instead of all the drama surrounding her demanding job. It would be good for both of them.

"I have an idea." Shifting her in his arms, he raised them to a sitting position, lifting a pillow behind her back. "And I want you to hear me out."

"I'm ready." She practically glowed from their lovemaking, so it was probably as good a time as any to pitch his idea.

"That night Cameron proposed to you, we were so focused on damage control that we never really talked about why he was in such a hurry to find a wife."

"I thought he was an impulsive guy." Frowning, she raised one bare shoulder in a delicate shrug.

"That's part of it. But he was also unhappy with our grandfather for writing up new terms in his will that dictate each of his three grandsons marry in order to secure a third share of McNeill Resorts. He thought it would ensure the company's future." Quinn felt bad he hadn't told her about it before. But there'd been a lot to learn about each other in a short space of time. He'd been busy trying to acquaint himself with her world while she'd been preparing for her audition and managing the fallout of Cameron's public proposal with the media.

"That sounds…heavy-handed." Sofia straightened beside him, her slight withdrawal feeling like an absence. "Why would he think that forcing his heirs into marriages would give his business more stability? Surely he must know those unions won't necessarily be durable."

"He refused to elaborate on his motives before he left for a month-long trip overseas. Privately, I've wondered about his state of mind, and whether my father's very expensive divorce from my mother was a factor in Gramps' decision." The legal termination of their marriage had made her a rich woman able to live anywhere in the world she wanted. Unfortunately it wasn't anywhere near her sons. "But Gramps had his lawyer unveil the new will three weeks ago and so far he's refused to change it. As it stands, each of our portions of the company will be sold at auction if we don't follow the rules and stay married for at least a year."

The air between them stilled. He felt her body tense further, like a wound spring.

"So Cameron wanted to marry me to save his shares

in the company?" Her voice hardened, her eyes wide as she swung on him. "He really was looking for a modern-day mail-order bride. And you knew this all the time? Oh. My. God."

Quinn hadn't expected such a strong reaction, especially since she'd met Cameron in person. His brother—while headstrong—wasn't a bad guy.

"Cameron was the most incensed about the terms because he is close to my grandfather and is most invested in the family business. I think he hoped a rash engagement might make Gramps see he'd pushed us too far." At least, that was the reasoning as Quinn understood it. With Cameron, who knew?

Cameron had yet to give him an explanation that made any sense in his mind.

"So, basically, to hell with me and my feelings. I was just supposed to be the wife of convenience for him." Sofia shook her head, then took a deep breath as if trying to hang on to her patience. "I hope he's not going to try that again with someone else."

The silences between her words seemed to grow longer, more deliberate and awkward. Was he being shut out?

She paused, her voice getting quieter. "What about you, Quinn? Are you going to marry and follow your grandfather's rules?"

He couldn't read her right now. Didn't know if she was already thinking he was ten kinds of ass for considering it. Or if she could possibly have the same idea in mind as him: that a marriage between them could be beneficial all the way around since she'd been pressured by her father to settle down, as well.

"I wasn't planning on it." He chose his words carefully, well aware he was walking on thin ice here, not wanting to lose what they'd just shared. He still wanted to explore where it might lead. Might? Where it damn well was heading at the speed of light. "But I'll admit that having my grandfather's health in question now makes me rethink how much I want to dig my heels in about protesting the will."

"Meaning?" She lifted an eyebrow in silent question.

"Meaning…" He was in too deep to turn around, but he realized midstream he probably should have prepared more. Had a real ring that was from him and not Cameron. Thought about what to say. But, too late now. He'd come this far already and he was a man used to making executive decisions quickly, firmly, decisively. "Why don't you and I get married?"

How could a man she'd only just met break her heart in such a short space of time?

She'd known Quinn for a week, but it had been an intense time with a lot of personal upheaval for her. Maybe that's how she'd come to care about him far too much, far too quickly. The turmoil had forged a bond between them, yoked them together. The heat of their passion and the high stakes of preserving her public relations campaign had driven her into the arms of a man that could not emotionally provide for her.

He'd slipped around tattered defenses when she was battling injuries, professional jealousy and worries her career could end before she had a plan B in place. Before she knew it, she was opening her heart to a man wholly inappropriate for her.

It wasn't his fault that her heart ached so fiercely she wanted to hold on to her chest to try to ease the pain. No. The fault was all hers for not protecting herself better, especially when she'd known that he was getting under her skin and making her care.

"Sofia?" Quinn's fingers brushed along her jaw, tipping her face up so he could see her better. She wanted to fold into his touch, melt into him again. But things between them had changed. Everything had. "It could solve a lot of problems for both of us. Quiet the speculation about our engagement with the reporters and with your peers so you can focus on the art that's most important to you. And, of course, it would secure my grandfather's legacy and fulfil his lifelong dream for his grandsons to run the company. At least where I'm concerned."

"If he'd really wanted that," Sofia interjected, leaning away from Quinn's touch, the chill of the apartment flooding the space where his fingers had lingered, "he could have just given you each a third of the business."

"I think he wanted to—"

"No," she said, forcing strength into her voice. She couldn't pretend to listen seriously to this idea when Quinn had crushed a piece of her by even suggesting it. "I know I agreed to hear you out, but I understand what you are proposing."

The thought ripped through her, wounding her more deeply than any injury dance could ever give her. Ballet could never betray her like this.

"It would only be for one year," he clarified. "Like dating with incredible benefits for both of us. I could help you solidify your career plans during that time so when you're ready to quit dancing you have a future you're excited about."

He understood her practical needs so well. Unfortunately he didn't have any idea about the emotional end of the equation.

"Most people don't put a time limit on a marriage, but

thank you for making that perfectly clear." She shot out of bed, dragging a sheet with her, unable to sit quietly by while he spouted more ideas that were like small knives to the naïve vision she'd had of continuing a relationship. "I really thought we had a connection, Quinn."

Stepping behind a screen, she flipped the sheet over the top because damned if she was baring any more of herself to him. She found her tank top on the floor and yanked it back on. Then she slid her pants into place, desperate to put boundaries between them, any sort of boundary at this point.

"We do. I never would have suggested this otherwise." She heard the creak of the mattress and the whisper of his clothes as he slowly got dressed. "I don't understand why you're so upset."

"I'm upset you never mentioned this will and the need for all the McNeill men to marry, when it feels highly relevant to our arrangement." Stomping out in her tank and pants, she found her sweater and punched one arm through each sleeve. "You even suggested marrying if worse came to worst and the *Dance* magazine writer published something unsavory about me. That would have been the perfect time to clue me in about the will and how—by the way—it would check off some boxes for your goals, too."

"How is me using a marriage to satisfy the terms of my grandfather's will any different than you using an engagement to smooth over your public relations agenda before a big audition?" Quinn stood, his clothes on but his shirt unbuttoned, the tie loose around his neck.

"I was trying to maintain focus on my career during a drama that had *nothing* to do with me. You're trying to protect your bottom line." She lobbed the accusation at him and hoped it found its mark.

"No." A new stillness went over him, alerting her that she'd at last gotten through to him. "Actually, it's about protecting family, which is the most important thing to me."

Watching the pain flash across his face sent a tiny prick of regret stabbing through her. She couldn't forget how devastated he'd looked when he'd walked into her apartment tonight. But, damn it, he had hidden the truth from her.

"You told me that billions of dollars of investments would be at risk if people don't trust you, but how are you worthy of trust if you treat a person as deceptively as you've treated me?" she reminded him. Reminded herself. She kept having to do that. "So, to a certain extent, it is about the money."

"If it was just about the money, I would find another way. I know it doesn't mean much to you, but I'm fairly good at making it." His mouth twisted. His jaw flexed. "I only care about making sure my grandfather's life's work is not lost to strangers because of his desire to see the family settled."

He waited for her to say something. But she was at a loss, empty after a night where passions had run high. Her emotions were spent and she didn't know what—or whom—to trust.

She stared at the rainbow colors leaping from her engagement ring in the muted light of her bedroom. It was the physical manifestation of every lie and deception.

With more bravado then she felt, she twisted the ring from her finger, hoping that with its absence, she'd be able to focus on why she was here in New York. On why she didn't get involved.

"I'm sorry, Quinn. But I don't know how to move forward from this. I know I asked you to pretend we were engaged to help me, but I release you from our agreement." Handing back the ring, she was done with false promises and a relationship that was just for show.

She'd finally learned to put some trust in her partner, and it had been a mistake that had cost her dearly.

Quinn stared at the ring in his open palm for a long moment.

The moment echoed between them. Her heart hammered; she was wretched. If he would just walk away now, she'd be able to curse him, move on. But he just stood there, a lingering shadow of what could have been.

"I know that people are important, Sofia, not the bottom line." His hand closed into a fist around the ring, the whites of his knuckles showing. "Has it occurred to you that you're so busy seeing the bottom line—in my case, a wealthy one—and that you're not seeing the person behind it?"

His eyes held hers. Challenging her.

"I don't know what I see anymore," she said tightly, barely hanging on to the swell of raw emotions seething just below the surface. She wrapped her cashmere sweater around her like shrink wrap to hold herself together. "I don't know what to believe."

"I'm not going to be the one to break our engagement." He set the ring on a whitewashed narrow console table by the bedroom door. "Keep this in case you need it to stem unwanted questions from reporters about its absence. And good luck tomorrow."

He walked out of her bedroom. Out of her apartment. The door shut quietly behind him. Only then did she allow her knees to give out beneath her. Curling on her bed, she wouldn't let herself her cry. Not when she had the most important audition of her life tomorrow.

There would be time enough for heartbreak afterward.

But as she closed her eyes, a tear leaked free anyhow. Despite her famous iron-clad professional discipline, her body had its limits for what it would do based on sheer will. She could dance on stress fractures and bunions, pick herself up after her dancing partners dropped her on a hard, unforgiving floor that would leave her body bruised for weeks.

Yet she'd discovered tonight that her eyes would go on crying even if she told them not to. And her heart would keep on breaking the longer she thought about Quinn. In spite of all reason and practicality, she'd fallen head over heels in love with this man.

Twelve

Turning around the stage in petit jeté jumps, Sofia prepared to dance for Idris Fortier. The choreographer sat in the middle of the small practice theater, which would be a closed set for the next hour. He'd allowed Delancy to sit off to one side with her camera, but had requested she not film during the session.

Even Delaney had been too cowed by Fortier to gainsay him. Sofia smiled to think how quietly the journalist had slunk to the sidelines to watch Sofia perform.

"Are you ready, darling?" the choreographer called up to her now, his accent lingering over the endearment even though his eyes were still on his tablet screen.

"I'm ready." She'd barely slept the night before and wondered if her parting with Quinn was going to cost her this audition, too.

The role of a lifetime. The cementing of her place in the ballet world. Some dancers were principals twelve, fifteen or even more years. Sofia knew her knees were on borrowed time. She might come back after the surgeries she would one day need, but a dancer never knew if she would be as skilled afterward.

She needed her career on fast forward in order to have the kind of post-dance life she envisioned for herself. To still work in the field and be able to hold her head high.

"What will you be dancing for me today?" He put his tablet aside and adjusted the small, round spectacles on his nose, giving her his full attention.

Sofia had planned for weeks to dance one of Fortier's dances. A flattering compliment. Plus, dancing a younger choreographer's work meant that there were fewer ballerinas she could be compared to. New pieces allowed a dancer a little more room for interpretation. But after the tears she'd shed last night, she'd arisen from bed this morning with the Black Swan in her heart and ready to burst through her toes.

"Black Swan. The final act in the Grigorovich version." She could dance that one without a partner since there was less emphasis on the pas de deux so important in the Balanchine version.

"An interesting choice, Ms. Koslov. Wholly unexpected."

She had no way of knowing what he'd expected. But most experienced dancers left the world's most well-danced pieces alone for situations like this since they left too much room for comparison. Today, Sofia did not care. She strode to the side of the stage to start her music, which gave her a twenty-count of silence to walk to position. She wanted to dance the hell out of a virtuoso piece and demonstrate the technical skill her critics all agreed she possessed.

And if she couldn't add the extra layer of emotion that

some say was occasionally missing from her work? She didn't deserve the part. Because today, she was nothing but raw emotion with Quinn's parting words still echoing in her head.

You're so busy seeing the bottom line...you're not seeing the person behind it.

As if *she'd* been the one to focus on his wealth.

Banishing the thoughts from her head, she took solace in the music and let Odile's seduction blast away everything else. She didn't want to be hapless Odette who lost Siegfried even though she hadn't done a damn thing wrong. Right now, she needed the fiery passion of Odile to lure Siegfried to his lonely end.

With multiple pirouettes spinning her across the stage, Sofia articulated every phrase, letting the music fill her as she poured out the role. Space-devouring leaps ate up the stage. Fast fouettés flowed naturally, one after the other. She didn't dance so much as she burned—all the heedless energy and longing of the night before torched through this one outlet she understood.

When she reached the end of the coda, the final fouetté perfectly timed, Sofia held her position into the silence, her breathing so heavy the pull of air was the only sound in the theater.

Until one person clapped. The fast, excited clap of genuine praise. And since Sofia could see her evaluator seated, unmoving, before her, she knew it hadn't been him doling out enthusiasm. Had Delaney truly been impressed? It didn't matter, but after tossing and turning about this dance all night, Sofia felt gratified to think someone had liked it. The journalist might be motivated by gossip scoops that would sell more magazines, but the woman would certainly know her ballet.

"Thank you, Ms. Koslov." Idris Fortier rose to his feet

and glanced sharply to his right. "I'd like a moment alone with my dancer, please?"

Sofia went to shut off her music while she heard Delaney making moves to leave the theater. As she wiped down her face with a clean towel, Sofia caught her breath and turned to find Idris standing very close.

"Oh." She stepped back to give herself room. "I didn't hear you." Her shoulders tensed; she hated to feel crowded and had anxiety in social situations where the professional pressure was high. For a split second she wished Quinn would show up—

And how ridiculous was that?

Her brief engagement was over, her ring still at home on the console where he'd left it.

"You have my full attention for this position, Sofia." Fortier's accent—French by way of Tunisia—had a peculiar but pleasant inflection.

"I realize you still have several dancers to audition." She should be pleased, she knew. She'd hoped to impress him and she seemed to have accomplished that.

But why was he standing so close? She folded her arms.

"The part is yours now if you are willing to work hard for it." He took her arms and unfolded them, extending them. He studied her body. "Black Swan really shows off your Russian training. You have beautiful extension."

Her body was part of her art, she reminded herself. Ballet was incredibly physical and she'd been touched often in her career by other dancers, directors and choreographers. So while Idris's touch felt a bit too informal for their first true professional meeting, it certainly wasn't out of bounds.

And…he'd said she had the part? Excitement trembled through her as she became aware of rehearsal music in the next studio over. A group was working on an interpretation of Vivaldi's "Four Seasons."

"I am prepared to devote everything to the project," she told him sincerely. She'd pinned all her professional hopes on it.

His hands lingered on her wrists as his dark eyes met hers.

"What will your new fiancé think of you spending all your time with me?" He didn't move. Didn't release her.

She stepped back, pulling her wrists from his hold but easing any offense with a smile.

"He will be proud of my success." She refrained from mentioning that her engagement had ended. With the strange dynamic at work in the room, she felt that it would be good protection from any misguided notions Idris might have about her becoming his lover, the way his last two featured performers had.

"Will he?" The choreographer narrowed his gaze and backed up a step. "Many new relationships are full of jealousy. That can destroy a dancer's focus."

It would destroy anyone's focus. But she could see his point. Besides, using her relationship with Quinn for show was exactly what she'd said she wouldn't do anymore. She'd wanted honesty about their relationship, not more subterfuge.

"Actually, our engagement is off," she confided. "We aren't announcing it to the press, but it was all so sudden—"

"This is very good news, Sofia." He smiled in a way that unsettled her.

It was almost as if he'd been expecting her to say that. She'd known the man for less than an hour and already she didn't like him. Artists could be strong personalities though. Maybe that accounted for it. And sometimes, the more successful, the more eccentric. Backing up another step, she bent to retrieve her phone, disconnecting it from the external speaker that had played her audition music.

"For me, as well. I couldn't be more pleased to work with you on a new ballet." When she straightened, he was still there, closer than ever.

His eyes were fastened to her left hand. He picked it up and kissed her ring finger before she could yank her hand back.

"Just happy to see this place is bare and that you are free," he explained, finally stepping away from her. "Let's go to lunch and celebrate the launch of our new partnership."

"I can't today." She hadn't even showered. She'd barely slept. And she had a very strange vibe from him that she needed to seriously consider. "I have another appointment."

"And I thought you were prepared to devote everything to this project?" The man's tone withered.

Damn it. She wasn't going to play this game. She'd worked too hard for her spot at the top of the company to be treated this way—even by a major star of the industry.

"Everything within the bounds of professionalism. And since I knew you had two other dancers to audition, I haven't cleared my schedule yet to begin working on new development."

"Perhaps you shouldn't bother. I can see you're not excited to begin." He gave her body a meaningful look, one she'd seen too often leveled at a dancer desperate for a break.

"If you're looking for a creative partnership, Mr. Fortier, I can't wait to begin." She didn't want to lose the role on a misunderstanding or because she was admittedly testy today.

Then again, she wasn't going to let him touch her, kiss her finger and stare at her body without calling him out.

"What if I'm looking for more, Ms. Koslov? What if I've read your reviews about passionless performances and I think I could be the man to inspire a creative fire that would make you unforgettable in every viewer's eyes?"

Anger simmered. She knew her Black Swan had just contained so much damn passion she'd burned down the room with it.

"How exactly would you accomplish that?" she asked, hearing a scuttling noise in the backstage area.

Had someone else entered the small theater or was that just wishful thinking?

He leaned closer, not touching her, but lowering his voice considerably. "Put yourself in my hands, Sofia, and you will see."

She didn't know if that was intended to be seductive, but she'd had enough of walking the edge of creepiness with him. And maybe her time with Quinn had given her enough confidence in herself to know she had all the passion she needed inside. This man couldn't undermine her with his smarmy insinuations.

A voice niggled at her, making her wonder if she could have walked away so confidently a week ago.

"I wonder if you actively seek out the most insecure women for your games, Mr. Fortier?" She backed away from him. "But I am not one of them, I assure you. I know my own worth. And I can admire your artistic excellence without being madly in love with you. I hope you will respect me enough to do the same for me."

Padding across the floor in her ballet shoes, Sofia left him to splutter condemning warnings about the future of her career. He threatened to tell the world she'd flubbed the audition and that's why she didn't get the part. And while that hurt, she refused to engage with him any further. She gathered her dance bag to change in a more private dressing room when she ran into Delaney.

The reporter held up a quieting finger as if she didn't want to be discovered, then waved her out into the corridor while Fortier ranted about naïve girls who didn't understand the way the world worked. What a disappointment the man had turned out to be. Usually news about people like him—a lecherous creep in the ranks—traveled along the dance grapevine quickly. She wondered if she'd alienated her fellow dancers too much in the past and that's why she hadn't already heard it for herself.

"Sofia, I taped a little of your audition," Delaney confided privately. "And I stayed behind even when he told me to leave—"

"My God." Sofia slammed through another door into a private dressing room empty except for open bags and discarded street clothes; everyone else was rehearsing right now. "Are there any lengths you wouldn't go to in order to get a story?" she fumed.

"No." The reporter set a small disk on the makeup table in front of Sofia. "But in this case, you should be thrilled since this can prove you danced your freaking toes off. You were amazing back there."

"You think so?" So maybe the self-worth she bragged about to Idris Fortier wasn't quite as steadfast as she'd pretended. Who didn't love to hear good reviews?

"I know so. And the footage I got shows it." She tapped the disk. "I heard that bastard threaten to tell people you flubbed it. I couldn't hear everything that happened before that, but it sounded like he was coming on to you?"

"Yes." Sofia dug through her bag for her facecloth. "I tried to tell myself he was just eccentric, but in the end, there was no mistaking he was angling for me to kiss his ass. And more."

"Bastard." Delaney frowned. "I took the footage hoping to use it to persuade you to give me a story about Cameron McNeill using a matchmaker."

"Excuse me?" She set down the cleansing cloth, shaking her head in disbelief.

"I moonlight for a gossip magazine on the side. It pays better." She shrugged, unapologetic. "It's expensive to live anywhere near this city. I was a dancer once, you know. A halfway decent one. But after I got hurt, my options were limited. I'd like to write about ballet and only ballet. But there's no money in it."

"What did you hear about Cameron using a matchmaker?" Sofia asked, needing to know what she was up against. Now that she'd ended her relationship with Quinn, she wouldn't have his help figuring out what to do next.

"Just that he hired Mallory West to find him a bride. I'm going to publish that much, but if you can give me anything else to add…"

"You're trying to trade the audition footage for information?" Sofia was going home and going to bed for a week. She couldn't deal with this toxic environment. Especially not with her heart breaking over Quinn and her career very likely in the dumps now that she'd told off the most respected choreographer of her time.

"I thought about it. But I can't do it." The journalist shoved the disk closer. "I can't stand it when guys try to use their position to manipulate women. Consider this me cheering on your rejection of his slimy suggestions."

"In that case—" Sofia put the disk in her bag along with her pointe shoes "—thank you. I can't help you with any information about the McNeills, though."

"Is your engagement really over with Quinn?" the other woman asked. "Or were you just saying that to convince Fortier you could do the role?" Delaney pointed to Sofia's bare ring finger.

"No comment." Sofia smiled brightly to hide the fact that just hearing Quinn's name hurt today.

He'd been such a generous lover the night before. Could a man so giving in bed really want to deceive her as thoroughly as she'd accused him of doing? She wished she had some perspective on the situation. Later, she would call Jasmine and ask for her best friend's advice. For now, she needed to go home and wrap her sore knees.

"Fine. But if you want my two cents, I would not let that man go." She shoved the strap for her black leather satchel onto her shoulder and checked her phone. "Besides being one of the city's most eligible bachelors, he seems to only date people he really cares about, you know? You won't see his name in the gossip rags, that's for sure." The woman headed for the door, shoving her phone into the back pocket of black jeans under a quilted blue parka. "And there was an older woman looking for you backstage earlier. With an accent. Oleska? Olinka?"

"Olena?" Sofia stilled. Olena Melnyk was one of her father's oldest friends from Ukraine. They'd visited with her briefly in Kiev after one of Sofia's performances. What was she doing in New York?

Delaney snapped her fingers. "That's it. I told her you'd probably be in the main theater after this."

Grabbing her bag, Sofia left the dressing area to peer inside the main theater. She didn't feel guilty about going home for the day. She didn't have any rehearsals scheduled and she'd substituted her audition for a class to keep her limber. The audition had been as physically demanding as two classes—a fierce workout for certain.

"There you are." A voice sounded behind her, the thick Ukrainian accent familiar since it still colored her father's speech.

"Olena." Sofia turned to find the petite, round-cheeked woman pacing the halls outside the theater. "My father didn't mention you were coming to New York. How nice to see you."

Olena wore a red scarf around her head and tied under her chin, the bright silk covering hair that had faded from blond to gray, but still gleamed with good health in the bright overhead lights.

"I go to Des Moines to visit my son. But I stop in New York when I find out your father, he is angry with me." She gestured with her hands, agitated.

Sofia spoke very little Ukrainian, so she was grateful for Olena's English. Although, at the moment, she wondered if her father's childhood friend had chosen the right words. Why would her father be mad at her?

"I can't imagine why he would be." Sofia hadn't spoken to her father since the flight home from Kiev, letting Quinn intervene on her behalf because she'd been so upset with him. She'd been ignoring his calls for days. "He was so glad to see you the night after my performance—"

"He is furious I did not choose Ukrainian husband for you. That I allow New York rich man to meet your plane." Her round cheeks deflated with her frown. "I am so sorry, my girl."

"*You're* the matchmaker he hired?" Sofia leaned into the back of a nearby theater seat, revising her perspective on her father's underhanded scheme.

Something about "hiring" his good friend from the old country—a woman who had helped him with his history homework in grade school—seemed far more forgivable than if he'd contracted an expensive global dating agency.

While still underhanded of him, at least there was something personal about the approach.

"Yes." She gave an emphatic nod. "He told me, 'Olena, find our girl a good man.' But afterward, Vitaly very angry I did not choose man from old neighborhood."

"He never told me that he wanted to hire a matchmaker." And the more she thought about that, the more she remembered how his pressure to get married had undermined her. As did his insistence she take his money. Had her father been holding her back from becoming self-confident all this time? Yet a voice inside her persisted; something had changed to give her a newfound strength and belief in herself. "And then, my photo and contact information ended up on a web site for men seeking wives—"

"I did this." Olena patted her chest to make it clear. "Come, we walk and talk. I explain where walls do not have ears." She glared at a young ballerina who had come out into the hallway, probably just trying to find a place to smoke.

The girl skittered back into the theater while Sofia tried to process what the woman was saying.

"You posted my photo on a site for men seeking a quick marriage?" Sofia asked as they walked out into the chill of a New York winter, a crust of snow covering most of Lincoln Center.

"My nephew helped. But I am very clear." Olena pounded one fist against the palm of her hand, her heavy silver rings glinting in the sun. "I say, my girl only date men ready to marry."

Sofia closed her eyes briefly, letting that news wash over her. Her father had asked an old friend to find her a Ukrainian husband. Instead, Olena had gone online to advertise her. No wonder Cameron had only gotten half of Sofia's details. The older woman was hardly a professional matchmaker. Just a well-liked woman from her father's hometown.

"So you told someone about my plane landing in New York?" Sofia wasn't ready to fight her way through the crowds on the subway yet. Maybe she'd walk for a while to let the fresh air clear her head and sooth the ache in her heart.

"First, I check the name of the man who asks about my Sofia. Very rich. Very handsome. I give details of flight." She shrugged her shoulders. "But you are not happy?"

Halting on the sprawling mezzanine outside Lincoln Center, Sofia let the snow fall on her as she watched the lunchtime traffic fill the streets. She wasn't about to delve into a long explanation of why she hadn't want her father in charge of her dating life. But she didn't mind sharing why she wasn't happy.

"I am only unhappy that my father thinks he can control my life. That he could manipulate me into marrying a wealthy man who moves in the same kind of circles as him." Her hands fisted inside the bright yellow mittens that a fan had knitted her long ago —a young ballet student who hadn't been invited into the company after graduation. The girl had moved back to Nebraska, but had given the mittens to Sofia as a thank you for inspiring her.

Oddly, looking down at them now made her realize that was a little bit of magic in her career. She'd told Quinn there wasn't any—only hard work. But that wasn't entirely true. Touching someone else's life, making a difference—that was beauty and magic combined. An insight she wondered if she would have realized without Quinn.

"It is not the point to be rich." Olena gripped her shoulders with her weathered hands. "It is the point to be a good man. And this McNeill, he is smart and successful. His smile is kind."

"So the fact that he is wealthy was incidental?" She shouldn't be hung up on it. The fact that she protested it only proved Quinn's point that she was too focused on the bottom line and didn't see him for himself.

Had she made a horrible mistake in sending Quinn away?

"Rich man focus on you instead of struggle to make life for himself. But there are good men everywhere." Olena spread her arms wide to point to the whole city. "You look beyond this small corner where dance is all you do. Find different men who give you new look at world, yes?"

"Yes." Sofia agreed, although in her heart she knew that search wouldn't be happening for a long time.

"Good. Then I have done my job." Olena patted her cheek. "I will not help anymore, as you ask. Tell Vitaly that we spoke, yes? He will forgive me then, I think." The older woman pulled her in for a hug and a kiss on each cheek. Exchanging goodbyes, she turned on her furry boots and stalked toward the subway station through the crusty snow.

Totally spent on every level, Sofia turned toward downtown to start the walk home. She might give in and get the bus in a dozen blocks or so, but right now she needed the fresh air. Striding across the mezzanine, she neared the crosswalk when a black Escalade rolled to a stop at the curb. She wasn't sure why her eye went to it.

But when Quinn McNeill stepped out of the back door of the chauffeured vehicle, she felt his presence like an electric shock.

"Sofia." He beckoned her through a veil of snowflakes. "Can I give you a ride home?"

Her pulse sped, her mouth going dry at the sight of him. How had he gotten more handsome since the night before?

"No. Thank you." She could hardly resist him from ten yards away. She would have no chance of denying him anything if she sat beside him in the warm comfort of that luxury SUV. Especially after Olena's pep talk about finding someone who made her see beyond the confines of her narrow world.

She questioned her feelings for Quinn, what she'd learned from him, but, damn it, this was still so new.

But her refusal didn't make Quinn jump back in his ride and leave. He exchanged a word with the driver before dismissing the vehicle. Then he strode toward her, his long, denim-clad legs covering the space quickly.

Even before he reached her, she knew she was toast. She'd stood up for herself to Idris Fortier. Held her ground with Delaney the nosy reporter. Danced the best piece of her life.

She didn't have the reserves for the temptation that Quinn McNeill presented.

He paused a few inches away from her.

"We need to talk."

Thirteen

Quinn had had his driver circle Lincoln Center for the last hour so he wouldn't miss Sofia after her audition. Jeff had promised to keep an eye on the exits so Quinn could work, but he couldn't have concentrated on anything else anyway.

Thoughts of the woman now standing in front of him had consumed him ever since he'd walked out of her apartment the night before. He'd felt that she'd needed him to leave, so he had. And he'd been offended that she'd reduced their relationship to economic differences that didn't matter. But, apparently, they mattered to her. Today, he realized that if he was serious about her, he needed to take her concerns seriously, too. That meant he was going to do a better job listening and paying attention, not just lining up his questions while already thinking ahead to his next move.

He had a few ideas for how to show her he was committed to her and not some temporary marriage to fulfill the terms of a will. But that's all they were—vague ideas. And he hated not having a solid game plan to win her back. In a short space of time she had become his most important priority and he was shooting from the hip with her.

She defied business logic.

She was art.

She was magic.

And, by God, he wanted her to be his.

"I was going to take a walk," she told him, looking so damn beautiful in her dark bomber jacket with a shearling collar pulled up to her heart-shaped face. Her hair looked like it had been in a ballet bun at one point, the ends all wavy and still a little damp. Tall boots covered most of her leggings, so she looked warmer than the last time they'd taken a walk together. Her bright yellow mittens reminded him of the sunny teacups she'd used the night before when she'd made him tea. But she was full of those contrasts—the worldly sophistication next to her more bohemian tendencies made her who she was.

A very special woman able to stand on her own feet.

Or tiptoes.

"I'll go wherever you like," he assured her. "But if we walk through the park again, we might have more privacy."

Also, he hoped traveling that route held happy memories for her, too. He needed every advantage at his disposal to ensure she didn't turn her back on him forever.

"That's fine." She nodded, heading toward Central Park the way they had after the meeting at Joe Coffee the week before.

"How was the audition?" he asked, knowing how much it meant to her. He reached for her bag, but she didn't give it to him to carry and he didn't press her.

"I nailed it," she said flatly, snowflakes swirling around them. "He offered me the role."

"That's incredible, Sofia. Congratulations. But I would have thought you'd be more excited." Maybe she was as tired as him.

Had she spent half the night thinking about the way they'd parted, too? He wished she would have agreed to join him in the Escalade where he could have spent his time watching her expression and gauging what she was feeling instead of looking out for traffic.

"It was clear to me that he expects to have an intimate relationship with his feature lead." She shoved her yellow-mittened hands into her coat pockets. "I made it clear to him I would be thrilled to work with him if our relationship is strictly professional. But honestly? I didn't like him, and I'm not sure I'd work with him even under the best of circumstances."

Anger surged through Quinn and he vowed right then and there he would make that man pay. Somehow. Some way.

But for now, he needed to focus on Sofia.

"Bastard." He wanted to pound the crap out of the guy. "Who the hell does he think he is?"

"A man who hasn't heard 'no' very often." She walked fast, giving away how angry the incident had made her. "An entitled, self-centered man who has let his reviews go to his head."

"I'm so sorry you had to deal with that. For what it's worth, it sounds like you handled it well."

"That reporter, Delaney, was lurking behind stage and overheard what happened." They crossed Central Park West and headed south to find entry onto a walking path. "At least if Fortier tries to discredit me or lie about what happened, I have a witness."

Hell. That hadn't even occurred to him. Sofia really could take care of herself and he respected the hell out of her for that.

"Would she tell the truth?" Quinn didn't know what to expect of the journalist who had seemed happy to sell anyone out for a story.

"To my surprise, I think she would." Sofia turned into the park ahead of him, still walking fast, as though demons followed close on her heels.

"Sofia." He took her arm gently, needing to get a better handle on what was happening here. "Please slow down. Should we go back there now and confront him? I'd be glad to—"

"No." She shifted her weight from one foot to the other, as if she had too much energy and didn't know where to put it all. "Definitely not. I'll call the ballet mistress tonight and tell her what happened. But I wasn't nervous. I was cool and professional. I danced the best I ever have. So, on some level, it was a good day because I drew on new strengths I didn't know I had." She stood still again, her wide blue eyes landing on his and seeming to really see him for the first time. "I'm only getting nervous again now because...you're here. And you said we needed to talk?"

Right. He'd asked for this audience, not realizing she'd just had one of the hardest days of her life. He tried reaching for her bag again.

"Please. Let me carry this for you."

She bit her full bottom lip for a moment, then passed him the bag. He felt like some medieval knight who'd just gotten his lady's favor tied to his sword.

They kept walking east, roughly following the same path as last time without ever discussing it.

"First, my IT connection put me in touch with the web site that posted—"

"I saw Olena, the matchmaker my father hired. She is just his old friend, by the way, and not a professional. That's probably why my father didn't tell you anything about her when the two of you spoke. I'm sure he didn't want to throw a friend under the bus. But she was the one who gave Cameron my contact details." She waved away the incident like it was no longer a concern. "She didn't understand the kind of site where she posted my photo. She meant well, but she knows I'm taking over my dating life. I will be choosing all future dating prospects."

The words punched a hole through his chest. He felt the sting of cold winter air right in the center of it as they walked down the slope near Tavern on the Green. This time, there was no talk of beauty surrounding them. No mischievous attempts to taste beauty on her tongue.

"About that." He willed all his persuasive powers to the fore. "I didn't sleep last night, thinking about what you said."

"That makes two of us." She wrapped her arms around herself.

He hadn't expected that hint of vulnerability from her after the way she'd ended things the night before.

"Sofia, I didn't mean to mislead you," he said, his boots crunching the frozen patches of snow. He'd dressed casually in boots and jeans today, taking the day off from work to focus on her. He'd take all damn month off if he needed to. "I understand how it might seem that way, but everything between us happened so fast. We went from planning how to stop a media storm to figuring out our dating history, and then getting to know each other for real in those phone calls—which I very much enjoyed—to trying to figure out where the matchmaking leak came from."

"I was focused on recovering from jet lag and impressing a lecherous ass." Her voice wound around him with a comfortable intimacy that he wished could last a lifetime.

She was that damn special to him.

"But we never lacked for conversation, did we?" he prodded, trying to justify his actions. "I didn't mention my grandfather's will at first because I didn't plan on following through. I planned to put his feet to the fire about the thing when he got back from China. Make him see reason. Marriage is too important to use as some bargaining chip in a business transaction."

Sofia glanced at him, giving him an assessing look through her lashes.

"If you really believe that—"

"I swear it. I sat up all night thinking about how I could convince you of it. I woke up my attorney and had her write up contracts to show you where I would renounce all rights to McNeill Resorts so you'd believe me." He opened his coat to show her a sheaf of crumpled papers. "I signed them, then discarded them an hour later, remembering how dismissive you sounded about using contracts in a personal relationship."

She nibbled a snowflake off her bottom lip. "Was I?"

"You suggested we should be able to arrange for dates without the help of a legally binding agreement." He withdrew the crumpled papers and handed them to her. "I'm only showing them to you now to illustrate how hard I tried to figure out how to convince you."

Heading east onto quieter pathways, they passed a horse-drawn carriage full of tourists snapping photos, but other than that there wasn't much traffic here.

"Convince me of what, exactly?" Sofia stopped near a field full of halfhearted snowmen, a few of which wore empty coffee cups for hats.

"I hadn't thought through what it meant to bring up marriage last night since I was wrecked after hearing about Gramps' condition." He reached for her free hand, pulling it from her pocket so he could hold it in both of his. "You haven't known me for long, so you couldn't know how unusual it is for me to talk without having any kind of agenda. But that is what has been so great about you. I got comfortable thinking we could talk about anything. But I had no business putting you in that kind of position."

"So you never meant to propose." She seemed to be tracking the conversation carefully, making him realize she was very much paying attention now.

Because she cared? Because she shared some of his feelings?

Fresh hope filled some of that hole in his chest and he took his time to get the words right for her.

"My brain was telling me to find any way possible to keep a ring on your finger so that that we could keep exploring whatever is happening between us. I sure didn't want to break off our fake engagement right when I realized I'm falling in love with you."

Sofia held a contract in her hand—signed by one of the country's wealthiest men—that stated in no uncertain terms he would relinquish all rights to his grandfather's legacy.

For her, he'd done that incredibly foolish thing.

That had floored her on a day when she thought she couldn't be any more surprised by life.

But then he told her he was falling for her and it was like what her mother had told her about beauty—you didn't see it. You experienced it all around you. She stood inside one of those beautiful moments right now with a man so important to her she could no longer imagine life without him.

"I know it sounds crazy," he started.

She tucked the contract into his pocket and squeezed his hands tightly through her beautiful yellow mittens that made her happy.

The mittens that made her think she had inherited some of her mother's joyous outlook on life.

"It doesn't sound crazy. I was there, remember?" She echoed his words from the night before when she'd told him the sex was so good the first time she'd thought she dreamed it.

"I remember." His voice deepened as he stepped closer.

"I was falling in love, too," she admitted, her voice hoarse in a throat clogged with emotions.

"Was?" He stood toe-to-toe with her now. She had to look up at him.

"Am." She breathed the word between their lips as they stood together in the snowfall. "I am falling in love with you, Quinn. And I do see you for the man you are."

He kissed her, answering all her questions and easing all her doubts. Her heart swelled with new joy that crowded out everything else, making her wonder how she could have ever believed there was any other place for her in the world than at his side.

His arms wrapped around her, sheltering her. She breathed him in, his scent and touch already so familiar to her.

"I don't want to lose you, Sofia," he said between kisses. "Whatever it takes to convince you, to keep you, I will do it." He sealed his mouth to hers and only broke the kiss when an older lady rode past them on a bicycle, ringing her bell at them and giving them a thumbs-up.

Sofia laughed, feeling a ghost of her mother's happy spirit in that sweet, romantic gesture.

"You're not going to lose me." Her whole world felt new and full of possibilities, their lives as mingled as their puffy breaths merging in the cold air.

"Then it's the happiest day of my life so far. How should we celebrate?" he asked, tucking her under his arm to walk past the pond toward East Sixty-First where the Pierre waited.

His home.

"First, we're going to burn that contract." She patted the pocket where she'd shoved the papers. "Because I want you to support your grandfather's business and fulfill his legacy with your brothers."

"That's generous of you, but it sounds too tame for a celebration." Quinn dropped a kiss on top of her hair.

"Then we're going to make love all day," she whispered in his ear as they walked.

"I can't wait for that." The husky note in his voice assured her how much he meant it.

"Then we're going to come up with a plan to help me find a way to have a career after dance that doesn't involve Idris the Idiot."

"I hope it involves me punching him into next year." Quinn's jaw flexed.

"Probably not, but we'll leave it open for negotiation." Sofia let him lead her into the beautiful building where he lived, wondering if she'd ever get used to this kind of opulence.

"Can I make a suggestion?" Quinn asked, hitting the button for his private elevator.

"Of course." She bet he had a hot tub in that extravagant place of his. Her knees, at least, would get used to luxury in a hurry.

"I'd like to replace that monstrosity of a ring from my brother with something that looks more like you." He must have seen the surprise she felt because he rushed to explain. "Not that it's a proposal. We can take all the time you want to date. But as long as the world thinks we're engaged…"

"You weren't kidding about keeping a ring on my finger, were you?" She stepped into the elevator, grateful when the cabin doors shut behind them, sealing them in privacy.

"We don't have to comment on it, or issue any statements, or explain anything to anyone. We can just date and be mysterious about our plans." His blue eyes sparkled with a happiness she hadn't seen in them before. Also, a hint of sensual wickedness that she *had* seen before. And thoroughly enjoyed.

She had the feeling it was the same look in her eyes.

"Right. Because what we do is no one else's business. And we each have a partner we can trust." She felt dizzy from the rush of the elevator up to his floor. The rush of love for a man who knew her better than any other.

A man who had spent all night thinking about how to show her he loved her.

When the elevator door opened and let them out into his apartment, Sofia fell into his arms, dragging him toward the first bed she found.

"I'm going to make you happy, Sofia." He kissed the words into her neck while she walked backward, peeling off her coat.

She smiled against his shoulder as she pushed off his jacket, too.

"You already have."

* * * * *

If you loved this story,
don't miss the next two installments in
THE McNEILL MAGNATES:
THE MAGNATE'S MARRIAGE MERGER
(June 2017)
HIS ACCIDENTAL HEIR
(July 2017)
then
pick up these other sexy and emotional reads
from Joanne Rock!

HIS SECRETARY'S SURPRISE FIANCEÉ
SECRET BABY SCANDAL

Available now from Mills & Boon Desire!

MILLS & BOON®

Desire™

PASSIONATE AND DRAMATIC LOVE STORIES